BACKLASH BLUES

AMULYA MALLADI

Copyright © 2024 by Amulya Malladi

All rights reserved.

No part of this publication may be reproduced, distributed, or transmitted in any form or by any means, including photocopying, recording, or other electronic or mechanical methods, without the prior written permission of the publisher, except as permitted by U.S. copyright law. For permission requests, contact [include publisher/author contact info].

The story, all names, characters, and incidents portrayed in this production are fictitious. No identification with actual persons (living or deceased), places, buildings, and products is intended or should be inferred.

ISBN: 9798866413584

BACKLASH BLUES

"There are two ways to be fooled. One is to believe what isn't true; the other is to refuse to believe what is true."

                                              Søren Kierkegaard

"We are our choices."

                                                  Jean-Paul Sartre

PROLOGUE

March, 2018

Raisa Chaban, a seasoned investigative journalist for the Russian magazine *New Times*, met Nikita Poletov, first Deputy Chairman of the Russian Central Bank, for the first time at Café Louise in Nørrebro in Copenhagen. One of the first and few faces of Russian financial anti-corruption, Poletov was in Copenhagen for a Financial Econometrics conference sponsored by the Department of Economics at the University of Copenhagen. Raisa, who was covering the conference, had started an email conversation with Poletov six months prior, building a connection with him.

That he had finally agreed to meet her face-to-face was huge. She knew that to get Poletov to talk to her, he had to trust her, which was why she hadn't even told her editor about the meeting.

Raisa was a petite woman with long, black hair that she tied into a ponytail. She was dressed for the weather in a dark gray woolen dress, black knee-high boots, an oversized black woolen coat, and a black beret. She made up for what she lacked in stature with a larger-than-life personality.

Poletov was waiting for her at Café Louise. He sat in a far corner, below a large Tuborg beer sign, nursing a pilsner with a cigarette in hand. His suit jacket was draped across the back of his wooden chair, and he had loosened his red tie. His thick brown hair was disheveled, and it had been a few weeks since his last beard trim. He did not look like the carefully coiffed man Raisa had seen in videos and photographs. She knew he was in his early forties but looked ten years older.

When he looked up at her, she noticed his blue eyes were red-rimmed. He stood up and held out his hand.

"*Zdravstvuyte.*" Raisa shook his clammy hand. He nodded but didn't respond to the greeting; instead, he directed her to sit across from him with his chin.

It was another busy Tuesday night in March at the café. Smoke filled the café's claustrophobic rooms, along with kitschy eighties music. Madonna was asking *her papa not to preach*. Greasy bar food smells mixed with tobacco, cannabis, and stale beer. No one would expect one of Russia's and Europe's most prominent financial figures to be in a place like this.

Since he was appointed Russia's Central Bank's Deputy Chairman two years ago, Poletov had spearheaded an aggressive campaign to close down banks accused of money laundering. His anti-corruption agenda had secured him powerful enemies, but he was not deterred.

They spoke in Russian, but they needn't have bothered because the café was loud, and no one was sitting close to them. Raisa thought the noise to be a protective blanket because Poletov had insisted on meeting without his security detail. He wanted no one to know he was talking to a journalist. Not even those who would protect him from the death threats he'd received since he started closing down suspect accounts in and out of the Motherland.

"Would you like something to drink?" he asked.

She nodded and waved to the server, a young blond with tattooed sleeves, and piercings in his eyebrows, nose, upper lip, and earlobes. When he strolled over, she ordered a Tuborg in Danish.

"You speak Danish?" Poletov noted.

"Yes, my mother is half-Danish." Raisa pulled out a notebook and her lucky blue Montblanc rollerball pen, a gift from her father when she'd graduated from journalism school. She would not ask Poletov if she could record the meeting. What was the point? He would refuse, and the place was so noisy that she would catch only about two out of three words on her recorder, even if she turned it on surreptitiously.

"But your father is Russian." He was dawdling, Raisa thought.

She smiled at him and nodded.

He looked at her without expression, and then shrugged after a long sigh. He pushed his half-drunk beer to the side, and leaned forward.

"Before I came to Copenhagen, I met with Maksim Lõhmus," he whispered.

"The Secretary General of the Estonian Finance Ministry," Raisa confirmed.

"Yes, and the Finance Minister's right-hand man." Poletov sat up as if getting ready to salute and march. "I told him I wanted several non-resident bank accounts closed."

"Non-resident?"

The waiter came back with Raisa's beer, and they both fell silent until they were alone again.

"Non-resident to Estonia. Russian accounts," Poletov continued.

"How much are we talking about here?"

"Somewhere between 10 and 15 billion."

Raisa picked up her glass of beer and her eyebrows rose in surprise. "Rubles?"

"Euros. Could be more...." Poletov ran a hand through his already mussy hair.

Raisa set the beer down without drinking it. *Did he just say 10 to 15 billion euros?*

"How much more?"

Poletov's shoulders slumped as if he was giving up. "I thought this would be easy, but it isn't. I hope you understand that. None of this is easy now and won't be easy later. The shit, as the Americans say, is hitting the fan."

Raisa controlled her excitement. "I don't reveal my sources, Nikita."

"You won't have to. They'll know. I'm the only one who could tell you what I'm about to tell you. There is some I can prove and much I cannot."

"Okay."

"But you can't go public until I give you the green light," he warned. "And I'm going to need you to help prove what I cannot."

"I understand," Raisa said with a feral smile. "I'm an excellent investigator."

A WEEK AFTER MEETING with Raisa Chaban, Nikita Poletov was murdered on the highway on his way to his hotel in Tallinn from Kadriorg Staadion. The home ground of the national football team had been hosting a friendly soccer game for the employees of the Estonian finance ministry, and Poletov had played for the winning side. He had a bruised shin and a wide smile when he got into his Mercedes sedan. He was joking with his driver about his football prowess, according to his wife Lucya, whom he had been on the phone with when the bullets hit the driver first, then Poletov.

Two months after the violent murder, Raisa disappeared—even her family in Moscow didn't know where she went. She didn't publish the story she'd meet with Poletov about.

CHAPTER 1

Friday Night, October 6, 2023

It wasn't unusual for Eymen to see me play the guitar at Mojos, a Blues Bar in the center of Copenhagen. It also wasn't uncommon that a blonde woman accompanied him because he sometimes brought his wife, Clara. But this blonde was not his wife. But she was clearly comfortable with Eymen. Her hand was on his forearm. His arm was around her shoulder. His head dipped close to her face to hear her over the music when she spoke.

Now, I'm not one to jump to conclusions. As a private investigator, it's a professional necessity to be objective. I also knew what Eymen was and wasn't capable of, as he and his wife, Clara Silberg, were some of my oldest and closest friends. It had been a scandal when an old-money Silberg married the son of a Turkish immigrant. Although he was now the CFO of a pharmaceutical company, he was still a *perker* to many in her family, a word that fell short of the N-word in English, arguably one of the most offensive ethnic slurs in the Danish language.

The band wound down to a break with Hendrix's *Born Under a Bad Sign*. Bobby K, a skinny dude, who called himself a mongrel because he was half Danish, a quarter Middle Eastern, and a quarter something else (there had been a dalliance or two in the family tree), sang with soul angels and led our band of musicians.

Nuru Kimathi, our drummer, waved at Eymen, and then leaned over. "That ain't his wife."

"No," I agreed.

Nuru nodded. "She's pretty hot, though."

"Who's hot?" Valdemar Vong, who played the sax, asked as he drank whiskey from a Starbucks coffee cup. He was a self-admitted functional alcoholic but didn't want to announce it—though everyone knew what he carried in his worn-out green and white plastic cup.

"The blonde who's not Clara." Our bassist, John Reinhardt, who was about a hundred years old, pointed at the couple.

We'd been playing together for the past decade and knew each other well, which meant we knew each other's friends and families.

"She's probably a friend," I suggested.

"If not, he'll be dead, and you won't have to investigate that." Bobby K shook his head in pity.

Victor Silberg, Clara's father, a banker who had more money than God, didn't give a shit about societal rules and did what he pleased, how he pleased. Still, the murder of his favorite (and only) son-in-law would probably not happen.

"Let me find out what's going on before we condemn Eymen to his death," I joked.

They laughed as I walked up to Eymen. We hugged, and he introduced me to Flora Brandt. He called her an ex-colleague.

"I'm here to watch you play. She's here to meet you," he grinned.

"My whole band was wondering if you'll be murdered by Clara or her father. My money is on Victor." I waved to the band, who watched us keenly.

Eymen nodded at them with a smile, and they called out, "*Hej*, Eymen."

Bobby K added, "*Flot pige.*" Good-looking girl.

"Flora is an ex-colleague. We went to business school together and worked our first jobs at McKinsey," Eymen explained.

"And...I'm a good friend of Clara's," Flora beamed. She wasn't as good-looking as Clara, but she was no slouch. She had nice legs covered in skintight jeans that fit her well.

"We'd like to buy you a drink after you're done," Eymen offered.

"Maybe I should be the one buying drinks. Because it looks like you're bringing business my way." I winked at Flora as I walked back to the band to ease their mind about the longevity of Eymen's life, and play our last set.

I was right about the *business my way* part.

We went to Drop Inn, a bar on *Kompagnistræde*. I knew the place well as they did open mic nights, and I'd played jazz with some other bands during their After-Work Jazz events on Friday afternoons. We sat outside where people huddled in jackets, smoking cigarettes around barrels lit with fire on the cold October evening. We were warmed by infrared lights, wrapped in jackets and blankets that all cafés liked to keep for outdoor seating.

The music of Kita Menari and The Vices, a garage pop band from the Netherlands, filtered through the smoke.

Eymen eyed my mineral water with curiosity. He had ordered a Glenmorangie because, according to him, it was a scotch kind of evening, and Flora, asked for a glass of the house red.

"It's my dry month," I told him.

I did a "no alcohol" month once a year, not in January like everyone else after the gluttony of Christmas, but after the debauchery of summer with beers, champagne, gin cocktails, and too much wine. I also didn't smoke during my dry month, which was more challenging to give up than alcohol, but I convinced myself that it built character.

This year, the month was October, and it had been exactly seven days since I'd gone dry. I watched enviously as the server placed my companions' drinks before them, aching for a cigarette. Even during my non-dry 11 months, I only allowed myself two cigarettes daily. One in the morning after my run with my coffee and one in the evening before I went to bed. It was something to start the day with and look forward to at the end. Smokers never got over that desire for a nicotine hit—and this was the only way I knew to avoid becoming a chain smoker with an iron lung without actually giving it up
.

"I don't know if I can trust a private investigator who doesn't drink." Flora was uncomfortable making the joke but made a valiant effort to mask her nervousness.

"I'm on a break. It's not permanent," I assured her.

"And thank god for that," Eymen retorted. "He does a dry month once a year, and it's hell on all of us."

She was probably here because Clara had suggested it and sent Eymen to hold her hand. However, she was still debating whether she would hire me. I had detected this through my insightful private investigator skills and the fact that she kept chewing her lower lip, which was raw, and not because of the bite in the October air.

"Where's Clara?" I asked, giving Flora time to make up her mind about whatever it was she wanted me to do for her. Probably take photos of a cheating lover. Those were the most embarrassed clients as they didn't want to be vulnerable because they suspected their spouse was fucking someone else. These were my least favorite jobs, but they paid the bills, and I had plenty of those stacked up as I was still neck-deep in renovating my house.

"Packing," Eymen caught on and answered casually. "There's a Silberg family thing in Cannes. She's taking the kids tomorrow morning. They'll be back Monday night."

"You're living the bachelor's life this weekend." I took a sip of my mineral water. *For Satan*, I needed a real drink.

"Oh, yeah." Eymen lifted his glass of whiskey in salute.

Eymen and Clara were the most balanced couple I knew. Clara didn't pressure Eymen to do things her large and influential family wanted him to do, and Eymen didn't drag her to his family events in Istanbul or Brønshøj. But for Clara's father, Victor, who loved Eymen as his own son, as he did me (he called us "his boys")—the Silberg family would've kicked Eymen to the curb. But Victor didn't give a crap that Eymen was Turkish or that I was a bald, disreputable ex-cop and hence out of his socioeconomic circle. That helped Eymen and Clara have a marriage where family interference was minimal.

"I work at Copenhagen Bank," Flora suddenly spoke. "I'm their CHRO."

"Good for you." The Chief Human Resources Officer for one of the prominent Danish banks was impressive.

She smiled nervously. "I have a situation that I don't know how to manage."

I waited.

She looked at Eymen as if for permission, and he shrugged. "This is your call. You know what Clara and I think. But if you don't want it to go beyond a drink that Gabriel pays for, that's fine."

"I'm not paying for drinks if there's no business coming my way."

"He'll pay," Eymen assured Flora. "He looks like a deviant, but he's actually alright."

"Deviant? In my Orlando Palacios fedora?" I lifted my hat with a flourish, then let it fall back on my head.

Several years ago, I decided to give up on the hair on my head before it gave up on me and sported a clean-shaven look, which luckily worked because I had a round, bump-free skull.

"I think she was probably thrown by the sequined jacket," Eymen remarked dryly.

"This jacket is vintage Balmain," I said in mock offense. "It's my blues musician uniform."

"It has sequins." Eymen shook his head. "There are times, Præst, that I wonder how I can be friends with someone who struts around like a peacock."

"A peacock with impeccable fashion."

"Okay, okay." Flora raised both her hands as if in defeat. "If I talk to Gabriel, will you stop the comedy routine?"

"We'll try, but we've been doing it for so long it's a habit." Eymen's eyes were soft as he patted her hand.

"Before I say anything, I need you to know that I don't want Copenhagen Bank to know that I want this investigated."

"It would help if you'd tell me what you want investigated that your employer shouldn't know about." I drank more mineral water even though I wanted a Laphroig 10 neat. Eymen was right; it was a scotch kind of evening.

"A Copenhagen Bank employee committed suicide." She said it flatly, without emotion, but her eyes told a different story.

I didn't say I was sorry because there was nothing good to say about suicide.

"Noor is…was from Pakistan—born there but raised in London. She interned with us while doing her MBA at the Copenhagen Business School, and after graduating, we offered her a job. She was a Chief Strategy Consultant of Business Banking for our Baltic region."

"Okay."

"She killed herself in early May. I should've said that at the start." She took a sip of her wine. It was something to do with her hands, I knew. Then she cleared her throat as if she had decided, straightened her spine, and continued. "As devastating as it was, it wasn't a matter that needed investigating. She had left a suicide note."

"What did it say?" I huddled into my Reiss shearling leather jacket. The bite in the air had sharp teeth that dug past the flesh to chill the bones.

A cigarette I couldn't have would've taken the edge off the cold.

"That she was sorry. It was written to her family. I spoke to her cousin who lived with her. The family was devastated and shocked. Afsana told me that there was no way Noor would commit suicide. She was only twenty-five, full of possibilities. But the police said that it was clearly a suicide, and that was that."

"Who is Afsana?" I wished I had a notebook to take notes, though I wasn't sure if my fingers could construct words, considering they were ice blocks.

"Her cousin. She found her. Afsana is a chef at Sapor. It's a restaurant in Christianshavn."

I nodded. "It just got awarded a Michelin star." It was on my list of restaurants to try; I was thinking of taking Sophie there for her birthday in December.

"Two weeks ago, I received an email," Flora continued and then looked at Eymen for support.

"She talked to Clara and me, and we thought you could look into it," Eymen finished.

"An email?" I prompted.

Flora nodded. "From an anonymous source. The email address is defunct. I tried to reply, and it bounced."

She pulled out a printed sheet and gave it to me.

I didn't look at it. It was too dark to read. I folded it and put it in my coat pocket. "What does it say?"

"Copenhagen Bank killed Noor. What will you do about it?" Her voice shook slightly, and it wasn't because of the cold.

"Okay. Who did Noor work for at the bank?"

"She was on Silas's team."

"And Silas would be?"

"Silas Haagen is the Head of Eastern European Business Banking at Copenhagen Bank," Flora explained.

"Do you know Silas Haagen?" Eymen wanted to know.

I shrugged.

"He's the businessman-philosopher," Eymen offered.

I shrugged again.

Eymen sighed. "So, you know him?"

I shrugged yet again. "I know *of* him."

"Be careful; one day, you'll dislocate your shoulder with all that aggressive shrugging," Eymen mocked.

I smiled.

Silas Haagen was famous in Denmark. The philosopher banker with his dark, shoulder-length hair in contrast with most bankers' salt-and-pepper, manicured, gel-soaked hair. He spoke with passion about the meaning of life, and wrote books about honest banking.

I couldn't stand him.

But it didn't help me tell Flora that I knew of Silas Haagen from the television or social media. I had learned a long time ago that as a PI, my job was not to tell people what *I* knew but to find out what *they* did. Keeping my mouth shut had never gotten me into trouble.

"I wouldn't have given it much thought, but the night Noor killed herself, we'd had a party at work, a celebration for crossing the 100% growth mark for the Baltic business. We had champagne and hors d'oeuvres in a conference room. I saw Noor and Silas arguing in his office. Our offices have glass walls, so I could see she was angry, and he was trying to calm her."

Flora's hands shook as she picked up her wine glass. "I'm sorry. I didn't realize how upset I was."

"Not a problem. We have all the time in the world," I assured her, though I wasn't sure if we did, because I suspected hypothermia might soon become a reality for me.

"She stormed out of his office, and he followed her, gripped her arm, and dragged her back in. I thought that was too much, so I walked in without permission. I asked if anything was wrong, and they both denied it. Silas said something snippy about me knocking before entering his office. I left. There just wasn't much I could do. Noor said she was alright. The next morning, I found out she was dead. Maybe if I had pushed…maybe then…I don't know. Noor went home that evening and took too many pills. She was being treated for depression; the police detective who investigated told me. The police weren't even interested in knowing what happened with Silas. And I didn't tell him, either. What could I say? She had an argument at work?"

"What pills did she take?"

"Xanax."

"How did she get them?"

Flora shrugged. "Apparently, they were prescribed to her. I mean, everyone takes something. I'm on Lexapro."

I nodded. "You can't know why she killed herself. And once someone decides to kill themselves, you don't always have the power to stop it. I have seen enough suicides in my line of work. Sometimes people are so unhappy and desperate that it's not a matter of why do it, but why not."

She frowned. "My therapist said the same thing."

"The therapy comes free with the PI work." I gave her my *I'm so funny and yet so kind* smile. The one that had gotten me plenty of female company in my youth. It worked. Flora softened.

"Why do you think she committed suicide?" I probed.

"I think Silas Haagen was sexually harassing her," she said hesitantly.

"How do you know?"

"He has a well-deserved reputation for being a sleazeball. I've seen it since I started working at the bank three years ago. I didn't know the dynamics initially, but everyone can see that too many young women leave when they work for Silas—and some stay and get promoted. I brought it up with our CEO, but he says that banking is not everyone's cup of tea, and those who leave do so because they can't cut it. And it's not like he doesn't have women on his team; he does, and they're successful. I tried to bring it up when Noor died, but our counsel, Harald Wiberg, warned me…no, that's not the right word; he threatened me. Nicely, you know. I could lose my job and never find one again if I went against the Copenhagen Bank boys. He said I should not smear a legend, the youngest and one of the most famous executives at Copenhagen Bank and Denmark."

"Have you shared the email with them?"

She shook her head violently. "No. It would be pointless. I know what they would say if I did. They would say that it's nonsense or that I made it up. They'll kick me out of my job if I push this too hard. I'm okay with losing my job. I want to be clear about that. I'll be fine. Financially. But I can't let a young woman's death go without some acknowledgment of what happened. I need to know why she killed herself."

"What will you do with that information?" I asked.

"Depends on the information," she countered.

Eymen shot me a "do what you must" glance. These were the no-win cases, and truth be told, they didn't bother me. Just this summer, I'd tackled one that, while it eventually went my way, left me with a souvenir: a bullet scar on my shoulder that still twinged in cold weather. Oh, and let's not forget the wreckage that used to be the ground floor of my home, or the PTSD diagnosis my therapist so kindly bestowed upon me. Here's the thing, though—I wasn't your typical private eye who dodged bullets. Most of my days were spent aiding lawyers in unraveling their cases: messy divorces, corporate embezzlements, financial skullduggery, and the like.

This case probably would not get me beat up or wounded, but the fact was that no matter what I found, we'd never know why this young woman really killed herself.

"Did her cousin know about the sexual harassment?"

Flora shook her head. "I talked to her. She said that Noor was stressed about work. Worried. Didn't sleep. Worked late. Was on the phone all the time. But that's all of us these days, isn't it?"

"Was Noor in a relationship?"

"According to her cousin, Noor was too busy with work for men."

I finished my mineral water. My hands were reaching the point where I wanted to tuck them into my underarms to heat them. But I didn't do it. I maintained my macho "nothing can touch me" dignity.

"Will you take the case?" Flora's voice was shaky.

"It was never a question," I told her softly. "Clara and Eymen want me to do it, so I will."

Flora's face lit up. "You will?"

"Yes."

"Thank you," she said gratefully.

"Well, I won't not do it for free…or am I doing it for free, Eymen?"

Eymen grinned. He knew if he and Clara asked me, I'd do anything…and not ask for payment.

"I'll pay you," Flora interjected. "What will your services cost?"

I told her, and since she didn't seem displeased or surprised. I wished I had upped my rate and not given her the friends and family discount.

"I'll send you an invoice," I explained. "I bill once a week."

"How many weeks do you think this will take?"

"I don't know." I raised my cold hands, palms up.

"Guess?"

I shook my head. "Maybe I'll find something within a day or a week, or maybe I'll never find out. But you'll be able to assess status once a week and terminate my services whenever you see fit."

"And you'll not let anyone at Copenhagen Bank know?" The fear was back in her eyes.

"I'll let no one know you hired me to investigate," I evaded.

"But they'll know you're investigating." Her voice was shaky and low.

I wanted to calm her, and used the firm but soft tone that got people to tell me everything I wanted to know. It worked about fifty percent of the time. "I'll be as discreet as I can be, but when I ask questions about Noor, there's a chance people may surmise that I'm investigating, considering my line of work. I will, however, protect your identity."

"He's careful," Eymen assured her.

"Scout's honor," I affirmed.

"You were never a scout." Eymen narrowed his eyes.

"But just as honorable." I stood up. "Is it okay if we walk and talk? I'll lose fingers and toes if I don't move."

"It's not *that* cold," Eymen remarked.

"I don't have any booze in my system to heat me up from the inside," I retorted sarcastically.

Flora rose, and then extended her hand to me with a small smile. I shook it. Her hand was warmer than mine.

"Thank you."

"No thanks needed, but once you see me in action, you'll want to thank me profusely. I request now that you don't get too effusive. It embarrasses me."

Flora didn't seem impressed with my sense of humor. I didn't let it hurt my feelings.

Chapter 2

Saturday Morning, October 7, 2023

It was a tradition that I had breakfast with Sophie, my daughter, every Saturday when both of us were in Copenhagen. We had been having Saturday breakfasts in restaurants, my townhouse, or her mother's apartment since Sophie was four and her mother, Stine, and I separated. Since we were never married, Stine and I didn't have to divorce, but many of the same traumas applied. However, shortly after we split (or maybe there was some overlap, I never asked), Stine started to date a lawyer. Erik, her *new* husband, and I were friends. In fact, I leased my office from *Dall og Digman* Advokater, the law firm at which Erik, last name Digman, was a named partner. The law firm used the entire floor atop the French restaurant Pastis and an Aldi supermarket about fifteen minutes by bike from my townhouse.

Since it was my *Far*, father's birthday, we were having breakfast at Sophie's mother's apartment on Rothesgade, a *herskabslejlighed*, a master's apartment in Østerbro. *Far* was visiting from Bourgogne, where he now lived with his French girlfriend, who was nearly twenty years junior to his seventy-five, and he helped run her family's vineyard. I didn't have Viggo Præst's penchant for younger women—but Stine accused me of having my father's roving eye, which I disagreed with. I was scrupulously honest with the women I had sex with.

Viggo and my mother stayed married until she died a decade and a half ago, but it was common knowledge that my father took his pleasures where he could find them, and he seemed to find them almost anywhere. Since he'd met Clémence nearly six years ago, however, he'd found (according to him) his soulmate, and had not strayed since.

"Once you find yours, you won't mind giving up your freedom," he told me when he introduced me to Clémence for the first time.

For some strange reason, Clémence and Stine got along well and were friends. Usually, when my father and his girlfriend came to visit, they stayed with me, but after a firebomb tore up my just-completed living room that I had been putting together for a decade, they stayed with Stine and Erik. It had been a couple of months since the incident, and only now had the smell of musty fire dissipated.

I stood in line at *Myers Bageri* to pick up pastries and rolls for my father's birthday breakfast, responding in the affirmative to texts Stine sent about all the things I needed to not forget to buy at the bakery.

I smiled when I got a message from Nico: *You free tonight??*

Me: *Maybe. My father is visiting.*

Nic responded immediately: *Is he staying with you?*

Me: *No.*
Nico: *Do you want me to come over?*
Me: *Yes.*
Nico: *See you at 8.*

I slipped the phone into my Burberry coat pocket and advanced in line toward the bakery counter.

Nico and I had been friends for many years. She was a journalist at *Politiken*, and we occasionally shared information to help each other. We were also friends who had good sex without the burden of romantic or emotional encumberments. There were no expectations beyond friendship. If I told her I was busy, Nico wouldn't consider it a rejection or even ask me for a reason. And when I asked her if she wanted to meet, whether for sex or just her company, I was comforted in knowing that she'd only accept if she wanted to and not because she didn't want to upset me or hurt my feelings. My relationship with Nico was the least complicated one in my life.

CLÉMENCE WAS A PETITE blonde with a body fit from working outdoors in the vineyard where her family grew Chardonnay and Pinot Noir. Clémence made sure that I was always stocked with wine from Chateau Marchand. I liked her very much.

Before my father had met her, he'd been wasting away just a little, and I worried he'd die soon, but now he was back to being as energetic as he'd ever been. His face was weather-beaten as if he spent too much time in the sun, which I knew he did, and his eyes were bright—happy—something that I'd not seen when he'd lived in Denmark.

"*Mon chéri*, Gabriel." Clémence hugged me and kissed me on both cheeks.

"*Ça fait du bien de te voir*, Clémence." I held her close for a minute and then released her.

"You forgot the cheese," Stine complained as she emptied the bakery bag on the dining table.

"I'm sorry," I said pleasantly. "Do you want me to go back and get some?" I had learned long ago to not respond in kind to Stine because she would not change, and it would only make things unpleasant.

"You always forget things." Stine placed the *rugbrød*, rye bread, on the cutting board and piled the *rundstykker*, Danish breakfast buns, in a basket lined with a tea cloth.

Sophie hugged me and then joined her mother at the table to arrange the chocolate croissants and *kanelsnegl*, cinnamon buns, on a plate. She smiled at me and winked when she saw I had bought two *hindbærsnitte*, raspberry bars, her favorite, which she left inside a paper bag near her plate.

My father came out, sniffing the air. "Ah, the food has arrived. Did you bring coffee, Gabriel? Your daughter's mother makes terrible coffee."

Stine straightened and looked pointedly at Viggo. "I make excellent coffee. Erik, tell him."

Her husband, Erik, patted my shoulder companionably and said almost reflexively, "Absolutely excellent."

My father and I were not huggers. We were the *hej* from a distance kind of people who nodded at one another. My mother had been the hugger and kisser.

We sat down to eat, and my father regaled us with stories about his life in France. He put his arm loosely around Clémence, and touched her hand or stroked her hair. I'd noticed it before, the easy affection between them. I'd not seen him like this with my mother, and I wondered if he'd changed or if he'd always been like this, waiting for the right woman to make him fall in love.

"*Gammel Dansk*, Gabriel?" My father held up the bottle of the Danish bitter, and I shook my head.

"It's his dry month, *Farfar*," Sophie told him.

"You still do that?" My father was surprised.

"Yes." I buttered a slice of rye bread and put a slice of cheese on top, which had come from Stine's fridge. She'd repeatedly mentioned that it would not be enough for everyone because I forgot to buy cheese.

"But why?" Clémence wanted to know.

"Because I like to drink, eat, and smoke, and this way, I know I can stop when I have to."

"How long do you do it for?" Clémence asked curiously.

"A whole month," Erik and Sophie said in unison.

"It's traumatic." Sophie bit into a raspberry bar.

Erik broke open a chocolate croissant and joined her. "He's a complete jerk the entire month. I wish he'd stop doing it. He stops drinking, doesn't smoke, and loses his sense of humor."

"I don't think you get worse when you don't drink," Stine assured me, and then added with a grin, "You're always a jerk."

After breakfast, while Erik and Sophie cleaned up, I joined my father on Stine's small balcony, closing the door behind me. My father had a pack-a-day habit, and Stine had put an ashtray out for his benefit. She would've preferred he went down to the street but had relented because she had a soft spot for Viggo.

I breathed in the tobacco and wondered why people complained about secondhand smoke. It was glorious.

I didn't bother with a jacket or hat; the cool October air stung my face and arms. I wish I'd at least put my woolen hat back on. A bald head was sensitive to the elements.

"How are you? How's the shoulder?" Viggo blew rings. He always fascinated me by being able to do that.

"Fine."

"Bullet wounds are nasty. I had one...."

"I know." Viggo had gotten shot in the ass in the line of duty nearly three decades ago. As if remembering, he stroked his right butt cheek. "At least you got shot in a dignified place. It was embarrassing to have my pants down every time the doctor poked and prodded."

I grinned, remembering his indignation.

"Sophie says she's proud of you. I know the man died, but at least he's no longer marked as a murderer. You cleared his name."

In the summer, I had investigated the murder of a politician who had purportedly been killed by Yousef Ahmed, an Iraqi refugee. It had been a tough and painful journey to victory, which included a few fists in my face and a bullet in my shoulder, but the real murderer went to jail; the politician whose bidding the killer had been doing still thrived as cockroaches do, even after a nuclear explosion, but Yousef and his family had been redeemed.

I stuffed my hands in my pockets and waited for him to get to where I knew he wanted to go.

"Have you heard from Leila?"

There it was.

"No." I didn't want to discuss Leila with my father. The one who got away and came back and then got away again. Though she didn't leave memories behind this time, perfumed by distance. Now, I remembered clearly why Leila and I had never worked as a couple and never could.

"She's a good-looking woman. Strong and...."

"*Far*, she's getting married to that British guy," I stopped him. *The one she'd cheated on me with.*

"Are you seeing anyone?"

"You know what Kierkegaard said, '*Woman is and ever will be the ruin of a man, as soon as he contracts a permanent relation with her,*' and that's why I maintain my single status."

"It's different when you're in love."

"And as good old Søren K said, *love hides a multitude of sins*," I replied smugly.

It irritated him when I quoted Kierkegaard because my father found him misogynistic, which good old Søren unapologetically was. For a policeman in uniform who epitomized the meaning of the term blue collar, *Far* was a well-read man.

He countered me with an old Danish saying. "They are most cheated who cheat themselves."

I missed my father, I realized. Missed this, the banter, the intimacy of knowing each other so well that we could talk in quotes and understand each other.

"Since you found Clémence, you have become suspiciously interested in my love life."

Before Clémence, my father didn't care who I was with. He'd told me when I was a teenager that he didn't mind me having girls over for sleepovers as long as I made sure that I only invited the ones who'd stay for longer than a couple of nights to the breakfast table. He didn't want to remember everyone's name. As it was, he called every girl who ever had breakfast with us Pernille, after my first girlfriend, whom I held hands with when I was eleven.

"A good woman can change your life," he gushed with such pleasure that I had to smile. "Clémence changed mine. I wish you'd meet someone who will do that for you. And soon. I was too old when I met Clémence. If only I'd met her when I was younger. I wasted so much time not knowing what it means to be…truly happy."

"I don't think everyone is meant to meet someone. Maybe I don't have a Clémence in my destiny." *And I don't want one.*

"I refuse to believe that." Viggo crushed his cigarette in the ashtray and turned to me. He put his hands on my shoulders. "I want my only child to be happy. I want you to be as happy as I am."

"*Far*, I *am* happy."

"But you could be happier, trust me, I know. You could be a whole lot happier."

Chapter 3

Saturday Evening, October 7, 2023

Nico floated in the antique cast-iron, eighteenth-century French bateau clawfoot tub, with a hand-burnished natural iron exterior in my master bathroom, which was on the third floor of the *Kartoffelrækkehus* I had inherited from my grandmother over a decade ago.

I was slowly renovating the potato townhouse, and unfortunately, right when I completed the ground floor where I had what they called a "conversation kitchen"—an open kitchen open to living and dining areas—a Molotov cocktail had decimated it.

The kitchen was the first thing I got back in order after the incident. I couldn't compromise on coffee. On the counter gleamed my brand-new Jura coffee machine that Clara had bought for me. The floors were not finished. Plastic covered the broken and charred floor. I was going to fix the floors this month. I had bought the wood and rented the equipment I needed. And every weekend, I was going to lay part of it. Slow and steady.

The bathroom was still a work in progress—and had been for many years. The bathtub took center stage and stood on a partially tiled floor. I had found just enough of the right black and white antique Spanish ceramic tiles to cover half the bathroom. I was on a mission to find same tiles (and the funds to buy them) for the rest of the bathroom, where a functioning modern toilet stood on the cement floor.

"I love this bathtub." Nico laid her head on the tub's edge and closed her eyes. "It's been such a long day, and this is just what I needed."

Unlike Clémence, Nico was tall…and, like her, blonde and beautiful, but only half French; the other half was Danish. Her hair was piled on her head in a messy bun, and she made quite a picture, tanned, naked, and relaxed.

I leaned against the doorway and poured champagne into a glass. I held the glass out to her, and she took it.

"You can stay," Nico offered with a smile, her eyes still closed.

"Take your break. I'll be in my office."

She sipped her wine and sighed in relief. "Præst, you know how to make a girl feel special."

I went into my office, which adjoined the master bedroom, and started my research on Noor Mallik.

I called my ex-boss and current friend, Tommy Frisk, *Chefpolitiinspektør*, Chief Police Inspector in Copenhagen.

"I need some information on a suicide case."

"Hello to you, too," Tommy said gruffly. "What's the case?"

"Suicide. Happened in Hellerup."

"Send me details, and I can see what I can find. New case?"

"Yeah. What do you know about Silas Haagen?"

"The Copenhagen Bank guy? Just what's in the news."

Since he couldn't help me with that part of the investigation, we talked a bit about the weather and Tommy's daughters, and made a tentative plan to meet for beer on a free evening in a few days.

While I waited for Nico to get done with her bath, I listened to a speech Silas Haagen had given on YouTube. He talked about how the answer to the world's problem of depression and anxiety was not more work-life balance but blending work and life in pursuit of existential well-being. Whatever the fuck that meant. Silas Haagen had recently published a book on the topic, and was hocking it in front of a large audience at some auditorium in Copenhagen.

Nico came into my office, wearing one of the T-shirts she left in my apartment for such occasions. She was barefoot and held an empty glass of champagne. She peered at my laptop screen over my shoulder. I paused the video.

"Why are you listening to this guy's blather?" She held her glass as I filled it with golden, bubbly liquid.

"That's not what the five hundred people in the audience think," I pointed out. "What do you know about him?"

She took a sip of champagne. "Just what I hear from the business desk in the newsroom. He's the youngest executive at Copenhagen Bank, turned things around in the Baltics, and is up for a promotion. He's Leif Timmermann's golden boy."

Leif Timmermann was the CEO of Copenhagen Bank, and had joined the bank seven years ago after a long career at Barclays in London.

"What's so special about him?"

Nico shrugged. She hoisted herself onto my desk next to my laptop, facing me. "What exactly are you investigating?"

Nico had helped me with cases before, and I had helped her with her work. I trusted her. So, I told her.

She shook her head and sighed. "Poor girl. We're late on the Me-Too bandwagon here in Denmark. I was talking to a colleague, and she said that Danish women got screwed because we believe we are an egalitarian society, therefore there must be no sexual harassment in Denmark. But there is. The number of times I've had to joke around a completely inappropriate sexual innuendo at workplace or sidestep a come-on…. And he looks the type, doesn't he?"

She turned her head to look at the frozen video image of Silas Haagen. "He obviously dyes his hair but not his beard. That's so pretentious. I've heard nothing about misconduct at Copenhagen Bank, well, not related to sexual harassment or a hostile work environment. I can ask around."

"That would be great." I closed the laptop and pushed it aside. I pulled her on the desk toward me.

She smiled as she put her feet next to my thighs on the chair and kissed me softly.

"Why don't we take the bottle of champagne to bed?" she suggested. "I'll drink wine, and you can do other things."

"Have I told you how much I adore how you think?"

"No. Why don't you show me?"
I did exactly as she asked.

Chapter 4

Sunday Morning, October 8, 2023

The next morning, as I ran around the lakes, a row of three rectangular water bodies curving around the western margin of the city center and one of the oldest and most distinctive features of Copenhagen, I planned my Sunday. I started my day every day at around six, rain or shine, snow, or sleet, by running the six kilometers around the lakes with others who walked, strolled, and jogged.

I returned from my run, made myself a cup of coffee, and *missed* my morning cigarette. Another twenty-three days to go, and then I could go back to my two cigarettes a day, and wine after 5 p.m. routine.

Nico joined me for coffee, dressed in jeans and a T-shirt. She had to get home to pick up her son, who had spent the previous week with his father.

"You know you can tell Lena not to take my t-shirts to the dry cleaners. It's really not needed." She drank coffee as she looked through her text messages.

Lena took care of my laundry and housework. She had been with Stine and Erik for nearly a decade and, a few years ago, had started coming to my place once a week to take care of cleaning, changing sheets, laundry, and everything else in between.

"You leave your clothes here and she does what she does." I raised my cup to her. "I'm really not involved."

Nico looked around the living room, and her face tightened. "It still pisses me off you lost your turntable."

My vintage Victrola Jackson had crumbled under the force of the Molotov cocktail that came sailing through my window, and the water had damaged the records. I hadn't bought a dining table yet, so I didn't need to replace that. But I did hate losing my blue Arne Jacobsen original swan sofa and a Flag Halyard chair, which I probably couldn't afford ever again. Also irreplaceable was the blue and white ceramic tiled coffee table designed by Severin Hansen in 1955 for the Royal Copenhagen Hotel. It had been one of a kind.

I surveyed the room. "I'll make it mine again."

She put her coffee cup down and came to kiss me. "I've got to go."

"Thanks for coming."

We didn't make plans for next time because that wasn't how we worked.

After Nicole left and I got ready for my day, I got a call from *Politiassistent* Freja Jakobsen. I had gone to the academy with Freja and we remained friends.

"Tommy asked me to call you."

"On a Sunday?"

"I'm on call this weekend."

"The suicide was your case?"

"No," she told me. "It was Ditte's."

Politiassistent Ditte Bentsen was Freja's colleague at the Hellerup Police Station, where they worked on crimes against people.

"I can come down and meet Ditte, if she's on this weekend," I offered.

"Ditte is on maternity leave; she'll return in eleven months. And I don't think it'll help. I looked through the file, and there's nothing here. Straight-up suicide. I can send you what we have."

"Thanks."

"Hey, question, why are you looking into a suicide? You think it's murder?"

"No," I said as sincerely as possible, so she'd know I wasn't bullshitting her, because I sometimes did. "Client wants to know why she killed herself, worries it was sexual harassment."

"No sign of that in the suicide note. But if that's the route you're taking, then no *problemo*. I will send it to your email."

"I owe you a drink."

"Drink...sssss."

After the call, I poured myself another cup of coffee and reviewed the file Freja emailed. As she'd said, there was nothing suspicious. It was cut and dried. Too many antidepressants with a bottle of California Pinot Noir. The 1-1-2 call had come from Noor's roommate and cousin, Afsana Mallik. The medical examiner had ruled it a suicide, no hanky-panky.

It was what I'd expected.

Not having much to occupy me, I went to Sapor to meet Afsana Mallik as she'd be in the kitchen by around noon to start prep for the Sunday evening service. I thought it would be easier to meet her at her place of work rather than the apartment where Noor killed herself.

IT WAS THE WRONG month to quit drinking and smoking. Entirely the wrong month, I thought, when Afsana Mallik took one look at me and told me to go fuck myself without using profanities.

"This is my place of work," she hissed in a prim English accent, tying her apron tighter around her waist.

I had gone into Sapor and asked for her, and the busboy had not even glanced at me before going into the kitchen to tell Afsana she had a visitor.

Afsana Mallik was born and raised in London, and graduated from *École de Cuisine Alain Ducasse*, a Paris-based French culinary school. In her short career, she had already worked for Sous Chef Chandan Taneja at Amaya, the Michelin-star Indian restaurant in London in the heart of Belgravia. I had been there once a few years ago, and it was still one of my top three food experiences. She was now a *Poissonnier*, the Chef de Partie responsible for preparing all fish dishes, working for the Basque Chef de Cuisine, Thiago Echeverria, who was in his early sixties.

Rumor was that Afsana worked in Thiago's kitchen at a Michelin-star restaurant in London as a *Commis Chef*, had an affair with him, and then joined him in Copenhagen. I had gotten most of this information from Nico's friend and restaurant critic Rasmus Frank, who was advertised to write "frankly" about restaurants.

Afsana led me outside the restaurant and looked at me disdainfully, her chin jutting up as we stood on the sidewalk on Wilders Plads right next to the Christianshavn Canal.

"I'm a private detective looking into your cousin's death," I explained in English.

She was beautiful. Very striking. She came up to my chest in her kitchen clogs, so I guessed she stood about five feet, five inches. She wore all white with splatters of something orange and yellow on her apron. Her black hair was tied back from her makeup-free face, intensifying her youth and beauty. Her eyes were big and black—and irritated. Shakespeare might have said beauty lives with kindness—but here it lived with fire. I preferred it.

How old was she again?

"Why?" she demanded.

"Because I've been hired to find out why Noor died by suicide." I was deliberately patient, probably annoyingly so, because she was getting increasingly flustered. In some perverse way, I was flirting with her, and as soon as I realized that, I stopped. Based on my research, she was twenty-five, a few years older than Sophie. I felt like a lecherous old man.

"Why?" she asked again.

"Because..." I sighed. "Same answer as before." I stopped flirting.

"And the same question as before," she retorted.

"I just need a little bit of your time—"

"No." She glared at me and then turned around. She took two steps toward the restaurant, and then looked back at me. "You are a complete stranger, and I will not discuss my family with you. This is personal and sensitive. I say this in the nicest way I can: get lost."

I stuck my hands in the pockets of the Burberry, camel-colored, cashmere coat that I had paired with a dark blue suit. I had worn a high-neck cashmere pullover with the suit to avoid wearing a tie. I looked down at my brown Kiton wingtip loafers and waited for inspiration to strike as I watched her leave.

"Of all the gin joints in all the towns," a voice heavy with Aussie came from behind me, and I turned and saw a familiar face.

"What a surprise." I shook hands with Simon.

"I'm the bar manager here." He grinned at me. "I can't believe it's you, Gabriel. Wow!"

Simon and I went to college together in Copenhagen. He was from Sydney, and we'd become friends because he knew how to party.

"You lost your hair, man."

Simon was slightly taller than my six foot three and, unlike me, had a full thatch of hair, which in Danish was called the color of *leverpostej*, Danish liver pâté. He used to be a gangly youth but had turned into a man who fit his skin well—even though most of what I could see had a tattoo on it. It suited him. He wore a white dress shirt that had been pushed up to his elbows, a snake's head tattooed on one hand, and a fire-breathing dragon on the other. He wore an apron, the same white as Afsana, but his was pristine.

"What are you doing here? We don't open for an hour. Do you have a reservation?" He ushered me in.

I put my fedora on the bar counter, and settled on a stool as he took his place on the other side of the counter.

"How about a drink? What do you like? You know, I've won awards for my cocktails."

It would take too long to explain my dry month, so I inclined my heard toward the Nuova Simonelli coffee machine as I sat down on one of the barstools. "I wouldn't say no to an espresso."

"Sure, mate. You look good. I heard you were a cop and then a private detective. I don't know any private dicks." Simon turned on the espresso machine, and expertly made me a cup. "Are you investigating something here?"

"I need to talk to one of your chefs," I explained.

He wrinkled his forehead in quest.

"Afsana Mallik. I'm looking into her cousin's death."

He frowned. "Looking into it? I thought she committed suicide."

"I believe she did. I've been hired to find out why."

"Why?"

I sighed. "Afsana asked the same question, and then asked me to take a hike."

"Right. She would. She's private. Not the silent type but doesn't reveal much about herself, you understand. Doesn't tell her business to anyone. She told us about the cousin because she needed time off, and when a chef needs a week off, we all find out what's up. She's close to Chef Echeverria; they used to, you know…have a thing. But not anymore, or at least that's what they tell everyone. All I know is some of the crew asked Chef about her cousin's death, and he told them to mind their own business."

I listened intently but didn't respond. I didn't have much to say.

"You married? Have kids?" Simon put my espresso in a small cup on a saucer with homemade biscotti, and placed it before me.

"Not married. Single. I have a daughter. Sophie's studying psychology at the University of Copenhagen. How about you?"

Simon shrugged. "I *was* married—got divorced. I have a girlfriend. She's great. Works here as a hostess. We live close by and have a great place. I have two kids in Viborg. I used to go there every other weekend, but now they're teenagers, so they love coming to the big city. Burns the ex's ass. It was…*hell*…it was *hell* with her. But we moved on. You divorced?"

"Sophie's mother and I separated when my daughter was four. It's been a while. Sophie is twenty."

"You want to stay for dinner? I can get a table for you. Friends and family rate on the menu," Simon offered.

"Thanks. Next time. I have dinner plans."

"What a blast from the past." Simon was bemused. "Hey, mate, do you want me to put in a good word for you with Afsana?"

"Would you? That would be great."

Simon went through the kitchen doors, and by the time he returned, I was done with my espresso.

"Some of the crew goes to No Stress on Nørregade after service. She said she'll see you there at around one."

"In the morning?" I knew No Stress, a bar that was open until 4 a.m. After a gig, I had been there a few times with my blues band.

He laughed. "She's going to make you work for it."

"Right." I stood up and held out my hand. "Thanks, Simon. It's good to see you. I'm glad you're doing well."

"Yeah." He shook my hand. "You know, you were always cool. I feel you still are. Let me know if you want me to get you a table here. We got busy after that first Michelin."

I promised him I'd reach out when I was ready to fork over fifteen hundred kroner for a meal.

I bicycled from Sapor to my townhouse by the lakes on the narrow Eckersbergsgade. Thanks to Inderhavnsbroen, a bridge exclusively for pedestrians and bicyclists that connected Nyhavn and Christianshavn, I was in front of my small white gate within 10 minutes, despite the post-work rush hour bicycle traffic.

"Hey, Gabriel, did you get the block party announcement? Are you coming or what?" my next-door neighbor, Jorgen, called out. He was in his seventies. He and his wife, Margarethe, were the glue that held our small community on Eckersbergsgade together. They'd been organizing a block party at the start of spring in April and one at the end of October when the days became shorter for nearly a decade and a half.

"Of course, I'm coming." I parked my bike and walked up to Jorgen. "I'm bringing Sophie's famous potato salad, and I promised Esther my gas lamp heater."

Esther lived at the end of the street. She was a single mother with two teenage sons I'd hired to help clean my living room after the incident.

"She's in charge of the heat." Jorgen nodded. "We're hoping it won't rain. If it's cold, it's fine. But if it rains, we're fucked." I had been to one of the block parties with umbrellas. Rain or shine, we ate, drank, and danced.

Jorgen was nearly six feet tall, and his back was straight despite the years. His white hair circled a bald center, and he wore black-rimmed glasses that were too big for his face.

"How's the renovation coming along?" he asked right when Margrethe's voice reached us.

"Who are you talking to?" She stepped out, wearing comfortable jeans and a t-shirt that said *Hvem kalder du bedstemor*, "who are you calling grandmother."

"Oh, hi, Gabriel. I thought he was talking to himself. You know what they say? Once they start talking to themselves, it's the end. That's when the husbands go completely senile." Margrethe patted Jorgen's shoulder.

"Stop calling me senile, old bat," Jorgen said good-naturedly, putting his arm around his wife. "Just because she's ten years younger than me, she thinks she's all that."

"I *am* all that."

I enjoyed the couple's banter. They'd been my neighbors for the entire time I had lived in the Kartoffelrækkehus, and for thirty years, my grandmother had also lived in the townhouse.

"Are you working on another big case?" Margrethe asked. "Can you tell us about it?"

"I keep checking the streetlights now since those Russians beat you up and bombed your house," her husband assured me.

"They didn't bomb his house; it was a Molotov cocktail." Margrethe jabbed him with an elbow.

"Isn't a Molotov cocktail a bomb?" Jorgen frowned.

Margrethe shook her head. "He's getting senile."

"She's the one losing her mind," Jorgen told me. "How's your shoulder, Gabriel? Giving you trouble? If you need help renovating, call me, okay? I used to build houses. Still can."

"You can't even fix the toilet anymore," his wife mocked him.

"Thanks. I certainly will," I assured him.

I walked past the picnic table and small children's playhouse in the middle of the street to my gate. I liked living here. It was unusual for neighbors to even talk to one another in Copenhagen, but here in the *Kartoffelrækkerne* neighborhood, there was a sense of community. If you fell off your bike, someone would come and help you up, and offer you a band-aid and a shot of something alcoholic. And if some Russian thugs beat you up, they'd call 1-1-2, keep your guitar safe, and hold your hand until the medics arrived.

The Potato Rowhouses, or *Kartoffelrækkerne*, comprised of 480 townhouses built in the late 1800s by the *Arbejdernes Byggeforening*, the Workers' Building Association. The association had bought the land by the Copenhagen lakes, where there used to be an agricultural farm. The nickname *Kartoffelrækkerne* emerged when the construction began, and the townhouses were strung in narrow rows, looking like potatoes. Even now, most of the façades had the old look and feel with yellow brick.

A variety of people lived on Eckersbergsgade. Some were single, some married, some married with children, some retired, a mix of age groups and skin colors. We had a Turkish family at the end of the street, a Nigerian couple had bought a townhouse recently, and a gay Spanish couple with a penchant for watering their plants (and doing everything else) naked had moved across the street from my townhouse.

I liked living here. This was home. I just had to make my townhouse mine. I'd done it once, and I'd do it again.

Chapter 5

Sunday Evening, October 8, 2023

Without warning, Victor switched our dinner venue at the eleventh hour. Instead of Hellerup, where Eymen, Clara, he, and I planned to meet, he texted saying he'd snagged a reservation at the trendy Restaurant Grimal. I was already on my bike when I got the message. Pulling up Grimal's address, I realized it was on Istedgade, the very street where I'd been shot just months earlier. This was my first time returning since the incident, and I took a moment to check in with myself, gauging any emotional upheaval. To my relief, I felt nothing.

Istedgade was a one-kilometer straight street that went from Hovedbanegården, the Copenhagen Central Station that featured cheap hotels, porn, drugs, and prostitution, to the modern part of Vesterbro, where 1900s tenement-style blocks had now become stylish and chic.

I locked my bicycle in the cycle stand by the restaurant. I'd wanted to try out the new restaurant since it opened a few months ago and touted a 200-strong wine list. It *really* was the wrong month to go dry.

Clara said as much when we were seated. She was petite and fair next to her tall and dark husband. She'd tied her hair away from her face in an artful bun, which probably took more effort to look messy than if it were not. She wore a black silk skirt with a long slit and a rust-colored sweater. But it was her boots that she showed off.

"Aren't they precious?" she asked me as she lifted both legs to show me. They were Chanel, brown leather, fold-over knee-high boots.

"For what they cost, they *are* fucking precious," her husband remarked, but there was no heat. Clara had money, and they didn't fight over *Kroner* as a couple. You didn't have to when you had as much as Clara did and were as generous as she was.

We were all dressed to ward off the cold. Victor wore a gray sweater with dark pants. Eymen was the only one in a suit, probably because he came straight from work. I had changed from my work uniform, which I considered a suit, into a pair of Todd Snyder cashmere olive dress pants with a classic vicuña crewneck sweater from Loro Piana. And since my skull needed warmth, I found comfort in a cashmere, camel-colored beanie from Brunello Cucinelli. When we sat, and it got too warm, I took off the cap and stuffed it into the pockets of my coat that hung over my chair.

"I'm sure you're wondering why I changed the restaurant at the last minute." Victor put down the wine menu and looked at me. "Does anyone want to venture a guess?"

"You're an eccentric man who thought it would be great to torture me by bringing me to a restaurant with an excellent wine list during my dry month?" I offered.

"*That* is a *capital* reason." Victor pursed his lips. "But I didn't think about it until you just mentioned it. Next time, I will. However, this evening, I discovered that someone I know you'd like to meet has dinner reservations at Grimal. So, I called Anders, and he said no problem and got us a table."

Anders Vendelbo was the owner of Grimal. Victor Silberg knew everyone there was to know in not just Denmark but all of Europe. He was your man if you needed to get into the three-Michelin-star Noma in Copenhagen or Arpège in Paris. And he was also your man if you wanted to invest a billion Danish *kroner*.

"Who do I want to meet?" I asked as the server came to our table.

"Silas Haagen," Clara announced, and then smiled at the server. "I'll have a gin and tonic."

"Me too," Eymen decided.

"Yeah, sounds good," Victor agreed. "We'll get some wine with dinner."

The server looked at me. "Tonic water with a twist," I said sullenly.

I looked around the minimalist restaurant with its white tablecloths and clean lines. Most of the tables were occupied—and there was a hubbub—a sense of excitement at discovering a new restaurant. It was palpable, and I decided to enjoy the food and not let the lack of wine interfere with my pleasure.

Bull fucking shit!

The lack of wine interfered with *all* pleasure, period. I wasn't an alcoholic; my dry month proved that to me, but I *was* a heavy drinker who enjoyed his drink, and the dry month was always way too fucking long.

"His reservation is at eight. Table for four. Copenhagen Bank had a weekend team-building meeting, so he's taking some of his team out for dinner. I thought if we were here earlier than him and seated where he'd see us when he passes by, he'd come and say hello," Victor explained.

"Team building over the weekend?" Clara asked. "I would hate to have to spend my weekends with my colleagues after spending all week with them."

"And that's why you don't have a corporate job, *skat*." Eymen kissed his wife's cheek.

"What can I say? I'm a quiet, little homemaker." Clara fluttered her eyelids dramatically.

Victor snorted.

Clara managed the Silberg Foundation. Many people who didn't know her thought of her as a trust fund baby, blonde, petite, and pleasant—she, in fact, had a master's in economics from the London School of Business, and could stand toe to toe with her CFO husband.

"What can you tell me about Silas Haagen, since you obviously know him?" I asked Victor.

"I don't know him; *he knows me.*" Victor nodded to the server, who brought our drinks.

"I can't believe you just said that. *Far*, you're such a snob." Clara shook her head in amusement.

Victor's blue eyes sparkled. He was a tall man who took up space physically and with his presence. "I know a little about him. Can't say one way or the other if he's sleeping with his secretaries or chasing them around conference rooms."

"They're not called secretaries anymore." Eymen grinned and drank some of his gin and tonic. It looked just the way it should, dry and tight, I thought enviously.

"It's better than calling them *tøsse*, which is what we used to call the girls. Either way, I don't know if he misbehaves with the *assistants*. Is that an okay term to use? I don't even know what to call them anymore," Victor finished exasperated.

"Women," Clara clarified. "*Far*, I know you want to behave like an old-fashioned hick, but you know better. I know you know better."

"Did you ever chase *tøsse* around conference rooms?" I asked Victor and heard Clara predictably groan.

Victor ran a hand through his full head of gray hair. "My daughter is here, but when it's just us boys, I'll tell you stories that'll make you realize you've wasted your youth."

Clara laughed. "*Far* likes to tell stories. *Mor* is definitely not the type who'd tolerate...what do you call it? Oh yes, adultery."

"Now, adultery is too extreme a word. I mean, a man pinches a woman's ass, that's just fun and games. I'm sure Eymen does it all the time," Victor said.

Eymen raised his hand. "You want to rile up your daughter, do it without involving me. I pinch no one's ass, not even my wife's…without her permission. And now, returning to Haagen, he's considered a creative banker. Made a lot of money for Copenhagen Bank managing the Baltic desk."

Victor snorted. "A lot of money is an understatement; he's made the bank fucking rich. He'll be the main speaker at their yearly conference for investors in New York in a couple of weeks. That means he's being groomed for the next big step. If it comes out that he's been bedding an employee who then killed herself, he'll lose his job and any other jobs he'd ever think of getting in Europe for the rest of his life."

"Or unless people forget, and people have short memories." Clara perused the menu.

"I don't think so, *skat*." Victor was affectionate and earnest. "I think men need to pay for their sins. I sit in many meetings, and you should see how men in boardrooms talk about women. And speaking of men in boardrooms, there are hardly any women there. Danish society needs a kick in its male-dominated ass, and I think the Me Too movement is just the ticket."

"Good thing, then, you didn't actually pinch a secretary's ass," Clara joked.

"I'm a gentleman and would never tell."

Clara put the menu down. "I'm starving. What're you planning to get, Eymen?"

The menu was small but varied enough to please everyone around our table.

"I'm thinking of the rabbit for the main, and I've heard excellent things about their terrine with pork and duck for the starter." Eymen pushed the wine menu toward me. "Since you can't drink, you can at least order the wine."

"Just rub it in, asshole." I looked through the wine list and groaned in despair. There were some beautiful wines listed, and Victor was paying.

After hearing what everyone was ordering, I suggested the Domaine Dujac Vosne Romanee's "Beaux Monts," 1er Cru 2016.

"It should work with your food. It's got a perfumed bouquet mixed with cold limestone. The taste is cherry and strawberry but tight and focused. Clara will like it for sure. There are some others I know of, but you'd be better off talking to the Somm."

"Why talk to a Somm when we have you, and it is so much fun to watch your eyes go big as you read through the wine list." Victor wasn't a wine guy; he leaned more toward whiskey but appreciated a decent red.

The wine was tasted by Eymen because I did not want to torture myself, and when he accepted it, the server filled all glasses but mine.

Victor had just taken a sip and hadn't even commented on the wine when the door opened, and in walked my quarry.

Silas Haagen entered with two men and one woman in suits, his face stern—which changed into a smile when he saw Victor. The others, all three of them, mirrored his expression.

"Victor." Silas extended his hand, and Victor rose to shake it. "What a pleasure."

"Of course." Victor managed to look genuinely surprised to see him.

Introductions were made, all hands were appropriately shaken.

"Why don't you join us?" Victor suggested.

If I weren't a trained investigator, I would have missed the flicker of excitement in Silas's eyes. He had not expected such a cordial welcome. He probably had met Victor on other occasions when he'd been ignored with the snooty Silberg look that Clara and Victor had perfected over the years.

"We would love to," Silas answered for his colleagues and himself.

Victor waved a hand, and the host immediately arrived. "We want to extend our table with four more seats."

Three servers and the host moved furniture quickly to get us all seated.

Victor and Clara maneuvered with ease so that I was seated between Silas and his female colleague, who introduced herself as Juula Saks. She was a Financial Institutions Relationship Manager for Copenhagen Bank in Estonia. She reported to someone who reported to Silas, who was head of Copenhagen Bank for the Nordics and Eastern Europe. Juula had a bachelor's degree in commerce from the London School of Commerce, and started working for Copenhagen Bank three years ago.

"Silas is my mentor," she gushed. "He's changed my life."

Investigators loved people like Juula. They were a mine of information, and you had to prod just a touch to get them to spill anything and everything.

Sitting next to Victor, Haagen was not paying any attention to me and singularly engaged Victor in a conversation I heard in my periphery about the pitfalls of the new compliance laws the EU was recommending for banks. According to Haagen, it was going to destroy banking as we knew it. I didn't think that was such a bad idea.

"How do you like living in Tallinn?" I asked Juula.

"I love it." Her smile was broad, and she sipped some of the wine I had picked. And we now had two open bottles of Domaine Dujac Vosne Romanee "Beaux Monts" 1er Cru 2016 at the table, not a drop of which I had drunk. "But," her voice dropped to a whisper, "Silas is working on getting me transferred here. I should know in a couple of weeks. I am so excited."

"You like Copenhagen," I prompted.

She flushed. "Yes, but more than that this is a chance to work even closer with Silas. He's brilliant, and I can learn so much from him. I'd move to Siberia to work with him. You understand?"

"Oh, yes."

"And," she whispered again with barely restrained excitement, "he'll soon take over all of Copenhagen Bank's business banking as Senior Vice President. I'll be on his team, and that's just going to be amazing."

Dessert came around, but I opted for a double espresso instead. Meanwhile, Haagen paid me no mind, which allowed me to listen to Juula recount her entire life story. So, this was Haagen's type: young, around mid-twenties, and eager to please.

I waited for a pause in conversation as everyone enjoyed the *pâte à choux* with praline *crème mousseline*, and then I went for the kill.

"I know a colleague of yours. She was from Pakistan. Noor Mallik." I enunciated each word carefully.

Pin drop, as much a cliché as it may be, aptly described the silence that fell. Clara hid her amusement, while Victor didn't.

"Copenhagen Bank is a big bank, Præst. Not everyone knows everyone." Victor raised the glass of port he was having with his dessert.

"She worked the Baltic Desk," I continued.

All three of Silas's colleagues looked at him and waited.

"Yes, we all know…knew Noor," Silas finally spoke after unnecessarily clearing his throat. "She passed away six months ago."

I waited a beat and then revealed, "Yeah, I know. I've been hired to investigate her death."

"Why?" Haagen asked calmly, but my trained investigator's eye could see he was rattled. *Gabriel Præst, master detective.*

"Because someone doesn't think she killed herself and wants confirmation," I lied.

Juula gasped. The other two suits stared blankly at me.

Silas remained composed, and then, as if talking to an inferior, imparted his wisdom, "I think you're wasting your time. The police confirmed she killed herself."

Juula couldn't hold on any longer and let the reins on her tongue go. "This is absurd." She spoke decent Danish, but as she got flustered, she lost her words, slipping into Estonian. "It's just absolutely...*rumal...idiootlik...idiotic.*"

Silas held up his hand. "This is a shock. You think someone killed Noor?"

I shrugged. "I don't know. That's why I'm investigating. But now that I have you here, I have some questions."

Victor leaned forward eagerly; he knew, as I did, that Silas knew he was trapped. If he didn't answer, he'd lose face in front of one of the most powerful financial figures in Denmark, and yet, he couldn't take the risk of what questions I may have in front of so many witnesses, including one of the most powerful financial figures in Denmark.

"This is neither the time nor the place. Your name is Præst?"

"Gabriel Præst," Victor put in, telling Silas that I was his man.

"Right. Præst, why don't we meet at my office tomorrow?" he suggested. He pulled out his phone and looked at it. "Shall we say around 10 in the morning? I have a 20-minute slot open."

Yeah, dude, we know you're busy as fuck.

I nodded and thanked him profusely and disingenuously.

The Copenhagen Bank people left immediately after that, and Victor asked for his favorite whiskey, a triple cask matured 15-year-old Macallan, to "celebrate how much fun this evening had been."

Eymen joined him.

I asked for more tonic water with a twist.

"So, this is how you work?" Victor asked. "I've always wondered."

"Usually, I have to hustle to meet people. I have an appointment tonight at one a.m. to see the victim's cousin. And sometimes, when I'm lucky, someone helps me as you just did."

"He uses his network," Eymen confirmed for Victor.

"And his friends help when they can." Clara was all smiles. She enjoyed being involved in my investigations and even accompanied me on several stakeouts when I was gathering evidence of infidelity. "*For satan*, did you see his face when Gabriel said he was investigating whether Noor was murdered? The man went pale under his tan."

"He did." Victor nodded thoughtfully. "And do you think he's the type who sleeps with his female colleagues? Is that the right term, Clara?"

Clara stuck her tongue out at her father.

"I think he's sleeping with that blonde that was sitting next to Præst," Eymen said.

"Oh, come on, that's obvious and sexist." Clara put her glass of cognac on the table with some force. "Just because she's good-looking and a blonde doesn't mean she's getting ahead by getting on her knees. I expected better of you, Eymen."

"Actually, it's because of how she talked about Silas," Eymen explained, leaning over to kiss his wife's cheek.

"She's absolutely smitten," I agreed. "And there's a possibility that she's sleeping with him, but I don't know for sure. Sometimes people just like their boss."

"And sometimes people fuck them," Victor tossed back his drink. "I think this is going to be an interesting case, *søn*. Let me know how else I can help. I can't stand that asshole."

Chapter 6

Monday Morning (Very Early), October 10, 2023

I reached No Stress a half hour before my appointment with Afsana so I wouldn't risk missing her in case she got there early.

It was a 10-minute bicycle ride from Grimal, where we'd literally closed down the bar and the restaurant. Victor's car had picked him up while Eymen and Clara had bicycled home to Frederiksberg.

No Stress was conveniently located right by Nørreport Station. The original Norwegian version of the bar had won awards for cocktails, so it was no surprise that the bar in Copenhagen was known for its mixologist. I'd never been a fan of mixed drinks, but as things stood, I didn't even bother to look at the menu and ordered a black coffee as I sat at the bar. The place was buzzing for a Sunday night. It was a cozy space where pictures of patrons with their friends decorated the walls, and I knew patrons often played the many board games on offer.

The first thought I had when I saw her was that she looked different, with her shoulder-length hair in curls around her face. She wore a simple black dress that hit mid-thigh where, if I wasn't wrong, comfortable thigh-high Givenchy clog boots began their journey down to her toes. She wore a black woolen coat and had a Prada backpack slung on one shoulder. Obviously, it wasn't her restaurant job paying for her wardrobe, so either she had a wealthy boyfriend or a rich family. My money was on the family. She looked like she was used to wearing the money she was adorned in. I knew the difference because I'd had to learn.

I stood up. She nodded and walked up to me, her eyes tired and slightly irritated. I had the urge to pull off my beanie and bow to her. I resisted it. If I had been honest with myself, and I wasn't planning to be, I'd say I was smitten. I needed to book an emergency session with Ilse, a therapist whom I'd been seeing for the past three years, so I could become a better version of myself. I figured if I was contesting making a pass at a woman nearly my daughter's age, I was nowhere close to being even a remotely decent version of myself.

She threw her backpack on the counter, and then removed her coat.

If I believed in God, I was sure he or she would smite me. The black dress hugged every inch of a *very* nice body. But she was twenty-five, all young women had nice bodies, didn't they? And what was I doing looking at one? Slightly disgusted with myself, I smiled my most platonic smile.

"May I buy you a drink?"

"Sure," she said without looking at me, and settled on the barstool. She turned to the bartender. "I'll have a Yamazaki 12, neat."

She'd definitely grown up with money, I decided, because she thought nothing of ordering a drink that went for seventeen hundred Danish *kroner* a bottle.

"You ordered that because I'm paying or because you—"

"I always have a Yamazaki at the end of the day," she cut me off. "Ask what you want so we can be done with this. Oh, and before we start, who hired you to look into my cousin's death?"

Gorgeous or not, I needed an attitude adjustment from her. Of course, she behaved exactly the way many people did when I poked my nose into their business. It just irked me she looked at me with such contempt.

"Someone who wants to know why she did what she did," I evaded. "I don't want to pry into your family's business, but my client is concerned that Noor was dealing with something difficult at work that pushed her to harm herself."

She nodded at the server, who poured her drink, and then looked at me. "You want to know why she killed herself?"

"Yes. Well, my client does. And I'm trying to find out."

"You think you can?"

I shrugged. "I can do my best. But only Noor can tell us what happened and why. I would only draw conclusions from facts I can uncover."

She took a sip and closed her eyes like I did when I had a Laphroaig or a good glass of Bordeaux. My coffee had gone cold, so I waved to the server, asking for a refill.

Afsana eyed my cup of coffee. "No drink?"

"I'm on a break."

Her lips twitched into a smile. "It's your dry month, isn't it?"

I narrowed my eyes. "How do you know that?"

She laughed. "I do a dry month every January, and I watch others drink like you're watching me. But if you can't stop, then you have a problem, so you have to do the dry month, right?" She had a snobbish but lilting British accent.

Lilting? Fuck, Præst, she's a kid.

Well, she's twenty-five. That's grown up, right? I had a kid by the time I was twenty-five.

And that kid is twenty-one years old. Four years younger than this woman whom you're eyeing with very non-paternal eyes, you pervert.

"I don't have a problem...with alcohol."

"Neither do I." She raised her glass to me, and I touched it with my cold cup of coffee. "Let's start fresh. I was annoyed in the kitchen because of some supply issue, and I took it out on you."

"What kind of supply issue?"

"Why would you want to know?" Now, she was flirting with me. *Great.* This was just great.

"Maybe I can help."

"You can help me get my hands on a sea urchin from Faroe Islands?" She tilted her head in challenge, her eyes lit with amusement.

Oh, yes, Præst, you're smitten.

"Maybe." I picked up the cup the bartender had just refilled with fresh coffee. "I have friends in Tórshavn, and in fact, someone who owes me a favor sells shellfish in the Bryggjubakki fish market *and* is the president of the Faroe Fish Farmers Association."

She stared at me. "You're making this up."

I put my right hand on my heart. "Absolute truth."

She finished her whiskey, and tapped on her glass when she had the bartender's attention. "So, you're a private detective, and you know people in Tórshavn. What else?"

It was an invitation. If good old Kierkegaard was around, he'd say: *there are two situations—do it or do not do it, you will regret both*.

"I play the guitar," I said, ignoring Kierkegaard's warning.

"Do you?" She was surprised, enthusiastic, and interested.

Are you trying to impress this kid now?

"I'm in a band; we play at Mojo." And I have a daughter who is nearly your age.

"I love Mojo." Excitement replaced the amusement in her big, dark, and beautiful eyes.

"And I have a twenty-one-year-old daughter," I blurted out. *Fuck!*

Her smile widened. "Really? And is there a wife?"

"No."

How would I explain this to Sophie? *Hey, skat, I'm having sex with someone half my age.* But she's only sixteen years younger, the man who wasn't a father inside me countered.

She picked up her glass of whiskey and ran an unpainted finger with short nails around the rim. "Do you think I'm flirting with you?"

I wasn't used to this generation, I thought. They were too bold.

"Why don't we talk about your cousin?" I proposed.

"Okay," she said soberly. "You know, she left a note."

"Yes."

She nodded thoughtfully. "I have been struggling to come to terms with the idea that she might have taken her own life, yet I can't ignore how despondent she seemed in recent months. Her life revolved around her work; no matter how late my day stretched, she was still working when I got home. She often had late-night phone calls with associates in the US. I must admit, my own schedule was packed—I would wake to find she'd already left for the day. The truth was, our time together had diminished; we just weren't present with each other anymore."

"I'm so sorry for your loss." There were no words to assuage guilt when you lost someone to suicide. There were doubts, painful analyses, and that question, which can never be answered to anyone's satisfaction: *Could I have saved them?*

Afsana nodded sadly. "That is the hard part. Her mother and mine are sisters, so they expect me to have answers. And what am I supposed to say? We were living together, but I didn't know her life, and she didn't know mine? I knew she was depressed because she told me. We argued about something in the kitchen...like you do with a roommate. I can't remember what it was about. What I remember is flippantly telling her to see a doctor and get some chill pills. Then, she kills herself by overdosing on Xanax. I mean, talk about a mind fuck."

I said nothing and just waited for the fresh onslaught of grief and guilt assaulting her to pass.

"And the only reason I'm talking to you is because you're cute." She sniffled but kept the tears at bay.

"That's what they all say."

"I'm sure they do. And I like your coat." She indicated to my Burberry camel-colored cashmere coat resting on my bar stool. "It's...handsome."

"They say that, too."

Her lips curved, and she looked at me. "How old are you?"

"Forty-one."

"Thank God. For a minute there, I worried you were in your fifties."

I sighed.

She laughed out loud at that. A rich and clean laugh. "You don't look like you're in your fifties. You said you had a daughter, so...you don't look *that* old...I mean...I'm going to shut up and drink because I'm obviously making this worse."

She was charming and I was *charmed*.

"Why was Noor talking to someone in the US? I thought she worked the Baltic desk?"

Afsana thought about it for a minute and then shrugged. "I knew little about her job. But you could check her phone to see the calls she made, couldn't you? They do that in the movies all the time."

Yeah, I could so that, I thought. That was next on my list. In the initial investigation, once the medical examiner had ruled Noor's death a suicide, there had been no effort made to look at her phone logs or emails.

"You have her phone?"

She looked confused. "No. Should I?"

"They gave her effects to you, didn't they?"

Her shoulders sagged. "They're in a box. I didn't touch it. I left the apartment when it happened, and I haven't returned. I should pack up her stuff, but I just can't. And our lease is until the end of the year, so why bother now? I thought I'd do it when I have to."

"Where are you staying now?"

"Hotel Skt. Petri."

"For six months?" I raised my eyebrows. *Family money, for sure.*

She shrugged. "I thought it'd be a few weeks, and then it turned into a month, and then another."

"I have to ask. How can you afford it?"

"I can't," she replied honestly. "My parents can. My mother is a big deal at an insurance company in London, and my father has pots of money because he owns a lot of real estate in the UK and Pakistan."

"Ah."

"Ah, indeed."

I finished my coffee. "You said she had Xanax, do you know which doctor prescribed it to her?"

"I don't know. I am still seeing my doctor in London. If I need something, I fly back and see her. I don't know what Noor did. We were close as kids, but now it's the rat race years, you know? She was trying to make it in banking, and I'm working in a restaurant where you get about five hours of sleep a night if you're lucky. And I have no weekends, just Mondays when I sleep and get my life in order. We didn't chat late into the night about our lives and boys."

"So, you wouldn't know if she was having trouble at work?"

"Not really. She talked about that guy she worked for. The famous guy..." she thought about it for a moment, "Silas, something."

"Silas Haagen?"

She nodded.

"Were they..." I trailed off.

"No," she protested. "It wasn't like that. And she would never sleep with a married man. Noor was discerning about the men she had relationships with. Careful. She was always critical of my...it's not like I sleep around, you know, it's just that I'm maybe a little less restrictive about who I have sex with."

I smiled. *Yeah, me too.*

"If you are Simon's friend, I'm sure he talked about Thiago…Chef Echeverria. Everyone at Sapor does. I sometimes feel like I'm wearing a scarlet letter. Thiago is the one who was married, not me. I owed his wife nothing. In any case, they were separated when we were together."

"I'm absolutely in no position to judge, and even if I were, I wouldn't." My interest in her had nothing to do with her affair with an older man. It made me wonder, though, if she had a type…and it was older men.

Stay away from her, Præst. She has what they call "daddy issues".

"I'm not with him anymore," she said emphatically. "I ended it when he asked me to join him at Sapor. It was hard enough back in London, you know. I didn't want to deal with that here. But news travels fast in the restaurant business…quicker than Twitter."

"Was Noor dating anyone?"

"Not that I know."

"Would you mind if I checked her room?"

Afsana looked at me critically. "Can you go without me?"

"Yes."

"Then, fine. I can give you the keys, but I'm not going there."

"That's fine." I put my hand on hers. It was instinctive. She was distressed, and I wanted to comfort her.

"Have I been of any help at all? Or...."

"Everything helps." I let go of her hand.

Tacitly, we decided it was time to leave. I paid the bill, and as I did, I pondered the question: *to walk her to her hotel or not*?

"Will you walk me to my hotel?" she asked, and I, a gentleman, acquiesced.

I put my bicycle between her and me as we walked into the quiet October night.

"Where do you live?"

"*Kartoffelrækkerne.*"

"I love those buildings. I've never been inside one." She hitched her backpack on her shoulder.

"You can see mine." We were doing this, I decided. We were two grownups. One way more grown-up than the other. "A warning, my living room is being renovated, so it's messy."

I didn't tell her that someone had destroyed the living room with a hand-thrown incendiary weapon, hence requiring it to be fixed up.

She paused momentarily and then, with a tone full of self-deprecation, said, "I was going to say something coy, like, but your bedroom is all good, isn't it? But I decided it was too much."

I wanted to tell her I was nearly old enough to be her father.

No, you're not. You'd have to have a child when you were sixteen to have a daughter her age, the voice in my head with the two red pointy horns said.

We were thankfully soon in front of her luxury hotel. Skt. Petri was in the Latin Quarter of the city and was once upon a time a department store. The hotel had a lovely New York-rooftop-inspired garden where it was easy to while away an afternoon with friends and colorful drinks with umbrellas.

We stood by the stairs to the glass doors of the hotel, a doorman poised to let her in.

"Thank you for talking to me."

She looked at me with speculation in her eyes and then smiled slowly. "Do you want to come in?"

I took a step away from her, bicycle, and all, obviously and without hesitation. I would not be an asshole. I'd just asked her about her dead cousin, and she was, whether she knew it or even liked it, vulnerable. And there were rules.

"I should go home."

"Yes," she agreed tightly. "What do you think you'll find out about Noor?"

"I don't know," I replied honestly. "But I can probably piece together enough of her life in her last months to paint a picture."

"I'll leave the key to my apartment and the address at the hotel lobby tomorrow. You can pick it up whenever you want." Her tone indicated she'd decided upon her next steps, which included not taking one toward me. "It was nice meeting you, Gabriel Præst." She held out her hand, and I shook it.

"Again, thank you for talking to me and allowing me to look through Noor's belongings."

I watched her go up the stairs to the hotel, and at the glass doors, as the doorman held it open, she turned around. "Take off your cap."

I gave her a puzzled look, and then slowly took off my beanie.

She grinned. "Still cute."

I whistled Nina Simon's *Feeling Good* as I biked home.

Chapter 7

Monday Morning, October 10, 2023

After my morning run and sorely missing my morning cigarette, I stood in front of my closet, thinking about what to wear to meet Silas Haagen. His assistant had sent me an email bright and early to give me 15 minutes with the busy man at eleven a.m.

The obvious answer was a power suit, but that would turn this into a pissing contest. I wore a Tom Ford Prince of Wales wool suit in charcoal gray with a heather gray high-neck cashmere sweater. And just for fun, I added a burgundy Gucci wide-brimmed, felt fedora. I liked the look. If he was a businessman philosopher, I was a businessman cowboy.

I bicycled to Holmens Kanal, where Copenhagen Bank's headquarters were housed since the bank came into existence in 1871. I loved this part of the city. It was right across from Magasin, the department store, and Hotel D'Angleterre, close to Nyhavn and all the delights of Kongens Nytorv. This was tourist heaven but also quintessentially Copenhagen.

In the summer, locals mingled with tourists by the colorful buildings in Nyhavn, enjoying a seafood lunch in cafés and restaurants that had been around for over a hundred years. But summer wasn't even a dream right now. The sky was a dull gray, matching my sweater, and those who walked and bicycled the sidewalks and streets hunkered down, the collars of their coats high, thick woolen scarves as added protection, hats covering their sensitive-to-the-cold ears, and lips that were chapped and blue. The wind was relentless. My non-Danish friends never could understand how Danes bicycled all year round. It was torture during the winter, they'd say. *That's what separates the men from the boys*, I'd say. Not to mention the way I ate and drank without restrictions; if I didn't run *and* bicycle, I'd be three times my size and none of my clothes would fit me.

Silas Haagen's office was on the third floor, the good-looking blonde woman dressed in a pencil skirt suit and very high heels at reception told me. She smiled brightly and added, when I introduced myself, that she knew who I was and that I had an appointment with Silas Haagen and Harald Wiberg.

I smiled back at her. I had thought I only had an appointment with Silas Haagen, but apparently, I had an appointment with him and Copenhagen Bank's chief legal counsel. As good old Billy Shakespeare's King Henry IV said, the game is afoot.

I felt triumphant. Something was *up* because why on earth would Silas bring in the big legal guns to talk about an employee who had killed herself?

A young brunette woman in another skirt suit introduced herself when I stepped out of the elevator. She took me to a meeting room with a money view of Copenhagen. Even dark and gray, the city thrummed with a bright energy. The red rooftops, the green copper domes, and the tall chimneys told a story rooted in a rich history. The meeting room was more of a boardroom, not deserving of a lowly private eye—and I guessed that Copenhagen Bank was flexing its considerable muscles, showing me they had a lot of power. What they actually had was a lot of well-dressed, skinny assistants old enough to be my daughter. No, not old enough to be Sophie's age, probably more like Afsana's age.

A slight four years older *than your daughter*, said a cautionary voice inside me.

"Silas is in a meeting, but he asked me to take care of you," the brunette informed me. "He won't be long. Would you like a cup of coffee?"

"Thanks. I take my coffee black," I told her.

She walked up to the end of the room and used one of those environmentally destructive high-end coffee capsule machines. I only winced inwardly when she discarded the used plastic coffee pod unceremoniously in "general" trash and not the blue recycle bin. Would there even be recycling in this mecca of financial corruption? It was probably because Eymen was a finance guy that I'd learned to distrust the entire industry. "You can be in finance, or you can be ethical; they are mutually exclusive," he'd once told me.

"How do you sleep at night being unethical?" I'd asked.

"They pay me a shit ton of money. I sleep like a baby."

Eymen was practical. He would never work for a bank, but enjoyed working for a pharmaceutical company. "They *mostly* save lives."

"They gouge money in the name of innovation," his wife, Clara, protested.

"And they also save lives, skat," he'd countered.

Silas and Harald made me wait. *And* they orchestrated their entrance. Harald came in first. He was a big man, nearly six feet, two inches shorter than me, and broad, about 120 kilos to my 80. His blue suit wasn't precisely ill-fitting, but he didn't look comfortable in it. He wore a white dress shirt with a blue and yellow tie. His hands didn't match his office outfit. They were large, rough, unmanicured, and strong. He felt less like a lawyer and more like a thug. The handshake wasn't innocuous. It was one of those I can break your bones, Putin-style ones.

I didn't get into a pissing contest with him and pulled my hand away as soon as I could. I wasn't drinking this month; I didn't need a single broken bone, because everyone knew when you broke bones, you drank whiskey to drown the pain and discomfort.

"How do you know Victor?" He sat in a chair on my side of the table and angled himself to face me.

I knew all the tricks. I'd chosen to sit with my back to the window because, during an interrogation, you always put the person you were questioning with the sun in their eyes. Not that there was any sun today; it was just practice for me, and it appeared for Harald as well.

"I went to university with his daughter and son-in-law."

He nodded. "Eymen. He's one of the good ones."

"Good ones of what?" I kept my tone light. I'd heard this before. Eymen was the good immigrant versus the ones who lived in the ghetto.

Harald grinned. "Chief Financial Officers."

"Right." I finished my coffee and then looked at my watch. Silas was now twenty-five minutes late.

"Are you in a rush?" Harald sat lazily in his chair, which contrasted with how he watched me, like a fucking hawk does its prey.

"No, I was more concerned about Silas's time. His assistant said he only had fifteen minutes for me."

Harald smiled waspishly. I didn't like the man at all. His teeth were very white. His hair was red and combed neatly with gel. His glasses were round on top of a nose covered with freckles. He was perfect casting for a serial killer.

"Katrine," he called out through the open door of the meeting room. "En kop kaffe."

The skinny brunette rushed inside to make him a cup of coffee. And as she made the coffee, he watched her. She'd made coffee for him before because she put a sugar cube in his black coffee and politely asked, "Will there be anything else, Harald?"

"Nej tak, skat," he said, and I felt like, if I weren't there, he'd have patted her ass.

She smiled uneasily and left the conference room. I couldn't stand men who thought they could call women darling in the workplace. It reeked of chauvinism.

I didn't have much time to ponder the lack of progress when it came to women's rights in corporate Denmark because Silas Haagen strolled in. He wore a gray suit, Armani, I guessed. His beard was combed and glossy, as was his shoulder-length hair.

"I'm so sorry I got delayed." He rushed in and shook my hand. "Thanks for keeping...ah Præst, right...company, Harald."

Harald shrugged.

"Harald is our legal counsel," Silas continued. He walked to the coffee maker and made himself a cup of espresso. He also drank it black.

He sat across from me. "Thanks so much for waiting for me."

"Not a problem."

He smiled and leaned back. "You said that you're investigating Noor's death. The police did that. We checked, didn't we, Harald?"

Harald nodded. "I spoke to a pregnant broad. She was the lead detective. It was suicide. She left a note. What exactly are you investigating, Gabriel?"

He would not pretend he didn't know my name the way Silas had tried to. The power structure in the room was clear. Harald came first, Silas next, and then sad little PI Præst.

"My client wants to know how she died *and*, if she killed herself, why she did so."

Silas shook his head and then looked at Harald. "Is this Noor's family? I hear they're wealthy and influential...in Pakistan."

"And London," Harald added.

I sat stone-faced for a long moment.

"He will not tell us who his client is." Harald stood up and leaned toward me on the table. If I were a weaker man, I'd have been intimidated. "We have no liability for Miss Noor Mallik's death. Do you understand?"

I shrugged. I could shrug with the best of them.

"What's that supposed to mean?" Harald demanded, his eyes narrowing.

"I understand."

"I know you think you're a hotshot because of what happened with Yousef Ahmed. I heard you almost died." Harald looked me straight in the eye. "Now, that witch hunt may make you think you're some kind of hero. You're not. You come after any of mine, I won't go easy as Elias did."

By Elias, he meant ex-Danish Prime Minister Elias Juhl. I couldn't hide my surprise. The man was showing me all his cards right away. I guess he was no bullshit.

"I appreciate your candor." He didn't scare me. I wanted him to know that. "The bullet only caused minimal damage.

Thank you. It wasn't a witch hunt. Neither is this." I turned away from Harald and toward Silas. "Bringing your lawyer for a casual conversation makes you look like you have something to hide."

"I just came to say hello." Harald put his hand out again, and this time, I decided to risk the broken bones when I shook it. "I hear you're a stubborn son of a bitch."

"I compensate for that flaw with my good looks." He let go of my hand. I resisted the urge to rub it.

Harald guffawed. "You're alright, Præst."

I didn't respond in kind, partly because it would be disingenuous and secondly, *fuck him.*

He left the conference room and slammed the door shut behind him like a toddler having a snit.

Silas Haagen and I smiled at one another. He was uneasy, but I was smug. I had absolutely no reason to be self-satisfied, but I was going to fake it till I made it. I decided to stay silent until the other person spoke. With Harald, it probably wouldn't work; lawyers knew how to remain silent. Silas was no lawyer.

"So…Noor?" he started.

I waited.

He shook his head. "It was a huge tragedy."

I drank some coffee.

"Huge tragedy," he repeated, and then sighed. "There was no impropriety on the part of Copenhagen Bank. I want to be clear about that."

I raised my coffee cup in acknowledgment.

"She was a good employee. Solid performer. It's a major loss for the team."

"I spoke to her family, and they said that before her death, she was talking to someone in the US every night. Do you know what that could be about?"

Silas kept his face stony—the apologetic smile, the steely eyes, and the uncomfortable jut of his jaw. "I see no reason she'd talk to anyone about work in the US. She managed the Baltic desk."

"That's what I thought."

"Maybe it had nothing to do with work," Silas suggested.

"The person I spoke with thinks it probably was work."

"Who did you talk to?" he demanded.

I smiled sheepishly. "They spoke to me in confidence. You know how it is."

"No, I actually don't." His voice was now firm. "I'm a banker, Præst, not some detective."

Some detective? He was certainly putting me in my place.

"I understand. Do you know who Noor's friends at work were?" I changed the subject. But I knew I hit a nerve. He didn't like that I knew Noor was talking to someone in the US.

"No." His tone said this conversation was over.

"Colleagues?"

"Please don't disturb my people, who are doing their jobs. If you have questions, you can ask me."

I picked up my Gucci fedora from the table and rose. "I have no more questions for you."

"I repeat, please do not bother Copenhagen Bank employees with—"

"With due respect, you can't tell me who I can talk to and who I can't," I interrupted him smoothly. "You can choose to not give me information, and I can choose to talk to anyone and everyone I want about Noor. You're welcome to let your employees know not to discuss Noor with me, but then people will wonder what you have to hide."

"I have nothing to hide." Silas rose, his temper shone on his face. His nostrils flared. His loose hair around his shoulders seemed to flutter as he shook angrily. He didn't have Harald's suaveness.

"Then you have nothing to worry about." I extended my hand, and he shook it after a moment of indecision. "Thank you for your time."

I left him in the conference room with the money view and went to find the exit that would take me out of the fucking revered bank.

I learned little about Noor, but I did find out that Silas Haagen and Harald Wiberg were concerned about an investigation into her death.

I unlocked my bicycle, and before getting on it, I emailed Flora's private email address, requesting her to call me at her convenience.

I had lunch at FIAT on Kongens Nytorv because it had a good wine list, was close by, and was not Café Victor, which was my go-to lunch place where I had gone twice the previous week.

FIAT was a trattoria that served shaved black and white truffles during the season with pretty much anything you wanted. They'd even put it on gelato if you requested it, at a cost. The restaurant was a staple in Kongens Nytorv, and had a lovely heated and covered patio that was ideal for the finicky Copenhagen weather.

I'd just parked my bicycle in the stand next to Espresso House on Kongens Nytorv when I got a call from Afsana.

"Hi." I ignored the blood rushing to all the wrong places.

"I have opera tickets. Two of them. It's for Carmen tonight." She talked like she was running a hundred-meter race.

"Okay." I didn't even think about it. Didn't flip through my mental calendar to check if I had a gig anywhere in the evening or plans or anything.

"I'll meet you at the Operahus at six-thirty," she said and then added as an order, "Don't be late. I'll go in without you."

"Yes, ma'am." I couldn't resist it.

She hung up.

I went into FIAT with a big smile, which vanished when I got a harried call from Flora.

"Where are you?" she asked flustered.

"At FIAT, having lunch."

"I'll be there in ten minutes."

I was looking forward to eating alone but decided that it wasn't a bad thing to meet Flora right away and get some insight into the people Noor worked with and also get a pulse on why Harald Wiberg was at my meeting with Silas.

I decided against pasta and black truffles and went for the grilled octopus with 'nduja, potatoes, and rucola. I ordered a glass of sparkling water with a twist and wondered, browsing the wine list, about what I would get if I were drinking. I decided it would be a glass of Pinot Nero Franz Haas Alto Adige. I would admire its ruby red color and finely marked nose of raspberry and clove and it would go perfectly with my spicy octopus.

I'd just torn a hunk of table bread to dip into olive oil and balsamic vinegar when Flora arrived. She looked as flustered as she'd sounded on the phone. She looked around the restaurant to find me. I had let the front desk know to send her to the covered and heated patio where I liked to sit because it made the dreary gray seem bearable in the winter and was refreshingly cool in the summer.

Her hair was tight in a severe ponytail, so tight that I feared that her hair was going to snap off her scalp. She paired her hair with a black skirt suit. She had nice legs, and her high-heeled black booties made them look like they were miles long.

"Did you meet Harald today?" she asked even before she sat down.

I raised my glass of water. "Hej, hvordan har du det?"

She took a deep breath and sat. "I'm fine."

"Thank you, as I am."

She sighed. "I was barking at you, wasn't I?"

"I wouldn't be so rude." I waved a hand at the server. "What would you like to drink?"

"I'm at work," she protested, and then shrugged. "I need a glass of something strong."

"I recommend a glass of the Pinot Nero Franz Haas Alto Adige."

We ordered when the server came. She decided on the beef carpaccio, which I also recommended because I thought it would go well with the Pinot Nero.

"I had a meeting set up with Silas Haagen, which Harald Wiberg gate crashed. They wanted to know what I was investigating and why, but mostly, they wanted to scare me."

"Did they succeed?"

"I'm harder to scare than most."

"Harald called me. He told me you were investigating Noor's suicide, and I was to let everyone related know not to talk to you."

"I asked Silas to give me names of people Noor worked with."

She licked her bright-red-painted lips. "You want me to give you those names."

I leisurely dipped a piece of bread into the olive oil, and then into the balsamic vinegar, savoring each bite, giving her the much-needed time to make a decision: whether to tell me who to talk to at Copenhagen Bank, going against the wishes of the general counsel.

"I could get fired." She broke off a piece of bread and did the dipping thing absently.

It would be a lie to say, no, they'll never fire you. I never trusted corporate Denmark. They were all a bunch of mercenary bastards, and the banking industry was worse than most.

The server brought our food.

"You'll have to talk to them after hours." She stabbed her fork into the carpaccio and ate a few bites, but I felt she wasn't doing justice to the finely sliced meat medley the chef had put together.

"Okay."

She nodded. "This is very good," she told me. "I've never been here before. I see it all the time but have never been."

"It's a good place." I didn't want to push, but I was pretty close to asking her to give me the names…now. I was running out of patience.

"Achim Suotamo was at her level, and they worked quite a bit." She took a sip of wine and set it down. "Marlene Bendixen was an assistant. She went on maternity leave and never came back. Her husband has a startup that went public. She quit three months ago. Noor and she went out and had drinks several times. She was distraught when Noor died."

The octopus was grilled to perfection, and the only thing that would've improved the meal was a glass of wine. I finished my glass of sparkling water and waved at the server for another. I was indulging hydration.

"There is Juula Saks," she continued. "They didn't get along. And…."

"I met Juula," I told her. "She's a Haagen acolyte."

"I'm sure they're sleeping together." Flora bit her lip. "I know I'm HR, I'm supposed to say nothing until I have proof blah blah, but…between you and me, it's almost like she's ready to go on her knees for him."

I grinned. "You may be right."

"How did you meet her?"

I didn't want her to know about Victor's machinations, so I said, "By accident. Silas and his colleagues were at the same restaurant where I had dinner with Eymen and Clara."

Flora didn't think it was suspicious. She probably didn't know Clara or her old man well enough. Between those two, they could run the world. They probably already ran the country with no one knowing about it.

"If you talk to Juula, you want to be careful." Flora then rolled her eyes. "But the way you look, she'll probably be easy. She's a complete slut."

"I have no objection to anyone's sex life as long as they don't practice it in the street and frighten the horses," I kept my voice steady.

"What?"

"Oscar Wilde said that. I don't remember about what, but that's my philosophy as well about people's sexual activities." There was a slight note of warning in my voice. I didn't approve of women being slut shamed.

"That's not what I meant…." Flora was immediately contrite. "She…she is just…"

"Let's leave it at that." I did not want to dislike Flora, we had to work together.

"I sounded like a judgmental bitch," she confessed. "I'm sorry. But I can't stand her…and not because of the sleeping around or maybe because of it, I'm not sure."

"I'll be circumspect."

"Eymen mentioned that's your middle name," she tried to joke to lighten the mood.

I shook my head. "Discretion is my middle name. Circumspection? Now, that takes some work."

CHAPTER 8

Monday Afternoon, October 10, 2023

I CALLED ACHIM SUOTAMO and when he didn't pick up the phone; I sent him a text message, asking him to call me back. I didn't tell him why, just what my name was and that I needed to speak with him. I had learnt that if I kept it vague, people became curious and got in touch.

I had better luck with Marlene Bendixen, the assistant who had quit working because her husband hit it big. She lived on the tree-lined Frederiksberg Allé in a renovated building that was home to Frederik the VI, a beer bar on the ground floor that offered over twenty-five beers on tap, both Danish and foreign, and served traditional Danish food. The restaurant was named after the Danish King Frederik the Sixth who used to summer in his castle in Frederiksberg with its vast gardens at the end of the street.

When I was in university, I had dated a theatre major before I met Stine, and she and her friends frequented Frederik VI, not just because it was inexpensive but also because it was on Copenhagen's theatre street. I had learned then that Dan Turèll, one of my favorite Danish authors well known for all his books (though I enjoyed his *Mord Serie*, Murder Series, best), was a regular patron, and his photograph still hung on the wall above his favorite table in the bar. The Mord series comprised ten books, each featuring an unnamed journalist-detective and his team. This included his girlfriend, lawyer Gitte Bristol, *Politiinspektør* Ehler, bartender Bob, and server Soffy. Set in the eighties, the books vividly portrayed an era of analog phones, urgent telegrams, casual smokers, and Copenhagen's seamy side. It had been a while since I last read *Mord i Mørket*, *Murder in the Dark*, Turèll's first and my favorite in the series. Feeling nostalgic, I decided it was time to revisit it.

While I waited by the apartment doorbell for Marlene to answer, I wondered if Afsana liked to read—and if she did, what were her favorite books. Learning about Afsana's reading choices would help determine her level of maturity. And then I could decide if we should...or should not....

"*Hej*, Gabriel?" a voice inquired through the intercom.

"Yes."

"Could you come to the *baggård*," the voice requested.

Like many apartment buildings in the city, this one featured a courtyard at its center, surrounded by flats. It was equipped with picnic benches, barbecues, and sandboxes for children. The space also provided areas for parking bicycles, storing trash bins, and offered a perfect spot for sunbathing in the summer.

At the edge of the courtyard, as was customary, four prams with sleeping babies were parked. The prevailing philosophy held that babies slept better outdoors, turning these prams into essentially portable baby beds. I recalled walking many miles with Sophie in her pram to help her sleep and ensure she stayed asleep, before she graduated to sitting in the bicycle's baby seat.

Marlene sat alone on a picnic table bench, enveloped in a bright red Patagonia puff jacket. A red cap covered her flowing, curly, blond hair. With a leather-gloved hand, she gently pulled and pushed a pram, soothing the small cries of an almost asleep baby, her movements filling the quiet space.

"Hi," she said apologetically. "Nina is just about to fall asleep. Please sit."

I sat across from her on the picnic bench. It was a cozy courtyard, probably cozier in the summer months than now when the grass was past the first frost, and the trees were bare.

"Thank you so much for seeing me." I huddled into my jacket. I had already pulled my fedora around my ears when I bicycled from FIAT. It was fucking cold.

"*Det er ikke noe problem.* I'm not doing much; just taking care of Nina. She has a cold, that's why she's not at *vuggestue.*"

I had seen a daycare at the edge of the street and predicted that little Nina spent a few hours a day there.

"How can I help you? You said you were a private detective."

I explained that I'd been hired to investigate Noor's death, carefully skirting around the subjects of suicide and murder.

She didn't seem to notice my evasion, as she immediately launched into expressing her feelings.

"I was devastated when I heard the news. Just a few weeks earlier, she had visited and seen the baby. She brought this adorable little Georg Jensen blanket for her, which I now use in her bedroom. It's my way of keeping Noor's memory alive."

Marlene dabbed at her eyes with her gloved hand.

Nina's tiny cries gradually subsided into silence as she fell asleep. Marlene continued to rock the pram, speaking softly so as not to disturb the baby.

"Do you want coffee?" she asked when it was obvious that Nina was out for the count. "We can go inside the apartment. She's going to sleep for at least two hours."

She quickly checked the baby monitor and, confirming it was working, led me upstairs to her elegantly appointed six-room flat on the second floor. The entrance opened into a sleek kitchen, complete with access to a spacious balcony boasting views of the Frederiksberg Gardens—likely a real estate agent's dream of *the perfect spot for afternoon sun*. The living and dining areas were expansive, furnished in Danish minimalist style. A bassinet was nestled beside the sofa in the living room, surrounded by various baby-related knickknacks, announcing the presence of a little one in the home.

She quickly took my coat, gloves, scarf, and fedora, hanging them alongside her own in the entrance closet. After removing our shoes, we proceeded inside.

I settled on a barstool at the smooth, beautiful oak kitchen counter, admiring its intricate woodwork despite the maintenance it likely required. Beside me were two more barstools and Nina's Trip Trap baby chair, designed to adapt and grow with her over the next eight to nine years.

Marlene set a kettle to boil and prepared a French press with ground coffee, carefully placing it on a cutting board to protect the oak counter. This reminded me why I preferred granite countertops in my own kitchen, they were less fussy about heat.

"Noor was lovely and so kind," Marlene said as she poured boiling water into the French press. "She always bought me a present for Christmas, and not just some stocking stuffer, but a proper one. Once, it was an ornament from Royal Copenhagen. I can't believe she's gone."

She opened a cabinet and brought out two Royal Copenhagen cups and saucers.

"Milk, sugar?"

I shook my head.

She poured mine black, and added some milk to hers. She came and sat next to me at the counter, and turned slightly to face me.

"Did she have a lot of stress at work?"

"It's a bank, there is always stress." She took a sip of her coffee.

The baby monitor she placed on the counter sizzled, and she listened for a moment, and when silence ensued, she turned back to me.

"Sure, Noor was stressed. She was working close with Achim to sort out the accounts at our Estonian branch. We bought Finba bank in Finland and they had a branch in Estonia, so Copenhagen Bank took that over, as we did several others all across Eastern Europe. The Scandinavian banks were merged with ours as we're so much bigger. There was so much excitement when we did that acquisition. Silas was amazing…he's such a…great leader."

I noted that she still called Copenhagen Bank "we" even though she hadn't worked there in several months. And there was a wistfulness to her tone.

She smiled wanly. "I loved working there. But then Nina came along, and Carsten sold his company to Microsoft, so we thought, why work? But once Nina is a little older, I think I'll go back. What am I going to do all day? And the kids, they say, grow up fast."

"They do," I agreed. "My daughter Sophie is nearly twenty-one, and just a minute ago she was a baby like Nina. I feel like no time has passed, but it has. I had more hair then."

She laughed.

"Noor worked a lot with Silas," I probed as gently as I could. I was keeping my demeanor casual. Drinking coffee. Talking babies.

"Oh, yes. We used to call her his work wife." She grinned. "Even Silas's wife…Anja…she's so beautiful…used to joke that Silas spent more time in restaurants with Noor than he did with her. They worked together all the time. There were others who were more senior, but Noor was his right hand."

Interesting, I thought, that Silas didn't mention that. Interesting but not surprising.

"I spoke with her family, and they said that Noor was talking to someone in the US a lot before she died. Do you know anything about that?" I poured some more coffee into my cup and, when she nodded, added some to hers. She didn't add extra milk to her coffee, just drank it a little darker now.

"I don't know why she would be," Marlene said, perplexed. "I mean…maybe she was talking to the merger and acquisitions people. They are spread around the world, and two of them were in our New York office. They were pretty instrumental in the acquisition of Finba. But that was a couple of years ago. Maybe it was personal. She could have family there. Noor had family everywhere. Do you know her cousin is a chef? Lives…lived with her."

I nodded, not wanting to let Marlene know I had talked to the chef cousin and was in fact contemplating having sex with her.

"Did Noor have any problems at work or personally that you knew about?"

Marlene looked thoughtful for a long moment. "Well, her family kept wanting her to get married to some Pakistani guy in London. She told them she wasn't interested in an arranged marriage. You know what I think?"

I leaned closer. *Yes, tell me what you think.*

"She had a crush on Silas." Marlene's smile was one that every office gossipmonger sported when they were ready to talk about something truly juicy.

I raised my eyebrows. "Was something going on between them?"

"I don't know," she said cheekily. "But they traveled a lot together. Lots of closed-door meetings. You never know. And Silas is so handsome and charismatic. I mean…Carsten doesn't worry about me and trusts me, but even he knew that Silas…well, he's special."

Special? That *asshole?*

"But you don't know for sure."

She shook her head. "Honestly, it's just…I don't know. I *really* don't…and I shouldn't have said that. It's awful of me. Noor is dead and I'm calling her a homewrecker."

"I think he'd be the homewrecker; she isn't the one who is married." I couldn't help myself. Whenever there was an affair, the man was almost a victim alongside his wife, but the woman he had an affair with, the jezebel, was the family-shredder.

The worst part about an affair, Nico, who had divorced because of it and many other reasons, told me once, were the lies. "If he lied about this, did he lie about everything? I felt like I was nobody to him. Just this woman at home he lied to."

As Sartre said, *the worst part about being lied to is knowing you weren't worth the truth.*

"You're right," she stated. "I used to do his expenses and there were a lot of double breakfasts when he traveled—and not with his wife. She has a yoga studio in the city. His wife does."

"Do you know Juula—"

I didn't finish saying her name when Marlene pounced. "Bitch! Now, she would probably sleep with Silas, Achim, anyone who can help her—and even Harald, though I think he's too old to get it up."

"Did you work with Harald?"

Marlene blinked at the change of topic. "Not really. I mean, I wasn't his assistant or anything. But I did sub for him if his assistant was out or if he needed something from the Baltic team."

"What's he like?"

"Scary," she said instantly. "*Very* scary. I remember there was lots of noise when *Politiken* wrote an article about banking irregularities in Eastern Europe, and they called Silas who gave them a quote. Harald was pissed. He closed the door into Silas' office, and we could hear him scream at him across the whole floor. He has a reputation of dressing you down in private...in public he's all lawyerly and polite. He was always nice to me."

I asked Marlene some more questions about Noor, but they didn't get me anywhere. I thanked the former assistant for her time and took my leave. As she handed me my coat and other belongings, she said absently, "Noor told me she had bought a present for Nina in Tallinn. She'd gone for a meeting at Copenhagen Bank there. We didn't make plans, but she told me she was going to come and see me. And then, suddenly, I find out that she killed herself. Why would she buy Nina a present then? Do suicidal people do that?"

I put my hand on her shoulder. "I don't know why she killed herself. But I *will* try to find out."

"Thank you," Marlene said. "It was nice meeting you. I hope you're able to give her family closure."

Chapter 9

Monday Evening, October 10, 2023

I LIKED THE OPERA. I didn't get season tickets because that was expensive, and I didn't like *all* opera. Puccini, yes; Bizet, absolutely...Wagner, no way. Wild or winged horses (pun intended) couldn't make me sit through five hours of Wagner's *Die Walküre*.

Now, *Carmen* was truly a delight. I had researched the evening's performance and discovered that we were in for a treat: a cabaret-inspired rendition of Bizet's opera.

The Royal Opera House stood as an iconic landmark. At its opening, it sparked much debate and criticism. Descriptions ranged from a fly to an alien ship, or even a helicopter landing pad. The most striking critique came from the architect Henning Larsen himself, who likened it to a toaster. To me, however, it was breathtaking—grand, a gateway to extraordinary journeys. Its façade, a spectacular blend of a metal grid encasing limestone, stretched across five of its fourteen stories, submerged below sea level. For me, the magic of a performance always began the moment I stepped into its opulent foyer.

Before the construction of the *Inderhavnsbroen*, the inner harbor bridge, my journey to the Opera house involved a ferry bus from Nyhavn, bypassing the congested traffic and meandering roads of Amager. However, with the bridge now in place, I opted to cycle to the majestic building on the harbor. The opera house, strategically aligned with Amalienborg Palace and Frederik's Church, usually captivated me with its marble floors, gleaming wooden walls, chandeliers in a diamond pattern, and bronze reliefs. But this time, my attention was elsewhere. Afsana had let her hair cascade over her shoulders, complementing a floral tulle halter gown in shades of pink, green, and purple. My guess was it was a Marchesa piece. She juxtaposed this feminine ensemble with Balenciaga's military-style black boots and a leather jacket, and accessorized with a Gucci handbag, featuring a bamboo handle. She looked effortlessly beautiful.

"I like the hat," she said as she walked up to me. She turned her wrist to look at her Apple Watch and grinned. "And you're on time."

I leaned down and brushed my cold lips against her warm cheek. *That was harmless, wasn't it?*

All day I had contemplated calling Sophie and asking her what she thought about her father dating a woman in her mid-twenties, but the asking seemed worse than the doing.

I dressed with more care than I normally did to see a woman. I settled on a crisp white dress shirt paired with a new Balmain asymmetric double-lapel blazer, striking in black and white, complemented by black dress pants. The shoes were a particular choice, Mauri alligator and calfskin monk straps in black and white, a vintage find from two years ago. The hat posed a bit of a dilemma. I opted for a Loewe calfskin leather bucket hat, a blend of warmth and style. And it looked, I thought a little pathetically, like what a younger man would wear.

We strolled to the cloakroom, where we checked in our coats, hat, scarf, and gloves. Afterward, as I offered my arm, she gracefully placed her hand on my forearm and leaned in close to me.

"I love the opera," she told me. "We have time, and I was wondering if you'd like to buy me a glass of champagne."

"The least I can do since you…scored…the tickets."

Was scored the right thing to say?

I found myself fumbling over some of my words, as I hadn't conversed this extensively in English in a long while. I still needed to switch my thoughts from Danish to English, requiring a mental translation before speaking.

I got her a glass of Ruinart *blanc de blanc*, and ordered tonic water with a dash of bitters for myself.

"What's that?" She wrinkled her nose.

"Delightfully refreshing. I find various ways to make my dry month go down less painfully, and this is one way."

She took a sip of my drink and nodded appreciatively. "It's not as bad as I thought it would be."

We took our drinks to the first floor and stood around a high table facing Holmen.

"Thank you for inviting me."

She smiled. "I thought you'd turn me down."

"Did you want me to?"

She shook her head, and I noticed her long gold earrings that had small bells on them as they tinkled.

"You're very young," I found myself saying. "I feel…very—"

"I'm not as old as you but I am a consenting adult," she interrupted. "Are you uncomfortable because you have a daughter in her twenties?"

I chuckled. "Probably. I almost called her to ask if she thought this was okay."

"Would she care?"

I thought about it. "No. But you are someone's daughter, and that makes me think about fathers and their responsibilities."

She sipped her champagne, looking at the lights of Nyhavn twinkling at a distance, and then turned. "You are not my father or even close to being a father figure. You're a man I'm attracted to, and since that doesn't happen very often…I want to see."

"See what?"

"Whatever this is."

"There may be more beautiful times, but this one is ours." The words slipped out in English as if they had always existed in that language in my mind.

"Hmm…that sounds like…" she closed her eyes and I watched, "like…I have no idea."

"Sartre."

"Do you come to the opera often?" She smoothly changed the topic.

"Maybe two-three times a year, depending upon the calendar. Last time I was here was for Tosca, last season."

The bell rang, and we found our way to orchestra seats. We sat down as silk rustled against chairs and people brushed past each other.

"The opera subtitles will be in Danish. Is that okay?"

"I know *Carmen* almost by heart. It's my favorite." Then she looked up at the ceiling and sighed. "It's a stunning opera house. I first visited it two years ago when I moved to Copenhagen, and it was love at first sight."

"Do you know that the ceiling of this main auditorium is covered in 24-carat gold?" I whispered.

"No." She tilted her head up again and then said sweetly as she looked into my eyes, "There may be more beautiful things, but this one is ours."

As the silence fell and the curtains rose, the music wafted slowly through the opera, bouncing off the well-crafted walls. The set was minimalist, compared to how I'd seen *Carmen* before. On the stairway, a soloist stood, playing, and singing along with the Royal Danish opera chorus and symphony orchestra.

"I wonder how it was a hundred and fifty years ago when they first produced *Carmen*," Afsana whispered.

I nodded, transfixed by the scene, as dancers and singers came together on a square in Seville, with the tobacco factory on the right and guardhouse to the left. The slow and ominous notes of *sur la place, chacun passe* strummed, and Afsana put her hand on mine.

After José was arrested for dereliction of duty at the end of Act 1, we went out and she got another glass of wine, and I got a glass of tonic water, this time without bitters. I was all about variety.

"I've watched videos of Maria Callas singing *Habanera*, and no one does it better," Afsana said to me. "Have you ever been to Verona?"

"Many years ago. I saw *La Traviata* and *Aida* during the *Arena di Verona* Festival."

"We should go," she said brightly, impulsively. "When is it?"

"Summer through September."

She grinned. "Maybe next year, then."

"Maybe." I didn't want to say it was highly unlikely we'd be going to the *Arena di Verona* festival or anywhere else together in a year's time. My relationships didn't last that long.

She didn't notice or at least pretended not to my reticence. "How goes the investigation?"

"It goes. I'm talking to some of Noor's colleagues. Do you know any of her friends outside of work with whom I could speak?"

Afsana shook her head. "They're in London not Copenhagen. She talked about a guy called Achim. They went out for drinks. He was a colleague. I thought she was sleeping with him, or at least hoped, but then she told me had a girlfriend."

"I talked to Noor's boss today," I added.

"The guy with the long hair? God, he sounded pompous, but Noor was a big fan. She called him a businessman with humanity. She'd tell me how he was a people-first leader. And here I was spending my time skinning fish all day in the cold outside, or something just as laborious. The restaurant business is definitely *not* a people-first business, unless we're talking about the paying guests."

We came out during each of the two breaks, and I found Afsana charming. Despite her youth, she was worldly, well-read, and possessed a knowledge of food and wine that surpassed mine.

After José killed Carmen and sang, his heart broken, *"Ah! Carmen! ma Carmen adorée!"*—and we gave the artists a standing ovation, I decided to walk her to her hotel.

"I'm hungry," Afsana announced as we came to my bicycle.

"You'll know better than I what is open this late at night that works for you." I unlocked my bicycle and added, "How did you get here?"

"Taxi."

"You don't have a bicycle?"

She wrinkled her nose. "I'm not Danish."

I laughed softly. "True. Can you walk in those shoes?"

She glanced at me, a hint of annoyance in her voice. "Gabriel, I wouldn't be wearing these shoes if I couldn't walk in them."

"You ride that everywhere?" she asked as I walked my bicycle.

"I do."

"Even in the winter?"

"Yes."

"When it rains?"

"Yes."

"Why?"

"Because it's the only exercise I get outside of my morning run."

"At what distance do you decide to drive?"

I thought about it for a moment. "Last time I drove was to go to Berlin. I borrowed a friend's car." It had been Clara's new Porsche, and I had scratched it as I was being chased by the Russian mafia. She was probably *never* lending me a car again.

We walked past Nyhavn to the hot dog stand at the corner of Gothersgade and Borgergade. There was already a long line of people waiting after a Monday night of partying.

"What hotdog do you like best?" she asked as we waited in a fast-moving line.

"*Ristet.*"

"Agreed."

I noticed the man in a black bomber jacket and a woolen cap when it was our turn to order. He stood by the 7-11 across the street, smoking a cigarette. There was nothing distinctive about him. He could be anyone. He could be no one. But his gloves were a dead giveaway. They were black with some kind of colored fingertips, designed to allow the glove wearer to use his touchscreen phone. Of course, lots of people had gloves like that. But I couldn't shake the feeling that this man had been with us since the opera.

We were being followed. I had to get Afsana back to her hotel with its security.

She ordered two fully loaded hot dogs with all the works, mustard, ketchup, softened onions, raw onions, fried onions, and pickles.

We ate with the others, holding napkins in our hands, her back to the 7-11, and with me facing the man who didn't know he had been spotted.

"There is no elegant way to eat a hot dog," she claimed as she got some ketchup on her nose. I wiped it with my napkin. "Wait until I'm done, then you can wipe my whole face."

Like you were a child, I thought and sighed.

When we were done, and before she could suggest a nightcap or *anything else*, I said, "I think it's time to get you to your hotel."

She narrowed her eyes. "I can get myself to my hotel."

"Agreed." I wondered if it would be better to send her on her way alone and let the man follow me. But what if he didn't? What if he went after her? "But humor me, will you?"

"Why?"

I smiled easily. "Because I've been told that when the date ends and I leave the girl by her door, I get to kiss her."

That did it. Her eyes twinkled again. I knew she wanted to ask if I'd come to her room this time, but she wouldn't. I'd already gotten to know her some and, even though she was direct and open, she was *young*, and not experienced enough with rejection or with me to know if I'd reject or accept.

"I really enjoyed spending time with you." She tried to sound casual, but I could feel her interest in my response, her curiosity. *I like you; do you like me?*

"Me too."

We walked in silence. She seemed to get emotionally distant with every step and my focus was divided. I wanted her safely inside her hotel, I wanted to know who was following us.

I had met Silas Haagen this morning and now someone was tracking me. They would know that Afsana is Noor's cousin. Had I now put her in danger?

"Well, this is my stop," she said when we found ourselves once again at the glass doors of Hotel Skt. Petri. The same doorman, observing us with an impassive gaze, was the one who had let her in previously.

I locked the bicycle stand with my right foot and freed my hands. I walked up to her and put my hands on her cheeks. "I had an absolutely wonderful time tonight. Thank you so much for inviting me."

She smiled brilliantly. "Is this the part where you kiss the girl?"

I leaned down and kissed her. I would've taken my time but there was an itch in between my shoulder blades. Someone was watching, and I didn't know who it was and what this could mean for Afsana. Last time I had been less cautious, someone I cared about had ended up in the emergency room, this time I would not take that risk.

I set her away. "Sleep well."

She looked confused. "Okay," she said huskily, and then she added, shaking her head, "I don't understand."

"I know your evenings are booked with work. But will you have lunch with me some day this week?"

"Text me and I'll think about it." She turned around and walked into the hotel.

She was *very young*. But regardless of her age, I was giving her mixed signals, and it was reasonable for her to think I was a fucking moron.

I made a big production of getting myself up on my bicycle and saw the glimmer of a man in the shadows.

There he was.

Unsure of the stranger's identity, whether he was armed, or his intentions, I couldn't tell if it was paranoia or real danger. The scar on my shoulder, a reminder of a bullet wound from a few months ago, itched as if sensing the peril. Fear enveloped me, echoing the days of hospitalization and unconsciousness after being shot—the dread of never seeing

Sophie again, the prospect of a life unfulfilled, and being lost in eternal darkness.

In his book, *Fear and Trembling*, Kierkegaard wrote, "If anyone on the verge of action should judge himself according to the outcome, he would never begin."

So, I tamped down the fear and took a page out of Sun Tzu's *Art of War*. "If you know the enemy and know yourself, you need not fear the results of a hundred battles."

I needed to find out who was behind me, literally. This wouldn't be possible if I kept cycling at top speed. So, I took a deep breath and slowed down, embracing the gentler night air, a stark contrast to the harsh, cold winds funneling through the opera's architectural corridors earlier. The streets were alive with people, some in groups, others alone. Their laughter and conversations pierced the night, seemingly louder than they would be under the day's usual cacophony of life.

Crossing Nørre Voldegade, past the bustling Strøget, I glanced back. The empty street behind me brought a mix of relief and unease. Was this all in my head?

Gliding down Nørre Voldegade, the light traffic and midnight calm steadied my heartbeat. Turning onto Sølvgade, I shrugged off the slight unease, despite memories of a brutal encounter with Russian thugs on Eckersbergsgade. "No Russians in Noor's case, Præst. Focus," I reminded myself.

But as I cycled down Øster Farimagsgade, the roar of an engine shattered the quiet. An instant later, I knew it was gunning for me. I swerved my bike onto the sidewalk, barely escaping the black Audi A5 as it barreled down the road.

In a split second, I leapt from my bike, diving into the safety of a doorway between the coin laundry and barber shop. The car crunched over my bike, the tinted windows concealing the driver. My attempt to note the license plate was futile; there wasn't one.

Panting, my heart racing, I looked at my mangled bike. This year alone, I'd lost one bike to theft, another rendered useless by bullet holes, and now this. My insurance premiums would skyrocket— if they didn't drop me altogether.

But the real sting was seeing my Loewe bucket hat, a casualty of my leap, lying crushed beside the wreckage of my bike. Bikes come and go, but that hat was irreplaceable.

CHAPTER 10

Tuesday Morning, October 11, 2023

"Do you know how many black Audi A5s are on the streets of Copenhagen? And do you really think it's appropriate to call the chief police inspector of Copenhagen to report a traffic accident?" Tommy asked me when I called and told him what happened the previous night.

"It wasn't a traffic accident." After my run, I was drinking my morning coffee and was desperate for a cigarette. "I think I've stepped into something I don't understand. And I need to talk to someone who does financial white-collar crimes."

"Walk me through it."

I did. I shared with him everything about Noor, detailing my discussions with Silas Haagen and Harald Wiberg, and the insights I gained from Afsana and Flora, Noor's colleagues. Then, I recounted the incident that occurred on my way back from the opera.

"Who did you go to the opera with?" Tommy wanted to know.

"How the fuck does that matter?"

"Maybe they were following that person and not you," Tommy retorted.

I sighed. He had a point. "Afsana."

There was a long pause. "The dead girl's cousin?"

"Yes."

"And we're sure they were not following her?"

"Then they would have stayed with her, not tried to run me over."

Another pause. "How old is this girl?"

"How the fuck—"

"As old as the dead girl?"

Now, it was my turn to pause. I took the plunge. They'd find out, eventually. "More or less."

Tommy whistled. "You getting inspired by that Hollywood guy Leonardo DiCaprio?"

"Will you get me in touch with someone in financial crimes?"

"Or maybe vice," Tommy laughed at his own joke. "She's legal, right?"

"Tommy." Fourteen was legal in Denmark.

He laughed some more. "Does Sophie know?"

"You know, I'll ask Freja to help me because you obviously are not mature enough to handle this situation."

"Which situation?" Tommy could hardly speak because he was so entertained. "The one where you're cradle robbing or the one where someone is trying to kill you...*again*?"

If any of my single friends were going out with a woman Afsana's age, I'd be right there with Tommy.

"Anyone working with financial crimes and banks will do. You have someone?"

"You're not going to like it," Tommy cautioned.

"I'm already not liking it," I drawled.

"No, I mean you're *really* not going to like it. Remember Eskola?"

I sighed. "Come on, Tommy!"

"She's with the NSK. If it's banks, she's the one working it."

"NSK?"

"National Unit for Special Crime. It's brand new. They combined all economic and organized crime under this agency, including part of your favorite organization, SØIK."

SØIK used to be the State Prosecutor for Special Economic and International Crime, the agency that, nearly a decade and a half ago, had helped bring down Karina Jensen, then the Chief of National Police. I kickstarted that investigation as a police inspector in the financial fraud division. I also leaked information to the media to ensure the investigation took place after I was blocked from doing so. Tommy, my then boss, fired me for sharing information about an ongoing investigation with a journalist, and I found my new life as a private detective.

"And what's her role?"

"Jorun Eskola is the *Chefpolitiinspektør* for the *National Enhed for Særlig Kriminalitet*, specifically economic crimes."

Besides being the top dog, now at the same level as Tommy for economic crimes across all of Denmark and not just Copenhagen, Jorun Eskola absolutely hated my guts. She had been, and probably still was, a good friend of Karina Jensen, and believed that I had helped the left-wing activists frame Karina (who was tough on crime, against immigration, and pro-ethnic profiling) for corruption. She never accepted that Karina Jensen was rightfully convicted for embezzling nearly six million kroner of the Danish people's money by falsely claiming friends and family members were contractors.

"Anyone else I can talk to?"

"Not if Eskola doesn't allow it. It's her team. Your old squad is part her team, and they all think you're a rat."

"Of course, they do," I grimaced. "Will you convince her to talk to me?"

"Sure." I could hear the laughter in his voice. "You know what? I'll do you a solid. I'll even show up for the meeting."

"You just want to see her kick my ass."

"Yeah. I'll bring some popcorn."

"Well, that's something."

"Whatever her feelings for you are, Præst, Eskola is stand-up," Tommy said seriously. "She's a good cop and investigator. I'm not saying she wasn't wrong about the whole Jensen situation, but she knows her job."

"I know," I agreed. "But it's still going to be unpleasant as hell."

"For you, yes, for me, though, pure entertainment."

Since I had no meetings in my office, I decided to go to Hellerup to look through Noor and Afsana's apartment. I wasn't expecting to find much, but it still needed to be done. In my career, I'd often found clues in the least obvious and unlikely places.

However, I needed a bicycle, so I called my friend Bør. He had kindly bought me my last bicycle after my house was bombed, and I asked if he had one I could borrow. He usually did, as he always kept some for his employees.

Bør and I grew up together in Brøndbyvester. Our fathers, mine a policeman and his, a mechanic, were good friends. Bør became an outlaw biker and ended up in prison for five years. Now, he owned a media company where he hired former gang members to help rehabilitate them. He was married to Malte, his husband, and they had two adopted children from Africa; James was five, and Una was seven. Our friendship never wavered. Even when he was in prison and I was a cop, we saw each other as often as the rules allowed.

"What happened to the one I bought for you?"

"It got mangled."

"How did that happen?"

I sighed. I didn't mind lying to my friends, but it never ended well for me when they eventually found out, so I'd decided long ago to stick to the truth as much as I could.

"Someone tried to run me over."

"What the fuck trouble are you in now?" Bør sounded exasperated.

"I don't know. I am investigating a girl's suicide, and I don't know what this is about."

"That's what you said last time. Is it the Russians again?"

"I can't see how."

"You've got to stop pissing people off. Do you need someone to protect Sophie? Anyone else—"

"Bør, I don't know what I'm into. I need a bicycle, that's all," I cut him off.

"But if you were in trouble, you'd tell me."

"Yeah."

"You know, before you took that Yousef Ahmed case, the most trouble you got into was a neighbor seeing you take pictures of someone fucking someone they're not married to. Now, people are trying to run you over. What the fuck, Gabriel?"

"Tell me about it."

Bør sighed. "I'll send someone with a bike. I'd like to say keep it safe, but I don't give a fuck about that piece of metal, so I'll tell you to keep yourself safe. If something happens to you, what will I tell Sophie?"

I assured him I was not in any trouble that I knew of. But I had an inkling I'd stepped into something bad for my health when I'd walked into Copenhagen Bank the previous day.

While I waited for Bør's man to bring me a bicycle, I tried to catch Achim Christiansen again. This time, he picked up the phone.

"You the private detective?" He spoke in Danish with a heavy Finnish accent.

"Yes."

"I don't have time to see you. Just ask what you want over the phone."

Had they gotten to him, I wondered. "Look, I just want to meet for fifteen minutes, no more. I'll come wherever is convenient."

"Why can't we talk now? The phone is fine." He didn't sound scared; he sounded irritated. That was something I could work with.

"Noor was your friend, and she killed herself for what looks like no reason. Don't you want to know why she died?" Emotional blackmail was a handy tool in the private detective toolbox.

"People kill themselves all the time." His voice wasn't as firm as it was at the start of our conversation, so I pressed on.

"Actually, people don't commit suicide all the time," I corrected him softly. "They do it when they're pushed. And..." I paused dramatically, "sometimes it's not suicide, but it just looks like it is."

I heard him gasp. Score! *Gabriel Præst, expert white liar.*

"You mean...you mean she was...," he couldn't say the word, and I didn't help him, either. I really didn't think Noor was murdered. I had no reason to believe that the police report wasn't correct in their assessment, but it did me no harm to let him think so.

"I just need fifteen minutes. You pick the place."

"My girlfriend works at Nørrebro Bryghus. I go there evenings after work to hang out with her. I can meet you there at around five thirty today."

"I'll be there."

"How will I know you?"

"I'll be the bald guy," I quipped.

"These days, lots of dudes are bald," he retorted.

"I've seen your LinkedIn page; I know what you look like. I'll find you."

That had been easier than I thought it would be. Now, I just needed to make sure no one followed me, so I didn't put this poor guy's life at risk, too.

CHAPTER 11

Tuesday Morning, October 11, 2023

I picked up the keys Afsana had left for me at the Skt. Petri reception, and bicycled to Noor's place. I went down Østerbrogade which turns into Strandvejen in Hellerup.

The great thing about bicycling was that you could see who was following you because cars would have to drive too slowly, and a person who was walking couldn't keep up. So, it would be someone who would be on their bicycle. The not-so-great thing was that on a bicycle, I was an alluring open target if anyone wanted to take a shot, run me over, or trip me off my cycle to hurt me.

I decided to play it by ear. The day was a good one. The sun was shining, even if it was cold and windy, and the clouds would swallow the ball of fire by midafternoon.

Noor and Afsana's *villa* apartment, as it was called because it was within a house split into two homes, was on Evanstonevej in Hellerup. Occupying both the third and fourth floors of the villa, it boasted an excellent location just off Strandvejen, conveniently close to the Waterfront Mall and Tuborg Havn.

I parked and locked my bicycle outside the gate of the villa. I had a story prepared if a neighbor stopped me. Afsana had left for me a keychain with two keys. I assumed one was for the main entrance into the villa and the other for the apartment.

Their place was gorgeous, with a balcony and a view of the Øresund. The entrance hall on the third floor was spacious and opened into two bedrooms and a bathroom.

Upstairs was a bright kitchen with a dining table, that flowed into a large living room with the balcony. From the window, I could see Hellerup School.

The apartment, unlike my place, was fully renovated—and the furniture was high quality but without emotional connection to the apartment. It looked like an interior designer had put it together. A sofa here, a coffee table there.

I had also expected the apartment to be dusty, but it seemed like there was a cleaning crew that had been coming in regularly.

I texted Afsana to ask her about that. She replied immediately: *I forgot all about that. They come once every two weeks. I guess I should cancel.*

I read her message and opened the camera app. I took pictures. I stopped when I noticed there was no mail on any of the counters in the living room. Usually, even I who got little mail, had something lying around.

I texted Afsana again: *Is your mail being sent to your hotel?*

She responded: *Yes. Even Noor's, but I don't open her mail. It's just sitting there. Do you want to see it?*

I grinned. Sometimes you found clues in the most unlikely places. *Yes, please.*

I walked around the house and entered what I assumed was Afsana's room. The room was neat and tidy except for some photographs on the dresser of Afsana with whom I assumed were her parents.

I opened her closet, aware that I was not just going through her room as part of my investigating Noor's death but also to know Afsana better.

Some of her clothes and shoes were still there. A bra was neatly folded on a pair of panties on a shelf in the closet. Feeling like a pervert going through a woman's underwear drawer, I walked to her desk. There was a mousepad on the table and some wires, one an iPhone charger and an Apple MacBook Air charger. And two blue sticky notes.

One said, "Call *ammi*." She had underlined *ammi* twice.

The other said, "Don't forget Noor's birthday, March 2." My heart clenched. Noor died on April 17. She had just turned twenty-seven.

In the drawers underneath her desk, there were papers, and some looked like important immigration papers. I pulled them out and set them aside. There were also articles from London newspaper websites about the restaurants she had worked in. There were printed emails with recipes in them. Some notebooks with notes taken during work meetings. She doodled, I noticed, made little sketches of vegetables and animals—*à propos* for a chef.

There was a bookshelf next to the desk. She had taken no books with her. There were five shelves, and each had at least fifteen to twenty books. She had the usual assortment of mysteries and contemporary fiction, and then she had poetry by Pablo Neruda, Rupi Kaur, Maya Angelou, and Amanda Gorman. She had several cookbooks, which didn't surprise me. I pulled out the *Grand Dictionnaire de Cuisine* by Alexander Dumas and smiled. Of course, she'd have this book next to *Les Trois Mousquetaires* and *Le Comte de Monte-Cristo*, all in French. So, she spoke and read French. Another thing we had in common. I had several works of Sartre in French.

I went through Afsana's room thoroughly and clinically. I put a few things I suspected she'd want in my backpack. An android phone that looked new, some chargers, photographs, and her immigration papers.

Then I went into Noor's room.

It was a mirror of Afsana's room. A king-size bed made up so stiffly you could flip an øre coin on, two side tables with bedside lamps, a desk, and a chair, a bookshelf, and a closet. There was the same assortment of orphaned chargers but no electronics, probably still with the police.

I texted Afsana: *Did you ask the police for Noor's belongings? If not, could you? If you can send them an email allowing me, I can get them for you.*

In Noor's room, I was ruthlessly thorough.

Noor's fashion sense was more like mine—more corporate and less creative than Afsana's. She favored Hugo Boss suits, Prada sneakers, pumps, and Balenciaga bags. I found nothing in her clothes, not even an old tissue or an errant øre coin in a jacket pocket.

In Afsana's room, there were sticky notes, papers, but here, there was nothing.

I stood at Noor's room's doorway and realized it had been picked clean. Someone had been here. I doubted we'd find anything on her phone or laptop. Someone would have erased all content on them as well.

A chill ran up my spine. I had thought I had been lying about Noor maybe not killing herself, but now I wondered if there was unwittingly some truth in my lie. And someone who could pull off making a murder look like suicide was a professional.

Præst, what have you gotten yourself into this time?

SINCE I WAS ALREADY in Hellerup, I called Freja to see if she'd have coffee with me at the Emmerys on Strandvejen. She agreed if I'd buy her a really big café latte and a chocolate cinnamon snail.

"What do you want?" she asked as soon she joined me at the table where I was waiting for her.

"I'm hurt, Freja. Maybe I just wanted to say hello to a friend."

Freja raised an eyebrow and flattened her full lips. Nearly five-eleven, Freja was a woman with a toned body, thanks to being on the police handball league, and that body combined with an attractive face sometimes made some men foolishly think she wasn't a bad-ass cop. I was no fool.

"Fine, if you only want to see me when I need you, then so be it." I grinned.

She laughed. "What's up?"

"I need to see Ditte's report on Noor. Everything you have."

"Præst, trust me, there's nothing there," she promised. "I sent you the most relevant stuff."

I didn't know how much I could tell her, mostly because I wasn't sure what I had. I trusted Freja. A few months ago, when I worked the Yousef Ahmed case, she'd come to me with vital information that she'd found out from a man she'd been sleeping with.

"I need to see photos of Noor's room. I just went there...," I raised my hands when she was about to yell at me, "Legally, because her cousin gave me permission and the keys. She shared the apartment with Noor. She's still paying the rent."

A server brought my black coffee, and Freja's latte and cinnamon snail.

"You will not get any of mine," she warned, pulling the plate with the cinnamon snail toward her.

"I like my fingers, thank you very much."

She tore a piece of the pastry and slipped it into her mouth. Her sigh told me just how good it tasted. Since I'd eaten those rolls before, I concurred.

"This is better than sex...but that could probably be because I haven't had sex in a while."

"What happened to the guy from PET you were seeing?"

PET, *Politiets Efterretningstjeneste* (PET), Police Intelligence Service was the Danish national security and intelligence agency that focused on domestic security.

"It's on again and off again. He might be a *little*...married."

"A little?"

"His marriage is also on again and off again," she remarked dryly. "He has two kids, and that makes it complicated. I asked him to figure his shit out because I can't go on this roller coaster ride with him. I mean, the sex is phenomenal, and we get along like a house on fire, but if he's conflicted about his marriage, then it's just not going to work."

I took a sip of my coffee. "I think someone *professionally* cleaned Noor's apartment. There are absolutely no papers anywhere. I've asked her cousin to get her belongings from you guys, but I don't know what was there and what wasn't. I'm sure you didn't go poking into her life."

"Probably not after the medical examiner ruled it a suicide. And we had a note," Freja agreed.

"Look, something is strange. I went to meet her boss at Copenhagen Bank and that evening someone follows me around and tries to run me over—"

"*Whoa*," Freja squealed. "Someone did what?"

I told her.

"Who were you at the opera with?"

I sighed. "Noor's cousin."

Freja's eyes widened and then snorted out a laugh. "How old is she?"

I caught myself before I said something like, *she's a very mature young person.*

"Can we get back to the fact that this guy who was following me probably tried to kill me?"

"Maybe they just wanted to break a few bones, and can you blame them?" she chortled. "But it's shady as fuck."

"I need to see the report, Freja."

She nodded. "I'll get it to you by the end of day. Just keep me out of it, and don't get me fired."

"Deal."

"Now that we finished the official business, tell me about the cousin. What's her name?"

"Afsana."

"Nice." Freja finished her cinnamon roll and wiped her hands on a napkin. She picked up her latte and took a sip.

"In Urdu her name means a fable, a story."

Freja coughed a little because the coffee went down the wrong pipe. As she banged a fist on her chest, she wheezed, "You looked up the meaning of her name on the Internet?"

I nodded.

"That's *really* pathetic." Her voice was a whisper as she tried to clear her windpipe, but the censure was loud and clear.

"Tell me about it," I agreed.

Chapter 12

Tuesday Evening, October 11, 2023

Nørrebro Bryghus, a stylish craft brewery renowned for its excellent organic beer on tap, was nestled on Ryesgade. This vibrant street was a mosaic of contrasts, where dusty antique shops neighbored contemporary art galleries, and cozy bodega-style bars stood alongside elegant French cafés, complete with *prix-fixe* menus and enviable wine cellars.

I arrived early and took a seat at the bar. The bartender, Linnéa according to her nametag, approached me. In her early twenties, she had a charmingly crooked front tooth and freckles dotting her nose and cheeks, exuding a vibrant energy that mirrored the brewery's lively atmosphere.

"I like my beer hoppy, what do you recommend?" I asked in Danish.

She responded in English with a Swedish accent, a common occurrence in Copenhagen these days, where your server was probably from across the Øresund, living in Malmö or Lund in Sweden.

"The Bombay IPA is popular. It's a fruity ale with lots of classis hops aroma. Intense malt flavor. There is the Kings

County Brown Ale. It's our first guest brew. Classic American. Lots of chocolate and dried nuts. Do you want to try them?"

I liked a bartender who knew their stuff.

"Maybe next time," I told her, shifting to English. She looked disappointed. I was sorry to have raised her hopes. "For now, I just want something nonalcoholic. What do you recommend?"

"The Stuykman Weissbier is *very* light," she promised.

"It's my dry month," I apologized.

"We have some non-alcoholic beer but it's complete shit. I wouldn't drink it. I have an organic *hyldeblomst saft* that's not horribly sweet," she offered sympathetically.

I accepted the elderflower cordial and as she had sworn, it was actually not horribly sweet. And that was the most charitable thing I could say about it.

Achim's LinkedIn profile revealed that he was a thirty-year-old Finn, having relocated from Helsinki to Copenhagen a decade ago for university. He held a bachelor's degree in economics from the University of Copenhagen and an MBA in finance from Copenhagen Business School. Straight after graduating from CBS, he joined Copenhagen Bank, where he had been promoted thrice, the latest being six months ago when he took over Noor's position.

While LinkedIn didn't provide his height, his Facebook page indicated he was around five-nine. He had blonde hair, a receding hairline styled with gel, and a slightly overweight build. He was slightly overweight, wore wire-rimmed glasses and appeared to favor department store suits.

I'd finished about half of my not-horribly sweet drink when he arrived. I waved at him.

He came and sat next to me at the bar and nodded at the bartender.

"That's him?" Linnéa asked Achim.

He nodded. *Ah, the girlfriend,* I deduced thanks to my keen investigative skills.

She looked at me and then shrugged. "My boss is out if you want to use his office."

Achim shook his head. "That would look even more suspicious."

"No one followed me, and no one is watching us here," I tried to assure him, but he was so tense that I didn't think anything I said would make him feel better.

"What do you want? Let's do this fast. I need my job. Alright?"

"Alright."

Linnéa placed what looked like a lager in front of her boyfriend. He took a sip with hands that shook slightly. I felt bad for scaring the poor kid.

"Was Noor under any stress at work around the time she died?"

He looked at me like I was nuts. "You know we work in a bank, right? She died in April, so yeah, probably stressed out of her wits with quarter-end stuff from March and quarter-start stuff from April. It's *always* fucking stressful at Copenhagen Bank."

If it's so fucking stressful, why do you all work there?

"Anything unusual she was working on?"

He shrugged. "I'm not sure if this counts, but around that time, we were working on something *incredibly* stressful. We had to verify the account information of non-Estonian national accounts for Finba Bank in Tallinn. She handled most of that, while I did the same for Latvia. It was a divide and conquer strategy. She mentioned concerns about some companies appearing non-existent beyond their LLC documentation. I continued the same work for Latvia and then Lithuania after she passed away. It was all grunt work."

"What do you mean some companies didn't exist?" I asked calmly, but I could feel my heart race. This was the first time I'd heard of something tangible connected with her job that was a red flag.

"Sometimes, companies make errors in their paperwork, either in spelling or other details, or we might make mistakes. Many of these accounts are old, and as executives come and go in companies, ensuring everything is legitimate takes time. It's not a major issue." Achim seemed calmer.

My questions were easy, *plus* I had not taken out my rubber hose...yet.

"Her roommate said she called the US a lot. You know what that was about? Was she calling to check on the companies?"

He thought about it for a moment. "No. None in the US. Most were incorporated in the UK or Poland...mostly Europe."

"Who would she be talking to?"

Achim took a sip of his drink. His girlfriend came back and asked me if I wanted a refill. I shook my head. It may be drinkable, but only for *one* drink.

"Are you sure she was talking to the US? We worked late a lot, and I never saw her call the US."

"Never?"

"No." He shook his head. "I mean...maybe she had a friend or something, but never for work. I mean, if you use your work phone it better not be for personal stuff. They're pretty strict about that stuff."

"Did she have a personal phone?"

"I don't know."

"But you do?"

He nodded.

"So, if she called the US, it wouldn't be from her work cell?"

Achim sighed. "Of course, she would if it was work related. We're careful about using the work phone. There was a whistleblower in our UK office last year and he used the work phone to call the authorities or whatever. The rumor was that Copenhagen Bank knew. Since then, there has been a running joke about our phones were bugged."

He looked at me then, fear back in his eyes.

"Do you think our phones are bugged?"

How the fuck was I supposed to know?

"We talked on your personal phone, which is likely not bugged," I said, though I wasn't certain. If Copenhagen Bank was tapping employee phones, they probably wouldn't hesitate to bug personal phones as well as corporate ones.

He liked that answer. "Right. Right. So, this one time we got an email...both of us did on our private email accounts from a journalist in New York asking us to talk to her about Copenhagen Bank and Finba. It happens but we know we cannot speak with media. That's the media relations people. We just deleted the email but joked that if we called the reporter from work, they'd fire us."

"A journalist?"

Achim made a dismissive sound. "Do you know how often that happens? All the time."

"I'm sure it does. Do you remember the name of the journalist or the media?"

He looked at me like I'd lost my mind. "It was spam. I get about a million emails a day that are spam. They go straight to the spam folder. This just escaped the filter."

After that the conversation veered into how Copenhagen Bank is a soul-sucking place. I advised Achim to get a new job, and his girlfriend who joined our conversation agreed.

"Working at this bar is less stressful than what you do," she said.

"But the pay, Lin," he said.

"It's not worth it," she said.

We all nodded.

After I left the Nørrebro Bryghus, I texted Nico to ask her if I could buy her *and* a colleague who worked the financial crimes beat a drink.

Nico responded: *You want someone who writes about hanky-panky in banks?*

I smiled and wrote back: *Yes, please.*

Nico replied: *I know just the person. Let's meet at Curfew, say around nine? I have a work dinner.*

CHAPTER 13

Tuesday Evening, October 11, 2023

Sophie called me as I headed toward Vesterbro to find a place to have dinner before meeting Nico and her journalist friend.

"Where are you?"

"On my way to Vesterbro."

"Where?"

"I don't know, *skat*. Somewhere near Curfew. I'm meeting Nico and a friend of hers there."

"When are you meeting them?" she insisted.

"Sophie, what's up?"

"I spoke to Bør, someone crushed your bike." There were tears in her voice.

For fuck's sake.

"My meeting is at nine. How about I take you out for dinner at Les Trois Cochons?" I suggested.

"I'll be there in fifteen minutes."

I rode my bicycle to Værnedamsvej, where I parked and locked it in front of the quaint French restaurant Sophie and I both adored. Nestled in the heart of Copenhagen, this charming spot was like a slice of Paris and had once been a butcher's shop.

I waved at the maître d', François Duplantier, who had been at the restaurant since it opened its doors in 2005.

"*Ça va*, Gabriel? It's been a long time since we saw you," he said in his slightly snobbish and very Parisian French accent.

Les Trois Cochons had been a staple for Sophie and me for a long time but with the opening of many new restaurants in the city, we'd expanded our horizons, and it had been a while since we'd come here.

The décor of Les Trois Cochons was dazzling, with a wall flanked by glazed bar windows from an old porcelain factory. The chandeliers and candles added to the coziness with soothing yet opulent lighting.

"*Bien, merci*, François." I shook his hand, and he clasped mine in both of his.

"How is *petite* Sophie?"

"Not little anymore, and she's joining me for dinner. I'm so sorry, I haven't made a reservation."

"*Pas de problème*," he protested. "There is always a place for you and Sophie at Les Trois Cochons."

He put me at a table for two by the window.

Sophie arrived a few minutes after I did, and after François and she did their "hello it's been a long time" routine, she came to me, worry in her eyes.

"What's going on?" she asked when I hugged her.

"I don't know," I admitted honestly.

We sat down, across from each other, and I picked up a menu.

"*Av for satan, far.*" She took my menu and set it aside.

Before I could formulate an answer, François came to talk about the menu.

"Today, I recommend the *escargots à la Bourguignonne* for apéritif and *filet de veau aux truffes* for the entrée. For dessert, we have a beautiful *café au lait pots de créme* with *caramel Armagnac*. And for wine, a glass of *Crémant de Bourgogne* on the house and—"

"It's my dry month, François," I interrupted.

He looked at me in shock, and then at Sophie. "He's still doing this."

"Every year." She gave an exaggerated sigh. "I'll have the crémant and whatever else you suggest with the veal."

François looked at me with disappointment and then turned back to my daughter. "You, my dear Sophie, will have a beautiful *Mas des Bressades Costieres de Nimes*. It's 55% grenache, 40% Syrah, and 5% cinsault. *Très beau vin.* Aged in concrete tanks so it's dark and juicy without the sweet. You, Gabriel, will have water. Sparkling or still?"

"Sparkling with a twist would be nice."

François made a disapproving sound and left.

"I didn't order," I whispered softly to his back. "I guess we're both eating what he decided."

"You want me to call him back?" Sophie laughed.

"I don't have a death wish. We'll eat the escargots and the veal...*ah the hardship.*" I put my hand on hers. "It's bloody good to see you."

"You can't *not* tell me these things, *Far*."

I leaned over the table and kissed her cheek. "*Jeg elsker dig.*" I whispered the words that I said often to her. *I love you.*

I sat down and smiled at this child of mine. Beautiful, smart, and loving. Stine and I had gotten our relationship wrong, but we'd raised one hell of a daughter.

"I don't know what I've gotten myself into," I began and told her everything I knew, which wasn't much.

"Was someone following you today?"

"I don't think so."

"Don't think so? What does that mean?"

A server brought my sparkling water with a twist of lemon and Sophie's crémant.

"I can usually tell if someone is following me, but I don't know for sure. It can happen without me knowing about it. I'm not a super sleuth, just pretending to be one," I said after the server left.

Sophie smiled at that.

"Remember the time I told you stop calling yourself superman?"

I put my hand on my heart. "And it still hurts."

I used to tell Sophie when she was little that I was superman. One day, when she was around eight, she told me to stop saying that because she knew I was not.

"I think you're a super sleuth. You're the man who toppled a government. Not that we can tell anyone." She took a sip of her crémant. "Why did we stop coming here?"

"Lots of new places opened, and we had to explore them."

"You know, I'm pretty sure you didn't go to the opera alone. Who did you go with? Nicole? What did you see?"

Ah, here it comes!

"I saw *Carmen*. I went with Afsana."

"And who's that?"

"She's Noor's cousin."

Sophie's eyes glittered. "The cousin? The chef?"

"Yes."

"Are you dating her?"

"I'm forty-one years old, *skat*, we don't date. We have...I don't know short companion...something."

"Nico and you have been seeing each other for a *long* time."

"She and I are friends. Entirely different."

Our escargots arrived, and I rehearsed in my mind how to tell Sophie how old Afsana was as we ate and talked about Sophie's classes at university.

After our table was cleared of the appetizer, I took the plunge.

"I have a question. If I was to say...*spend time* with a younger woman, how would you feel?"

"How young?" Sophie took a sip of her red wine, which had arrived after the table was set for the entrée.

"Twenty-five or so."

"Or so?"

"Twenty-five, then."

"Okay. Is that how old Afsana is? The cousin you went to the opera with?" She was smiling now.

"Yes."

"And you're seeing or *whatever* her?"

"You're enjoying this, aren't you?"

She laughed softly. "Oh *Far*, it doesn't matter how old she is, or you are. You're both grownups. As long as it's consensual, it's no one's business but yours. But if you married her, I won't call her *mor*, I'm going to say that right now."

I laughed, the fist around my chest loosening. "She's *very* young. But she's…and I sound like an old fool when I say this, a mature young person. That sounds like the crap all older men who date younger women say."

"And older women who date younger men probably say," Sophie added. "Would you care about the age of the man I was sleeping with?"

I thought about it for a moment and shrugged. "It's none of my business."

"Exactly. And who you sleep with is none of mine."

"Are you sleeping with someone older?"

She shrugged. "Maybe. It's just sex and maybe some companionship, but not a relationship. My friends are in relationships. Remember Arianna? She's moving in with her boyfriend. She's twenty-one, and I think that's way too young. But she doesn't. It's a personal choice."

"You don't have to have a relationship to have sex," I told her.

"I like that about you. Lots of fathers put on this whole 'my daughter is having sex, woe is me' façade even though everyone knows everyone is having sex if they can have it."

"You're twenty-one years old. If you're not having sex, we need to go see a therapist."

We finished our meal, and I felt that I had calmed Sophie down about my mysterious stalker and attacker. She wasn't exactly comfortable with me, not knowing what I was doing and why someone tried to run me over, but then, neither was I.

She gave me a hug outside, bundled in a big black coat. She smelled of cold air and Sophie. Of daughter, warmth, and home. I kissed her forehead and smiled at her.

"You keep getting more and more beautiful."

"I think you feel that way because you're related to me." She leaned into me for a long moment and pulled away. "I never worried about your work before this summer. Now, I feel something has changed. I don't think it's bad because you seem more excited about your job than you've ever been. *But* you got shot a few months ago, and you left me a letter because you didn't think you'd come home. This is hard for me. I can't stand the idea of a world where you're not there."

"I'm being careful, Sophie. I promise. I just need to let this play out."

We said our goodbyes and made plans for Saturday breakfast. I watched her cycle away, and then reached for my own.

I felt a movement at the end of the street and this same gnawing feeling that I'd had when Afsana and I had been at the hot dog stand after the opera. *He* was here. I was certain of it. And he'd seen me with Sophie. He'd know who Sophie was.

Even as I turned, I knew I wouldn't see him. It had been a fluke that I had seen him at all. *If* I had seen him.

I called Bør as I rode to Curfew Bar where I was going to meet Nico. Would I put Nicole in danger now? No, it was just me having drinks with friends. Nothing more. If this man was a professional…and I believed he was, he already knew about everyone in my life, because whoever had killed Noor was skilled enough to make it look like suicide to the elite Danish police.

"A man is following me," I said even before Bør could say hello.

"Why?"

"I'm working on a case that I don't understand."

"Describe them."

"I can't. He is *nobody*. Just average. I just…*feel* him."

Bør was silent, and I added, "I think he's a professional."

"A *he*?"

"I think so."

I heard Bør breathe deep. "I'll ask around."

"I had dinner with Sophie, and he saw us. I don't want her to worry. She can't know."

"I'll put a man on her she won't see. And even if she does, the hell with it, we can't risk her," he said gruffly.

Bør loved Sophie. She'd been in his life since she was a baby. If she was in trouble and couldn't tell me, she'd go to him and *had* the one time she'd been arrested at a climate change march that I had explicitly told her not to go to.

"It's even more important that the man following me doesn't know that I have spotted him. It takes my advantage away."

Bør growled. "You have *no fucking advantage* if he's a pro. And you haven't *seen* him. You have a *fucking* feeling. Are you even carrying your gun?"

"If he's a pro how will a gun help me?"

"My point exactly. Can you drop this case?"

"No."

"Here we go again," Bør commented, resigned.

"Just take care of Sophie. I'll take care of myself."

"Okay."

"Don't put someone on me, because I'll notice, which means *he'll* notice."

"On one condition."

I waited as I stopped at a red light.

"You need to come to the shooting range with me and to the gym at least twice a week for hand-to-hand training."

"Fuck no."

"Then I'll send a big guy to follow you around like glue."

I sighed.

"Tomorrow afternoon, be at the range at four and we'll go straight to the gym from there," Bør ordered flatly.

By "the gym," he meant his old-biker, gritty, bare-bones, no-frills gym called Kæmpe, which means "fight" in Danish. Kæmpe was on Birkedommervej in Nørrebro, and was once a beacon for fighters but fell into decay in the late nineties. It became a place where transients and substance abusers gathered around until Bør and his gang took it over. Now, it was part club house, part fitness center and boxing ring. In all honesty, I preferred the grittiness of Kæmpe over some over-polished fitness center in the city, where it was all muscles, tits and ass, and spandex.

"If the guy is a professional, do you really think training in your gym is going to make a difference?"

"It could be the difference between life and death."

I told him he was a dramatic asshole. He agreed and told me again to be at the range the next day. "And don't bring that silly Glock. You are going to need your SIG Sauer."

I didn't like guns. I wasn't ashamed to admit that they scared the hell out of me—both when they were pointed at me and when I pointed one at someone. I had recently shot a man to his death, and it didn't sit well with me. When I didn't feel I had a choice, I carried my baby Glock. It was small. It was light. I had a license for the Glock and a SIG Sauer P320, which was the police standard issue in Denmark. I also possessed an unregistered gun, kept for situations where I might need to use it without the shooting being traceable to me. Fortunately, I had never found the need to use it.

By the time I finished speaking with Bør, I was at Curfew on Vesterbrogade.

The space had been a bar since the 1940s and was popular with officers during World War II, I had learnt when this past summer I'd had to educate myself about the Danish Nazi collaborator history. These days, however, Curfew had a speakeasy chic feel—and a true dedication to Scandinavian cocktails with a Portuguese twist.

I waved to the bartender, and he nodded at me. I knew Humberto Marques from when he was making cocktails at 1105 and winning awards.

"Heard you're going to Ruby's for your cocktails these days," Humberto accused me.

"Only when a client wants me to." I raised both my hands in a gesture of peace. "I'm meeting Nico. I need a table."

Humberto looked around and waved at a server. "Daniel, take him to table five."

"Thanks."

"What do you want to drink? On the house."

I sighed. "It's my dry month."

Humberto laughed. "I can't believe you're still doing that."

"Why does everyone say that?"

"Because it's *ridículo* for someone like you who loves the liquor," he explained.

I texted Nico to let her know where I was sitting. When the server came by, I ordered tonic water with orange bitters *and* a twist. He kept his tone flat and polite, but I detected some judgment in his eyes.

As I waited for my drink, I looked around the bar. It was filling up nicely—as the crowds, regardless the day of the week, trickled in around eight or nine in the evening, and kept the party going until one or two in the morning.

My phone pinged. I smiled when I saw a message from Afsana. She thanked me for dropping off her belongings. *But I don't know whose phone this is though.*

Me: *I found it in your room.*

Afsana: *It's not mine.*

I thought back to my search of Noor and Afsana's apartment.

Me: *Do you think it's Noor's?*

Afsana: *Possible. But why would it be in my room?*

Me: *Do you mind if I take a look at the phone?*

Afsana: *I can get it to you. And also give you Noor's mail. Where do you want me to drop them off?*

I was about to respond when my drink arrived. I took a sip of my *fucking* tonic water and bitters, and stared at her message for a moment. Then, deciding, I grinned.

Me: *How about lunch tomorrow at Pastis? My office is upstairs. Noon?*

Afsana:

Feeling a little brighter despite the lack of a proper cocktail in hand, I raised my glass to no one in particular.

"*Salud.*"

Chapter 14

Tuesday Evening, October 11, 2023

Nico's friend, one of the better-known financial journalists for *Politiken*, Dag Sorgenfri Kjær was as tall as me, and sported a manicured, dark brown beard, and trim haircut. He paired his jeans with a T-shirt that announced it was from Tiger of Sweden, all of which fit him well. He had green eyes and a firm handshake. He draped his black jacket on his chair and Nico did the same, though she took longer. She was wrapped in far more layers than Dag because I knew she got cold easily.

"It's criminally cold out there," Nico announced as she rubbed her gloved hands together and sat down next to me. I took her gloves off and held her cold hands in between mine to warm them. "He's a human furnace," she said with a broad smile.

"It's her early childhood in Provence that has made her blood thin," I remarked.

"I hear you," Dag said. "I grew up in the Middle East."

We ordered drinks and talked about where we grew up—Nico and Dag had more interesting stories than mine, and then as I drank tonic water with a twist and they alcoholic cocktails, we got down to business.

"Nico tells me you're going after Silas Haagen." Dag took a sip of his Negroni, which I wasn't a big fan of, so it didn't bother me…much.

Nico ordered a Hemingway Death in the Afternoon, a beautiful cocktail that brought together absinthe and Perrier-Jouet champagne, which I did like. I tried to not ask for just a sip because there was no such thing as just a sip during a dry month.

"It's not Silas Haagen I'm interested in. It's Noor Mallik."

Dag raised his eyebrows. "And who's that?"

I told him. The one thing I had learned from Nico was that the more I told reporters who liked to hold their sources close the more I got out of the conversation.

"You think Silas was sleeping with her?"

I shrugged. "Got no clue."

Dag nodded.

"I don't think they'd send a professional after you to cover up an office affair gone wrong," Nico reflected. "It's something else."

"I'm working on a story about European banks money laundering rubles for the Russians." Dag set his glass down on the table. "I'll keep you as deep background, but if I show you mine, you'll have to show me yours."

I had little to show, so I agreed easily.

"In 2012, Nikita Poletov, the first deputy chairman of the Russian Central Bank, was murdered, and we suspect it was because he was asking legitimate EU banks to investigate and close fraudulent foreign, specifically Russian, accounts that had one and only purpose, to launder money," Dag explained. "He was killed in Tallinn. According to his wife, Lucya Poletov, who got asylum in the United States, it was the SVR. Obviously, the Russians deny any involvement."

"Okay." I didn't understand how any of this connected to Noor. So, I nodded, made assenting sounds, and hoped, eventually, I'd get a clue.

"Have you heard of Alexander Litvinenko?" Dag asked.

I nodded. "Ex Russian intelligence officer killed in London."

Dag smiled. "Yes. He defected, and they laced his tea with polonium-210, which killed him. On his deathbed, Litvinenko said that Putin ordered the hit. Putin denied it. The Strasbourg court investigated and said they *think* but cannot conclude that two Russian intelligence agents, Andrei Lugovoi and Dmitry Kovtun, killed Litvinenko. Now, these two guys also say they know nothing, and say that maybe Litvinenko poisoned himself."

"Not likely," I offered.

"Polonium is a bad way to go," Dag stated. "Now, Poletov was shot dead along with his driver. He was on the phone with his wife, so a little different from Litvinenko but ultimately all part of Putin's deliberate policy to 'liquidate,' traitors. The Kremlin saw Poletov as a defector because he was going after their money."

"How is Copenhagen Bank involved?" Nico sighed. "Get to the story, Dag."

"Let him tell it his way," I reassured Dag that he was doing just fine.

"Dag wants to be the Danish Rachel Maddow," Nico teased.

"I *am* the Danish Rachel Maddow," Dag contradicted, "in print that is. The link to Copenhagen Bank is Maksim Lõhmus, former Secretary General of the Estonian Ministry of Finance and ex-aide to the finance minister during Poletov's anti-corruption efforts in Russia. Poletov, after meeting Lõhmus, went to Copenhagen and reportedly met key European figures to combat Russian money laundering. Shortly after these meetings, Poletov was killed. A few months later, Lõhmus was appointed head of Copenhagen Bank in the Baltics, a role that significantly increased his wealth. His wife, who lives in Paris, recently purchased Joan Miró's *Femmes et Oiseau Devant le Soleil* at a Sotheby's auction in London for two million dollars."

Dag finished his drink and then raised his glass to ask the server to get him another Negroni.

"In 2018, Copenhagen Bank scrapped its plan to shift its Baltic banking operations to the group's IT platform, a decision approved by Silas Haagen. Some sources suggest this might have been to enable the Estonian branch to bypass standard Copenhagen Bank anti-money laundering, transaction, and risk monitoring procedures. While there's no concrete proof, it's notable that the revenue from the Baltics surged from nineteen to twenty-seven billion euros during that period."

I whistled. "A forty-two percent increase."

"Since acquiring Finba, a Finnish bank with significant Baltic assets, in 2012, the leadership team at Copenhagen Bank, including Silas Haagen, has consistently received substantial bonuses. I have absolutely no proof of this, but my gut says that Silas Haagen and the whole Copenhagen Bank leadership is consciously and knowingly laundering money for the Russians, and are using the Baltics to do this, where there is limited oversight on purpose," Dag concluded.

I finished my tonic water and decided to not get a refill. I was all about restraint. "Noor was calling the US a lot in the weeks before she died. Who would she be calling?"

Dag thought about it for a moment. "If I'm suspecting Copenhagen Bank, then I won't be surprised if the Americans have already launched an investigation or two. The NSA would be all over this—"

"I thought the NSA was a national organization?"

Nico shook her head. "Yes and no. They work with European agencies. Denmark was an outpost for NSA agents spying on German Chancellor Angela Merkel and other politicians in France, Norway, and Sweden between 2012 and 2014."

"They'd work with the PET or the DDIS?" I asked.

The PET was equivalent to the US FBI, while the DDIS, the Danish Defense Intelligence Service, called the *Forsvarets Efterretningstjeneste* (FE), was the Danish CIA.

"Probably PET. But who knows? And from the American end, it could be the NSA or even the Secret Service who get involved in financial crimes," Dag said.

"So, Noor could call the FBI, NSA, CIA, or the Secret Service," I said grimly.

"Or an old boyfriend who she was having phone sex with," Nico pointed out.

"She doesn't seem the phone sex kind," I contended. And then I looked at Dag and asked the question that was burning a hole inside me. "Would this be worth killing for?"

Dag didn't hesitate. "Yes."

"Who would they send?"

"If you're going after Silas Haagen, Harald Wiberg, and Copenhagen Bank, yes, they'll kill to protect themselves and the pots of money they're making in the Baltics," Dag confirmed. "And based on their pattern, I'd say they'd send SVR or ex SVR."

"That means Russians, Gabriel," Nico said.

"Russians, yes, but specifically the SVR, which is worse," Dag assured me.

"Last time it was the Russian mob," Nico sighed.

Dag raised his eyebrows in query.

"They shot him."

"The SVR is worse," Dag said. "Much worse."

It really was the wrong month to go dry, I thought once again.

Chapter 15

Wednesday Afternoon, October 12, 2023

"Did you know that Croque Monsieur was popularized in the 1900s in a bistro owned by a chef called Michel Lunarca. The story goes he didn't have fresh baguette to make his sandwiches one day and used regular bread, and toasted it a little so it would have the same crunch as a baguette," Afsana informed me when I ordered a Croque Monsieur for lunch at Pastis.

I treated the restaurant like an extension to my office, especially in the summer. But now the café doors to the patio were closed, and we were huddled in the table by the colored photograph of a naked woman looking at a naked man lying in bed. I held meetings, did paperwork, and entertained friends at the restaurant. Since it opened in 2006, Pastis has had nearly the same menu, with French hits like *terrine de foie gras, soupe à l'oignon gratinée, steak frites, and tartar*. Besides the food, they had an excellent wine list, which I enjoyed eleven months a year.

"Did you know that Croque Monsieur was mentioned for the first time in text by Marcel Proust?" I countered.

She grinned. "But which one of the seven volumes of *In Search of Lost Time* did he mention it in?"

"I have absolutely no idea."

"It was *À L'ombre des Jeunes Filles en Fleurs*."

I translated it in my head. "In the shade of...."

"*In the Shadow of Young Girls in Bloom*," Afsana supplied. "It was published in 1919. Now, before you seem too impressed with me, I worked for a French chef once who was a big Proust fan."

"And what about the Croque Madam?"

Afsana shrugged. "I guess they put a poached egg on top of the sandwich and called it something else. In Normandy, they call it *croque-à-cheval*."

"Food for the horses?"

She laughed. "Exactly. But let's face it, the master's sandwich was invented before the madam's or the horse's."

She pulled out a plastic bag from her Prada purse and pushed it toward me. "Noor's mail and that phone. I charged the phone, but it has a passcode. I tried some of my codes and those of Noor's I know about, but nothing."

I put the letters and phone inside my Tumi messenger bag. "That's okay, I may have a friend who can help with it."

"Do you do this a lot? Hack into phones?"

I shook my head. "Not exactly. I'm a pretty regular detective...no fancy stuff. It's the usual background checks, financial fraud, and cheating spouses—like in the movies."

Afsana wore a pair of jeans with a black turtleneck sweater, which was undoubtedly cashmere. Her hair was tied back.

She had some makeup on, mascara and lipstick, but nothing more. As Nico said, "when I was young, I didn't need make up. The skin took care of itself. It's now, in my old age, that I need it to hide the damage."

Our food was served, one sandwich for the monsieur and one for the madam. I drank tap water, while she drank Perrier.

"Do you have family in the US?" I spread mustard on top of the sandwich for an extra kick.

"Sure."

"Anyone Noor would talk to?"

"You mean on those calls I told you about? I don't know. We have some cousins and uncles...no one close. The really close relatives that Noor would talk to are in London."

Afsana took a bite of the croque madam and chewed thoughtfully. "I wish I could tell you something of value, Gabriel. But the fact is that we talked little. We worked a lot, and our working hours were different. In our business, we find it very difficult to have relationships of any kind outside of the restaurant. I mean, I can have dinner once a week with someone and, usually, that day, I want to stay home and order takeout bullshit of some sort. I don't want to cook or go to a restaurant if I can help it. And on weeknights, I'm home after two in the morning most days. I'm not particularly chatty even if I'm awake."

"I can cook for you next Monday." The words were out before I could weigh them. "And...why don't you come to my place tonight after work?"

She looked at me speculatively. "Like a booty call?"

I laughed. "I'm too old for those. But let's say I'd like to make you breakfast tomorrow morning. I can make a pretty good omelet, and my specialty, according to my daughter at least, is crepes."

"I won't be there until one-thirty-two," she warned.

"I'm playing at the La Fontaine tonight."

"Playing what?"

"The guitar. They usually have live music on the weekends, but they have a special concert tonight with an American jazz singer, and I'm filling in for her guitarist, who couldn't make it," I explained.

"So, you'll be at your place by the time I get there?"

"Yeah."

She set down her silverware and leaned toward me. "Are we having a romance, Gabriel?"

"Yes."

"And that's why this isn't a booty call."

"Yes, and because booty calls are crass."

Satisfied, she went back to her food.

After I got back to my office, I went online and bought all seven volumes of Proust's *In Search of Lost Time* with the promise to read them during my Christmas break.

Chapter 16

Wednesday Afternoon, October 12, 2023

After demonstrating my passable shooting abilities with my SIG Sauer at the gun range to Bør's satisfaction, we bicycled to Kæmpe.

I'd changed into my running clothes before I went shooting so I stayed in them while Bør changed in the gym's locker room. I walked up to Small Bo who was throwing punches at a boxing bag. When he saw me, he stopped and gave me a big bear hug.

Small Bo was anything but small. He was six feet tall and 100 of his 195 kilos were pure muscle. He distinguished himself as small because Big Bo was six feet two inches tall. A few months ago, Small Bo had been my bodyguard for a hot minute, while Big Bo and his friend Luc had protected Sophie when my face had met with the fists of some unsavory Russians.

"How are you, man?" Small Bo pulled his gloves off and picked up a bottle of water. He wore red and white Denmark soccer shorts and a wife-beater of the same colors. "Luc and Big Bo went to a Kashmir concert last weekend with Sophie."

I nodded. Luc and Big Bo had become friends with Sophie. They were ex-bikers in their late thirties who had been to prison for crimes against persons. Sophie was twenty-one with no tattoos, that I knew off at least. I felt, again, a puff of pride at how Sophie navigated any social setting with remarkable grace and authenticity.

"I heard."

"I'm supposed to train you."

"For what?" I asked, eyeing the boxing bag skeptically.

"We start with the bag." He smiled broadly. "And then we move to Brazilian jiu-jitsu. I'm a brown belt. I learned it in prison from a black belt. I'll earn my black belt by next year, if I keep at it."

"Brazilian jiu-jitsu?" I shook my head. My idea of fitness was simple. Go for a run every morning, rain or shine, and bicycle everywhere.

"It's an offshoot of Judo. More *ne-waza* ground techniques, though. We felt it would be best for your needs. Very focused on self-defense, grappling, and submission holds," he explained. I had no idea what the fuck *ne-waza* meant.

Bør joined us, also now in the same outfit and colors as Small Bo. He probably bought the workout gear in bulk. "BJJ is the best form for controlling an opponent. You want to gain a dominant position and get the enemy down," Bør added, his arms folded.

"Enemy?"

Small Bo smiled. "They're trying to kill you, man. They are the enemy."

I used to box many years ago, so I knew the basics.

Stand within arm's distance, hold hands in a tight fist in front of my face, and aim the hook at the jaw of the purported enemy, though I preferred the liver when I'd had the few occasions to use my training in my police officer days.

We started with shadowboxing. I threw short, solid, fast punches—though Small Bo kept calling them lazy.

"Focus on your footwork," Bør yelled.

After building up a good sweat and new aches and pains I hadn't experienced in a while, I drank from a water bottle Small Bo held out to me.

"You're out of practice."

"No shit," I gasped. It had been more than a decade since I'd used my fists.

Small Bo led me to the heavy bag he was working on, while Bør went into the ring to practice with another boxer.

"Think this is the enemy," Small Bo taunted as he held the bag still, "And go for it. Don't worry about practicing combos or your footwork. Just start hitting. You need to build up to form."

I punched the bag for five minutes before I was winded. I thought I was in shape, but hell, I was way *out* of shape. I could barely stand up straight after.

"Come on, let's get back to it," Small Bo persisted. "The enemy won't care you're tired."

I ran and cycled, which kept my legs in decent shape, a crucial factor for maintaining stability in boxing. However, even with this conditioning, my legs struggled to maintain the fighting stance after just five more minutes.

After twenty minutes, sweat covering my bald head and face. "I'm totally out of shape," I muttered.

Small Bo shrugged. "You're in decent shape for a dude with manicured fingers sitting at a desk—but not to fight some guy who's out to kill you. That's going to take some work. Bør wants you here three days a week for an hour. I think you need to be here every day. You can run from your place, do the work out and run back."

If I hadn't felt like an old man bent over at his waist ready to wheeze his lungs out, I'd have asked Small Bo to go fuck himself.

"I'll be here at six thirty tomorrow morning," I said huskily, still catching my breath.

"Good," Small Bo nodded. "Bør knew you'd be more cooperative once you found out how fucked up your body is."

"I thought you said I was fit." I took my shirt off and wiped my head and face with it.

"For a desk, not for the *real* world. And you're in the real world if a pro is after your old ass."

Chapter 17

Wednesday Evening, October 12, 2023

After my workout, I felt as though I'd been run over by a truck when I joined Freja for a beer at Godt Øl, a bar that had recently joined the craft beer craze. I was acutely aware that as tough as I felt at that moment, the next day would be even more challenging. To prevent my sore muscles from completely giving out, I realized I'd need to increase my visits to Kæmpe to daily sessions, rather than just three times a week. Just as Bør had demanded.

Godt Øl was on the most Instagrammed street in Copenhagen: the cobblestoned Magstræde. One of two oldest streets in Copenhagen, Magstræde still had the original cobbling, and was quaintly squeezed between old crooked and colorful townhouses and apartments.

When I texted Freja that I needed a contact within PET to talk about Copenhagen Bank, she recommended we meet. God Øl was a good choice as it was just a hundred meters from La Fontaine on Kompagnistræde where I was playing in an hour.

She was already at the bar when I got there, chatting with the bartender.

"I come here a lot," she explained when she suggested I come back after my dry month was over to try a beer called Rasputin from *Brouwerij De Molen*, a famous Dutch brewery in Bodegraven, which was a good stout that she thought I'd enjoy.

"How come?" I drank my sparkling water with a twist.

She looked uncomfortable as she stared at her Pilsner. "*He* got an apartment on Nybrogade after he moved out of his…ah…wife's place."

"Okay. I thought you weren't seeing each other anymore."

She cleared her throat and looked sheepish. "We're on *again*…as of last night."

"Are you happy about it?"

She shrugged. "Yeah, until I'm not. And then we'll be *off* again. I don't think this is a healthy relationship."

I kept my expression noncommittal.

"This is why I like you, Præst, you never judge."

"Not my place."

"I'm assuming you want to meet *him*."

I nodded. "Does *he* have a name?"

She uncharacteristically blushed, which I found charming. "Valentin Jørgensen. He's been with PET for twenty years. What do you want to talk to him about?"

"Financial fraud."

"He's with organized crime, not financial fraud."

"That's okay. If he can lead me to the right person, I'm good with that, too."

"I'm meeting him for dinner at Tight if you want to join us," she offered.

I shook my head and tilted my chin toward my guitar that was resting against the bar at my feet. "I'm playing at La Fontaine tonight. The set starts at seven, I've got to be there by six."

V ALENTIN LOOKED NOTHING LIKE I thought he would. So much for not being judgmental. Standing three inches shorter than Freja, who was five feet eleven inches tall, he sported glasses so thick they seemed to call for laser surgery. His attire consisted of baggy jeans and a large t-shirt, likely chosen to conceal his paunch. However, as soon as he began to speak, it became clear why Freja was attracted to him. Valentin was intelligent and articulate, with a notable knowledge of beer. He chose a Danish New England IPA, its hoppy appearance aligning perfectly with my expectations.

"I know some of what's going on, but I'm not supposed to talk about it. You understand? A PET agent who is a blabbermouth doesn't stay an agent very long," he announced after his beer was served.

We moved to a small table in the corner. The tables had filled, and some regulars were playing a game of Partners, a four-player strategy board game.

"You can trust him." Freja finished her beer.

"You're the man who brought down Elias Juhl."

I shook my head. "Elias Juhl is secretary of NATO."

"Rumor is that he left because you had something on him."

"You know in my business, a blabbermouth doesn't stay a PI for very long," I countered.

"Want another?" Freja asked, looking at my empty glass. *Well, why the fuck not.*

"Sure." *I'll have another glass of fucking sparkling water with a fucking twist.*

Freja left to get us our drinks, and Valentin took a deep breath.

"PET is *very* interested in Copenhagen Bank, but we're not talking about it because we're not investigating. The NSA is investigating. We're in a supporting role."

"The American NSA?"

"Any other NSA you know about?" Valentin remarked.

I nodded.

"The NSA is scrutinizing Deutsche Bank, Copenhagen Bank, and various other European banks, focusing on non-native accounts. There's a proliferation of dummy accounts, especially in the United Kingdom, Monaco, and other locations, set up by Russians for money laundering purposes." Valentin briefly diverted his attention to his phone when it beeped, then returned his gaze to me.

He was a serious man. And I liked his straight forwardness.

"Why would Copenhagen Bank go after an employee?"

"If the employee knows about what they're doing in the Baltics. We suspect that nearly eighty percent of the Copenhagen Bank revenue from the Baltics is from illegal Russian money."

Freja came back with my water and her beer.

"If you know, why haven't you done anything about it?" I demanded.

"We suspect. We *know* fuck all. And what we suspect is from a Russian journalist the NSA had been working with, who disappeared after Nikita Poletov was murdered. At PET, we think he or she is now in the states."

I felt a headache coming on. This investigation started with an innocuous suicide of a young woman who I thought Silas Haagen had maybe sexually assaulted. Now, it looked like the cluster fuck of all investigations.

"Do you know the name of this journalist?"

Valentin shook his head.

"I think...and maybe I even know that there is someone following me since I met with Harald Wiberg and Silas Haagen," I told him.

He nodded. "Not surprising. Did you make sure no one followed you here?"

"Yes."

"Good, so you know how to *behave*."

I didn't respond. I wasn't an idiot, but I didn't want to sound defensive. "What can you tell me about Harald Wiberg?"

Valentin smiled. "Most people think Silas Haagen is the leader of the pack."

"He's a dilettante."

Freja laughed. "Only you'd say that."

"He's right," Valentin confirmed. "Wiberg is the...*consiglieri* as they'd say in the movies. He's a thug. He's a good lawyer. And he's a good criminal. PET has been looking at him for years. We have nothing on him."

"A contact of mine said that if Copenhagen Bank sent a professional, it would be ex SVR."

Valentin drank some beer and thought about it. "Yes. But they also are close to Israel, so a pro could be ex Mossad, who I think are more dangerous than SVR. I know, odd bed fellows."

I gave him a blank look. I understood the Russian-Europe connection, but Israel was way out of my realm of knowledge.

Seeing my confusion, Valentin explained. "Israel has become a hub for money laundering for Russian organized crime. Billions in illegal money is flowing from Russia and former Soviet republics, South America, Africa, and Europe through Israel, which is now one of the world's leading money laundries." Valentin picked up his phone again to check something, and then set it down.

"Anything on your phone of interest?"

"Yes. Your friend *Chefpolitiinspektør* Tommy Frisk cleared you. He thinks you're a stubborn asshole but that I can trust you."

"It's embarrassing how he praises me," I said.

Freja snorted.

"Israel's relaxed money-transfer laws, originally intended to attract Jewish immigrants, are now being exploited by Russians, Venezuelans, and others for money laundering. Just last year, a Chechen was apprehended while attempting to open an Israeli account with 50 million dollars in Venezuelan checks. A few years earlier, an Israeli citizen with mob connections was convicted in Florida for operating a money laundering scheme for a Colombian cartel. Israel has become a significant hub for laundering a large percentage of recycled cocaine cash."

I raised my hand. I pulled out a notebook from my Tumi bag, along with a pen, and began to take notes. This was whole hell of a lot of information to commit to memory.

"Look up Gregory Lerner. He defrauded Russian banks of millions to open a bank in Israel. He didn't go to jail. He just paid a few million in fines and went on with his business. Russian money is everywhere. And it's a lot of money. What is it you're trying to achieve by putting your life in danger?" Valentin wanted to know.

I sighed. "A woman killed herself. She worked for Silas Haagen, and I'm trying to find out what happened."

Valentin's eyebrows came together. "They sent a professional after you from maybe Mossad or SVR. Maybe you should stop investigating this woman's death."

"I can't. I want to, but I can't."

He looked at Freja as though enquiring if I had lost my mind. She chuckled, "He's ethically weird."

Valentin cleared his throat. "Walk away. Let PET and NSA…the experts do their jobs."

"He will not walk away, Valentin," Freja assured him. "We tried with the Yousef Ahmed case, and he got shot."

"You may get shot again," Valentin warned. "Is that worth it?"

"No," I said honestly. "But if I can be run off cases, I need to find a new line of work. And the only thing I'm good at is this…and picking the right wine. And I don't think I'll like being a floor sommelier at a restaurant."

"This is fucking serious, you understand?" Valentin said sharply.

"Yeah, I do."

"What are you going to do?" Freja asked.

I put my notebook away. I stood up, shook hands with Valentin, and gave Freja a hug.

"Præst, what will you do?" she insisted.

"I have no fucking idea," I told her sincerely.

Chapter 18

Wednesday Night, October 12, 2023

"I'm playing at La Fontaine. You want to come by?" I told my American friend Cézar Doucette who worked for a FinTech company that made financial software for banks. I knew Copenhagen Bank was one of his company's customers, and I was hoping to dig up some financial dirt.

"*Cher*, I've got an *envie* for some jazz," he said in his New Orleans accent. "Who's playing?"

"An American jazz singer from the Blue Note in New York. Her guitarist fell sick so I'm filling in."

"She sing some Nina?"

"I'll make sure."

"Then I'll see you at the *fais do do*."

Cézar, hailing from New Orleans and of Haitian descent, embodied the *laissez les bons temps rouler* spirit. He frequented jazz clubs and blues bars, and during the American football season, he was a regular at sports bars, passionately supporting the New Orleans Saints. His Creole accent would surface or fade as he wished. Fluent in Danish with a Copenhagen accent, he seamlessly switched to English for more serious conversations.

I first met Cézar a few years back while handling an embezzlement case at a Danish IT company for *Dall og Digman*. He had been head of IT there, and we'd worked together to clean up the mess. It had all been handled hush hush, and no police were involved. People were fired and people were transferred, and Cézar left the company and was now working for a Danish FinTech company that developed and sold banking regulatory compliance software.

La Fontaine was one of Denmark's oldest jazz clubs. I had come here many a Sunday night for their jam sessions, and was one of the lucky ones who, during the Copenhagen Jazz Festival in 2015, witnessed Lady Gaga drop in for an impromptu rendition of *La Vie En Rose*. Sophie is still jealous, because I not only got to see the singer live but was also playing the guitar when she sang.

I was not what one called a *professional* guitar player. I liked to play, and I did it as often as I could, but Bobby K wanted me to practice more. A professional guitar player would practice nearly four to five hours a day, but I fell into the eight to ten hours a week category. There was a time when I played every day, but I had become lackadaisical in my old age. I wasn't exactly rusty, but I wasn't great, either.

Ella Simone Parker, the singer from New York, was beautiful and charming. She spoke with that distinct air of a jazz musician and the Big Apple, where she was born and raised in East Harlem.

Ella, the sax player, piano player, and I practiced for a good forty-five minutes, understanding each other's cues, getting a feel for how we'd jam. I loved to play the guitar, loved that moment when it was just the music. It was my meditation.

It's a cliché, but a guitar is like a woman's body. And the Gibson ES-335 Figured Semi-Hollow with its mahogany neck and rosewood fretboard was delicious, not only to look at, but also touch and play. Now, I could use the Gibson for both jazz and blues but when I played the blues it had to be on my Fender Vintera '50s Stratocaster.

Eric Clapton, Jimi Hendrix, Stevie Ray Vaughn, amongst many other blues greats, worshipped at the altar of Fender, which was why I preferred the Fender Vintera series as it dripped old-school charm, thanks to its period-accurate neck tint, a vintage synchronized tremolo, locking vintage tuners, classic off-white control knobs, and a two-color sunburst finish. But for jazz, I wanted a perfect blend of form and function, which the Gibson offered.

Every time I tested my mettle against new artists like I was doing now, I knew I was not as good as I used to be or as good as I could be. I could hear Bobby K's voice in my head, *"You have talent, but you don't practice, Præst."* And I'd respond with a, *"I've got a day job, Bobby. Got to make a living."*

We started with one of Ella's originals, *Welcome to My World* and then moved to many of the usual suspects, *At*

Last by Etta, *Lover Man* by Billie, and *I Put on a Spell on You* by Nina.

Cézar and I stepped out during a break.

"I'm guessing you didn't just want to spring free tickets for La Fontaine for me. So, what's up, *cher*?"

"Drop the Creole accent, will you."

He laughed. "Hey, the Danish girls love it."

Cézar had an air about him that subtly hinted at being a government agent. In our interactions, it felt like a mutual exchange of information, though he seemed to know more about me than I did about him. He was a good-looking man, possibly in his mid to late thirties, slightly shorter than me, with closely cropped hair and a neatly trimmed beard. His comments about Danish girls loving his accent left his relationship status and orientation ambiguous. He exuded a natural ease, equally comfortable in a suit or board shorts. I remember seeing him at an embassy party, seamlessly blending in, and at a barbecue at Bør's gym, mingling effortlessly with ex-bikers.

"I'm working on a case that involves a bank, and wanted to ask you for some information," I told him.

He nodded. "I'm going to need more than that to help you."

His white teeth shone in the dark and a woman who came out to smoke a cigarette looked at Cézar appreciatively. He smiled invitingly at her.

"I want to know what you know about Copenhagen Bank's Baltic business."

He shrugged. "Not a lot."

I thought about it for a moment, and then decided that if I gave him more, I'd get more. And it wasn't like anything I knew yet was top secret. In fact, it was pathetically sparse.

"A woman working the Baltic desk killed herself. I'm trying to find out why. I met with people she worked with, and the general counsel showed up for the meeting. And since then, someone has been following me. Busted up my bicycle, trying to run me over."

I watched Cézar and was convinced he was indeed some kind of American government official when he showed no emotion at all. No surprise. No shock. No, *oh my god, they're trying to kill you*.

"Who did you meet with?"

"At Copenhagen Bank?" I asked, and he nodded. "Lots of people—"

He cut me off. "Besides Harald Wiberg, who did you meet with about this woman?"

So, he knew who the general counsel for Copenhagen Bank was. "Her boss, Silas Haagen."

Cézar nodded. "And someone is following you? How do you know?"

"I know."

He nodded again. "Your instincts have always been on point. I'll give you that. I can find out more and report back to you."

I pulled out the Android phone I found in Afsana's room. "The phone is locked. The woman who killed herself probably used this phone to call some people she didn't want Copenhagen Bank to know about...or it's a phone she used to surf porn. I have no idea. I don't have the skills to work the phone. I hope you do."

Cézar looked at the phone speculatively, and then took it and slipped it into his jacket pocket.

"Someone sent an email to the CHRO at Copenhagen Bank. It was brief, just two sentences: *Copenhagen Bank killed Noor. What will you do about it?*" I said, taking out the printed email which Flora had received and set this clusterfuck in motion. "I can send you the digital copy. Could you trace its origin?"

Cézar took the printed paper and shoved it into his pocket without looking at it.

"It's not always easy to find out who sent an email, despite what the movies tell you," Cézar warned.

"Do your best," I said.

He nodded. "Why do you think they're following you?"

"I don't think they intend to have a conversation with me."

Cézar grinned. "Probably only with their fists. And you aren't working on anything else to piss anyone else off?"

I shook my head.

"Okay," he said, looking around and ignoring the woman who had given him the big come on. His Creole accent had also completely disappeared. "Now, I know you're not stupid."

"I'm glad someone knows that."

"I can guess why you came to me instead of many other IT people who you could go to."

I gave him my most innocent look.

He looked around as if uncomfortable. "If there's something on the phone, that's important...I may not give it back to you."

I nodded. I knew that.

"I'll give you what I can. For now, here's what I know. A man called The Ghost is in Copenhagen. We don't know why, but there has been some chatter about a hit out on someone. And it's connected to Russian money and—"

"Whoa," I cut him off and lifted both my hands. "Who the fuck is a ghost?"

"*The* Ghost is a professional hitman. His expertise is in making murders look like suicides or accidents. We don't know who he is. We suspect ex-SVR or ex-Mossad or...who the fuck knows."

"Wait, are you suggesting that someone put a hit out on me?"

Cézar shrugged this time.

"You've got to be kidding me. You are fucking with me, right?"

Cézar gave me his "does this face look like I'm fucking with you?" expression.

"I know nothing," I sighed. "Why are they trying to kill me when I know fucking nothing?"

"Because when it comes to Russian money, they're *very* sensitive. Now, if you dropped the case and walked away, *maybe* that'll be enough, but if they sent a professional after you…I don't think the chances look good no matter what you do," Cézar contemplated.

"I'm glad to see that you're all torn up about it."

Cézar laughed. "Maybe he's here to do someone else entirely. Or maybe he isn't here at all. He is after all called *The Ghost*. Look, let me look into all of this and find out who put a *gris-gris* on you."

"And a *gris-gris* is?"

"A curse," he said, his voice dripping Creole. "In the meantime, *cher*, try to keep a low profile, okay?"

"My goal in life."

CHAPTER 19

Thursday Morning, October 13, 2023

I FELL ASLEEP.

For the sake of everything holy!

I. Fell. Asleep.

I had a naked and willing woman in bed with me, and I crashed. For a man who was pondering his age versus the woman he's trying to bed, the embarrassment of falling asleep even before the foreplay cannot be exaggerated.

Afsana had come by after two in the morning. She'd insisted on a shower, and I lay down to close my eyes for a minute. Next thing I knew I was waking up at six in the morning with Afsana, naked, in my bed, under the duvet with me. She was asleep when I went for my run and workout with Small Bo at Kæmpe. Everything in my body hurt. I was feeling muscles I hadn't felt in years.

Esther, my neighbor from down the street, waved to me as I ran past her place.

"Hey, Gabriel," she called out.

I stopped, my lungs gasping for breath. Every step was agony, and it would be like this until I got my body to a place where it could handle the Small Bo's workout regimen for me.

"*Godmorgen*, Esther."

"Did you check if your heating lamp is working? We'll need it for the block party. It's going to be a cold night," she explained. Esther was a slight blonde woman, a single mother of two teenagers.

"I'll do it today and make sure it's working. I can also get some electric lamps from Mojo if you need them. They have extra in storage." I put my hands on her white fence and leaned.

"Who's the girl who came by last night?" she asked slyly.

I smiled. "A friend."

"Is that what we call them these days? What do I know, I haven't dated in years."

I laughed then. "Anything else you need for the party?"

She shrugged. "We'll know more as we get closer. You better show up. Okay? Or at least make sure the potato salad does. Tony is planning to cook pork shoulder on the grill for twenty-four hours. And he's making his own barbecue sauce."

Tony was an American who lived with his Danish husband, three townhouses down from me. He was from Texas and was educating us on the difference between grilling and barbecuing.

I took a shower and made some coffee. Freja had sent me Noor's file. I sat on one of the bar stools at my kitchen counter and read through it.

She'd taken pills. She'd written a note.

I am so sorry for doing this. But I have no choice. I can't simply go on like this anymore. I love you all. I hope you'll understand.

But now with my *ghost* wisdom, I wondered how much duress she was under to write that note.

My phone rang, it was Flora.

"They fired me," her voice was shaking. "Did you tell anyone?"

"No."

"Then they guessed. Those sons of bitches," she retorted.

Or they tapped your phone.

"I'm so sorry, Flora."

"Look, they didn't say it directly, but Harald Wiberg walked me out of the building and he...look, I think it may be best if you stopped investigating."

I took a sip of coffee and smiled when I saw Afsana come to the kitchen in one of my t-shirts. "I can't stop, Flora. I have another client who is also after the same thing. I have to do this."

Afsana leaned against the counter next to the barstool where I was sitting, and took my coffee cup. She sipped it and nodded in appreciation.

"But...."

"Flora, I *have* to do this. I'm really sorry about your job. I won't charge you for the work I have done," I explained.

"Of course, you'll charge me," her irritation came through loud and clear. "This isn't about money. I'm, well, there's no dignified way to put it. I'm scared. Is this *other* client, paying you?"

"No."

"So, if I stop paying you, you'll do this pro bono?"

"Yes."

She laughed softly. "Eymen was right. You're a weird one. I'll keep paying you, Gabriel. If you're not scared, then maybe I shouldn't be scared, either."

Well, that wasn't entirely true.

"Who fired you, Flora?"

"Leif Timmermann."

The CEO. "Did he say why?"

"At my level, they don't need to. He said it wasn't working out. We've had several HR issues. Anyway, they gave me a good severance, and Harald Wiberg walked me out of the building, telling me to mind my own business and be *careful.*" She sounded tired.

I couldn't tell her what Cézar had told me, partly because I'd sound like a moron who was cooking up stories about assassins called the fucking *Ghost*...and partly because I didn't want Afsana, who was listening to our conversation, to worry. She was drinking my coffee, looking out of my kitchen window at my patio, waiting patiently for me to finish the call. Her hair was mussed, and she'd not tried to put it right. She didn't have to. It looked just fine. Her face was clear of any makeup and looked soft and dewy.

Dewy? For pity's sake!

"Where are you, Flora?"

"At home."

"Do you want me to come over?"

"No. I'm fine."

I texted Eymen to tell him to reach out to Flora because she'd been fired as she had feared she would.

"You'll keep me posted?"

"Of course."

I hung up and smiled at Afsana, who was now finishing my cup of coffee.

"Would you like me to make you a cup?"

She set the coffee down and leaned. She brushed her lips against mine. She tasted of mint and coffee. "After."

"After?"

"Yes, after." She laughed and sat on my lap.

I held her. "I'm sorry I fell asleep."

"That's okay," she smiled mischievously. "As long as you make up for it."

I thanked her for giving me another chance…and made up for it.

Chapter 20

Thursday Afternoon, October 13, 2023

It took me forty minutes to bicycle to Glostrup to the office of Jorun Eskola, chief police inspector of NSK, Denmark's special crime unit. Tommy had offered to drive me, but I wanted to loosen my muscles.

When I had to meet Tommy, I went to Polititorvet, which was in the center of the city. I'd never been to the NSK building, which was completed in 2018. It was a modern building that housed, amongst other agencies, the special crime unit, the National Forensic Science Center, and the National Cyber Crime Center. Nearly 750 government employees called the building, which had three floors, a full basement, and an enclosed courtyard, their workplace. Like most new government buildings, it was *green* and came with solar panels.

I wasn't sure how I felt about the building as it looked like a cross between gray Soviet-era architecture and the genius of Bjarke Ingels.

I went through the secure gate and got my visitor's badge. The building was all light and glass, and I warmed to its minimalist Nordic design. Jorun Eskola's office was on the second floor, but I was asked to wait in the lobby for someone to come and take me upstairs.

I thought Eskola would send a flunky, but she came down to get me herself. She was an attractive woman in her early forties, who stood several inches shorter than me, but made up for her height with her intimidating demeanor. She wore her dark shoulder-length hair in a ponytail. Her eyes were a bright blue and her pale skin had just the right amount of makeup to give her that *"I don't care how I look but I know I look good"* effect. She was dressed in a dark blue pantsuit, paired with a white button-down shirt, looking as if she had stepped out of a Vogue magazine feature on stylish women in law enforcement.

For the meeting, I dressed conservatively in a gray suit with a turtleneck, dark gray Cashmere sweater. I'd removed my dark gray Falconeri cashmere coat, and had it draped on my forearm, and I held my Goorin River gray merino wool felt fedora in my hand when Eskola came up to me.

"Præst." She held out her hand, and I shook it.

"How are you, Inspector? Thanks for seeing me," I said politely. I understood she thought I was a snitch who had crucified her friend, and I couldn't change that, but I was hoping we could have a professional relationship.

"Before we go to the conference room, I want to make a few things clear." She tucked both hands into her slacks. "Tommy asked me for a favor, and I owe him a few. I don't like you. I don't want to meet with you. I don't owe you fucking anything."

I tried not to sigh visibly. "Then I thank you even more for your time and patience."

She narrowed her eyes. "Are you mocking me?"

"No," I said sincerely. "I am grateful that you're talking to me. I need help."

She nodded, still unsure about me. "Let's go." She led the way, and I followed her.

We didn't make small talk as waited for the elevator and walked to the conference room where Tommy was.

As we entered, he waved to me while on the phone. I chose a seat across from him, positioning myself so the windows were behind me. It was a habit of mine, always ensuring that the sun wouldn't be in my eyes and that I wouldn't get distracted by any outside activities visible through the window.

Eskola sat next to Tommy. The sides were declared. It was the cops against the poor PI. I wasn't offered coffee, tea, or water.

"We're in reporting hell at Polititorvet. Prime Minister wants to not look like she's soft on crime," he said jovially after ending his call, fully aware that Eskola hated my guts, and I was straining at the seams to keep my sarcasm at bay.

"Let's get this done with," Eskola said in her no-nonsense tone.

"I want to understand if you're investigating Copenhagen Bank and especially its Baltic division for financial fraud of any kind." I used my words carefully.

"Yes."

"Can you tell me what your investigation is about?" I asked even though I knew her answer.

"No."

Tommy smiled.

"I believe and I have it on good authority that the Baltic division of Copenhagen Bank, the former Finnish Finba Bank, is being used to launder money for the Russians," I tried another tactic. Perhaps if I shared more, they would reciprocate. Normally, I'd rely on silence to coax out information, but facing two seasoned cops, I knew the silent treatment wouldn't work on them.

"Really?" Eskola raised her eyebrows.

"On whose good authority did you come to ah...*believe* this?" Tommy wanted to know.

I cleared my throat unnecessarily. I didn't get nervous in situations like this, but Jorun Eskola was getting to me. In order to stretch the time I would have in this conference room, I asked, "Do you think I could get some water? It's a long bicycle ride from Gammel Mønt."

Eskola looked at me speculatively, probably considering if she should ask me to go fuck myself, and then, as if deciding, she picked up her phone. She called someone and asked them to bring in coffee and water.

I tried another line of information. "On Monday night, someone tried to run me over, this was on the day I had a conversation with Harald Wiberg and Silas Haagen at Copenhagen Bank, where I asked them about Noor Mallik, an analyst who died by suicide. Today, my client, Flora

Brandt, the CHRO of Copenhagen Bank, was fired and told to *mind her own business and be careful*. She'd come to me initially because she received an anonymous email that insinuated Noor was killed by Copenhagen Bank. She assumed it meant that something happened to her, and she suspected it was sexual harassment by Silas Haagen."

Before Eskola could give me yet another one-word answer, the conference room door opened and a young man in a suit that was too tight for him, which apparently was the latest fashion, brought a tray with a coffee carafe, water jug, three cups, milk, sugar, and three clear glasses.

Tommy did the honors, pouring water into the three glasses, and then coffee into the cups, while we watched in stony silence.

We all sipped some coffee. Eskola looked at her Apple Watch pointedly, and then back at me.

"Look, I just need information. Anything you can—"

"You're a fucking civilian and we don't share with civilians or rat ex cops," Eskola drawled, emotionlessly.

I stood up. Enough was enough.

"Well, then I'll thank you for your time."

"Sit down," Tommy ordered.

I sat down.

"Jorun, this man took a bullet a few months because we fucked up on the Yousef Ahmed case," Tommy whispered. "We owe him."

"He's a goddamn snitch."

"No. You're being bullheaded about Jensen, but we don't have time to dredge that crap up so let's stick to what we know now," Tommy continued on calmly. "Someone is trying to take you out. And you suspect it's Harald Wiberg and Silas Haagen?"

"Well, when you say it like that even I think it sounds crazy," I conceded.

Eskola drank some coffee and took a deep breath. "Officially, we're not investigating Copenhagen Bank, but our friends in the NSA are. We're supporting them...*very* actively. Nikita Poletov...do you know who he is?"

I nodded and mentally thanked Dag Sorgenfri Kjær for imparting some of his knowledge to me.

She continued. "Five years ago, Poletov met with a Russian reporter, Raisa Chaban, in Copenhagen. He was working on closing down non-resident and fraudulent accounts at Finba Bank in Estonia that was, we suspect, laundering what could be nearly two billion euros for the Russian government and friends of the government. After he died, Raisa disappeared. We believe she's in the United States in hiding and under the protection of the US government."

"What did Raisa Chaban know?"

Eskola shrugged. "We're helping the Americans. They're not helping us. And, your Noor Mallik is not on our radar or theirs."

"What if she was murdered?"

Tommy scoffed. "We're not amateurs. Do you know how hard it is to make a murder look like a suicide?"

"Yes, but what if you were a professional?"

They both contemplated that for a minute.

"What is your suspicion?" Eskola asked.

Nice! We were now partners.

"Someone emailed Flora Brandt about Noor. Someone wanted this to be in the forefront again."

I pulled out a printout of the email from my messenger bag, and laid it in front of them.

Eskola read through and nodded. "Send this to me by email, and I'll see what we can find out."

I opened my phone and immediately forwarded the email that Flora had sent me at the start of the investigation for the second time in two days. Last night, I'd sent it to Cézar.

"If you think someone is trying to take you out," Eskola continued, "you should consider removing yourself from this investigation, *and* try your best not to interfere with Copenhagen Bank. Let the experts handle this."

"No." I could also do one-word answers.

"We won't protect you," Eskola warned.

"I thought it was your job to serve and protect," I countered.

"That's only in the movies. In real life, we kick ass and take names," Tommy replied.

"Thank you. That makes me feel safe."

"Don't feel safe," Tommy barked at me. "Stay vigilant, you motherfucker. Whenever I turn around, someone is beating the crap out of you, shooting at you, or trying to kill you."

"What can I say, it's my pleasant personality." I beamed.

"And Præst, be careful if you're going to try to find Raisa Chaban. The US government will chew you up and spit you out," Eskola advised.

"I'll try my best not to get chewed up and spat out," I confirmed.

I thanked her and shook hands again with her.

Tommy stood up. "I'm going to give you a ride."

He wasn't suggesting. It was an order. I followed it.

CHAPTER 21

Thursday Afternoon, October 13, 2023

With my bicycle secured on the bike rack on Tommy's police-issue Volkswagen Touran, I got into the car beside him.

He remained silent for a while as we drove. I waited.

"Jorun's team has been looking into Harald Wiberg," he revealed. "He has traveled to Russia extensively in the past few years, including since the war began. Usually, that's not a problem, but he's been seen with certain people there that put him on the radar of the Americans…who told us. By *us*…I mean, Jorun's team. I know what I know through *other* sources."

This made sense, because Tommy was homicide and crimes against persons, not financial crimes.

"Okay."

Tommy slowed down as we hit traffic on Roskildevej.

"Now, what didn't you tell her?" he demanded.

I thought about it for a long moment. "Tommy, the less you know, the better." He didn't need to know about Cézar.

Tommy sped up and got on the *samkørselsbane*, the carpool lane. "What is your next step?"

"I think I'm going to find this Russian journalist."

"And what makes you think you'll be successful when the entire Russian government has not been?"

I grinned. "My charming personality."

Tommy sighed as an Audi A5 stormed to get in front of him, and then slowed down. "*Motherfucker,*" he cursed and slowed down.

We didn't talk as Roskildevej turned into Vesterbrogade and followed Kongens Nytorv and Gothersgade. He drove into the parking area of Pastis and parked in an accessible parking spot.

"I'll buy you a drink," he instructed.

We sat outside at a small table with two chairs. In the autumn and winter, Pastis became an indoor restaurant with the outdoors exclusively for smokers.

Tommy got a pack of his Marlboro reds out, and when the server came, he asked him to turn on the electric heater above the table. I ordered a cup of coffee, and Tommy ordered an Ardbeg 10.

"You seeing this dead girl's cousin?" he asked, lighting his cigarette.

"*Tommy,*" I protested.

I restrained myself from sinking into the smell of tobacco. Secondhand smoke wasn't the same as first-hand, but it was better than nothing when you were as desperate as I was.

"When I say seeing, I mean seeing naked?"

I sighed.

"So, that's a yes." He took another puff. I didn't respond.

"How old is she again?" Tommy asked.

The server came with our drinks and discreetly placed blankets on a chair next to us. Neither of us picked up the blankets as the electric heater was doing its job.

"Is that a good idea?" He took a long drink of his Ardbeg. I bet that scotch was heating him up nicely from the inside, I thought sourly.

I eyed him thoughtfully, and then did what I did very well. I shrugged.

"You think this Noor girl was murdered by a professional?"

I nodded as I warmed my hands on my coffee cup.

"The same professional you think is after you?"

"Yes."

He drank his scotch, and I let the coffee warm my insides and my extremities. It was a poor substitute for alcohol.

"Præst, what do you need from me?" Tommy asked as he finished his drink.

"Not this time, Tommy."

"Why?"

"This could really get fucked up and I don't want to involve you. I'm even keeping Eymen and Clara out of it...though Victor, as you know, is hard to keep out of anything."

Tommy pulled out three hundred Danish kroner and put it on the table to cover our drinks. He stood up and pulled his jacket close.

"Look, if you get killed, Sophie will make my life miserable, and Nadia will never fuck me again," he said soberly. Nadia was Tommy's wife, and she had a soft spot for me. "So, try to not get killed."

I stood up, and we shook hands.

"Thanks, Tommy." He gave me one last look, then left.

I sat down and finished my coffee, feeling a heaviness I hadn't felt in a long time. I didn't have a firm grasp on this case. I didn't know what I was doing.

As I got up to go to my office, I could suddenly feel a prickle at the back of my neck. I didn't have any hair to stand up in warning, but I could feel *him*. *The Ghost*. He was here. I was certain of it.

My phone rang then, it was Cézar.

"*Cher*, this is a cluster fuck," he said in response to my *bonjour*. "I can't keep what's on the phone hidden. You understand."

"Just give me a head start," I requested.

"That I can do. First, the easy stuff. The email to Flora Brandt came from Caja Hansen. She lives in Vesterbro. She used to work at Copenhagen Bank and quit a year ago. She used to work for Silas Haagen."

"Thanks." I pulled out my notebook and wrote down names and places.

"Now, the phone...I don't have it anymore. It's hit the chain of command, which means your PET or DDIS or some other fuckers are going to be at your door sooner than later. Your girl, Noor, was in contact with a Russian journalist called...."

Raisa Chaban.

"...Raisa Chaban. We have no text messages, just phone calls. And we have an email from Raisa to Noor setting up a time to talk. We know this because Raisa used to use a username, *mertvaya_devushka*," he finished.

"My Russian is a bit rusty." I kept my voice steady through my excitement. The pieces of this puzzle were finally coming together, even if I couldn't see the full picture yet.

"Dead Girl," he said coolly. "She's on everyone's hitlist and no one wants her to talk."

"Why not?"

"Because, politically, it'll be a shit show if the Russians know we're harboring an enemy of their state. The next time they kidnap an American, they'll use her for hostage negotiations, and we can't send her back, they'll first torture then kill her. We like to protect journalists—you know the First Amendment and all that. It's best they don't know she's with us," Cézar explained.

"But they know."

Cézar sighed. "Yes, but not officially."

"How do I find her?"

Cézar sighed. "You're not listening to me, *cher*."

"I'm listening. I'm just not agreeing with you."

"*Merde!*" he swore. "I don't know. No one knows."

"I guess I'll have to put those detective skills to work, then," I said solemnly.

And since a good detective knew how to use a source, I called Nico and told her to see what she could dig up on Raisa Chaban and if she could find me a lead.

CHAPTER 22

Thursday, Early Evening, October 13, 2023

*C*AN I COME BY *tonight? I'll let you sleep.*

I read Afsana's message after I locked my bicycle outside Caja Hansen's apartment building on Åbakkevej, and the day felt a little lighter.

Yes, please. I'll leave the door open. And I'll try to stay awake.

My research showed that Caja was single and in her late thirties. She lived in a brick building from the 1930s, which had around 300 rental units on three levels. Her apartment was a one-room apartment, which was fashionably called a loft, with a small balcony and a view of *Grøndalsparken*. She paid six thousand Danish kroner in rent, which she earned by working as a teacher at Børnehaven Slettegården, a nearby kindergarten.

This was obviously a big change in career for someone who had an MBA from Copenhagen Business School, and had been working as a Senior Business Manager for Large Corporations and Institutions with a focus on the Baltic region at Copenhagen Bank. Her LinkedIn profile had not been updated since she left Copenhagen Bank a year ago.

I followed some other tenants into the building, avoiding the buzzer, and knocked on Caja's door.

A slender, petite blonde woman opened the door.

"*Hej*," I said, holding out my business card.

She took it and a man, about twice her height and weight, came up to stand behind her, filling the doorway.

"What do you want?" he asked, looking at my card that Caja held.

"I want to speak with Caja Hansen."

"Why?" he demanded.

I looked at the woman and smiled sincerely. "Are you Caja?"

"*Hey*, I'm talking to you." The man pushed Caja behind him.

I sighed. This would not be a good day to try out my hand-to-hand training. I'd only had a few sessions, and every muscle and joint in my body told me I was not ready to take on this gigantic man with tree-trunk arm muscles.

"I want to talk to her about the email she sent to Flora Brandt about Noor."

Now the man pushed me further out. "Who sent you?"

I raised both my hands in my defense. "I'm investigating Noor's death for Flora and her family."

"I don't want to talk to anyone from Copenhagen Bank," I heard Caja say from behind the man.

"I'm not from Copenhagen Bank. I've been hired by Flora and Noor's family." It was a small white lie, but I didn't think Afsana would mind.

"Her family?" Caja moved the hulk of a man aside.

"Afsana Mallik."

She nodded. "It's okay, Peder. Let him come in."

Peder stepped aside.

We sat down in the small living room. They were on the sofa, and I sat across from them in an uncomfortable armchair. I removed my coat and scarf, and laid them on the arm of my chair, and placed my fedora on the coffee table.

I smiled. They smiled back.

"You want a beer?" Peder asked, as he stood up.

"No, thank you. But I wouldn't say no to a cup of coffee."

Peder looked at Caja and she nodded.

"How do you take it?" he asked.

"Black."

Peder left us in the living room and went into the adjoining kitchen. The apartment was classic Copenhagen. A living room that opened into a kitchen, a small dining room, and a bedroom. There was a small bathroom somewhere, probably next to the bedroom.

"How do you know I sent the email to Flora?" she asked. She was wearing a pair of blue skintight jeans, and her feet were stuffed into Ugg boots. She wore a Copenhagen Business School pullover. Her hair was loose around her shoulders. She wore makeup, as if she'd just returned from somewhere.

"A friend in IT helped me."

She nodded, and then sighed. "I hired Noor into Copenhagen Bank as an intern. She was my responsibility, even though she eventually reported directly to Silas. She was literally his right hand, even though she was inexperienced. I *used* to be his right hand, many years ago, so I know how that went."

I didn't need to ask; I could guess, and I dreaded realizing what she was implying.

She laughed then, a short almost hysterical laugh. "Have you met him?"

By *him*, she meant Silas Haagen, so I nodded.

"He's handsome and charismatic. When I started at the Baltic desk, it was like an explosion of energy. We had an affair. We were together for nearly six months, and then I found out that he was...well, that this was a pattern, and he did this a lot. I ended it. He didn't take it well and...." She trailed off as Peter came in with a beer and a cup of coffee.

I tentatively took a sip. It was one of those coffee capsule affairs. It was passable. He sat down next to her, beer in hand.

"Anyway, I thought he and Noor were having an affair. Many of us did. Then one day it seemed like it was over. He did to her what he did when he was dumped. In meetings, he'd belittle her...you know, ignore her, or shut her ideas down."

"Is that why you think she killed herself? Because they were having an affair, and he broke it off?"

Caja shrugged. She took Peder's hand in hers. "In the beginning, I thought that was what had happened. Trust me, I've seen what he does. He humiliates you and makes you feel useless. The rest of the team sort of also gets in on the bullying because well, the boss is doing it. A friend in HR told me that Silas Haagen is untouchable. He's Leif Timmerman's golden boy, and he can do no wrong."

"He's an asshole." Peder put an arm around her to draw her into him. He stroked her hair as she leaned into him. "After Caja left him, he humiliated her in meetings. He'd ask her to shut up, say how she was not good at her job. Tell her she was stupid. She went into depression and one day she...." Peder stopped speaking as well.

I felt for both of them.

"You know, it was my fault. I knew he was married, and I had an affair. I should've known. My team, who I had worked with for so many years, alienated me because of Silas, and it all became too much. I stopped sleeping and couldn't eat, and I had panic attacks every day. And one day I thought about killing myself. Just end it. So...I tried. I was lucky. Peder and I've been friends for years, and he's a psychologist. We talked and...now...I'm picking up the pieces."

Peder held her as she began to cry.

"I'm so sorry," I said helplessly.

Peder nodded. "He probably pulled the same shit with Noor."

"Caja, do you know of others who went through what you did?"

Caja looked up, her eyes red rimmed. "I think so. I mean, no one talks about it. I felt so ashamed of myself for sleeping with him and for getting hurt; for falling for the bullshit about what a great leader he is and all that."

"It's not your fault." I kept my voice level, even though I wanted to punch my fist through something, specifically Silas's face. "He used his position of power to mistreat you. That's on him, and he needs to feel ashamed of himself, not you. And he's the one who's married. He took the vows. He owes his marriage fidelity, not you."

Caja nodded weakly.

"I take care of her." Peder smiled at her. "We'll get through this, Caja."

"I'm so lucky to have a friend like Peder."

"We should all be so lucky," I agreed.

"Can you give me the names of other women who he's treated this way?"

"Why? What will you do with that information? You think you can bring Silas Haagen down? You can't. You think people have not complained before? Sure, they have. I was told that Noor took it all the way to the general counsel and CEO," Caja cautioned.

I nodded. "I know it won't be easy, but we have to do what we can. I have a daughter, she's twenty-one, and I want her to live in a world where she won't have to go through something like this."

They both looked at me like I had grown horns. So, maybe I had laid it on too thick with the daughter line. But I wasn't bullshitting them, it wasn't a line, this was how I felt.

"I'll have to think about it," Caja said.

"No problem. You have my card. Send me an email when you're ready. Whatever your decision, I'll accept it. But I hope you'll give me the names and I'll do what I can to expose Silas Haagen."

"You *really* think you can succeed?"

I smiled. "I won't know until I try."

It didn't take Caja long to remember the names of the women. By the time I biked to Salon 39 in Frederiksberg for my dinner with Nico, my email inbox contained the names of five women who had left Copenhagen Bank because Silas Haagen harassed them.

Chapter 23

Thursday Evening, October 13, 2023

At Salon 39, the music was jazz and blues, the cocktails perfection, and the food good. It was close to my house and had an old-time charm with its dim lighting. In addition, the chef made one of the best burgers in the city.

I ordered tonic water with bitters while I waited for Nico at a table close to the bar. Salon 39 was on two levels, one by the bar and one raised by a few steps. The bathroom was entertaining because when you stepped out to wash your hands, you expected to have a mirror over the sink, instead you could end up looking into the eyes of a fellow patron also washing their hands at a sink across from you.

I took a sip of my drink and found it surprisingly good, a clear sign that I had stopped drinking for so long that my taste for it had diminished.

I texted Flora and asked her if she could meet with me. She responded immediately and agreed to come by my office around noon the following day.

Nico burst into the restaurant, a whirlwind of motion, with her jacket billowing behind her, and her scarf completely covering her face. She pulled the scarf down and greeted me with a grin.

"The minute I have enough money, I'm moving to the Bahamas," she declared as she took off her coat, her scarf, her gloves, and her hat. She dumped them on an empty chair at our table, and leaned down to kiss me.

She sat across from me and sighed. "I've had the longest fucking day at work. How about you?"

"More or less."

She looked at me critically. "What are you drinking?"

"Tonic water with bitters."

"Ugh," she muttered and waved to the bartender. "The usual," she told him, and he winked at her.

She usually got an old-fashioned, which Salon 39 called an Old Funky Fashioned, made with a variety of rums and chocolate bitters.

Since Nico was starving, we ordered right away. She got the steak frites medium rare served with béarnaise sauce, while I ordered the burger.

"How's it going with the case?" she asked after her drink was served.

"It's going in a couple of directions," I remarked. "I stirred up shit with NSK, which is run by Jorun Eskola, and *apparently* there's a hit out on me."

She didn't choke on her drink, but it was close.

"Hit? As in someone is trying to kill you?"

I sighed. "I feel stupid even saying it because who the fuck would want to kill me so bad that they'd pay a professional. But apparently, someone has hired an assassin called *the Ghost* to kill me."

She peered at me.

"I'm not drunk," I assured her. "It's my dry month."

"Don't remind me. I'm never at a loss of words, but the only thing I can think of to say right now is: *are you shitting me?*"

"That was my reaction, too," I said, chuckling. "Someone tried to run me over and...well, that's one part of the story. The other is that Silas Haagen could become the next head to go up on the #MeToo pike."

"Wait. I can't get past *The Ghost*," Nico maintained. "What the fuck, Præst?"

"I can't explain it any better."

"You think it's a professional?"

"I think nothing. I was told it probably was."

"By whom?"

I smiled. "I must also protect my sources, *skat*."

She threw a paper napkin at me. "You're such a son of a bitch."

"But lovable?"

She grinned. "And now you want to know about a Russian journalist who has gone underground."

Her eyes lit up, so I knew she had found something.

"Now, before I tell you, I want to make clear, this is all very and I mean, *very* unsubstantiated," she stressed. "I spoke to a friend of a friend of a contact...blah, blah, blah, and a reporter at *The Atlantic* is your best bet at finding her. She lives in Manhattan, and her name is Kelsey Haines. She is working on an investigative piece about Russian money."

As we ate, I relayed to Nico what I had learnt from Caja Hansen, and Nico, as I had suspected she would, demanded to investigate the story.

"Why don't you come by my office tomorrow around noon and you can meet Flora," I suggested. "And between the two of you, I think you can probably come up with a way to bring this asshole down."

Nico smiled broadly. "It pays to know you, Præst, I'll give you that."

"I know, just call me Gabriel Claus."

She laughed. "And speaking of the benefits of knowing you...."

She smiled at the sheepish look on my face. We wouldn't be benefitting from our friendship carnally for a little while.

"Ah, so you're seeing this chef."

"Yes."

She cleared her throat. "Well, I'll be damned. I didn't think you'd get over the age difference."

"Neither did I."

"But...?"

"She was very persuasive."

Nico laughed. "I bet."

I CALLED KELSEY HAINES from *The Atlantic* as soon as I got home.

"Hi, my name is Gabriel Præst, I'm a private detective from Copenhagen," I introduced myself as soon as she said hello by identifying herself.

There was a long pause.

"Hi Gabriel, what can I do for you?" Kelsey asked.

"I have been investigating the death of a young woman who worked at Copenhagen Bank, Noor Mallik."

"Okay."

"Before she died, she was in contact with a Russian journalist named—"

"Gabriel," she interrupted me, "Is this a secure line?"

Secure? What the fuck? "I'm calling you from my cell phone."

"Gabriel, I can't talk to you over the phone about any of this."

"Okay. Will you talk to me if I come to New York?"

"Maybe."

"Where would you be?" I asked.

"You're going to come to New York?"

"Yes."

There was a long pause. "I'm going to be at our Madison Avenue office for the next week."

CHAPTER 24

Friday Morning, October 14, 2023

AFSANA MADE BREAKFAST. It was simple. Just scrambled eggs, with fresh breakfast buns that I picked up from Emmerys bakery down my street after my run and workout with Small Bo.

"I want to ask you something," she said as she sat down next to me on a stool at the kitchen counter after serving me.

"Shoot."

"Do you really not mind my coming here every night?"

"No."

"Would you tell me if you did?"

"Yes."

She smiled and then dug into her food. After her first bite, she drank some coffee and laughed suddenly, throwing her arms around me. She pulled back. "I feel so extremely gauche with you. You…you have it all figured out. And I'm still trying to understand myself."

"And I think you're *very* sophisticated…for your age."

"The sex is good, isn't it?"

"Yes."

"Is that a young person question?"

I shook my head. "It's just a question, Afsana."

"You mean like when *they* say there are no stupid questions?" she challenged.

"I'm not *them* and I do think there are stupid questions. But I ask enough of them, so I don't judge."

She ate some more of her scrambled eggs.

"I was supposed to make *you* breakfast," I reminded her.

"I know. But I'm feeling energized after a very long time. I'm excited, and I wanted to do something nice for you."

"I thought we already did something nice," I teased.

Her face heated, and I was charmed by the combination of confidence and shyness she exuded. *God, she was young!*

"I don't know how to do this so I'm just going to ask. What if I want to come back tonight?"

"Please do."

"And tomorrow night?"

"Yes."

"And the night after—"

I held up my hand to stop her. "Afsana, I'll give you an extra key. Come by anytime."

"And what if you're with another woman?"

"I won't be."

"Monogamy?" she probed.

"Yes."

"You expect it of me?"

I thought about it for a moment and specified, "I expect it of me. You are your own person."

She put her fork down, and asked cautiously, "So, you'd be fine if I was sleeping with other people?"

"I don't know," I replied honestly. "Are you?"

"Like when? Do you see my life? I barely have time to fuck you."

I put my hand on hers. "Two things I can promise. Respect and kindness."

She nodded as if she understood. "Yes."

"Do you get any time off?"

"Why?"

"I may have to go to New York in the next few days, and I wondered if maybe you'd like to come along with me."

Her face glowed. "I can't. I'm taking a week off during the potato break next week. I'm going to San Francisco to meet with…well, actually to interview for a sous chef job."

"Really. That's great."

"I…should I have told you earlier? This has been in the works for a couple of months and—"

I shook my head. "Don't overthink it, Afsana. I mean it when I say I think it's great. A sous chef role would be a great next step. What kind of restaurant?"

The excitement was back in her eyes. "French. Two Michelin stars."

"Amazing."

"You think I'll get it?"

"Yes."

"Why?"

"Because you make absolutely fabulous scrambled eggs."

She hugged me again, and kissed me. "You're never what I expect you to be."

"What do you expect me to be?"

"I don't know. A regular guy who gets jealous, possessive, and territorial."

I kissed her on the nose. "Some women would say that it showed a lack of interest or commitment."

"I'm not *some* women. I think it's a sign of respect."

Maybe she wasn't so young after all.

Chapter 25

Friday Morning, October 14, 2023

As soon as I stepped into my office, I saw I had a guest. He was seated in one of the client chairs, his phone on my oak desk, which was made from a tree my father had helped cut with my grandfather when he was a teenager.

"Hello, Harald." I put my Tumi bag on my desk.

"Good morning, Gabriel." Harald Wiberg wore a well-fitted black suit that nevertheless made him look like an overweight mob boss.

I went about taking my coat, hat, and scarf off, and took my time hanging them in the closet. I removed my laptop from Tumi bag then, as if Harald wasn't there, got settled in.

Finally, I sat down. "What can I do for you?"

"This is a nice office," Harald said.

"Thank you."

He stood up and walked up to the window behind me. I swiveled my chair as he stood with hands in his pocket, looking out at the stores across Gothersgade. I had a hand-waving relationship with the owner of the antique store Le Boheme

Interieur, and I bought superior Peruvian coffee at Café Boheme.

"I hear that you've been talking to several employees from Copenhagen Bank," he continued, still not facing me.

"Would you like a cup of coffee?"

Harald turned then. "I would."

"How do you take it?"

"Black with a teaspoon of sugar."

I went to get coffee and found Erik, in the kitchen.

"What's Harald Wiberg doing in your office?" he asked.

"I think he's here to tell me stay off the Noor Mallik case." I poured coffee into two cups.

"Why does he want you to stay off the case?"

I shrugged.

"What's going on, Gabriel?"

"I'm trying to find out."

I left Erik in the kitchen and went back to my office. Harald was still looking out of the window.

I extended his coffee cup toward him, which he accepted while leaning against the window. Settling back into my office chair, I faced him, and we both sipped our coffee.

"I can say a lot of things," Harald was the first to speak. "Things like, nice office, you wouldn't want anything to happen to it. Or nice house—"

"Someone already fucked that up," I cut in with a broad smile.

"I heard." He grinned. "So, we have assessed that we're both sons of bitches who know how to one up each other.

Now, let me tell you what I'm here to say. Noor Mallik committed suicide."

"These days we actually say died by suicide."

He chuckled. "If you try to talk to anyone at Copenhagen Bank, you'll be putting their jobs at risk, just as you did with Flora Brandt."

I drank some more coffee.

"I hear you've become good friends with Noor's cousin. The chef at Sapor. Nice restaurant."

I said nothing, just sat serenely, not showing that he had scared me by mentioning Afsana.

Harald set his coffee cup on my desk and sat down across from me. I knew he was making me follow him around the room. I didn't mind. I swiveled my chair to face him.

"I heard you got shot this summer. And you survived. That's not always going to be the case."

"Are you suggesting I may get shot again?"

"I'm saying that life is fragile. You should take care of yours."

I nodded. "Thanks. I do."

"What you've walked into is way above your pay grade."

I shrugged. "Most things are. But just so I know for sure, could you tell me what you think I've walked into? Because I don't know what the fuck is going on."

"You've walked into something you cannot influence or change." Harald rose.

Erik decided then that he'd had enough of listening through the door and opened it to step inside. "Erik Digman," he politely said.

"Harald Wiberg."

Erik stood as tall as Harald but was about half his size in girth. His blonde hair was slightly ruffled and, combined with his steel-rimmed glasses, gave him an air of casual intelligence.

"It's nice to meet you, Erik." Harald adjusted his suit jacket as he ambled to the door of my office. He turned and looked at me. "Take care, Gabriel."

"I will."

Erik shut the door behind Harald. "I couldn't hear everything, but what I did made it pretty clear that he was threatening you."

"Yep."

"Why?"

"I think Harald did something bad, and he's afraid that I may find out."

"Can you expound so I can get up to speed?"

"Yeah. But I'm going to need some *real* coffee."

We walked to the Coffee Collective at Kristen Bernikows Gade. Erik got a latte while I got a cortado, and we sat at a table close to the door. I told him everything I knew.

"*The Ghost*? You're kidding me, right?"

I shrugged.

"It sounds like the plot of a bad Hollywood movie."

"Unlike a good one?"

Erik grinned. "You have Bør looking out for Sophie, which is good. I mean...it's not good that you have to have someone look out for her, but at least that makes me feel a little less afraid. And how about you?"

"I'm scared."

"I mean what are you doing about your safety?"

"Small Bo is training me in hand to hand, and Bør is making me go to the gun range."

"And how is this going to help if this *Ghost* guy is a pro?"

"That's exactly what I said," I quipped.

"Stine is going to be so pissed with you when she finds out," Erik stated.

"Yeah," I agreed.

"And if the *Ghost* succeeds, she'll be pissed with me," Erik sighed.

"Yeah," I repeated.

"It'll somehow be my fault. You know that, right? For some weird reason she thinks it's my job to keep you safe. So, stay alive, Gabriel."

"Why does everyone say that like it's under my control?"

Chapter 26

Friday Afternoon, October 14, 2023

I introduced Nico to Flora at Pastis, where we met at one of the outdoor tables. It was an unusually good October day as the sun was shining, the sky was blue, and it wasn't windy, which made sitting outside palatable, even though the temperature was only in the high single digits.

We kept our coats on as we settled in between two gas heat lamps. Nico even kept her hat on and placed an extra blanket on her lap.

"We can sit inside," I offered.

"No," Nico protested as she pushed her sunglasses up her nose. "When I get to wear sunglasses in winter, it's a win."

I ordered coffee, Nico ordered coffee with cognac, and Flora ordered a glass of Kir royale, flouting the cold weather.

"I'm unemployed," she explained, "I think I have a moral obligation to have a champagne cocktail for lunch."

I shared with them the information I had gathered from Caja Hansen, including the names of the women she suspected had left Copenhagen Bank due to harassment.

"Don't you do exit interviews?" Nico asked Flora. "At Politiken, everyone who quits gets to vent their feelings to HR."

Flora nodded. "Absolutely, but nothing was flagged from these conversations, otherwise I would've seen it. Especially, if anyone even mentioned sexual impropriety, consensual or otherwise."

Flora went through the names Caja sent as our drinks were served.

"I looked at two of these employees," Flora said thoughtfully. "One because she left in under two years, and I usually got a report on those. And I looked at Maria Christiansen's file because she first went on sick leave due to work stress, and then never came back."

Our server served our drinks, and Nico continued to interview Flora, who had agreed to offer deep background and would consider being quoted if she felt it would add credibility to Nico's story.

I had expected Flora to be reluctant for a story to be written about sexual harassment at Copenhagen Bank while she was their head of HR, but she was all in.

"You suspected Silas was having affairs with female employees. Are there any company rules about this?" I asked, as I held the cup of coffee to warm my hands.

"According to the employee handbook, you can sleep with employees consensually, as long as you report it to HR immediately. Of course, we strongly recommend not sleeping with employees because the power dynamic is always tricky." Flora drank her champagne cocktail.

"Obviously, Silas didn't inform HR about any of his affairs," I concluded.

Nico took notes in her Moleskin notebook, and occasionally warmed her hands on her coffee.

After Nico had asked all the questions she could think of, she turned to me. "I'll look into it but, right now, it's all fluffy and unsubstantiated. Let me see if I can get these women to talk to me, and that will give us the layers we need. Would any of them have signed NDAs, Flora?"

Flora shrugged. "I'm not sure. I can't confirm if anyone was paid off back then. But if Copenhagen Bank had made any payoffs, I would know. Such transactions would have to be processed through HR."

"Unless Harald Wiberg did it without consulting HR or following whatever protocols you have," I pointed out.

Flora sighed.

"Do you have anyone on the inside who can do some digging for you?" Nico wondered.

Flora looked stricken. "I don't want to put their jobs at risk."

"I think that should be their decision." I finished my cup of coffee. And waved to the server to get his attention so I could get a refill.

"I agree. I can ask and, if they said no go, then that's that. But I think you'll be surprised at how many people might be eager to help. Sexual harassment in the workplace is not a

Copenhagen Bank issue…it's happening all over Denmark," Nico told Flora.

I got a text message from Afsana, saying that she was locking up and taking a key with her. She'd be back the next morning.

After Flora left, Nico and I went up to my office.

"If we can get these women to talk…it could lead to something important," Nico declared as she rubbed her hands together to warm them. She sat across from me on a client chair where Harald Wiberg had sat just a few hours ago.

"Caja Hansen was eager to talk to me, but I think she's still having some PTSD," I told her.

Nico shook her head. "So many people in Denmark think that sexual harassment is a *hygge* sexism issue. It's not a *real* problem but one created by emotional women. And that's what annoys me about political discourse in this country: we keep pretending that something bad isn't happening—we just define ourselves out of the issue. Like saying racism doesn't exist in Denmark and those who say otherwise are sensitive brown people. The US has been going after assholes like Weinstein like bloodhounds and we're sitting around pretending it doesn't happen here."

The #MeToo movement had come late to Denmark. It began when Sofie Lind, a host of a Danish television show who, during an awards ceremony speech, told the audience how when she was a young professional in 2008, a Danish Radio big wig had threatened her career if she didn't give him a blow job. A recent, much publicized survey showed that over half the Danish population thought the #MeToo movement was exaggerated.

I leaned forward and patted Nico's hand. "You're going to write a groundbreaking story."

"You think so?"

"I have absolute faith in you," I assured her.

She smiled. "You're always on my team, Præst."

"Always."

"So, tell me about this young chef you're seeing."

I grinned.

"Oh my god, you're absolutely smitten," Nico exclaimed.

"I *am* infatuated," I agreed.

"How come?"

"She's charming...refreshing. As they say, there's no fool like an old fool—and I guess I'm one. But it's time limited. She's looking for jobs in America, so, once that happens, she'll be on her way."

"And will you be heartbroken?" Nico asked, watching me as I considered her question.

"No."

"That's too bad. A little heartbreak is not a bad thing."

Chapter 27

Friday Late Afternoon, October 14, 2023

"What does it mean to break one's heart?" I asked my therapist, Ilse Poulsen, after lunch with Flora and Nico, at our regular bi-weekly session. We met at her home office, a room in her apartment above the French restaurant Le St. Jacques in Østerbro.

"It means different things to different people. What would it mean to you?" Ilse countered. She always sat on a chair with a table next to her, where she lay a notebook and sometime took notes. But most of the time, she kept her focus on her patient. She forgot nothing. She remembered each incident, the names of my friends and foes and now, after nearly a decade of working together, she knew me better than I knew myself.

I sat on the couch across from her, my cup of coffee on the Arne Jacobsen coffee table between us.

"I think Layla broke my heart, but I didn't realize it for a long time because I was angry with her for cheating on me. I loved her. I still do and I probably always will, but she can't break my heart now."

"Because she's gone?"

I nodded. "I have experienced her loss—and we had a chance that I walked away from because I knew we're not right for one another."

"And you and Afsana?"

I smiled. I noticed that every time I thought of her it made my heart lighter. "If I was younger, I'd say I was madly in love. I know I'm infatuated. It's a lot of fun to be in a new relationship, and she's exciting, different...."

"Young?" Ilse supplied.

"Well, that's front and center."

"Why are you so obsessed with her being young? Is it because she's just a few years older than Sophie?"

"Probably, but there's more to it than that. Wanting someone so young makes me feel like a pervert. But I've not had this much excitement in a new relationship. And I don't know if it's because she's young, or because she speaks French, or because she's well read...or because of all those things put together, she's one of the most interesting people I've ever met."

"You could say exactly the same things about Sophie," Ilse proffered.

I sighed as realization struck. "And that's what makes me feel uncomfortable."

"I think so. It's not her age or just not only her age. It's that bubbly excitement of youth, of possibilities, that reminds you of Sophie."

I drank some coffee, and then sat back. "This Copenhagen Bank case is tough, and she's a terrific distraction."

"Why do you need a distraction? You've never needed one before."

Had I really never wanted to step away from a case for a moment? No, I guessed not. But now I *wanted* to because that meant spending time with Afsana.

I rubbed my face with both my hands and leaned back, my eyes closed. "I'm forty-one years old. I'm an old fucking man. Do you know that when we have sex, I wonder about my age, creases, wrinkled balls...whatever. I've never given a shit, and now, a part of me wants to not be unattractive to her."

Ilse laughed at that.

"What's so funny?"

"I'm sorry. I think this is the first time since I've known you that you've mentioned any insecurity about your body."

"*For satan!*" I swore.

"Gabriel, relax and have fun. Just give in and enjoy. You're not a pervert. She's a grown woman, and this is completely consensual. And I can guarantee you she feels just as insecure. I'm sure she's thinking that maybe her sexual technique isn't good enough because she's inexperienced," Ilse crossed her legs and leaned back. "And maybe a little insecurity is healthy for you. Teaches you humility."

"Nico thinks it'd be good for me to have my heart broken."

Ilse smiled. "I think you need to stop worrying about broken hearts and wrinkled balls, and just live in the fucking moment. You avoid real relationships with women because you're scared that they'll make you feel as vulnerable as you did when Layla cheated on you. The thing is, Gabriel, you're always vulnerable in a relationship. Take Nico, if say, she *cheated* on you, not with another man but regarding ethics or her integrity, you'd be heartbroken. If say Eymen did something like what this Silas Haagen did with these women, it would break your heart. And—"

I raised my hand. "I get it. What you're saying is that every relationship has the potential to hurt me."

"It's wonderful how once in a while a patient has a breakthrough," she said cheekily.

I laughed. "Sometimes the line between a breakdown and breakthrough is pretty thin."

"Oh, Gabriel, you're such a drama queen," Ilse teased.

Chapter 28

Friday Evening, October 14, 2023

I joined Clara and Victor for dinner at MASH, an upscale chain restaurant at Bredgade that consistently offered good American-style steakhouse dishes.

We were seated in the middle of the restaurant, and the Friday hubbub cheered me immensely. I passed on an appetizer and went straight for their bone-in ribeye from Nebraska, with a garlic and thyme jus. Victor started with oysters for the table, and then settled on the Wagyu, A5 Striploin. Clara went with the steak tartar as a main course. They paired the oysters with a glass of Louis Roederer Collection 243 Brût champagne, and their dinner with a bottle of a 2018 Paolo Scavino Barolo. I drank my sparkling water with considerable envy.

"How's the case progressing?" Victor demanded.

"Well," I swirled my glass of water, "it looks like Silas Haagen *does* sexually harass his employees. And this morning, Harald Wiberg came to my office to ask me to cease and desist."

"Fascinating," Victor exclaimed. "I'm always surprised by how stupid some crooks can be. Harald is a smart man and yet he feels like he can walk into your office and threaten you without repercussions."

"And what repercussions would they be, *Far*?" Clara contended.

Victor thought about it as he poured some mignonette sauce on a raw oyster. He paused, holding it to his mouth, and then admitted, "I mean, Gabriel could kick his ass."

"Right, because he's so good at kicking asses," Clara said dryly.

"Hey, I'm working out every morning at Kæmpe."

"You're going to Bør's place?" Victor drank some of his champagne. "Did you know that Ingo Johansson used to train there?"

I nodded. Bør told the same story to anyone who would hear it, including Victor who'd made it his own.

Victor smiled as he reminisced. "He won a silver medal at the 1952 Olympics. They used to call his right fist the Hammer of Thor. Man, he was something else."

"And he died because he got hit too many times in the head," Clara added.

"The cost of art when you're a boxer," Victor said ruefully. "And why are you going to a gym every day when we know you absolutely hate it?"

"It's going to sound farfetched and nuts," I warned.

"Almost everything you say sounds that way," Clara said cheerfully.

I told them about *The Ghost* and my sixth sense I was being followed.

"That's exciting," Victor exclaimed.

"*Far*," Clara chided. "He could die."

"Well, darling, that's the cost of being a PI." He picked up his champagne glass and raised it to me. "It's the wrong month for you to go dry."

"Tell me about it." I raised my water glass and clinked it with his.

Our food arrived and, after the wine was tasted by Clara, and we were well on our way to the end of the meal, Victor asked, "When are you planning on going to New York to meet this journalist?"

"I don't know. Soon."

"Eymen and I are going to the Copenhagen Bank annual customer meeting in New York on Monday. You should fly with us," Victor offered.

"That's a great idea, *Far*. I wish I could come along, but I have appointments I can't miss," Clara said.

"Her mother will kick her ass and then mine if she does."

Clara sighed. "She's doing her girl's weekend next week. If I miss it, no joke, she will kill me."

"Girl's weekend?"

"Yes, we're going to Ibiza. She chartered a flight and...what? Why are you looking at me like Gabriel?"

I shook my head amused. "The life you live, Clara."

She flushed. "Right, this is so totally a first-world problem."

"Worse, it's a rich-man's first-world problem," Victor corrected and patted her hand in mock comfort. "But I'm sure you'll work through it."

As we were getting ready to leave, my phone rang.

"Afsana?"

Her voice was shaking. "Can you come and get me?"

"Where are you?"

"Rigshospitalet. Emergency Room."

CHAPTER 29

Saturday Morning, October 15, 2023

I CALLED TOMMY AS soon as I found out what happened.

"It's the middle of the night, Præst," he growled.

"Someone hurt Afsana while she was at the Christianshavn Metro station." I was furious and scared in equal measure. "They slapped her around, Tommy. She's just a kid."

"Is there a constable around?" Tommy asked.

"*Politibetjent* Borgen."

"Give him the phone."

Constable Borgen spoke to Tommy and then handed the phone back to me.

"You know the chief?"

I nodded.

"Nice."

I went back to Afsana, who was sitting on a bed in the ER, with curtains drawn around it for privacy. Clara was with her, while Victor stood guard outside. I had left my bicycle outside of MASH and we'd taken the short drive from the restaurant to *Rigshospitalet* in Victor's car.

"Can we leave?" Afsana asked me.

"Yes," I said. "Where do you want to go? The hotel or my place or…."

"Your place? Is that okay?"

"Of course." I sat next to her and took her hands in mine. "I'm so sorry this happened."

She was accosted outside the Christianshavn Metro station, deserted at one in the morning. Two men approached her, their faces obscured by surgical masks. They began by shoving her roughly. Then, abruptly, one of them slapped her.

"Tell your boyfriend to mind his own business," the other man had whispered to her in English.

Then they had pushed her down on her stomach, holding her down.

"I was so sure they were going to rape me," she confessed, her eyes bright with tears.

"Then a car honked, and people were screaming. The men ran away and…the people in the car…I didn't even thank them, Gabriel." She touched her face, her left cheek that had hit the ground was abraded, and she had a bruise along her cheekbone.

"That's okay. I met them and expressed my gratitude. I've got their contact information if you need to reach out to them later," I said. Her rescuers were two men returning from a work dinner at a nearby restaurant. They had heard Afsana's screams and immediately responded, honking their car horn to draw attention. Without hesitation, they rushed out to chase off the men who were assaulting her.

She turned into me, and I held her as she cried.

"I don't know why I'm crying," she sniffled.

"Don't worry about the reasons, just do what you need to do to feel better." I stroked her hair.

Clara watched us with concern as Victor joined us. "This is about the Copenhagen Bank case, isn't it?" She spoke in Danish, but Afsana immediately pulled away. She'd been living here for two years; she'd picked up enough Danish.

Her voice trembled. "I was asked to meet some guests at a table today. A man called Harald something. He said he was a lawyer for Copenhagen Bank and wanted to offer his condolences for Noor's death. He was with another man...the guy with the long hair and a beard. Noor's boss. I can't remember his name."

"Silas Haagen," I said, my heart sinking.

"Those sons of bitches went too far," Victor snarled in Danish, and then, realizing that Afsana was there, he explained in English, "I was cursing the assholes."

Afsana smiled and as she did, she winced as a cut on her lip probably smarted.

"What did those men mean when they said you, I'm assuming you are the boyfriend, should mind your own business?" Afsana wanted to know.

"They want me to stop investigating Noor's death."

"Why?"

"Because something is very wrong at Copenhagen Bank and I think it got Noor killed," I said, and added with no hesitation, "But none of that matters now, Afsana. I want you to not worry about a repeat performance. We'll get you some protection."

"What?" She looked at Clara and then Victor in confusion. "What the fuck is going on?"

"Your *boyfriend* here," Victor said flatly, "has once again stirred up a hornet's nest and made some powerful people angry. He has a penchant for that."

"You said you were going to San Francisco for your interview," I remembered. "Can you go right away?"

"No," Afsana said adamantly. "I have to work."

"*Skat*, you need to...."

"No," she repeated. "No way am I going to let some guys scare me."

"They are scary, so it's perfectly okay to be scared. I'm fucking terrified," I retorted.

Afsana pulled away from me. "Then you be terrified. I'm going to go live my life."

Clara grinned. "I like her, Gabriel."

Victor nodded appreciatively at Afsana. "Yeah, me too."

I sighed.

Politibetjent Borgen said, "Excuse me," as he stood on the other side of the curtain.

Clara who was closest to the curtain opened it.

"*Chefpolitiinspektør* Tommy Frisk is in the reception and wants to know if he can come in."

"I'll get him." I leaned down and kissed Afsana on the forehead. "He's a friend. Are you okay talking to him?"

She nodded. "As long as it doesn't mean I have to change my life. I won't live in fear, Gabriel."

"Yeah, I got that," I said wearily, and then went to bring Tommy to join the clusterfuck this case had become.

"Gabriel…can we talk to them at home?" she pleaded. "I don't like it here."

"You take care of Tommy, we'll take her to your place," Victor offered.

Tommy, along with a *Politiassistent* Simon Mikkelsen from Christianshavn, talked to Afsana. I gave her a glass of Lagavulin and tucked her into a cashmere blanket on my new-to-me vintage reupholstered Mogens Koch brown leather couch from the 1960s. I had only received it two weeks before and wasn't sure if I liked it as much or better than my old Arne Jacobsen couch, which was alas, irreplaceable.

"Did the men have an accent?" Detective Mikkelsen asked.

"I mean…yes. Doesn't everyone in Denmark who speaks English?" Afsana replied thoughtfully.

Tommy chuckled. "True. But was it a Danish accent or some other one?"

She thought about it for a moment and then carefully said, "I think they were Eastern European. But I have to be honest, my memory is really patchy. Mostly, I just remember being overwhelmed by fear, and not much beyond that."

"That is normal," the detective reassured.

After the detective left, I got Afsana into bed.

Once she was asleep, I picked up my laptop and went down two floors to my living room, where Tommy waited for me.

On my way, I stopped at Sophie's bedroom—and missed her suddenly. I had converted the second floor to be hers with a bedroom, a study, and a bathroom with a shower and toilet. It was the one floor that was completely finished and, thankfully, had seen no harm from the Molotov cocktail that a good humidifier hadn't been able to solve.

I wondered if Afsana should call her parents to tell them what happened. I would expect Sophie to do that with me. It would break my heart and scare the life out of me if she didn't. But we were close. I did not know what kind of relationship Afsana had with her parents.

"You want to tell me what's going on?" Tommy was drinking my Lagavulin. I ached for a cigarette *and* a scotch, so I turned on my coffee machine to make myself an espresso.

"Tommy, there's a lot of shit here that makes little sense and some that does...but you're the police chief and—"

"Don't fuck with me, Gabriel. Tell me what's going on."

He hardly ever used my first name and so I knew he was serious. I told him everything I knew, and he patiently listened.

"I'm going to get Mikkelsen to talk to Wiberg and Haagen tomorrow. Sons of bitches."

"Talk about what?"

"About them being at your office, and then at her restaurant and…," he trailed off. "We can question them, but they'll tell us fuck all. They'll say they went to a restaurant for dinner and wanted to say hello to a dead colleague's family member. And, let's face it, Wiberg said nothing to you that can be construed as a threat."

"Attacking Afsana is the threat."

Tommy nodded. "How do you do this, Præst? How do you walk into shit all the time?"

"What can I say, Tommy, I have mad skills."

CHAPTER 30

Saturday Morning, October 15, 2023

I CALLED BØR TO tell him I couldn't come to the shooting range or the gym as I didn't want to leave Afsana after what happened the night before.

She'd taken a painkiller and a sedative, so she was still sleeping peacefully. I hoped she'd take the day off work, but I doubted it. She'd think it as a sign of weakness to stay home and nurse her wounds. I'd think of it as being sensible.

And is that what you did when you were roughed up, Præst?

"I'll send Small Bo to stay at your place. Come for a coffee to My Brother's House in an hour," Bør instructed. "Toomas has something to say to you."

My Brother's House was a bar close to the main train station. It was divided into a main bar by the entrance and had three rooms with couches and seating areas as if they were big living rooms. I had once met Toomas Reznikov, formerly or maybe currently, of the Russian Bratva and the secret Brother's Circle in a backroom there. What Toomas didn't know, and I did, was that the bartender at My Brother's House, Emil, was a cop.

"Do you think I should tell Toomas that they have a cop watching the place?" I asked Bør.

"No," he said before ending the call.

I took a shower and checked in on Afsana. I gently woke her, and she looked at me sleepily. "Hey."

"Hey."

I kissed her softly, and she smiled. "Do it again," she demanded lazily.

I laughed and did as she asked. "I have to leave for a little bit."

I felt her stiffen.

"There's going to be a rather large man called *Små* Bo downstairs to make sure nothing happens to you."

"*Små* Bo?"

"Yes."

"Why is he called Small?"

"Because Large Bo is a couple of inches taller than him."

She closed her eyes. "You have the strangest friends. Police chief, crazy rich white guy, and now Small Bo."

"Go back to sleep. I'll be back soon. And if you need me, just call. Your phone is charging on the side table next to you." I wasn't sure she heard me because her eyes were closed, and she was breathing regularly.

***

I stepped into the room marked 'Private', the same place where I had first encountered Toomas a few months ago. I waved at Emil, who nodded at me but didn't smile. He didn't know I knew he was undercover, so I decided not to freak him out that his cover was blown, at least with me.

The private room boasted a bar and was furnished to accommodate about eight people comfortably. Each table was flanked by two or three plush leather chairs, creating an air of understated luxury. The mingled scents of alcohol and cigarette smoke filled the space, adding to its clandestine allure.

Bør followed me into the café minutes later. We both ordered black coffee, the rich aroma mingling with the murmurs of other patrons. As we sipped the hot, bitter brew, I filled him in on the latest with Afsana.

"This case is getting weirder," Bør concluded. "How's the girl?"

"She's sleeping it off." I had no idea how she was. I'd be pretty fucked up if someone slapped me around and tried to rape me.

"What do you think Toomas wants to talk to me about?"

Bør shook his head. "He didn't say. Just said it was urgent."

Toomas looked like Santa with his round body and big white beard, but he was far from jolly, and, unlike Father Christmas, he had big gang tattoos. He also didn't move like Santa, but like someone who knew how to move when the shit hit the fan. He wore a pair of jeans with a gray sweater. He had little hair but what he did have stood up in spikes as he pulled his woolen cap off.

"Emil, get me a Stoli," he barked and came to sit down next to Bør and across from me. He nodded at Bør, and then at me.

"Stoli?"

"You have to tell them what to drink or they'll serve you horse piss like Moskovskaya Osobaya."

He had told me this before. My question was more about vodka at eight in the morning rather than the specific brand. But I let it go. To each his own.

Emil brought Toomas' Stoli, which he drank in one go, and then asked for a refill.

"So, how's it hanging?" I asked with a smile.

He glared at me. "You shot a friend of mine."

"Yeah, well, he was shooting at me at the time." I'd had to kill a man for the first time in my life a few months ago. His name was Boris Labazanov, and I still had trouble with what I'd done. I wasn't the man who shot people...ever...well, mostly.

"He wasn't *really* a friend. He owed me money, which he now cannot pay," Toomas confessed.

Emil set another shot of Stoli on the table. Toomas looked at it for a long moment as if contemplating what to do with it. And then, as if deciding, he downed it as he had the previous shot.

He shook his head and cleared his throat. "There's a hit on you."

I nodded.

His eyes narrowed. "Brother, this is no joke."

"I know," I agreed. "Why do you think I'm carrying a piece?" I indicated the bulge in my jacket, where I had holstered my baby Glock.

"Your baby Glock is better than a stick. But that's about it," Bør stated levelly.

"You think you can outshoot an *ubiytsa*?" Toomas demanded.

"My Russian is a bit rusty, but I'm assuming *ubiytsa* means hitman. No, I don't think I can outshoot an assassin. But it makes me feel better and sometimes I have to, you know, indulge in self-care. Some people medicate, some meditate, I carry a gun."

Toomas looked at me like I'd lost my mind, and Bør sighed. "Toomas does not have a sense of humor, Gabriel."

It was my time to sigh. "Toomas, what can you tell me about *The Ghost*?"

He looked baffled. "You know about *The Ghost*?"

"You don't have to look so surprised. I'm a fucking private detective, so sometimes I fucking detect. I've been told that this man has been sent after me."

Toomas looked at me with new appreciation. "He's ex-SVR and spent many years killing for Putin. You know business executives and people like that. His specialty is making murders looks like accidents or suicides. When a rich Russian businessman jumps off balcony, we think it maybe was *The Ghost*."

I'd heard of the Sudden Russian Death Syndrome, where prominent Russian businessman who were not in Putin's good books were dying in so-called accidents and suicides.

Is that what happened with Noor? The Ghost made her write a note, and then forced her to consume the drugs that killed her?

"Can you tell me anything about *him*? Like...what does he look like? How old is he? Anything?"

Toomas laughed. "He is *The Ghost*. He can be anyone. Some say he in his thirties, and some say in his sixties. Some say he tall, others say he average height. Some say he blonde, and others say he bald like you. Some say he white, and others say that he Latin. That man is a *focking* chameleon. He becomes part of the background wherever he is."

"Sounds like you know absolutely nothing about him."

"You're an honorable man. I saw what you did for Yousef Ahmed. So, when I hear, I want to give you a warning. You probably will still get killed, but at least I'll feel better about having done what I could," Toomas said.

Bør snorted.

"Thanks, Toomas, your confidence in me is overwhelming," I said dryly.

Toomas lifted a hand. "Look, I'm telling truth. *The Ghost* is a *focking* monster—the one who hides under your bed and kills you silently."

I changed tack. "Do you know a reporter named Raisa Chaban?"

Toomas shrugged. "Don't know no reporters. Not same...ah...social circle."

"Thanks, Toomas."

He rose to leave, and then added, "There is one rumor I hear about *The Ghost*. He likes art."

"Art?"

"Yes. He likes art. Apparently, spends most of his money buying paintings. But then," he scratched his jaw, "some people say he spends most of his money buying hookers. Who knows?"

"Any specific art?"

Toomas shrugged. "Maybe Polish? Russian? Ukrainian?"

"Why?"

"They say he was born in either Russia, Poland, or Ukraine...but then some people say he was born in Jerusalem or Madrid. No one really knows."

"Well, Toomas, you've been *really* helpful."

"I try," Toomas said. "This one guy I knew was in prison with this Ghost. Wronki in Poland. He said the guy likes scary artists."

"Like who?"

"You know that director...what's his name...del Toro?"

"Guillermo del Toro?" I offered.

"Maybe...anyway, all the men in prison have naked picture of Angelina Jolie, this guy has a painting of an insect...something about crawling death. Anyway...I hope this helps."

Toomas put his hat back on, shrugged into his coat, and left.

"And I guess, I'm paying," I grimaced.

Bør grinned. "Toomas likes a free Stoli...or two."

I pulled out my wallet and left bills to cover our drinks on the table.

"Did any of that make sense to you?" Bør asked.

"Yeah, sure. The Ghost could be white, Latin, short, tall, Russian, Polish, Ukrainian, Israeli or...pretty *focking* anyone?"

"So, it didn't help."

"No."

"Well, it's a good thing you're practicing shooting and fighting then."

I tried not to snarl at my friend.

Chapter 31

Saturday Late Afternoon, October 15, 2023

Since Afsana insisted on going to work, Small Bo went with her. I asked Cézar Doucette to let me buy him a drink at Café Victor.

In the center of the city and one of Copenhagen's most iconic cafés easily identifiable by its green awning and outdoor seating with heated lamps, which smokers braved in the cold, Café Victor was the place to be if you wanted to rub elbows with celebrities, escorts, and regular corporate employees. The huge window front with its revolving door and open kitchen were both warm and appealing while being exclusive.

I hadn't had lunch so while I waited for Cézar, I ordered two *smørrebrød*, open-faced sandwiches, usually made with rye bread. *Kartoffelmad* was one of my favorites as it was completely unhealthy; a concoction of homemade mayo, served with boiled potatoes and potato chips—and to balance the unhealthy, I also ordered the gravadlax with honey mustard sauce on rye.

Since I knew Cézar didn't smoke, I chose a seat inside the restaurant, close to the circular staircase leading to the upstairs dining room and bathrooms. Here, round tables were snugly arranged, creating a cozy yet bustling atmosphere.

Cézar arrived after I finished lunch and was drinking coffee while reading through all the material Nico had sent me about Raisa Chaban. Almost all of it was from the public domain. I would learn more, I hoped, when I met Kelsey Haines at *The Atlantic*.

"How's it goin', *cher*?" He took his black wool coat off and hung it on the back of his chair.

"Someone beat up a friend of mine and asked her to tell me to stay away from the Noor Mallik case."

All humor left his face. "Which friend."

"Afsana Mallik."

The server in the Victor uniform of black pants and shirt and an apron with the café's logo on it came by. Cézar ordered a pilsner. I asked for a coffee refill—mine had gone cold.

"What do the police say?"

"They've got nothing. I'm sure they're going through CCTV tapes and whatnot. But they're probably not going to find anything."

Cézar nodded.

"What the fuck have I gotten myself into?"

He chuckled. "A lot of shit, *cher*."

"I need help, Cézar. If I get Afsana out of the country, will she be safe, or will they go after her?"

"I don't think she's the target of anything except shutting you down. So, my guess is that she'd be fine. Where are you planning to send her?"

"Out of Denmark. Am I still a target?"

"A big, flamin', bright red one," he assured me.

The server returned with his pilsner and my coffee. We waited until the server had left, and then Cézar continued.

"Two things, both I'm not supposed to share with you. Your NSK head, Eskola, knows about the phone and knows that you handed it to *us*."

"And *us* is?"

"The Americans."

"I handed it to *you*. You're a guy I know who knows IT."

Cézar smiled. "They know you know that I know that you know...."

"And what do I know?" I drank some coffee and wished it was a shot of whiskey. Hell, at this point, I'd drink Stoli.

"That's the first thing. She's going to *interview* you on Monday. So, if you want to *not* speak with her, you might want to find a way to avoid that."

"Thanks. The second thing?"

"There is or was a whistleblower at Copenhagen Bank. We don't know who. But someone sent information all the way through the chain of command to Leif Timmermann, the CEO, about the activities at the Baltic branch." Cézar picked up his glass of pilsner and toasted.

"Leif Timmerman fired Flora Brandt, their chief HR officer, who was the one who first came to me about this case. He will not do anything and is probably complicit," I pointed out. "And Harald Wiberg was in my office yesterday with a few veiled threats, and then someone attacked Afsana."

Cézar took a deep breath. "I don't have details on who *they* are looking into at Copenhagen Bank."

"Who's *they*?"

"Just *them*."

"This cloak and dagger stuff is getting old," I snarled. I was tiring of it all. I was afraid for Sophie, Afsana, Flora, Nico, myself, and everyone I knew.

"I only know what I know, and I can tell you about half of what I know," Cézar justified. "Do you have any leads on Raisa Chaban?"

"No," I lied and wondered about Kelsey Haines' question about my phone line being secure. How would I know if my phone was, how did they call it—*tapped*? Seriously! This was stretching even my bounds of reality.

"Well, if you do, let me know. I can help. In the meantime, I think you might join your girlfriend in San Francisco. The Danish cops are after you, an assassin is after you, and some thugs Harald Wiberg probably hired are after you." Cézar frowned.

"How do you know about San Francisco?" I asked.

Cézar only smiled. "This may have been the wrong month to go dry."

No shit, Sherlock!

I bicycled home in the cold and the stinging rain that had taken over the city, making it gray and unwieldly.

There was a note on my door from my neighbor Jorgen about the upcoming block party, and if I could make sure my heating lamp was working. Jorgen didn't have a phone and refused to get one, so he left handwritten notes stuck to doors with cellophane tape.

I went down in the basement to the small storage area I had, and pulled the heating lamp out. Thankfully, the gas tank was about half full, and the heating lamp, after sputtering a few times, came to life. I texted Jorgen's wife Margrethe, who had a phone. I told her that the lamp worked just fine, and I'd have it out for the block party.

She responded with a don't forget about the potato salad, and I responded to say I wouldn't. I texted Sophie to remind her she was making potato salad for the block party. She responded with a thumbs up emoji.

Since I had missed my run in the morning and my head was swamped with confusion, I put on winter running clothes and ventured out into the rain.

I had gone around the lakes once when I felt *him*, right in the middle of my shoulder blades. He wouldn't shoot me, that wouldn't look like an accident. What was his plan? Push me into the lake? The lake was artificial and not too deep.

I didn't look around because I knew I wouldn't be able to see him. This guy was a professional. He'd been doing this for a long time and would not slip up. And then I remembered what Toomas said. This man was unrecognizable—as in no one could determine who he was. He could be thirty or fifty or sixty, or he could be white or brown, or he could be...anyone he wanted to be. He could be one of the runners, and I wouldn't know. Would I?

On my second round, I was more mindful about who was running or walking by me. A couple walked their dog. A woman ran and looked good doing it. There were three people with umbrellas—probably tourists. Real Danes wouldn't have umbrellas for this kind of almost mist-like rain. You didn't get wet, you got damp. You didn't need protection for that.

As I went up the stairs from the lake to the sidewalk close to my street on Øster Søgade, I saw a man walk past me toward Fredensgade. He wore a black coat and black cap. A black scarf was around his neck. I could barely see his face. This wasn't suspicious. Nearly all of us dressed like this from October through May in Copenhagen. He was on his phone, tapping away with a gloved finger as he walked.

And right then, another man similarly wrapped up walked past me, also tapping at his phone, going the other way toward Østerbrogade.

I sighed. I was getting paranoid. Sure, they weren't following me but now fear had set in, and I looked at every stranger with a sense of foreboding.

I crossed Øster Søgade and went onto Eckersbergsgade, my street, feeling impotent.

I was drinking water in my kitchen when there was a knock on my door. I picked up my baby Glock, uncaring if the person knocking would freak out that I had a gun, and went to the front door.

Freja raised an eyebrow at my gun. I shoved it into my waistband at the small of my back, and opened the door wide for her.

"That's some welcome, Præst."

She tucked her scarf and hat into the sleeve of her jacket before draping it over the Menu wall hooks beside my own coat."

"Coffee?" I offered.

She nodded. "If you'll add some whiskey to it, I'll be your best friend."

I turned on the coffee machine and pulled out a bottle of Glenmorangie Signet Single from my liquor cabinet.

Since the firebombing, I had revamped my kitchen. In the dining area of my open plan, *'conversation'* kitchen, as they called it in Denmark, now stood a circular Jonathan Adler liquor cabinet. Unlike my usual preference for vintage pieces, this was a brand-new acquisition. Its versatility appealed to me: it could be wall-mounted for space-saving or, as it was now, rest on polished brass legs. What truly captivated me, though, was the hand-hammered brass relief on the doors, polished to a flawless finish.

"You're going to pour a fifteen hundred kroner bottle of whiskey into coffee?"

"That's all I got right now," I apologized.

"Fuck the coffee, then. Give it to me neat."

I let the coffee machine run for myself and poured her a finger of Glenmorangie into a whiskey tumbler for Freja.

She smelled it for a long moment, and then, as if she couldn't wait another second, took a sip. "Ah, beautiful."

"What's up?"

"I heard about your girlfriend getting hurt last night," she began.

I didn't correct her that Afsana wasn't my girlfriend. I was a forty-one-year-old man, we didn't have girlfriends.

"She's at work. Someone will drop her off and pick her up," I explained.

"Valentin wanted me to give you some information, which he's not supposed to do."

I'd just had a similar conversation with Cézar. "A lot of that going around."

"What?"

I shook my head and gestured for her to continue as I stared at my cup of coffee. I was getting pretty sick and tired of drinking coffee. When this month was done, I'd take a break from coffee for a while and only drink alcohol. Good plan!

"PET has been analyzing flight booking data to track the movements of several pro-Russian militants active in Donbas. This investigation has led to the discovery of several cover identities. The passports linked to these identities are issued by Russia, Belarus, and other pro-Russian countries. However, when cross-referenced with tax and residency records, there's no evidence of these individuals in the cities where their passports were supposedly issued.

She drank some whiskey and made approving sounds.

"We suspect that one of these passports or several of them are being used by *The Ghost*. Three weeks ago, a sausage executive, Grigory Semenov, who was critical of Vladimir Putin, was found dead at a hotel in New Delhi. He jumped. During that time, one of those identities PET has been tracking was also in New Delhi. This past August, a Latvian-born Putin critic fell from the window of his New York City apartment, a few days later the chairman of a Russian company took a fatal tumble down a flight of stairs at his mansion in Nice."

"These Russians seem to fall down a lot."

Freja nodded. "Don't they just. Another identity, who they have been tracking, showed up in New York and another one in Nice, coinciding with these deaths."

"So, these are the same person?"

"They think so. They don't know. They're tracking several identities, looking at flight data. Now, of course, it's possible that your friendly assassin could have identities we know nothing about. But Valentin wanted you to know what he knew."

"Thanks." I set my cup of coffee down on the counter. "Do you have the names of these identities that Valentin thinks *The Ghost* used?"

"I can ask Valentin."

"Thanks, Freja."

She looked concerned, and stood up from the bar stool she was sitting at, and came up to me. And then suddenly gave me a big hug.

"What was that about?" I asked when she pulled away.

"You looked like you need a hug."

"Thank you."

After Freja left, I took a shower, and went shopping at Irma on Øster Farimagsgade, which was a five-minute walk. I didn't feel like eating out and decided, instead, to make dinner. I needed comfort food.

Chapter 32

Sunday Night, October 16, 2023

Small Bo dropped Afsana off early because her colleagues could see she wasn't feeling well, and I told her sit her cute butt down and leave the cooking to me.

"I'm not in pain," she said militantly.

"Drink some wine and I'll make us dinner." I looked through my wine fridge that could house thirty bottles, and was right next to the dishwasher. I chose a bottle of Vigne de L'Enfant Jésus Premium Cru Bourgogne from 2014 because I wanted to impress her. I poured a taster's portion into a burgundy wine glass and handed it to her.

She tried it and nodded appreciatively. Then after I poured a full glass for her, she read the label.

"Very nice for a random Saturday evening," she exclaimed.

"Well, I'm trying to look good in front of a professional chef," I admitted.

"What are we having?" She peered at the kitchen counter where I had ground pork, apples, onions, garlic, and celery out by my six-burner induction stove.

"We are having *boller i karry*," I announced. "Danish meatballs in curry sauce." I paused, and then asked, "Do you eat pork?"

She nodded. "Unless I'm with my parents. Then I neither drink alcohol nor eat pork. I mean, they know I do but…it's out of respect for them."

I chopped the vegetables, facing her.

"Do you need help?" She picked up her wine and drank.

"I think today you let me do the cooking while you do the easy work of sitting there and looking pretty," I recommended.

She'd brought some of her clothes and hung them in my closet. She currently wore a pair of comfortable looking beige cashmere pants and a matching sweater. Her feet were warmed by a pair of Ugg slippers.

Except for the bruise on her cheek that was changing colors, she looked like a princess on vacation.

"My colleagues were horrified that I'd been mugged," she told me as I added olive oil to a Le Creuset pot to soften the onions, garlic, and celery. I diced apples as the vegetables cooked at medium heat.

"You're very proficient at chopping," she remarked. "I didn't think you knew how to cook."

"I can cook. I'm out of practice because I've been eating out a lot lately, but today, I felt like some comfort food, and nothing says childhood comfort like *boller i karry*."

"For me, comfort food is *dal* with *rotis*," she told me. "But I'm game for trying some authentic Danish home cooking.

This looks like something that would never show up on a restaurant menu."

I shook my head. "It's not fancy enough."

Once the vegetables and apples had softened, I added half of them to the ground pork along with some flour, eggs, salt, pepper, and panko. I used my hands to mix everything together, and then rolled a few small meatballs.

I washed my hands, and heated water to cook the meatballs.

"What happens next?"

"Next, I taste to make sure that the meatballs are seasoned right. My mother used to taste the raw pork, but I just can't get myself to do it."

"Well, I could taste it for you," Afsana offered. "I eat plenty of raw everything in the kitchen."

"Let's do this my way."

I hadn't yet replaced my turntable. All my records had been damaged by both the firebomb and the firehose. While I waited to get a new turntable, I joined the modern generation with a Bose speaker that connected to my phone. I set the volume at low and let the strains of *Time Out* by the Dave Brubeck Quartet fill the house.

I cooked some of the small meatballs, and then, after determining that I had indeed gotten the seasoning right, I added more meatballs and let them simmer in the water until they were done.

I made a roux with the remaining softened vegetables, added curry powder and thyme, and then added the liquid that I used to cook the meatballs in to make the curry sauce.

"What do you eat the meatballs with?"

"Rice," I said.

She grinned. "That's almost Pakistani. I didn't even know Danes ate curry."

"It's interesting, isn't it, that both curry and rice are not natural ingredients in Denmark, and yet, this dish has been a staple Danish meal for many years."

"What else do you use curry in?"

"During Christmas…have you been here for a Danish Christmas?"

She nodded. "Yes, I was surprised by the *karry* salat."

We served rye bread with pickled herrings and a curry egg salad for *julefrokost*, Christmas lunch.

It was comfortable to have Afsana sit at the counter while I cooked. I made some rice, and we sat on barstools and ate our dinner.

"This is nice," she said.

"The food?"

"Yes, but also, just sitting here with you and eating. I don't think I've felt this…calm, I guess is the right word, in a long while. I've been living in limbo at the hotel, not being able to settle. Since Noor passed, I've felt homeless. So, this is *very* nice, Gabriel. Thank you."

I took her hand in mine. "It's my pleasure."

After dinner, we sat on the couch, and she mentioned I didn't have a television.

"No," I agreed. "I've not had a television in many years."

"How come?"

I shrugged. "Habit. I am usually renovating or reading. I can't remember the last time I sat and watched something."

"No binging on Netflix?"

I shook my head. "I may have watched an episode or two of something with Sophie on her iPad. But that's about it."

She leaned against my shoulder, her wine glass in her hand, and I put my arm around her. "Will you tell me what's going on with Noor's case?"

"It's turning into something else, Afsana, and…I don't know how much I should tell you."

She looked up at me. "I don't understand."

"It's gotten complicated."

"So, what?"

So, I want to protect you because you're young and fearless. But you're not her father, Præst, you're her lover, so treat her like the mature woman you keep telling everyone she is.

"I think Noor was a whistleblower for Copenhagen Bank's money laundering activities, and they killed her for it."

She sat up suddenly, and I held her wine glass so its content wouldn't spill. I set the glass down on the piece of raw wood sitting atop some bricks that was serving as a coffee table until I could find the one I loved.

"Are you saying she didn't commit suicide?"

"I think she didn't, but I have absolutely zero fucking proof."

"And that's why these men don't want you to investigate her death."

"Maybe. But these are dangerous people, as you know. So, I need you to do me a favor."

She nodded. "You want to me to go away."

"Yes, for a short while. A week or two." I didn't know whether this will be resolved in a week or two, but at least she'd be safe during that time so I could focus on the investigation and not worry about her.

"I could go to San Francisco...."

"Can you leave tomorrow?"

"What?"

"Please. I have to go to New York on Monday, and I'd feel so much better if you were in San Francisco, far away from Copenhagen Bank and Copenhagen." I wasn't above begging but before I could go on my knees and grovel, she relented.

"Okay. I...I'll ask our travel agent to book me a ticket. Why are you going to New York?" She took her phone and sent someone a text message. Probably her travel agent. Clara and Afsana had more in common than she and I did. Clara and Victor had travel agents who did their travel planning and didn't go on apps like I did.

"I want to meet someone your cousin was talking to, probably about what was happening at Copenhagen Bank."

Afsana picked up her wine and drank some. "This is really something, you know. I mean…crazy as fuck."

"I know."

"This happens to you a lot?"

"No," I said immediately. "Though, this summer I had a difficult case and…I got shot."

She put her hand on my shoulder where the bullet had torn through flesh and muscle. "I wondered about that scar."

"I'm really sorry about upending your life like this, Afsana."

"Why? You're doing my family a huge service by finding out why and how Noor died. Please, you have nothing to be sorry about."

She put the glass down and kissed me. I tasted the dark plum of the Bourgogne in her mouth, and was planning to ask her about the condition of her aches and pains and suggest we go to bed when my doorbell rang.

Chapter 33

Sunday Night, October 16, 2023

"What the fuck are you opening the door with a gun?" Erik asked as he walked past me, an leather overnight bag in his hand.

"It's midnight, Erik."

"I need a place to stay. I need a break from *her*."

This happened a couple of times a year. Erik would have a fight with Stine and would leave for a few days. The longest he'd come and stayed with me was four days.

Right on cue my phone lit up with a text message from Stine: *Is he there?*

I replied: *Yes.*

Stine: *Ask him to go fuck himself.*

"Your wife wants you to go fuck yourself." I followed Erik into the living room.

"Hi," Afsana said.

"Hi," Erik replied, and then looked at me, obviously stumped that there was a woman in the house. "I...I...can...."

"It's fine," I said. "Afsana, this is Erik. He's Sophie's bonus father. He's married to Sophie's mother, Stine."

Afsana was amused. "Well, aren't you all a *very* happy and cozy family."

Erik threw his bag on the floor and slumped on an armchair across from Afsana. I gave him a glass of wine after I put my gun away in a drawer in the kitchen.

He drank it thankfully. "I didn't know you had company."

"That's okay," I said.

Afsana worked on her phone, and then smiled. "Looks like they'll be able to get me on a flight to San Francisco tomorrow afternoon."

"Excellent." I would get Small Bo to take her to the airport because I'd be leaving early to fly with Victor and Eymen to New York.

"When's your flight?" she asked.

"Early tomorrow," I said, and then looked at Erik. "You can't stay here because the way things are going some fucker might throw a firebomb in here again."

"Where are you going?" Erik asked.

"New York. I'm going with Victor and Eymen. They have a Copenhagen Bank meeting to attend, and I have work to do."

"How long will you be there?"

"Home by Thursday, I think."

Erik perked up. "I'll come with you."

"To New York?"

"Yes."

I sighed.

Afsana was smiling ear to ear. "So, you're both good friends?"

Erik looked at her suspiciously. "Yes."

"Fascinating," Afsana declared.

I texted Victor to ask him if his plane had room for Erik. He responded immediately with a: *More the merrier. Let Birgit know if you need extra rooms or whatever.* His text message included a link to the contact information of Birgit Poulsen, his travel agent.

I texted Birgit to let her know that both Erik and I would join Victor and Eymen, and if she could also book hotel rooms for him for the duration of the stay.

"What are you and your wife fighting about?" Afsana asked curiously.

Erik shrugged. "I told her that the floor heating is not working, but she tells me it's working *just* fine. I told her she needed to stop gaslighting me, and she said I needed to stop having such a vivid imagination. One thing led to another and, suddenly, the floor became a metaphor for our marriage, and I left before I said something that I couldn't take back or hear something she couldn't."

"And she knows you're here with Gabriel?"

"He does this a couple of times a year," I explained. "Last time we went to Christiania and Erik got *very* high."

"Good times," Erik nodded.

CHAPTER 34

Monday Morning, October 17, 2023

SINCE THE PLANE HAD just taken off when Jorun Eskola called me, I talked to her.

"Where the fuck are you?" she demanded.

"On my way to New York."

"You're at the airport?"

"*I'm on a jet plane…*," I sang.

"And when will you be back?"

"End of the week."

There was a long pause as if she was controlling her temper. "When you come back, and you get your ass in my office."

"Yes, *chef*," I mocked.

She hung up.

Eymen who was sitting next to me, raised his eyebrows. "The head of NSK. She's crazy about me."

He sighed. "What have you done?"

I raised my glass of orange juice at him. "So many things."

I had flown with Victor previously on a chartered plane but usually only for small hops to London or Oslo. This was a very nice way to fly across the Atlantic.

Once we reached cruising altitude, Victor joined Eymen at our bench seats to ask about Erik, who was in a seat at the back, lying flat, sleeping.

"What's his story?" he asked as he sat down across from us.

"He had a fight with Stine."

Victor nodded.

"And then he drank two bottles of wine at my place last night," I added.

"What I don't understand, and never will, is how you're friends with him," Victor said.

"He says it's because he never loved Stine," Eymen explained.

"What's love got to do with anything?" Victor snarled. "He's your ex-wife's new husband. It's indecent to be friends with him."

"Stine and I were never married," I corrected.

Victor shook his head. "You have a plan on what you're going to do in New York?"

"A vague one."

"Do you need help?" Eymen asked.

"Anything to get out of your boring meetings?" I grinned.

"Maybe," Eymen allowed. "But you should join a couple of the sessions. One of your old pals is a keynote speaker."

When I raised my eyebrows in enquiry, he answered, "Elias Juhl."

"I think I'll pass."

Elias Juhl, the former Prime Minister of Denmark, and current Secretary General of NATO, was no friend of mine. This past summer, we exchanged a few words. He'd emerged unscathed after being implicated in the murder of a politician and the framing of an innocent man for that crime.

"You sure you want to go alone to your meetings?" Eymen wondered.

Right then, Erik let out a loud snore that reached us over the sounds of the plane.

"I'll take Erik with me for moral support," I said.

When we landed in New York, I got a text from Afsana that she was on her flight safe and sound. I texted her back that I was in New York, and that she should call me if she saw or felt anything suspicious. She sent me back a middle finger emoji next to a heart. I didn't respond.

I loved New York any time of year. There was an energy in the city that was incomparable. I had come to New York many times and every time I found something new about it I loved.

Eymen and Victor had meetings scheduled from ten in the morning while I was hoping to catch Kelsey Haines at *The Atlantic's* Manhattan location.

We were staying at the Mandarin Oriental across from Central Park, and they'd had our rooms ready when we arrived, no bickering over check-in times.

Since Erik was still groggy, he got some more sleep while I went for a run in Central Park. It was a brisk 10 degrees centigrade. The sun was shining, the sky was blue, and the wind was a light breeze. This was the perfect weather for a run.

I jogged into Central Park, entering from West 60th Street near the Maine Monument. Deliberately ignoring the towering presence of Trump Tower to my left, I ran the mile up to the Ramble, weaving my path around the lake. My run paused at Belvedere Castle, its granite tower always managing to surprise me with its incongruous presence in the heart of New York City.

Erik was awake but surly when I got back. I took a shower, and then insisted he did the same. I told him I'd wait for him at the MO Lounge on the reception level on the 35th floor for brunch.

"Did Stine call you?" he asked as he sat down across from me at a table right by the tall windows that showcased the Big Apple in all its glory on a stunning autumn day.

"No. But she texted me again and—"

"And asked me to go fuck myself," he nodded. "I don't understand your ex-wife."

I lifted my cup of espresso and shook my head. "We were never married."

"That's just semantics. You had a mortgage and a child together, that's being fucking married," he muttered and looked through the menu.

When the server arrived, a perky blonde with dimples and a sunshine personality, he looked at her, almost pleading. "Do you make a Bloody Mary? Extra spicy."

She didn't even look at her watch. It was all of ten in the morning, but a man had to do what a man had to, and this man had to do a Hair of the Dog.

"Of course. What kind of vodka would you like?"

He looked at me confused. I looked at the beverage menu. "St. George Green Chile."

She smiled at my espresso, and I nodded. "I'd like another."

She pranced away.

"What do you want for breakfast?"

Erik looked at me dazed. "McDonald's French fries."

"We can do better." I perused the breakfast menu.

I ordered the pastrami hash for myself and the shakshuka for Erik. The server was kind enough to bring a bottle of Tabasco along with our food.

"Did you take a painkiller?" I asked.

Erik nodded. "I'm a grown man and I have a hangover. It's fucking embarrassing."

"We've all done things that embarrass us."

"She drives me nuts. Half the time I don't know why we're together. If we split up, Sophie would still be my bonus daughter, right? I just wouldn't have to put up with *her* bullshit."

Since he'd been giving this speech at least twice a year for the past decade. I didn't take it seriously. He wanted to vent, and I was happy to listen. It had been years since I was uncomfortable about the fact that my daughter's mother's new husband bitched about his wife to me.

After the Blood Mary and the food, Erik felt human, he informed me.

"So, what's on the agenda?" he asked.

"I'm going to meet a journalist at *The Atlantic*."

"I'll come with you."

I raised an eyebrow.

"I've gone on interviews with you before," he countered.

"Yes," I agreed. "But those people were your clients."

"I'm coming along. This is America. You probably need a lawyer."

I put on my prized felt and grosgrain fedora from St. Laurent. I'd dressed more casually as I was meeting a journalist who, knowing Nico, was probably wearing jeans and a sweater. I wore a pair of black wool dress pants, with a gray sweater and a black wool coat. Since I knew I'd walk a lot in the city, I'd put on a pair of Gucci Ace leather sneakers that Sophie had insisted I buy because they were hip.

Erik looked at my fedora, and then at me. "Why do you always have to wear designer shit?"

"I like clothes that are well made."

"That's such a snobbish thing to say." Erik pulled on his non-brand black coat. He wore a pair of jeans and a sweater with sneakers, not a label in sight.

"I like well-designed clothes."

"Everyone likes nice things, Gabriel, but everything you wear is *designer*. Those shoes, what are they?"

"Why do you care?"

He hissed. "You're such a fucking Swedish metrosexual."

We walked to the elevator of the hotel. "I do not wear tight pants. And I'd never wear a blazer with a T-shirt."

"This is what I mean," Erik sighed.

"Are you trying to pick a fight with me?" I asked as I pressed the button to get down to street level.

"How far is this place we're going to?"

"About three kilometers."

He groaned. "I'm not walking all that way, Gabriel."

The part of me that was feeling petty because Erik when he was distraught was such a bitchy diva wanted to tell him it was walking or nothing; but the other part, the part that liked Erik said, "We're taking an Uber."

"I never know how that app works."

Uber had been banned in Denmark, but the taxi companies had set up their apps to be as convenient as Uber.

"I do."

"Can we trust Uber?" he asked as we waited outside in front of the hotel as people in limousines and cars came in and out.

"Yes."

"You don't think they'll drive into an alley and kill us?"

I frowned. "Where the fuck did that come from?"

"I just watched *Collateral Damage* with Sophie."

The Uber, a Tesla arrived, and we got in.

The Tesla driver, a woman, Nancy Something, asked us where we were from and gushed about her love for Copenhagen as she had been there one time and saw the Little Mermaid.

"My friend here wants to know if you're planning to drag us into an alley and kill us?"

Erik kicked me.

Nancy Something laughed. "I don't have time for that. Got to make a living."

When we were at 60th Madison Avenue, I asked Erik if I'd be better off leaving him at a coffee shop because he was being testy.

"I'm a fucking professional," he objected.

I didn't bother to respond, and went to the reception and told them I was there to meet Kelsey Haines.

Chapter 35

Monday Afternoon, October 17, 2023

Kelsey Haines was a petite brunette with a shaved head and a tattoo of a snake that seemed to start on her right wrist and go all the way up to the right side of her neck. She looked nothing like LinkedIn and Google told me she'd look like.

"I know, my professional photos are about a decade old," she said when she saw my hesitation.

She was not wearing a pair of jeans or a sweater. She wore black leggings with knee-high boots, a magenta blouse, and a black bomber jacket.

We did the introductions, and she took us for a short walk to a coffee shop on Madison and 5th called Coppa Nomad. The café had funky art outdoors, and inside, it was a well-lit cozy space.

She ordered a latte, I ordered another espresso, and Erik got a Diet Coke with a *pain au chocolat*.

We sat down at the back of the small café and, after we'd passed some time in uncomfortable silence, she said, "I can't believe you're here."

"You told me if I came, you'd talk to me."

"I know," she ran a hand over her head, "but I didn't think you'd actually show up."

"I need your help."

She nodded.

"I'm investigating the suicide…the death of a woman called Noor Mallik. She worked for Copenhagen Bank. I think she didn't die by suicide but was murdered because she knew something."

Kelsey said nothing, just drank some of her latte.

I knew the trick she was using. I used it as well. The more I kept silent, the more the other person spoke. But I needed her more than she needed me, so I wanted to convince her that I was one of the good guys. That meant I had to be more forthcoming than I liked.

"She was talking to a Russian reporter, Raisa Chaban," I added softly.

Kelsey took a deep breath. "Raisa Chaban is in hiding. I can't help you find her. And even if I knew where she was, I wouldn't tell you…not that I know where she is."

"I understand. But you can communicate with her that I need to talk to her."

"Why?"

"Because someone is trying to kill me. Because they hurt a friend of mine to warn me to stay away from this case. And it all began after I talked to some people at Copenhagen Bank about Noor," I informed her.

"Who did you talk to?"

Before I could speak, Erik raised his hand. "He's telling you everything and you're telling him nothing. This not an equitable relationship."

She grinned. "Ah, the lawyer speaks. This is *not* an equitable relationship. I need nothing from Gabriel."

"I think you do. I think it would help your story if Gabriel told you everything he knows. And he has a ton of information on dodgy bank dealings and people who are ready to kill for it." There was absolutely no evidence of a hangover now. Erik was in true lawyer mode. He was also lying his ass off. I didn't have even half or even a quarter of a ton of information.

Kelsey tapped her hand on the table. "Okay. Here is what I *can* tell you. I have talked to Raisa Chaban as part of deep background. She won't go on record."

"How did you get in touch with her?"

"I need to make a few phone calls before I can tell you anything. To do that, I need to understand your investigation better," Kelsey confessed.

I believed her so I told her what I could do about Silas Haagen and Harald Wiberg, and the *Ghost*.

"I don't know this Noor person. *But* it sounds like, and I'm speculating here, that she might be the whistleblower Raisa was talking to. Because six months ago, Raisa went silent as well, and I wonder if that was her reacting to the death of this woman."

I felt literally every nerve in my body scream with adrenaline. This was it. Wasn't it?

"I *need* to talk to Raisa."

She nodded. "I agree. But I was telling you the truth when I told you I have no idea where she is."

"How did you talk to her then?"

She grimaced. "Give me a minute."

She walked outside the café, and we watched her on the phone outside, having an animated conversation with someone.

"If you were James Bond, you could tap her phone from here and know who she was talking to," Erik noted.

"I'm not James Bond."

"No shit."

"You know, you're a whole other person when you're on the outs with Stine. Usually, you're a nice guy, but when you're away from her, you're a bit of an asshole."

He rubbed his face with his hands and sighed. "It's such a cliché, Gabriel, but I think she makes me a better person."

"Now, if only you made *her* a better person," I quipped.

"Hey, that's my wife you're talking about."

"My ex," I countered.

"You were never married."

Before we could go further down that road, Kelsey came back.

She sat down and took a breath. "What I'm telling you can get Raisa killed. You understand?"

No, I absolutely do not *fucking understand.* "Yes, of course."

"You need to talk to Lucya Poletov...and she will decide if...let me put it this way, she's your first point of contact."

"Who?" Erik wanted to know.

I put my hand on his shoulder. "The widow of Nikita Poletov?"

"Yes," Kelsey nodded.

"She's not in hiding?"

"Not really. She lives in Princeton. They don't think she knows anything. She has two children, and she's careful. *But* she's agreed to talk to you," Kelsey frowned as if surprised that Lucya had agreed to speak with me.

"Okay. I appreciate that."

"I must ask you to be certain you're not being followed. I mean, an assassin is after you."

Erik snorted. "How can you say that with a straight face. It's so Hollywood!"

"You wouldn't think so if you were nearly run over by a car," I snapped. "Kelsey, I don't know if I'm being followed. I don't think so. *But* I don't know. I have an intuition sometimes but that's just instinct and not based on facts."

"And here we all thought he was some hotshot PI."

"Shut up," I said mildly to Erik.

"She'll see you tomorrow."

Then she pulled out a pen from her jacket and wrote an address on a Coppa Nomad napkin. "Read it, remember it, get rid of it. I don't someone to find it in a trashcan."

"We burn it, then, like spies." Erik rubbed his hands together.

"I'm sorry. I can't get rid of him. He's married to my daughter's mother."

Kelsey grinned. "Don't get anyone killed, Gabriel, otherwise I will write a story about nosy Danish investigators who ruin lives. Good luck working after that."

"Would that story be in *The Atlantic*?" Erik asked.

She gave him a baffled look.

"Because that would be good publicity for his business," Erik said.

"Shut up, Erik," I tried, again, to silence him. "I'm sorry. He's normally not an asshole. Normally, *I* am the asshole."

Amused, Kelsey left, and I watched Erik finish his pastry. "You know, I can't take you anywhere with me."

Erik shrugged. "I think we should rent one of them cool American muscle cars to go to Princeton. I think a red Mustang. What do you think?"

"A Mustang is a poor man's Porsche."

"You're such a fucking European snob," he said.

"I'm okay with that."

"I want to stick my tongue out at you right now but that would make me feel childish." He crossed his arms across his chest like an upset toddler.

"You're behaving like a juvenile weirdo."

"I'm not the weirdo. *You're* the weirdo."

I sighed.

Chapter 36

Monday Evening, October 17, 2023

"Where are you both?" Sophie asked us over the phone connected via Bluetooth to the rental car's audio system.

"On the road, driving to Princeton," I told her. "And Erik is backseat driving like an ass."

"*Mor* is pissed with you, Erik."

"Tell her I'm pissed with her, too," Erik snarled. "And tell her I'm not coming home until the fucking floor heating is fixed."

"He turns into such a foul mouth whenever they fight," Sophie grumbled.

"Maybe I should get him some weed. Last time they fought we went to Christiania, and he was in a great mood," I wondered.

"It's getting white outside," Erik claimed.

"It's snowing. That's why we had to get a car with winter tires."

"Sophie, he didn't want to drive a Mustang because it's the *poor man's Porsche*, and guess what he's driving?"

"What?"

"A Nissan Altima," Erik crowed.

"Can you drive in the snow, *far*?" Sophie wanted to know.

"That's insulting," I said in mock offense. "Did you forget I drove in Norway during a snowstorm?"

"No, I remember, and that's why I'm worried."

Erik laughed at that.

"Stop insulting your old man, *skat*," I growled. "And be a good girl and get your mother to make up with this asshole so I can get rid of him."

"I'm not the asshole. She's the asshole," Erik whispered.

"I heard that, Erik," Sophie was amused.

"This is going to be a long drive," I sighed.

Lucya Poletov resided in a sprawling American home along Barrington Drive in Princeton Junction, complete with a three-car garage and an expansive yard. There, the grass had faded to a dull brown. Leaves, tinting with the season's change, adorned the trees in her yard, encapsulating the essence of a Pleasantville-style suburban neighborhood.

The weather channel promised nearly fifteen inches of snow, thanks to a freak Nor'easter. It was going to start a little later in the night and extend through the next day. I hoped that we'd be back in the city before it came down.

The snow was falling lightly and slowly, covering everything in a thin layer of white. A couple with their dog chatted with a woman whose fully wrapped toddler was trying to make a snow angel in the barely there snow on the lawn.

"She's probably not going to want to talk to us," I told Erik. "So, let me lead this conversation."

"You're the PI, I'm just the *simple* European sidekick," Erik mused, digging his hands in his coat pockets.

I rang the doorbell and waited. Lucya, according to Kelsey, lived with her in-laws and two daughters in their teens.

A petite woman with silky, straight blond hair, and fully made face opened the door. She wore a pair of dark blue silk pants, with a soft cream-colored woolen blouse. As she walked, her beige pumps clicked against the wooden floor. I hoped she'd dressed up to meet with us because, if this is how she normally hung out at home, it was downright creepy.

"You're Gabriel Priest?"

"Præst," I corrected. "Yes. This is my colleague, Erik Digman. Thanks for seeing us."

"Can I see some identification?"

We fumbled in our pockets and pulled out our Danish driver's licenses. I hadn't thought to bring our passports along. She gave them back to us, and then took a long deep breath.

"Come on in."

We walked through a spacious entryway, bordered by two rooms. To our left, an office, and to our right, a formal living room. Beyond this, the space opened into a kitchen, seamlessly transitioning into a dining area and a cozy, informal living room, where a rerun of *Law & Order* flickered at a low volume on the television. A staircase ascended to the upper floor, from where the murmur of another television drifted down to us.

Lucya didn't look nervous or uneasy. She looked like she was comfortable having us in her home. It made me feel a little better about invading her space.

"Coffee?" she asked.

We both nodded.

She gestured for us to sit on bar stools at the granite kitchen counter.

"You have a beautiful home," I complimented.

She shrugged. "Poletov money."

"Your in-laws live with you," I said to say something. She might not be nervous, but I could feel some anger, and I wasn't sure if it was directed toward me or her dead husband or the Russian government.

"Yes." She watched the kettle as it made rumbling sounds. She had pulled out a French press and dropped two scoops of powdered coffee from a non-descript coffee tin. "My kids are with friends down the street. They're having a sleepover. School is probably going to be closed tomorrow because of the snow."

The kettle whistled, and she picked it up from its electric base, and poured the water into the French press. "If anyone finds out that you were here to see me about Raisa, you'll put my whole family in danger. You understand?"

We both nodded.

"If it's so dangerous, why did you agree to see us?" I asked.

She seemed to collect her thoughts as she watched the coffee steep. "Because I owe it to Nikita. And I owe it to his children and his parents. And I owe it to myself."

"Good enough."

"What do you want to know?" she threw back at me.

"Do you know how I can get in touch with Raisa Chaban?" I didn't want to prevaricate.

"Why?" She poured the now-steeped coffee into three white coffee cups. She added milk and sugar into hers, and milk into Erik's, leaving mine black.

I was expecting it. I had to convince Kelsey to let me talk to Lucya, and now I had to convince Lucya to let me talk to Raisa.

I told her what I told Kelsey.

"Noor is the woman who worked at the Baltic office of Copenhagen Bank?"

"She worked the Baltic desk but in the Copenhagen office," I corrected.

Lucya looked at her coffee cup. and then threw it across the kitchen into the sink. It broke with a cracking sound.

Someone's footsteps hurried downstairs. "Lucya?" a man's voice demanded.

I saw the weapon first. A *Pistolet Yarygina*, a high-capacity double-action, short-coil, semi-automatic pistol, popular in Russia.

"*Otets*," she exclaimed and then turned to us. "I'm sorry."

The man, I assumed was Lucya's father-in-law, Arkady Poletov.

"Put that away," she scolded.

He was a large man and not someone I'd like to meet in an alley, dark or otherwise. He was over seventy years old and built like a bull. He tucked the gun at the small of his back in a practiced move.

"I heard the noise. I thought there was trouble," he said in accented but clear English.

"This is how he lives...and makes us live. In fear," Lucya agonized. "You want coffee, *otets*?"

He shook his head and looked at Eric and me with cold blue eyes. "I hope you're not here to create trouble."

"No, sir," I replied.

He looked at Eric who also shook his head. "No, sir. No trouble."

He didn't smile, didn't give any sign he believed us. Just turned around and went upstairs.

"I can't believe those assholes killed her," Lucya's voice trembled with rage. "Raisa told me that woman committed suicide. We thought the pressure became too much. She checked with Danish police to be sure."

"Why was Raisa talking to Noor?" I asked, even though now I could guess.

"She was her source," Lucya confirmed. "She was a whistleblower. She knew that Copenhagen Bank in Estonia was laundering money for the Russians. She had found many accounts, leading to millions of euros that were not attached to a legitimate company. She took what she had to her superiors in the bank. They did nothing—well, they threatened her. She wanted to go to the police but wasn't sure if they could help, considering how powerful Copenhagen Bank is. Raisa has been following up on the story of Russian money laundering through banks across Europe. That's why she was talking to Nikita. She reached out to several people at Copenhagen Bank. And then, one day, Noor got back to Raisa. She was going to get proof for her. They were close to finding enough evidence that Maksim Lõhmus was corrupt, which they hoped would get him to talk to Raisa—so she could break the story."

Erik looked at me at the mention of a new name.

"Maksim Lõhmus was the Estonian finance minister's right-hand man and, after Nikita Poletov's murder, became head of the Baltic branch of Copenhagen Bank. He works for Silas Haagen, who is responsible for Eastern Europe," I explained.

"How do you know all this?" Erik asked, surprised.

"I'm a private investigator. I know stuff." I then turned to Lucya. "Did Lõhmus know about Noor?"

"I don't know." She shrugged.

"Will Raisa talk to me?"

"I don't know. Look, Raisa and I have been in touch since we left Russia. Two lost immigrants stuck in a foreign country. She's working as a fact checker for a newspaper. *But,* on the side, she's been working her contacts in Europe from Deutsch Bank, Copenhagen Bank, and others." She smiled wanly. "She hasn't given up on the story."

"We can help each other," I offered.

Lucya took a deep breath. "I have some protection. I have money. No one is after us. Not that I want to advertise that I'm talking to you or Raisa or any of the dissidents. But Raisa is on her own. She left her parents and sister. She had to change her identity to protect her family as well as herself. The Americans helped. I can reach out to her, but it'll be her call if she'll talk to you."

"Understood." I gave Lucya my card, which had both my phone number and email address.

"What is your endgame?" she asked me.

"I want to tell my client what happened to Noor."

"You don't want to bring the whole Danish banking establishment to its knees?"

"No. That would be a happy accident."

"Last time he was on a case, he was trying to prove a man's innocence and ended up getting the Prime Minister of Denmark to resign," Erik told her. "There's a possibility he *may* bring down Copenhagen Bank."

Her smile in response was feral, her red lipstick contrasting against white teeth. "I don't want *possibility*. I want revenge."

"Now *that* certainly would be a happy accident," I mused.

"I always told Nikita to play the political game, but he didn't want to. He wanted to do the right thing. Now, I want the right thing to happen for him. I want the people who killed him to pay for it," she stated.

"I'll do my best," I promised. "If I need to get in touch with you again?"

She pulled out a yellow stack of sticky notes and a blunt yellow pencil from a drawer. She wrote her phone number and email address on one and gave it to me.

"Thank you."

When we left the Poletov house, the snow had accumulated to several centimeters, blanketing the world in a hushed white. The sky, a deepening shade of twilight, stood in stark contrast to the ground, which glowed in the snow's luminescence.

"I liked her." Erik strapped himself in the passenger seat. "She's a tough cookie."

"Yes," I agreed as I started the car. "This sounds like a fucking sewing machine."

"Do you think the sewing machine can take us to one of those truck stop diners? I'd love a Philly cheesesteak sandwich," Erik mused.

"Maybe they'll have American pancakes."

"I think it behooves us to find out." Erik looked on his phone for an eatery suited to our appetites on the I-95.

Erik directed us to Legends Diner & Restaurant close to Secaucus, New Jersey, on our way back to the Mandarin Oriental.

The snow was coming down now and, even though our first instinct was to get to the hotel immediately, the other was to get something to eat at an honest-to-God American diner.

Legends was a classic diner where they served the breakfast menu all day. It promised to be nothing fancy, just down-to-earth, country-style cooking.

We sat at the bar, and a woman named Alice with a broad smile, white hair tied up in a bun, wearing a black shirt, asked us how she could help us, and then, when we answered, asked us where we were from.

"Denmark," Erik told her while I looked through my phone to see if I had any emails from Cézar or Valentin about *The Ghost*.

I knew, or at least I thought I knew, that no one had followed us when we went to see Lucya Poletov. But I couldn't say for sure. And if we had been followed, and I didn't know, I'd be putting Lucya and her family at some risk.

Alice served me coffee and Erik a Diet Coke. I ordered a stack of pancakes, despite it being dinnertime—all in pursuit of self-care. Erik went for a Philly cheesesteak sandwich and, even though I was tempted, I stayed on course with breakfast for dinner.

"Any news from back home?" Erik asked.

I shook my head. "Stine hasn't asked me how you're doing."

"I didn't mean that. I meant about your investigation."

I grinned. "Sure, you did. And no. Well, except Eskola sent me a formal request to appear in front of her on Friday morning or whenever I return, whatever comes first. Or she'll arrest me."

"Arrest you? On what legal grounds?"

"She's creative. I'm sure she'll find something."

Our food was served and, as Erik unwrapped his silverware and put the paper napkin on his lap, he wondered, "How do you do this? How do you end up getting involved in such serious shit?"

"I'm just one lucky son of a bitch," I told him as I gleefully spread butter on top of my stack, liberally poured maple syrup, and cut into my self-care.

CHAPTER 37

Monday Night, October 17, 2023

Erik went to his room to drink the mini bar, while I went to an actual bar. It was just after nine and I was wide awake.

Afsana called me as I walked out of my room toward the elevator.

"How did it go?" I asked of her interview before she could say hello.

Her crisp laughter came through.

"That well?" I asked.

"I don't know," she said. "I mean…it's good. We talked, and I'm going to work in the kitchen for the next couple of days, and then we'll see. They know I can cook but I need to fit with the team."

"Do you feel you'll fit?"

I heard the sounds of people and life at the other end of the country.

"I think so."

"Where are you?"

"Pier 39. I'm meeting some friends for dinner," she paused, and then added, "I miss you. It's peculiar because we just met but...I miss you."

"I miss you, too," I answered honestly. Despite the busyness of the day—and the excitement of unraveling at least part of the Noor mystery, Afsana was well and truly lodged in my thoughts.

I reached the bank of elevators but waited to press the button.

"Then...should I take this job?"

Ah, youth, I thought, and regretted telling her I missed her. I missed her, but I didn't want to mislead her.

"This is your dream job, isn't it?"

There was movement behind me, and I looked back to see who it was.

A blonde man with dark blue eyes was holding a saxophone case. I nodded at him, and he nodded back. He walked past me to press the button to go down.

"Yes, it is."

"Then you should take it."

She didn't say anything.

"Hey," I coaxed.

"No, of course, you're right. I was being...I don't know...romantically emotional for a minute," she said, and there was both amusement and sadness in her voice.

The elevator beeped. I heard someone call out Afsana's name at her end.

"My friends are here, Gabriel. Call me before you go to bed?"

"Yes."

She hung up as the elevator door opened. I let the man with the saxophone enter first.

"How you doin'?" the man said pleasantly as he held his saxophone case like a weapon, upright.

"Very well, thank you. Assassin or musician?" I wondered, amused.

The man raised his eyebrows and laughed. "Jazz."

"Is there a good place around here?"

"For jazz?"

"And a drink."

He nodded. "I'm doing a set at Dizzy's Club. It's a 10-minute walk from here."

I knew Dizzy's, it was in the Time Warner Center building and offered live jazz every night along with a stunning view of the Manhattan skyline.

"Are you going there now?"

The man nodded. "Why don't we walk together?" he suggested.

I loved this about New York. You met a stranger, and he took you to a jazz club with him.

The snow was falling steadily, but it didn't look like it was going to become the storm that the 24/7 newscasts had predicted.

We huddled into our coats, and I pulled on a cashmere beanie as we stepped into the bustling New York night. The snow made the city seem oddly silent, even though cars were still driving, people were still walking, and the lights still shining…but it was all just this side of mellow.

"So, where are you from? You don't sound to be from around here?" the saxophone guy said.

"I'm from Denmark."

We did the usual, *oh Denmark, I went there once and saw the Little Mermaid and went to Tivoli* bit. He didn't disappoint, though he added that he also went to Vega, where he saw Sonny Rollins, the American jazz saxophonist and composer, perform in 1985.

When I asked him where he was from, he replied as I'd predicted based on his accent, "Brooklyn. Born and raised. I now live in Connecticut. That's what we do here in New York City once we have a family. We move upstate. I travel a lot, so it works out."

We shook hands when we reached Dizzy's.

"Gabriel," I introduced myself.

"Charlie," he replied.

He wasn't a bad musician. But he wasn't great, either. It wasn't a performance that knocked my socks off, but that wasn't what I was expecting at Dizzy's on a Monday night. I got a glass of tonic water with bitters and enjoyed being part of the crowd and the music.

I called Afsana an hour and a half later from bed as I struggled to keep my eyes open.

"Did you have a good dinner?" I asked.

"Yes. And you?"

"I went to Dizzy's to listen to some jazz and drink some non-alcoholic beverages."

"You know what Proust says about alcohol, don't you?"

"What did he say?"

"I'm probably going to butcher it. I can't remember quotes word-to-word quite like you do. He said something about how wine makes us forget our problems but it's only temporary and probably not healthy."

"Well Kierkegaard, as you know, had a complex relationship with wine and depression. He said, '*nothing is as heady as the wine of possibility*,'" I recounted. "And I probably butcher the quotes as well because I read them in Danish and French, so when translating into English, I'm never sure if I get it right."

"Am I the first relationship you're having in English?"

"Yes."

"And?"

"And…well, I think it makes me a little self-conscious."

"You speak English very well."

"Sometimes I speak *Danglish*, and I'm aware of that. It doesn't prevent me from speaking, it just takes a minute to translate what I want to say in my head," I explained.

We talked some more. She didn't ask me about Noor, and I didn't tell her what I found. We were two lovers, talking on the phone at the end of a long day about nothing more important than some old dead philosophers and writers.

After the call, as I waited to sleep, I admitted to myself that I would miss Afsana very much when she left, and that it was a good thing she was leaving sooner than later.

CHAPTER 38

Tuesday Morning, October 18, 2023

At Victor's request, Erik and I joined Eymen and him for breakfast at the conference area where Copenhagen Bank had set up a buffet.

"Are you coming in with us today? Elias is speaking," Victor asked.

"Oh yeah, he and Gabriel are good friends," Erik mocked.

"I have to drop the rental car off," I muttered.

"I can drop it off for you," Erik offered.

As I was about to turn Erik down again, Eymen rose from his seat, as did Victor, to shake hands with the man of the hour.

Elias Juhl, ex-Prime Minister of Denmark, and current Secretary General of NATO, the smiling silver fox himself, had deigned to walk up to our table. Erik also stood up and shook Elias's hand, so I had no choice but to do the same.

"Gabriel, it's a wonderful surprise to see you here," he said, and I could tell he wasn't surprised at all. "I didn't know you were a Copenhagen Bank customer." Now, he was mocking me.

"I'm on holiday, Elias." I used his first name as a sign of disrespect, which wouldn't bother him at all. Elias didn't give a flying fuck what I or anyone else thought of him. Narcissists never did.

Victor grinned, obviously and unabashedly enjoying my discomfort and Elias's amusement.

A woman who I recognized as Elias's wife, Johanne Juhl, current Danish representative of the European Commission, joined us. There was one word that described her: handsome. While Elias was a pretty boy, Johanne was strong, with her short dark hair, shrewd eyes, and a face that commanded attention. She was nearly as tall as Elias's six feet in her Louboutin heels that she paired with a dark violet suit dress and jacket.

She did the cheek kissing thing with Victor and Eymen, and politely shook hands with Erik, and grinned widely at me when she gripped my hand with hers.

"I've heard a lot about you, Gabriel. My husband speaks *fondly* of you, and we're so grateful for the work you did to clear Yousef Ahmed's name." Her voice was cool and confident. She was fooling no one with her cheerleader smile.

In the dictionary, where it said "Power Couple", a photograph of these two probably showed up. Regardless of her taste in men, Johanne Juhl was smart with the brains to go after juggernauts like Google and Apple as part of her work for the European Commission's "A Europe Fit for the Digital Age" program, and the guile to tell me, in front of many people, that her husband told her *everything*.

"I did what I did for my client," I responded with as little emotion as I could.

"Elias needs to go prepare for his speech, but I was hoping, you and I could have a quick chat," she said softly. Then she did something most women didn't do with grace, which was to have me offer my arm to her so she could slide her hand through it and take me away from the table.

We walked to the other end of the room where the windows looked over Central Park. There were some empty tables and a sofa set. We stood by the windows.

"I love New York." She smiled. "Especially in the winter when it's almost bleak. There's a starkness to it."

"Is that what you wanted to have a quick chat about? New York?"

The smile faded, and she became serious. "No. I wanted to talk to you about the work you're doing for Copenhagen Bank."

"First, I'm not doing *anything* for Copenhagen Bank, and second, how would you know what I was doing?" I wasn't polite. She might be a knockout, but I didn't like her husband's politics, and I wasn't so sure about hers.

"I have an interest in Copenhagen Bank. My mother is a member of the Board of Directors. She used to be the CEO and President of the Danish NASDAQ," she told me. "Did you know that?"

"I may have read that somewhere."

"The thing is that the board is concerned about the—"

I held my hand up. "I repeat, I am not doing any work for Copenhagen Bank."

She smiled. "Of course. You're investigating the death of Noor Mallik."

I sighed. "You're well informed."

"I'm a politician," she replied as if that explained it. "I'm trying to help you, Gabriel."

I didn't respond, and went to the old faithful and shrugged.

"I understand you don't trust my husband, but I'm *not* my husband. I know that you're looking into what Copenhagen Bank is doing in Tallinn. The board...well, some members of the board are keen on finding out exactly that and are concerned that because of compliance loopholes, Copenhagen Bank may be a conduit for Russian money laundering," she explained.

I was now interested, so I nodded.

"Good, I now have your attention." She pulled out a card from her pocket. "If you need any help during this investigation, call me. Think of me as someone who can be an instrument of information from *some* members of the Copenhagen Bank board."

She waved at someone then, and I turned to see an older version of Johanne talking to Victor and Eymen. The older woman waved back. The mother, I presumed.

"And what do you want in return?" I took the card and slid it into a pocket of my dress pants.

"Gabriel, I am disappointed at your cynicism," she admonished. "I'm sincere. And I know that you'll need help. When you do, call me, and I can make sure that Harald Wiberg and that slimy asshole Silas Haagen get what's coming to them."

With that, she sashayed away.

Victor nodded at me as I walked up to him and Eymen. He had helped set up this meeting with Johanne, who seemed to know a lot more than I did about most everything, including the case I was investigating.

In the end, I let Erik drop the car off at the rental agency a few miles away and sat to listen to Elias Juhl speak about cyber security in a changing world.

"A few years ago, Estonia suffered directed cyber-attacks that shut down essential services, and as a NATO ally, we were called in to support. We are equipped to send a team in...," he went on, and I drowned his voice out when I saw a text message from Erik that increased my heartbeat. I kept calm as I whispered to Eymen that Erik had been in an accident and left after assuring him he didn't need to come along.

CHAPTER 39

Tuesday Afternoon, October 18, 2023

"Stine, I wasn't even there," I told my ex on the phone after she blamed me for Erik's accident and his broken right tibia.

"Why weren't you there?" she demanded.

"Because Erik is a grown man, and I don't babysit him. He was dropping the rental car off and a truck banged into him," I explained.

"Why?"

"How the fuck am I supposed to know? Drunk truck driver?"

It was a good question, I thought as I zoned out her angry retort to my sarcasm. Said truck had hit the car in an alley as Erik turned into the street where the rental drop off was. I asked Officer Chavez, a petite Hispanic woman, who seemed to have walked off the set of *Blue Bloods*, if she knew anything. She said she didn't...yet, but her team would check to see if there was CCTV footage, but that would take time. Eyewitness accounts were unanimous in their description of the incident: a truck had seemingly emerged from thin air, striking the car in what appeared to be a deliberate act.

"When are you bringing him home?" Stine demanded.

"We're getting on a plane tomorrow, so we'll be back home early Thursday morning our time."

"Make sure he's comfortable on the plane," Stine insisted.

"It's a private fucking plane, Stine, it doesn't get more comfortable."

After spending the morning and a good part of the afternoon at the New York-Presbyterian, I brought Erik to the hotel, cast and all. Stine and Erik had made up. Nothing like a broken leg to dissolve marital differences.

"This is great," Erik told me a little woozily, thanks to the painkillers he was on. "I mean, my leg is broken, and I need a cast for eight weeks, but Stine is feeling bad for me and she's blaming *you* for it. This works out nicely for me."

"Except for the broken leg," I pointed out.

"Well, as my buddy Will says, '*the course of true love never did run smooth.*'"

"Now you're quoting Shakespeare?"

"I think these pills are making a pseudo intellectual like you."

I left Erik to get some sleep and found my way to the hotel lounge, where Victor and Eymen were in deep conversation about the American debt ceiling with some other suits.

I left them to talk about money and sat alone at the bar.

The bartender, a guy who looked like he knew how to make a drink and had made a few in his time, asked me what I'd like to drink.

I'd *like* a very large scotch, I thought.

"Just some sparkling water with lime."

He raised an eyebrow and waited to see if I was going to alter my order.

"It's my dry month," I told him, annoyed with myself. Who had thought that this dry month shit was a good idea? Well, I had, nearly a decade ago when I was worried I was going from *heavy drinker* to full on *alcoholic*.

The bartender seemed sympathetic. "I can make you a mocktail? I also have some good non-alcoholic wine and beer."

I shook my head. "I don't want something that tastes like alcohol, I want alcohol. So, water will have to do."

He didn't argue because I think he saw my point.

I was about to take a sip of my fresh water with a fresh fucking twist of lime when a man sat next to me, and I was further tortured by what seemed like my endless no alcohol October.

Silas Haagen smiled at me. "How are you doing… Præst, was it?"

"I'm doing dandy. How about you?"

"I hear you've been talking to several Copenhagen Bank employees…some ex-employees," he continued, ignoring my sarcasm. "And so is a friend of yours. A journalist. She seems like a sweet girl."

Danes tended to call grown women "sweet girls." *The Crown Prince is getting married to a "sweet girl" from New Zealand*. But I always felt it was a way to mock women. *Girls are made of sugar and spice, and everything nice.*

"Nico is an award-winning journalist," I countered. "And, yes, she's talking to a bunch of women who you have sexually harassed. What I can't understand is that with all that fucking hair gel you use, and the suits...by the way, you need to get yours tailored because the one you're wearing is terrible—"

"It's an Armani."

"And yet.... Regardless of the money you seem to throw to make yourself look dignified, you go about making the lives of women at work who don't want to fuck you miserable. That is the *definition* of sexual harassment, and of a fucking asshole, which you are." I finished my water, even though the sparkles didn't make it easy, but I wanted to bang the glass down on the counter and I needed the glass empty for that.

"You're out of line," he wasn't yelling at me exactly, but it was close.

Several of the suits were watching us.

Although I was wearing a better fitting suit than Silas, no one would mistake me for a corporate shill, not with the Keith James red-rimmed, black wool fedora I was sporting.

I banged the glass hard on the counter for effect and garnered some more attention from the patrons at and around the bar. The bartender didn't bat an eyelid. Probably not the first time he'd seen someone lose their temper, and I, who prided myself on keeping my cool, was out of fucks.

"Next time, Haagen, don't get into a pissing contest with someone who thinks men like you should get their dicks cut off in public." I didn't bother to lower my voice. "And stop sleeping with your female staff. Despite your high opinion of yourself, women, as a rule, generally don't want to fuck men with small dicks."

I regretted I had nothing better than *small dicks,* but I was too angry to come up with something wittier. I couldn't stand this man and men like him. The Elias Juhl's and Silas Haagen's of the world, who never seemed to pay for their sins. And I was *furious* that Erik had gotten into an accident, which I suspected was not an accident, and that I was supposed to be the one with a broken leg not him.

The Ghost's signature style was making murders look like accidents and suicides. Yet, in this instance, I was inclined to believe their intent wasn't to kill Erik or me. Instead, it seemed they were aiming to incapacitate me, hindering my ability to delve into Noor's death.

I walked out of the hotel and spent the evening by myself. I was poor company.

I walked into Central Park.

It was five in the evening, and it was already getting dark. I strolled past the joggers, the baby carriers, and the tourists. I wasn't sure where I wanted to go but hoped that *The Ghost* was following me, leaving my friends and family alone.

My phone rang. It was an unknown American number, and since I was waiting to hear from Raisa, I picked up.

"Is this Gabriel Priest?" a voice asked.

"Yes, this is Gabriel *Præst,*" I responded.

"I'm Officer Chavez. We met today...."

"Yes, thank you for calling me. Do you have news?"

"We checked the CCTV at the rental car company, but it wasn't working, and we can't seem to find the truck, either," she informed me.

"Oh." I was disappointed. I had wanted her to say that it was a drunk driver. That this, indeed, was an accident.

"Is your friend alright?"

"He has a broken leg but, yes, he is. Thank you for asking."

I put the phone into my jacket pocket and felt my spirits plummet. I kept walking briskly, not paying much attention to my surroundings. Before I knew it, I was on fifth, right next to the Met. I loved museums, but I was simply not in the mood to stand in front of a Rothko to contemplate the depth of color.

I was going to go past the Met and find a restaurant, maybe get something to eat, when the painting advertising a special art exhibition hit me like a ton of bricks. It was one of the most disturbing paintings I'd ever seen, something that looked like it came from *Pan's Labyrinth*. It depicted a gaunt figure with elongated limbs and fingers, traversing a barren landscape. The figure, a fusion of rusted metal plates, pipes, and exposed veins and tissues, created a chilling tableau of eerie desolation. This haunting piece was part of Zdzisław Beksiński's exhibition, and a small notation informed viewers that it was unofficially known as *Crawling Death*.

It clicked almost as soon as I thought of Guillermo del Toro's fantastical movie. Toomas had said that *The Ghost* liked dark art. Wasn't there a poster of a painting *The Ghost* had on his wall in prison instead of naked women? Was it something like this? Or exactly this?

I didn't know Beksiński as an artist, but I appreciated his skill. There was something about his use of muted colors that enhanced the oppressiveness of this painting that embodied everything we thought about death and decay. It seemed just the kind of art an assassin would enjoy.

Even though I never imagined becoming a fan of Beksiński, I found myself purchasing a ticket. The Met, typically closed by 5 p.m. on Tuesdays, was hosting a special event that evening. Fortuitously, this allowed me to explore the Beksiński exhibit, where my luck doubled as I recognized *The Ghost*.

CHAPTER 40

Tuesday Night, October 18, 2023

I RECEIVED AN EMAIL from Valentin containing a list of potential aliases *The Ghost* might use, derived from flight booking patterns of pro-Russian militants. These patterns coincided with the locations and timings of mysterious accidents and suicides of Russians critical of their current leader.

I looked at the list once and then twice.

I called Nico.

"Missing me already?" she flirted.

"Oh yeah. What are you wearing?" I joked.

"I'm at work, Præst."

"I think I met *The Ghost*."

"Tell me."

"You're going to have to take a leap of faith," I said.

"Okay. So, how do you know you met him?"

"He's a jazz musician. Plays the saxophone. And he likes dark Polish art. He told me his name was Charlie. And now I know how he comes up with his aliases."

"You sound very confident."

"Because I am." I couldn't believe that I had identified *The Ghost*. I was certain I had.

And what irony that I had asked *The Ghost* in the elevator at the hotel if he was an assassin or a musician. But for the fact that the Met had been open, and Toomas had told me about *The Ghost's* love for morbid art, I wouldn't have made the discovery. He was careful. He was a master of disguise. But he was cocky.

I told Nico about him playing at Dizzy's.

And then I told her about what happened at the Met. I wasn't expecting to meet *him*. I was only going to look at the paintings and get some insight into my future killer's twisted head.

There were a few people milling around, standing in front of the paintings. I found all the art disturbing. However, I was captivated by the macabre untitled painting of a powder blue severed head eyes leaking tangled, blood-colored roots that sprawled over a white plain.

"Do you like it?" an older gentleman asked me.

He was leaning on a cane, wearing a dark coat and a checkered hat. He spoke with an Eastern European accent, and I surmised he was in his mid to late seventies.

"No."

"Why?" he asked.

"I find it unsettling," I told him.

"Beksiński was born in Sanok in Poland in the late twenties, which was decimated by Hitler. Sanok had a large Jewish population. The Nazis killed many of them, and those who remained were sent to Auschwitz—and then most of them died there. Beksiński was sixteen when the war ended, when the Russians came. His art comes from seeing that destruction," the man explained, as he watched the painting with appreciation.

An African American woman stood close to us, listening to the man. "You know, Beksiński was murdered?" she asked.

The man nodded. "Killed for a hundred dollars."

"Devastating," the woman agreed.

"Who killed him?" I wanted to know.

"Beksiński got into an argument with a man who wanted a hundred dollars, which Beksiński wouldn't give him. The man was 19-years-old. He knifed Beksiński to death. Seventeen stab wounds." The man shook his head at the tragedy.

"In 2006, when his killer was sentenced, *Burning Man* put up a *Beksiński cross*, in the T-shape he frequently employed, in his memory," the woman added.

I loved this about New York! This connection you could make for an instant and in a moment. In Copenhagen, you could go on the train with the same people for a decade and never say hello to one another.

"Do *you* like his art?" I asked the woman.

The woman smiled. "I'm studying art at Julliard; this is part of class work. I can't say I *like* his work, but I find it impactful. And art is supposed to make us feel. His art, regardless of whether you like or not, makes you feel…uneasy, unsettled, afraid…even disgusted."

We became a threesome as we walked the exhibits. By the end, I knew more about Zdzisław Beksiński than I ever wanted or cared to know.

Our small threesome left the exhibit together. I was feeling much better than I had when I came inside, despite the morbid and disturbing artwork.

The woman went to get her things from a locker, and the man and I walked out into the cold as we'd not put our coats in a locker.

"Do you know that Beksiński never visited museums or studied fine art, his inspiration came from music. He listened to classical and rock music," the man said.

"Maybe if he listened to blues and jazz, his paintings may have been a little brighter," I suggested.

The man laughed. "I like jazz."

I adjusted my hat against the cold and dipped my hands into my jacket to find my gloves. As did the older man.

"It was nice meeting you," I said and extended my hand to him. "My name is Gabriel Præst."

"Zygmunt Karasinski."

I may not know Polish art, but I knew my *global* jazz. Zygmunt Karasinski was the saxophonist who, along with others, formed the first Polish jazz band in 1923.

But even if that hadn't given him away, his gloves did. He really needed to be careful about carrying the same gloves in Copenhagen as he did in New York. The gloves were black with just one red tip on the right-hand forefinger so he could use his phone. It was the same glove I had seen after the opera near the Seven-Eleven. The glove could be coincidence, but the glove and the jazz connection...that was, as Hercule Poirot would put it, a clue.

"Then I went through the list of aliases that PET suspects are Russian assassins helping with the sudden Russian death syndrome that Valentin sent. Guess what I found?" I told Nico.

"I think you're a few beats ahead of me," Nico admitted.

"Names of Polish Jazz musicians."

"You're kidding me."

"Three names, Henryk Majewski, who used to be fondly called Papa, Tomasz Stanko, and Adam Makowicz."

"This is unbelievable."

"Everyone has a type. Jack Reacher used to check into motels under the names of Yankees players and US Vice Presidents."

"You know, Præst, Jack Reacher is a fictional character," Nico mocked. "And when I said this is *unbelievable* what I meant is that this is not believable. Not, *wow*, this is so exceptional."

"I'm telling you, it's him. If I need to find out the names of people staying in the five-star hotels in Copenhagen, how do I go about doing that?"

"All the names?"

"Yes."

"Why five-star hotels?"

"He's staying at the Mandarin Oriental here. I have a feeling Charlie has expensive tastes."

"Charlie?"

"It makes me feel silly to call him *The Ghost*. I think I'm going to call him Charlie."

Nico sighed. "And why do you think he picked Charlie when he introduced himself to you?"

"I think it comes from Charles Turner, Brooklyn-based jazz musician," I was guessing but I felt it was informed.

"You're reaching."

"No, I'm pretty sure about this, Nico. I...feel it in my gut," I lamely said.

"Well, since I can't convince you that you're in fantasy land. If you want names of everyone staying at a 5-star Copenhagen hotel, you may have to go hotel by hotel and beg...or...ask your friend at PET, or that guy who works at the IT company who does stuff for you...what's his name?"

"Cézar Doucette."

"Yeah. That guy is hot."

"That guy is US government," I informed her. "And he doesn't do favors for free."

"I'm sure you'll find a way to manipulate him. I need to go work on a *real* story about a man called Silas Haagen, who actually exists, unlike Jack Reacher."

"Oh, and speaking of Silas Haagen, he knows what you're doing, and I may have called him an asshole with a small dick." I told her about my exchange with Mr. High & Mighty Banker.

"Small dick? Seriously?"

I sighed. "I know. I couldn't come up with anything better. This is really the wrong month to stop drinking."

She laughed.

"Nico, am I on the right path?"

"What's up, Mr. Overconfident?"

"I'm in over my head."

"Aren't we all, *skat*. You're *always* on the right path, Præst. You got this."

"I don't feel like I got anything."

"One step at a time like every time. Big kiss." She made a loud smooching sound before ending the call.

I texted Afsana, who was still working the late service as part of her job interview, goodnight, before falling into a deep sleep.

CHAPTER 41

Wednesday Morning, October 19, 2023

I woke up to a message from Lucya Poletov that Raisa Chaban had agreed to get in touch with me.

I immediately let Eymen know I wouldn't be leaving with them and then extended my stay at the hotel by another night. I would fly back commercial, leaving Thursday afternoon and arriving Friday morning.

This case was costing more than my investigations normally did, what with international travel. I was hoping Fiona would pay me. Regardless, what had to be done, had to be done.

I helped Erik pack, and bundled him into a town car with Eymen and Victor.

Victor put his arm on my shoulder. "Johanne is not Elias."

I nodded. "She reached out to you?"

Victor shook his head. "I reached out to her after they hurt your friend. She confirmed that part of the Copenhagen Bank board is worried about the bank's activities in the Baltics. When it's time to bring Harald and Silas down, you *will* need her help."

I trusted Victor implicitly. He knew how the system worked, and thought of me as a son. "I don't know what I'm doing here, Victor. But if the time comes, I'll reach out to her."

"Was Erik's accident…," he trailed off and, when I nodded, he pursed his lips.

"Have a safe flight." I tipped my hat at him.

Eymen followed me as I went into the hotel lobby. "Do you want me to stay with you?"

And get a broken leg or worse? No, thank you.

"I'm here for just one extra day," I said easily. "It's going to be fine."

"If anything happens to you, between Sophie and Clara, my life won't worth be living."

"Thanks for taking Erik home; Stine is going to be on the warpath."

"Yeah, but she blames you for it, so I'll be fine."

THE CALL FROM CÉZAR Doucette arrived just as I returned from my run in Central Park, my breath still catching in quick, shallow drafts. I answered my phone, leaning against the cool facade of the hotel, the craving for a cigarette gnawing at me.

"Are you trying to get me into trouble?" he asked without preamble.

"Hey, Cézar, nice to hear from you. About getting you into trouble, you're going to have to be a little more specific," I remarked.

"Did you meet with Lucya Poletov?"

"No."

"Præst...."

"No," I repeated, keeping the panic I felt out of my voice. *How did Cézar know?*

"How the fuck did you get to her?"

"I don't know what you're talking about."

"Lucya Poletov is being watched. Which means you were watched going to her house. Which means, you're probably getting a visit from some of my colleagues," he indicated.

"When?"

"I don't know."

"I have nothing to say to anyone," I drawled. "Abso-fucking-lutely nothing."

"I heard Erik was in an accident."

"It wasn't an accident."

"That's what I thought," Cézar agreed. "What's your next move?"

"I don't know," I lied. "When you said Lucya Poletov is being watched, did you mean watched as in to spy on, or watched as in to protect?"

"*Mostly* protect."

"So, nothing has happened to them?"

"No."

I was relieved. "Cézar, what if I could find *The Ghost*?"

Long pause. "Can you?"

"Maybe."

"That would be very beneficial to a lot of governments."

"Hmm."

"Præst, have you found him?" Cézar probed.

I didn't want to help the US and Danish governments, I wanted to help Noor Mallik, I wanted to get justice for Lucya Poletov, I wanted to vindicate Caja Hansen, and I wanted very much to see Silas Haagen and Harald Wiberg brought down.

"He's *The Ghost*, do you think he'd be easy to find?" I prevaricated.

Another long pause, "*Cher*, you find him, you hand him over. Try nothing on your own. This man will kill you if he knows you can identify him."

"I know."

I promised Cézar, I'd catch up with him after I returned to Copenhagen, and headed up to my room. The sweat from the run had already dried, and I was all but shivering as I reached my room, wishing for nothing more than a hot shower to make my extremities come alive again.

The moment I closed the door behind me, I knew something was off.

She was a petite woman. About five feet one or two inches. She wore a pair of very tight jeans, knee-high black boots with a high heel, a turtleneck black sweater, and a lot of confidence on her fresh face. Her eyes were green and fierce. She was standing, leaning against the bar.

I walked up to her, hand extended. "Thank you for meeting me, Raisa."

She shook my hand. She had a firm, warm and welcoming grip.

"Do you mind if I make myself a cup of coffee?" I asked. "And would you like one?"

"Yes, thanks, black." She moved away from the bar and sat down on the armchair next to the sofa. The standard rooms in the Mandarin Oriental were a few notches above most hotel rooms with a king-size bed and a sofa set, coffee table, and armchair set to pretend to be a small living room space right next to the desk with enough the plugs to charge all your electronics at once.

I poured her coffee into a Mandarin Oriental branded cup and took it to her while the machine brewed mine.

I stood by the bar, where she'd been standing, drinking coffee, and watched her. This was her show, I thought. I'd wait.

"Both Lucya and Kelsey say that you're not an asshole." She was done with most of her coffee, and I was half through mine, when she finally addressed me. She spoke English with not a hint of her Motherland. If I didn't know any better, I'd think she was a New Yorker.

"I am not an asshole," I agreed.

"I also discreetly enquired about you in Copenhagen. You seem to have a penchant for getting into trouble, but you also seem to have a flair of breaking open investigations," she mused.

"It's my stock-in-trade," I replied. Thanks to speaking in English with Afsana, I was stumbling less on my English clichés and slang.

"I'm sorry to hear about Noor," she said seriously. "I couldn't reconcile the person I'd been talking to with a person who'd kill themselves. I even checked with the police."

"Have you heard of an assassin called *The Ghost*?"

The ripple of awareness and fear that went over her face told me she'd heard of the hitman and was afraid of him.

"Copenhagen Bank has deep pockets. *The Ghost* doesn't come cheap, now that he's gone private." She finished her coffee and held the cup up. I took it and brewed another cup for her.

"Did you think Noor's life was in danger?"

Raisa shook her head. "No. But maybe I should've. They killed Nikita...but Noor wasn't high up enough to be dangerous."

"What can you tell me?"

Raisa assessed me as I gave her a second cup of coffee. "Everything. I can tell you everything. *But*, if I do, I get to write the *whole* story, your side, Noor's side...all the sides."

The woman had been in hiding for many years. She'd earned this.

"Yes."

"What do you know about how the Russians are money laundering through Europe?"

"Whatever is in the papers," I admitted.

She nodded. "This began when Copenhagen Bank acquired Finba Bank in Finland. Most of Finba's branches seamlessly merged into Copenhagen Bank's portfolio, except for the one in Estonia. This outlier remained somewhat isolated, as Copenhagen Bank hadn't yet established a foothold in the Baltics. The acquisition aimed to bolster their Baltic presence, a move that was financially lucrative, raking in billions. However, the legitimacy of this windfall was under scrutiny. Nikita Poletov had previously alerted Maksim Lõhmus, then with the Estonia's Ministry of Finance, about the necessity of rigorous due diligence on all non-resident accounts to ensure their legality."

I held my cup with both hands to prevent them from shaking. Some of this I already knew, but to have *her* tell this had a profound impact on me. She put her coffee cup on the table and stood up, shoving her hands into the front pockets of jeans.

"Then Nikita died. I got death threats. I reached out to my contacts in the US and got asylum. I left my family behind. I couldn't get them out. I know they were threatened. My father was in prison for a few weeks...," she trailed off and stood still for a long moment. "I almost gave myself up then. But my father was freed. The Russian government concluded my family didn't know where I was, and they couldn't use them to bring me out of hiding. After a while, they forgot about me."

"I'm so sorry." Words were not enough, but I had nothing else to give her.

She nodded. "Nikita died. And Maksim Lõhmus became head of Copenhagen Bank Estonia. By the time I got in touch with Noor, she'd already uncovered over two hundred bogus accounts. These were companies that didn't exist and, according to her estimation nearly *two hundred billion euros* or more were being laundered through Copenhagen Bank in Estonia."

I knew the numbers were big but not this big. I whistled softly.

Raisa smiled. "Corruption is profitable."

"No wonder they're ready to kill to protect their investment," I breathed.

My phone pinged then. It was a message from an unknown number that I suspected was Cézar: *They say they'll be there in an hour. You have twenty minutes.*

I looked up at Raisa. "We have to continue this conversation elsewhere. Some of our friends from the US government are on their way here to have a chat with me."

Raisa shrugged. "It was inevitable. Why don't I leave now. You can take me out for lunch."

"Where?"

She grinned. "The Russian Tea Room."

"Isn't that a bit too obvious?"

"And that's the beauty of it."

Chapter 42

Wednesday Afternoon, October 19, 2023

Raisa left, and I went to the gym with my laptop and passport, and a change of clothes to avoid any of Cézar's colleagues in case they got there early. I took a shower in the well-appointed gym, got dressed and headed out, taking the service exit.

I walked briskly on 60th toward Broadway. and found my way to the Russian Tea Room on 150 West 57th, within ten minutes of leaving the hotel.

Raisa sat at the far end of the spacious room, adorned in brilliant red. I had always been fond of the Russian Tea Room, despite its stark contrast to my preference for Scandinavian minimalism. The restaurant's opulence was a tasteful blend of extravagance and elegance, its lavishness unmistakably signaling luxury.

We sat in a booth right below the 1925 painting *Russian Tea Room* by Otto Rothenberg.

"You're paying," she announced and ordered the afternoon tea with a glass of Moët & Chandon Rosé.

Not feeling much like tea, I ordered the lobster salad with a glass of sparkling water, non-vintage, like the Moët & Chandon.

"I love coming here." Raisa smiled. "Maybe because it's Russian. I come alone and watch as I eat. Do you like to eat alone? Many people feel embarrassed to eat alone."

"I love eating alone," I confessed. "There's serenity in it. I can focus on the food and no one else."

She nodded in agreement.

We clinked our glasses, her pink champagne with my plain sparkles.

"How are Harald Wiberg and Silas Haagen involved?" I asked as we waited for our food.

"When Noor discovered what was going on she talked to Haagen. He told her he'd look into it, and then she heard nothing. She then used Copenhagen Bank's anonymous speak up platform. Next thing she knows, she's being asked about career development and how would she'd like her next step to be in London so she could be close to her family." Raisa took a long sip of her champagne.

"And then someone threatened her." I offered.

"Yes. She gets invited to a meeting with Harald Wiberg, who scares the living daylights out of her. She's on a visa, she's not an EU citizen, she's a British citizen, blah blah. She gets scared, and then reaches out to me. We decide that she'd collect all the proof she could, and then quit, go back to London. A week after that conversation, she was...*gone*."

The server brought our food and explained all the delicacies on the various towers of Raisa's afternoon tea. Cucumber and smoked salmon sandwiches, caviar with blinis, small cakes of various kinds and, of course, green mint tea.

My food was easier to explain. Butter poached lobster with a beetroot salad. It would go very well with a Sauvignon Blanc, I thought, maybe something from the Loire. They refilled my water, and I made do with it.

"Did she find any proof?" I asked.

"Yes. She did a thorough analysis of all the non-resident accounts in the bank, and listed all those that were bogus. I have those and I can share them with you. That should trigger an investigation if sent to the Danish police, but I wanted to wait until we had more. I wanted the people behind those accounts and those who were helping to launder money. *And* I didn't trust the Danish police," Raisa explained. "Maybe…if I hadn't waited…."

I put my hand on hers. "They'd still have killed her."

"Yes. And, if I'm not careful, they'll kill me."

"Maybe once you write the story, you'll be harder to kill."

She grinned. "I'm already harder to kill."

I liked her. Despite all that she'd experienced, she still had faith in the universe that it would work out, that she would find justice and write her story.

"I feel they killed Nikita…no, I *know* they killed Nikita because he talked to me," she stated. "I couldn't do anything about that. I couldn't do anything about Noor. A part of me thinks I should stop and just live this new life that I have.

It's a good life. I have a nice place. Good colleagues. A whole new identity. But another part knows that Raisa Chaban wouldn't be who she is if she doesn't tell this story, because Nikita and Noor trusted me, and I don't want to fucking let them down."

I understood her sentiment well.

"I'll help you," I promised.

"What you need is someone who will talk. Harald and Silas won't, but I think Maksim Lõhmus is ready," she stressed.

"Why?" I cut into a luscious butter-drenched piece of lobster.

"Maksim likes to gamble, and he spends equal amounts of time at the Olympic casino and private card games," she revealed. "He owes many people a lot of money."

"So, he's desperate."

"Yes, and I think he's hoping to make a deal with the Estonian or Danish government to save his life. He'll tell them what's going on, if they'll keep the Russian mafia, who he owes money to, off his kneecaps."

"Or he could get more money from Copenhagen Bank—"

"He may try that, but I think that money train has reached its final station. This is not the first time Harald Wiberg has bailed him out. Right now, with all the speculation and American investigation into money laundering, they may find it easier to silence Maksim than pay him off," she specified.

"Maksim Lõhmus could very well be the next person to succumb to Sudden Russian Death Syndrome," I pondered.

"He's going to be in Copenhagen next week, and I think you should meet him, convince him to become a whistleblower, that this is the only way for him and his family to make it out of this alive."

"Okay," I agreed, though I had no clue if I'd succeed. I finished my salad and watched as she picked the next small cake on her tea tower to sample.

"You want one?"

I shook my head.

"I'll send you all the details."

"Do you think they have access to my email?"

"If you were stupid enough to allow a Trojan into your computer," Raisa speculated. "But we won't be using email."

"No?"

She helped me download some obscure chat software onto my phone and promised it was the most secure way for us to communicate. Since she had more to lose than me, I would do whatever she needed me to do for her to feel safe.

As we got ready to leave the restaurant, I asked, "How did you know my room number and how did you get into my room?"

"I can't tell you all my trade secrets," she grinned. "Let's say that I know someone at the hotel, and I had help."

"Can this person also help you get the list of all guests who stayed at the Mandarin Oriental this week?"

She narrowed her eyes.

"I'm testing a theory?"

"What?"

"The one that is *unbelievable*."

I didn't reveal more than that, mostly because I felt like an idiot telling a big-time journalist like Raisa Chaban that I was chasing names of jazz musicians to find *The Ghost*, who I now called Charlie. It was enough to make a grown man feel like a teenaged conspiracy theorist.

CHAPTER 43

Wednesday Night, October 19, 2023

According to the Mandarin Oriental guest information that Raisa sent to me through the secure software she installed on my phone, a Charlie Turner, with an address in Hartford, Connecticut, stayed at the hotel for one night, and had checked out this morning. The address he gave was that of a Walmart in Hartford.

I was now convinced that Charlie was *my* ghost, and that he had followed me from Copenhagen. Since I'd made plans to stay an extra night in a hurry, he was gone, while I was still here.

"I got the job," Afsana was breathless on the phone. "I got it. I'm going to be a sous chef at a two-Michelin star restaurant."

"That's amazing." I was walking to La Grenouille, one my favorite French restaurants in New York. I could already taste their three-cheese French onion soup and, even though it would be perfect with an acidic, earthy, medium-bodied gamay from Beaujolais, I would make do without the wine.

"I really like the chef here, Gabriel," she gushed. "And the food. If you're in San Francisco, promise to come."

"Absolutely." I wanted to ask but didn't; I didn't want to mislead, and waited instead for her to tell me when she'd be leaving.

"I start in mid-November. I was thinking of leaving Copenhagen in a couple of weeks. I can then spend some time at home in London, before going to San Francisco to find a place and…all that."

"Congratulations, Afsana." I felt a small gnawing feeling in my chest. The good ones always left. Leila went to Brussels with her soon-to-be husband, and Afsana was going to become a famous chef with Michelin stars attached to her name.

But you like it like this, I heard Ilse, my therapist's voice in my head. *And if Afsana was staying, how long would it last before you helped her leave you?* A month? Two? Maybe I wouldn't want her gone, I chastised Ilse. Maybe I wanted her to stay and do that *relationship* thing everyone talked about. Maybe not.

"I'm back on Saturday," she said. "And…I was thinking of moving out of the hotel until I leave."

"Yes," I whispered, answering her unasked question. I'd just met this woman and yet, I irrationally wished we had longer. She had such a zest for life that it buoyed me whenever I was with her.

"You don't mind?"

"Not at all. I'll make room in my closet for you. I'll even let you use my toothpaste."

I could feel her smile.

"What are you doing on your last night in the Big Apple?"

I told her, and the world traveler that Afsana was, she knew La Grenouille and told me I must not leave the restaurant without having their classic choice of soufflés. "The passion fruit is especially amazing, but really all of it, the pistachio, espresso...vanilla, *incroyable*."

A*mazing*, I thought as I ate the soufflés later that evening. Afsana Mallik was *incroyable* indeed.

Chapter 44

Friday Morning, October 21, 2023

"Even for you, Eskola, arresting me at the airport? Handcuffs? That's a bit much." I flexed my now-free wrists.

"It's standard procedure," she grinned widely.

Tommy had texted me before I left New York that Eskola would be waiting for me at the airport. What he didn't know was that the FBI had been waiting for me at JFK to have a *conversation*, which we had in a backroom of JFK.

They threatened me, I condescended them. It was a nice conversation.

The good news was that I was upgraded to business class. The bad news was that I would be handed over to Danish authorities in Copenhagen by the marshal on the plane.

Eskola had no reason to arrest me. Not really. She knew that. I knew that. She knew I knew that. *But* here we were in a bleak interrogation room in the NSK building with a metal table and two chairs.

"I want my lawyer." I sat down on a chair.

"Your lawyer has a broken leg, let's let him rest," Eskola muttered as she sat across from me and opened a file.

"I want a lawyer."

She sighed.

"*Lawyer*." I repeated.

"Fine, I shouldn't have had you arrested, but you pissed me off. How come you didn't tell us about Noor's phone. *And*, as if that's not bad enough, you give it to the US Secret Service? Where the fuck is your loyalty?" she demanded.

"Lawyer."

She picked up her phone and dialed. "Can you come by? Præst is being a downright git."

They gave me a bathroom break, a coffee, and a croissant—in that order—as we waited for who I suspected was Tommy.

"She had me arrested," I protested when Tommy asked me to shut the fuck up about a lawyer.

"Do you know what you've done? You've triggered a cluster fuck with the Danish PET, FE, the NSK, the US Secret Service, the FBI and, for some reason that I am not quite clear about, the Europol," he thundered. "So, don't be a d ick."

I shrugged. *Europol? What the fuck?*

"I need an apology for the arrest. I was *humiliated* at the airport."

Tommy kicked me under the table.

"What?" I looked at him with mock innocence.

Eskola glowered. "I do not know why this asshole is your golden boy, Frisk—"

"Fine, I'll behave," I interrupted. Fun was fun, but I really needed a shower, and I wanted to get back to my case. "What do you want to know?"

"Start from the start and don't miss any important details," Eskola advised.

I shook my head. "Look, Eskola, none of us has time for this—"

"I have all the time in the world," she cut in.

"What the fuck do you want to know? Asking me about the history of the earth will not get you anywhere."

"Why did you give Noor Mallik's phone to Cézar Doucette?"

"First, I didn't know it was Noor's. I got it from a search of her flat, which I did with her cousin's permission. I gave it to Cézar because he's helped me with such matters in the past. I didn't know he was US Secret fucking Service."

"He's FBI...we think," Tommy pointed out.

"And what did the phone tell you?" Eskola prodded.

I shook my head. "Ask Cézar because it didn't tell *me* anything. I gave it to him, remember?"

They both looked at me like they would a kid with his hand in the cookie jar, saying he didn't know *who took the cookies from the cookie jar.*

"I can't," I finally admitted. I would not say Raisa Chaban's name. Her life was in danger, and there weren't enough favors anyone could cash in with me for me to mention her in relation to this case.

"You *won't*," Eskola remarked.

"Yes, I won't," I agreed.

"Why?" Tommy asked, genuinely curious.

I shrugged. "I made a promise, and someone's life could be in danger. Don't you think enough people around me have been hurt? Someone tried to fucking rape Afsana. Erik has a broken leg. I won't risk more people."

"I can throw you in jail—" Eskola threatened.

"No, you can't," I contended. "What else do you want to know?"

"How are Harald Wiberg and Silas Haagen involved in...whatever this is?" Eskola asked.

"I think they hired an assassin who makes murders look like accidents and suicide to silence Noor." I rotated my neck as I could feel a tension headache make its way up from the base of my neck. I'd been able to lie down, thanks to being upgraded to business, but I hadn't slept. I'd spent the eight hours of flight time contemplating my next steps, which I could get on with once I left NSK.

"And do you have proof of that?"

"The proof will have to be the testimony of the hitman."

"And he's just going to walk in and give it?" Eskola jeered.

"I do have proof that over 200 billion euros worth of money is being laundered through Copenhagen Bank Estonia."

Tommy and Eskola stared at me.

Tommy was the first to find his voice. "You have proof?"

I nodded. "And I'm going to get corroboration next week."

"I don't believe any of this." Eskola flung her hands up in the air and sat down. She looked at Tommy. "Do you believe any of this?"

"If anyone else was saying it, I wouldn't. But I know him, Eskola. He doesn't bullshit." Tommy looked me in the eye. "Is this hitman coming after you?"

I nodded.

"What's your plan?"

I smiled. "I'm going to catch him."

"How?" Eskola asked.

"I haven't figured that out yet."

Both Tommy and Eskola sighed.

Chapter 45

Friday Evening, October 21, 2023

"You're nuts. What do you mean you're going to catch *The Ghost*?" Clara demanded.

After dinner at Eymen and Clara's, we settled into our usual spot on their balcony. The glow of a gas lamp heater enveloped us in a warm, comforting embrace, warding off the evening chill.

"Let me get this straight: you're going to look at the guest list of all the five-star hotels in Copenhagen, and look for names of Polish jazz musicians," Eymen asked incredulously.

"Maybe some four-star as well," I wondered, and then shook my head. "No, he'll stay...my guess is at Hotel D'Angleterre, Hotel Herman K, Nimb, or Nobis."

Eymen sipped his port, an exquisite Niepoort Vintage 2007 that was deep purple and hit the palate with chocolate and licorice. I especially enjoyed it with the most stinky stilton or Danish blue cheese. I looked at the port longingly and spread some blue cheese on a cracker, ate it, and washed it down with coffee.

"And what will you do when you find him?" Clara wanted to know. "Go to his room and say, *Viola! Here I am*?"

"Something like that."

"I can get you the names," Clara offered. "I can just call *Far's* executive assistant. Lars is very resourceful."

"What did you and Johanne talk about?" Eymen asked.

"Oh yes, I heard that *Far* allowed Johanne and Elias to crash the party." Clara's eyes glittered with excitement.

"She said she'd help me bring down Harald Wiberg and Silas Haagen."

"She's a lovely lady." Clara brought her hands together. "Isn't she?"

"Lovely like a piranha," Eymen shuddered. "She gives me the creeps. She's always smiling and happy, and then poof, she ends someone's career."

"That's why she's lovely," Clara remarked. "So, Gabriel, what's next for you?"

I had several balls in the air right now.

Maksim Lõhmus would be in Copenhagen on Sunday night, and my job would be to convince him to testify against his colleagues. Maksim was staying at the Radisson Blu Scandinavia Hotel, arriving Sunday, and checking out Wednesday.

I had Nico and Flora working on the sexual harassment case, which would be tough to prove in a court of law. Such cases always were.

I'd given the documents Raisa had received from Noor to Eskola so they could start the very slow ball rolling to look into money laundering through the Estonian branch of Copenhagen Bank.

I had my plan, albeit unbelievable to some, to find Charlie and, through him, get the proof I needed to show that Noor was murdered.

Of all the balls in the air, it was the ball called "Charlie" that would be the one that would get me what I needed to solve my case. And that was the ball I was focused on.

"A man's got to do what a man's got to do," I said evasively.

"You're determined to get to *The Ghost*?" Clara was concerned.

"If I don't find him, I can't find what happened to Noor."

"Are you sure Noor didn't die by suicide?" Eymen asked.

I shrugged. "I have wondered, but now that know her a little, she doesn't seem the type. But then I know many types who don't seem like they ever could, and then one day they do."

Sitting next to me, Clara put her arm around my shoulder and dropped a kiss on my cheek. "You're going to clear all of this up. I know you will. I believe in you."

I leaned into her, taking comfort in the hug.

"Afsana is coming back tomorrow afternoon. She's going to stay with me until she leaves for London."

"Is that to keep her safe?" Clara asked.

"Yes," I confirmed, and then added, "And because…I think I'm going to miss her when she leaves."

"You barely know her," Eymen protested.

I sighed. "I know. There's something there. Or rather, there *could've been* something there if there was time.

"And you were a different person." Clara hugged me closer.

"Yep."

"You're so fucked up." Eymen finished his port, and rose. "I'm going to bed, children." He leaned in to kiss Clara on her lips.

"He's feeling sorry for me," I told Clara.

"I think he feels responsible because he brought Flora to you," Clara reminded him. "Maybe I should join him in feeling remorse because it was my idea, but I don't. This is exactly why I wanted her to go to you. Have you talked with her?"

I shook my head. "I'll check in with her and Nico shortly. They're working together. It gave Flora something to do, and you know Nico, she's militant about sexual harassment."

"You think Charlie is already in Copenhagen?" Clara asked.

I nodded.

"Then we'll go through the list of names and find the ones that are…names of jazz musicians. You know that sounds ridiculous, right?"

I grinned. "I know."

"But we'll go through the ridiculous list, and then you'll meet this Maksim guy and convince him to rat his buddies out. Easy peasy."

"Piece of cake," I agreed.

Chapter 46

Saturday Morning, October 22, 2023

I took Sophie for breakfast the following day at Kalaset on Vendersgade, which looked like it had come straight out of the sixties, with old-school radios on the walls and the décor to match. The little basement café was usually packed, and service personnel with bandanas and tattoos served guests their famous hot cocoa, which Sophie called dessert in a cup as it came with whipped cream, cherry coulis, melted chocolate, and marshmallows.

I locked my bicycle at the stand in Nørreport station, and walked to Kalaset. I wondered if Charlie was following me as I went down the stairs to enter the café. Sophie was already there and waved to me from a table by one of the low windows.

I gave her a hug and a kiss on her forehead before taking a seat across from her. She'd already ordered a carafe of coffee, and poured me a cup.

"How are you?"

"A little jet-lagged," I confessed. "It was hard to run this morning and go to Kæmpe and workout with Small Bo."

"I'm impressed that you're learning to fight." Sophie drank some coffee as she browsed the menu.

She looked more like Stine than me, all blonde hair and light skin, whereas I had brown hair and a darker hue—but we had the same gray-blue eyes. Hers shone with more excitement than mine ever could. When she was born, I'd been madly in love with her. As she grew up, my daughter became her own person, someone I was incredibly proud of.

I ordered poached eggs on a brioche bun with hollandaise, sauteed spinach, and prosciutto, while Sophie went rogue and ordered pancakes with poached eggs and prosciutto, served with hollandaise and lemon ricotta.

"I had a stack of diner pancakes with maple syrup in New York," I told her, recounting our trip to and from Princeton.

"I think he's back to being the Erik we all love."

"But then he's not as funny or fun."

Sophie grinned. "True. He's a total riot when he's off balance. He cusses and is sarcastic. But I prefer the sane version of him. I mean, we already have *mor*. I don't need Erik to fly off the handle like she does."

"How's university?" I asked as I almost always did.

"I think my name may get on a published paper," she said excitedly. "We are doing a study on how isolation negatively impacts workplace creativity. I've been talking to people who work remotely versus those who are hybrid and those who come into the office. We've done a qualitative study based on that analysis, and we'll do a quantitative study. I think that I/O is what I want to specialize in. Maybe do a PhD.

What do you think? I could go to the US, study under Adam Grant."

"I think it's an ambitious plan and if anyone can do it, you can."

Since Sophie studied psychology, I'd learned more about it. A few months ago, if someone had said I/O, I wouldn't know the acronym from my ass. Now, I knew it stood for industrial organizational psychology.

"Wouldn't that be amazing?"

I agreed it would be. But I was a father in love. Everything and anything Sophie did was amazing.

The server came with our food, and we talked as we ate.

"I think I'm dating someone," she told me after her meal.

"You think?"

"Well…I don't know, *far*. We've been spending time and having sex. We haven't articulated the dating part."

"Tell me about him."

"He's American."

"Ah, that's why the desire a Ph.D. in the United States?"

She smiled. "Maybe he's influencing me. His name is Jadyn McNair, and he's doing part of his PhD in neuroscience from University of Southern California on aging. He's here collaborating with Dr. Abrahamsen, who's a rock star. He received a three-million Danish kroner grant based on this cool study he did with rats."

"And where's Jadyn from?"

"Memphis."

"The land of BB King," I said.

"Most people would say Elvis."

"I was never a fan of The King...but BB King and Beale Street, my kind of place. I'm assuming Jadyn hasn't met your mother yet."

"I want to wait until I *know* I'm dating Jadyn before I mention him to *mor*. And I know you and Erik don't care he's black, but I think *mor* will need some time to accept that," Sophie elaborated.

"And how old is he?" I asked in mock seriousness.

She laughed. "Older than your girlfriend. He's twenty-seven."

I grimaced. "She isn't my girlfriend, and whatever she is won't be for long. She just got a job as a sous chef at a two-Michelin-star restaurant in San Francisco. She's leaving at the end of the month."

There was some pride in saying this about the woman I was seeing. Look how cool I am that a freaking Michelin-star restaurant sous chef wants to spend her time with me.

"How do you feel about that?" Sophie asked as the servers came to clear up our table.

"Good. She's coming back today. She's been staying at Hotel Skt. Petri, but she'll move in with me until she leaves."

Sophie raised her eyebrows. "Excuse me? Move in with you?"

"For one week."

"Wow! Do you think she'll come to your block party? I'm bringing potato salad. Everyone has repeatedly reminded me by email, text, and WhatsApp."

"I don't know if she'll make the block party. This is a way to keep her safe and...stop smiling, Sophie."

Her mischief gave way to fear. "Is she in danger? Are you?"

I told her what happened in New York and what had happened since then.

"They arrested you. How come I didn't know about this?" She was livid. "Tommy let them arrest you?"

"I don't think Tommy can control what NSK does, *skat*."

"*Far*, you never had a dangerous job before. I mean, the most dangerous thing that could happen was some disgruntled adulterous husband wanting to punch you because you ended his marriage. But since this summer...are you picking dangerous cases on purpose?"

I put my hand on hers. "No. This was a favor to Eymen and Clara to help a friend who was grieving and wanted to know why Noor died by suicide. She was afraid, and rightly so, that Silas Haagen was sexually harassing women who worked for him. I didn't expect this."

Sophie picked up my hand and kissed my knuckles. "I worry about you."

"I know."

"I also know that Bør sent someone to keep an eye on me," she continued. "You can't keep walking into situations where people are trying to hurt you."

"I promise I'm not doing it on purpose."

"But you don't mind it."

I turned my hand and took both of hers in both of mine. "I feel good about the work I'm doing. I feel good that I can help bring closure or justice. It balances out the danger for me. If it was easy, *skat*, everyone would do it. This is worth it."

"I'm proud of you, Far."

"And that makes it even more worth it," I said, feeling like I was Superman.

Chapter 47

Saturday Night, October 22, 2023

"I'm going to miss the sex," Afsana announced as she lay naked on my bed, the comforter partially covering her.

I'd just come out of the shower, marveling at the fact that my sink was taken over by Sisley and La Mer makeup and creams. My Sauvage body soap was ensconced between a bottle of Shu Uemura shampoo and conditioner. She was here for a week, but my house already smelled like Afsana.

"I'm happy to serve." I went into my closet to find clothes.

I had to play at Mojo, and Afsana was going to join me—first for dinner at Damindra, and then drinks and music at Mojo. Interestingly, since I told Clara and Eymen about that, they'd also decided to come watch me play.

While Afsana took a shower and got ready, I spent time in my office, going through some of the work that I had to do for other clients and hadn't been able to get to.

I'd almost canceled this evening, but I knew Bobby K would have my ass as this would be the second time this month that I'd be abandoning the band. Previously, I had an excuse, I was in New York, but now I was home and, although I was distracted, I didn't want to *not* play. This was my *out*, my meditation.

I was packing my Fender when Afsana came into my office, looking like a dream. She wore a black and white stripped woolen skirt with a sheer black blouse and a faux fur jacket. Her booties had enough inches that I knew we'd be taking a taxi to Damindra.

"You look dapper." She came to me and kissed me.

I wore a dark blue Saville Row suit with a blue vest with gold flowers, and a pair of black Brunello Cucinelli leather brogues.

I took her face in my hands and kissed her lightly. "You are beautiful."

"Thank you," she beamed. "I'm starving. Let's go."

We took a taxi to Damindra, which Afsana had mentioned as one of her top Japanese restaurants in Copenhagen. Since this was her last week in the city, I wanted to take her to some of her favorite places, not that I knew many of them. The fact was that I barely knew this woman, having met her a recently. And yet, there was *this* undeniable connection.

We ordered the elaborate *omakase*, the chef's menu. And while she drank warm sake and me water, we ate several courses of sashimi, nigiri, uramaki, futomaki, lobster tempura, and finally a Matcha tea dessert.

"What do your friends think about you dating someone as young as me?" she asked.

"They've taken some cracks at me," I admitted. "But they don't judge."

"Really?"

"Yes."

"And if it were one of your friends dating me?"

I grinned. "Then I'd take part in the crack taking, think he was a damn lucky bastard and reserve my judgment. What are you worried about, Afsana?"

"I don't really know," she confessed, using her chopsticks to toy with a slice of pickled ginger. "Or maybe I do. I want them to like me even though I'm leaving at the end of the week."

"They'll like you."

"You're sure?"

I nodded. "And they'll think I'm a damn lucky bastard."

"My insecurities are showing, aren't they?"

"If I was meeting people who were important to you, I'd feel insecure and wonder if they'd like me."

Conversation, thankfully, diverted away from the personal to the professional, and I told her some of what happened in New York. I didn't tell her about Charlie. I didn't want to burden her with that. He'd probably killed her cousin, and I wasn't sure how and even if I could bring *him* to justice. I could tell Afsana what *really* happened, but I wouldn't be able to give any kind of closure with a statement such as "and the killer is in jail for the rest of his life."

"It's sometimes too painful for my family to talk about Noor, so we just don't," Afsana told me. "If she didn't kill herself, and someone else...was responsible, it's hideous, absolutely horrible, and yet so much better. It absolves all of us for not knowing we needed to save her from herself."

"I'm so sorry."

She shook her head. "It's just...I know that there will always be a hole in my heart, which will never fill. No matter *how* she died, that she *did* is painful. Every year I will wonder, how old would she be now? When I get married, I'll think, who would she have married? When I have kids...."

I didn't have any words of comfort, so I didn't assuage. Grief came in waves, some days you were fine and others it crippled you.

She was silent as we walked the short distance on Løngangstræde to Mojo. I wanted to ask how I could help but I didn't. I learned a long time ago, you can be there, you can even distract, but you can never ease the pain of loss. As Sartre said, *"we cannot escape anguish, for we are anguish."*

When we reached Mojo, I nodded at Thomas who was by the door. "She's with me."

Thomas looked Afsana up and down appreciatively. "Damn, you have all the luck with the ladies."

I ushered Afsana in, and she stopped so suddenly that she stumbled into me. "You, okay?" I whispered in her ear.

She nodded, and then gave me an odd smile. "This place is a bit of a dive. I was...I don't know expecting something...more like you."

"Which is?" I drew her inside to find a table that could seat four.

"Sophisticated."

I stopped by a table and gestured that she should sit. "I'm a lot of things. Mojo is just as much of who I am as anything else."

"I don't really know you, do I?"

I leaned and brushed my lips against hers because she looked so forlorn, and I wanted to comfort. "There are facets to all of us and we're not always the same person, either. As Kierkegaard would say," I paused, and she smiled as I wanted her to, "most people are subjective toward themselves and objective toward all others, frightfully objective sometimes—but the task is precisely to be objective toward oneself and subjective toward all others."

"And what does that mean?"

"It means that we know each other enough objectively and subjectively," I explained. "For the time we've had, we've met each other well. Don't you think?"

She nodded. "There may be more beautiful times, but this one is ours."

I had mentioned that Sartre quote to her when we'd gone to the opera. And it touched me that she remembered.

"Go on and play. I'll try to not embarrass you in front of your friends." She was smiling again, telling me she was okay.

"*Skat*, I'm more worried about them embarrassing themselves and me in front of you, not the other way around."

Clara and Eymen came shortly thereafter, and I did a quick introduction before I went to warm up with the band.

That evening, Bobby K took us around Muddy Waters with *Cold Weather Blues*, Johnny Winter with *Everybody Blues*, Joyner Lucas with *Winter Blues* and the audience saw the pattern. Bobby K was feeling blue about the weather, and he wanted company.

"Baby, it's cold out there," he announced after the first few sets. "Please give it up for Nuru Kimathi on the drums, Valdemar Vong on the sax, John Reinhardt on bass, and our friend, who abandoned us earlier this week to spend time in the Big Apple, Gabriel Præst on the guitar."

"He's still pissed at me?" I sighed.

"Oh, yes, because we had that weird guy Larsen or Carsten whatever on guitar, and it was a fucking nightmare," Nuru said.

Valdemar took a sip of whiskey from his Starbucks coffee cup. "I thought Bobby K was going to kill Mortensen."

"His name is not Mortensen. It's Mads Madsen," John piped in. "At least I think it is."

"I'm pretty sure it's Mortensen," Valdemar confessed. "But I was on my third cup of coffee, if you know what I mean, so who the fuck knows." He held up his Starbucks cup that we all knew contained whiskey at *all* times.

"Regardless of his name, he was a shitty musician." Nuru started to slowly work the drums as Bobby K went straight to Blind Willie McTell's *Cold Winter Day*.

I watched Afsana as I played. She *was* too young for me, not *just* by age and definitely not by experience, as she was better traveled than I—it was *life* experience. She was still at an age where you fell in love, you gave yourself away without thought, with confidence and hope.

She got along well with Clara and Eymen, who were both older than her. She was versatile, I had to give her that. And I was even more impressed during the break when I went to their table.

"You found yourself a wine snob at an even higher level than you," Eymen said to me. "Not above Clara, though."

Clara punched him lightly on the shoulder. "She has good taste, like me."

"I don't know. A chardonnay is a chardonnay is a chardonnay. I don't care whether it comes from Santa Barbara or some little village in Bourgogne." Eymen knew his wine a lot better than he liked to admit.

"You know, Gabriel's father's girlfriend has a vineyard in Côte de Nuits. They make a very nice Pinot Noir," Clara remarked.

I pulled up a chair and sat next to Afsana, casually putting my arm around her, getting a feel for what it would mean to be in a regular relationship where you did that kind of thing. I had friends with whom I had this ease, Nico and even Freja, but I was not in a romantic relationship with them.

"She's leaving at the end of the week, Clara," I reminded my friends.

Afsana looked as if she were about to say, *I can stay a few more days,* but something about the way I looked at her said quite clearly that I didn't want her to stay a few more days. How could that change anything? *She could stay a lifetime,*

Gabriel, I heard Ilse in my head, *and it wouldn't change a thing.*

As Sartre said, "*loving someone is a huge undertaking. You have to have energy, generosity, and blindness. And there is that moment, right at the start, where you have to jump across the abyss; if you think about it, you won't do it.*" I thought about it a lot. I had never done it but once, and that had been enough.

CHAPTER 48

Sunday Evening, October 23, 2023

AFSANA TOOK A TAXI to Sapor, and I bicycled to Kalvebod Brygge to first meet Flora for a drink at the Radisson Blu Scandinavia bar, and then wait for Maksim Lõhmus to check in. I got to BusStop lobby bar earlier than Flora, which gave me time to go through a list of names Victor's executive assistant had sent. A very large list of names of all the people who had checked-in or had reservations at five-star hotels in Copenhagen for the week.

About ten names had promise. I highlighted them in the PDF file on my iPad. Some were names of Polish Jazz musicians, some were partial—and then there were a few names that were of American jazz musicians, partial and otherwise. I sighed. This was a *long* shot and, as Nico said, *unbelievable*.

Flora looked happier than I'd ever seen her. She wore thigh-high boots, with a little black dress.

"I have a date," she announced as she sat next to me at the counter.

Her blonde hair was soft and fell in curls, framing her face. She'd had it done. The makeup was subtle, the lipstick fire engine red, as were her nails.

"Lucky date."

She grinned. "You know, what I didn't realize when I was working? That every Sunday afternoon I'd get this feeling in my chest, this heavy coiled piece of lead that all but crushed me. Since I stopped working, that feeling is gone because, come Monday morning, I don't have to go to that shitty place."

"I can track that." I had felt the same way when I'd been fired from the Danish police force. I could never go back to having a regimented job. I liked my freedom. Granted, I had more freedom than most because my expenses were limited.

My house was paid off, so I had no mortgage. I had no car, so no debt there. All I had was renovations, which I mostly did myself and slowly, when I could afford it—and so I had the luxury to control my spending, depending upon the health of my business. The business health was good lately, so I was ready to invest in luxuries, like a new record player to replace my Victrola Jackson turntable, which had died an ignoble death when my living room had been firebombed. This time, I was steering clear of the antiques and going for something modern, like a Wrensilva.

"I love your friend Nico," Flora revealed after she ordered a gin and tonic.

I continued to nurse my bitters in tonic water. *Another week to go, Præst. And the dry month will be over. Hallelujah!*

"Flora, Noor was a whistleblower." I didn't want to dampen her mood right before a date, but she was paying the bills, and had a right to know where I was in my investigation.

She nodded. "What did she find out?"

I explained what I could about the money laundering crimes Copenhagen Bank was committing.

Flora shook her head. "I can't believe it."

"I've seen the evidence and now NSK has it. It's going to take time to unravel it all, but what I can tell you is that Noor most probably didn't commit suicide."

Flora drained her drink and signaled the bartender for one more.

"This is fucked up, Gabriel."

"Yeah. Do you know Maksim Lõhmus?"

Flora nodded. "Of course. Don't tell me he's involved?"

"Up to his neck in it, I'm afraid. Can you tell me about him? I'm going to meet him tonight."

"Maksim is ambitious. His wife is French, and she and their two kids spend more time in Paris than with him. I think they're separated but who knows. He's good at what he does. Made Copenhagen Bank a lot of money…well, now it seems like he was making money by laundering it, so I don't know what to think. He's motivated by reputation. Very conscious about what people think of him."

"So, he'd care that people thought he was corrupt or if he was the hero who helped bring down a money laundering operation?"

Flora's phone beeped, and she ignored it. "I think he would. But only for appearances' sake. It's like…you wear these designer clothes because it makes you feel good to wear them. He wears them so people can see he's cool."

"What makes you think I don't want people to think I'm cool?" I asked.

"You're way too cool for that."

I laughed.

Flora was thoughtful for a moment, and then she said, "Look, we set out to find out what happened to Noor. Well, now we know. Let's end it now before someone else gets hurt or worse."

I shook my head. "It's too late for that. And like I said before, you can stop paying me, but I have to see this through."

"What does seeing it through mean to you?"

"That I can prove to the authorities what happened," I replied. "It doesn't mean much without it. Right now, it's just innuendo. And that's not good enough."

"I understand. I'll keep paying you." She shrugged when I narrowed my eyes. "I can afford it. Trust me. Whoring for corporate pays well. I feel like such a shitty head of human resources. I didn't know any of this was happening."

"Few people did, Flora, that's why the bad guys are able to do it and have been doing it for a long time. These people are smart. They know how to hide."

Flora got her new gin and tonic and took a sip. "I believed, probably naïvely, that there were checks and balances in place."

I nodded.

She pushed her half-finished drink away, and stood up. "Just keep sending me the bills, Gabriel."

"Oh, I will." *I had a new turntable to buy.*

Chapter 49

Sunday Evening, October 23, 2023

I wasn't surprised Maksim picked the Radisson Blu Scandinavia for his stay, as it had a casino attached to it. He'd either come down for a drink or go to the casino to feed his habit, both of which worked for me.

I watched him check in.

Maksim Lõhmus was a middle-aged man with short, dark hair, and a prominent chin. He was average in height and build; and wore a sad gray suit without a tie. He looked tired. From what I had seen on YouTube and other websites, his facial expressions could be intense, and his demeanor was serious, sometimes even confrontational.

He checked into room 1912. I knew enough people working at the Radisson Blu that this was information I could find without going through Victor's assistant. Once he entered the hotel, I set my iPad aside and focused on him.

As I predicted, he was at the bar fifteen minutes after he'd gone up the elevators to his room. Enough time to hang his suit and dress shirts, and empty his toiletry bag in the bathroom. Evidence of the emptied toiletry bag was in the cologne that wafted through as he sat three bar stools away from me at the bar.

He ordered a Macallan and asked the bartender about the casino, also as I had predicted.

Gabriel Præst, super sleuth!

They were a few people scattered across the bar this late in the evening. I moved bar stools to sit next to Maksim, who gave me a questioning look.

"My name is Gabriel Præst." I held out my hand.

His eyes flickered with recognition. He shook my hand, his expression flinty.

"What can I do for you, Præst?" He pronounced my name correctly, which was nice after all the times in New York where everyone got it wrong and called me *Priest*.

"You can talk to me about how Copenhagen Bank is laundering vast amounts of money for the Russians through your branch in Estonia."

He wasn't expecting the direct question and was taken aback.

"Excuse me?"

I shrugged. "I know you're here to see if Copenhagen Bank will bail you out one more time with your gambling debts. Knowing Harald Wiberg, that is probably not happening. I predict that you're close to becoming the next victim of the Sudden Russian Death Syndrome. I wonder if you'll die by suicide or accident. What do you think?"

He downed his whiskey. He was not moved by my little speech, and I admired a man who could keep his face as expressionless as Maksim was.

"It looks like you think you're some big shot but you're just a shitty private detective. Now, if you don't mind—"

"But I do mind," I hissed. "Maksim, stop being an asshole and let's talk. I can help you. I may not be a big shot, but I have access to several big shots. From a member of the Copenhagen Bank board to the chief of police, and even the current Secretary General of NATO; my reach is remarkable."

I felt insincere dropping all those names, but if contacts couldn't be used at a time like this, when could they?

He shifted uncomfortably on his barstool.

"They're going to kill you, Maksim," I whispered. "*The Ghost* is right now in Copenhagen."

"What do you know about *The Ghost*?"

Here goes nothing, I thought. "Harald and Silas hired him to get rid of Noor. Then they sent him after me. He's still here, waiting for a chance to help me into an ICU or a coffin, either will work for him. You go to Copenhagen Bank tomorrow and tell Harald that you want money or else, and you won't live to see the next day. You know that."

Maksim rose. I wondered if I needed to take a defensive stance. I didn't want this guy to throw a punch at me in the lobby bar of a hotel.

He smirked as he took his suit jacket off. He threw it on the counter next to him, and sat down again. His white dress shirt had sweat marks.

"Lay out your plan," he challenged me.

"You tell me what you know, and I get you protection. I'll have NSK guarding you day and night." I did not know if I could do this, but he didn't know that, and I'd figure it out if it came to it.

"No Danish police. I don't trust them. Wiberg has a long reach."

He wasn't an idiot, I thought. Harald Wiberg probably did have a long reach.

"And no one from the Copenhagen Bank board. One of them, I know for sure, is complicit."

"Who?"

Maksim shook his head.

I wondered if Johanne Juhl had set a trap for me, and it was her mother who was working with these assholes. Knowing her husband, entirely possible. "Ingeborg Hjorth?" I asked.

His confused expression told me that Johanne's mother was not the board member Maksim was worried about.

"No, not her. It's…Svend Bæk," he revealed as if giving up.

I remembered Bæk's profile from my study of all things Copenhagen Bank. He was sixty-three years old, came from old money, and his last job before he joined the Copenhagen Bank board was as Vice Chairman of the Finance Association at Copenhagen Bank. There had been a small scandal about a DUI some years ago—but that had had little impact on his reputation.

"How about Interpol? You trust them?" I knew absolutely no one at Interpol, or was it Europol in Europe? My knowledge was limited. I'd have to reach out to Johanne Juhl for her help, as Victor had predicted.

"I trust no one. I don't even trust you."

"I understand. Should we take this to your room?"

He nodded, and I paid the tab for both of us.

He had a suite. Of course, he did.

He opened the mini bar and emptied a mini bottle of Glenlivet into a glass. He looked at me enquiringly and I shook my head as I put my Tumi messenger bag with my iPad on the sofa by the bar.

"When did it start?" I asked, sitting down, hoping to make him comfortable because he was as jittery as Lucifer in a church.

Maksim gave a short, harsh laugh. "It was *always* going on, since Finba, since before Copenhagen Bank. Nikita Poletov was pushing us...the finance ministry, to stop letting Russians use our banks to launder money. Those days, Russians were trying to be honest. Now they're not even pretending. Copenhagen Bank was happy to be discouraged from applying their compliance regulations in Estonia, though in truth, it probably wouldn't have made a difference. Money is right now being laundered through the Copenhagen branch."

I was glad I'd turned on my phone's recording app because there was no way I could remember everything without taking notes.

"What about Harald Wiberg and Silas Haagen?"

Maksim finished his drink and looked for another bottle of something. This time it was Johnny Walker Black. He downed that and looked at me, flustered.

"Silas is an idiot. He just wants to fuck some employees and Harald lets him. Harald is the one. You understand? He's the one who's running this."

Oh, I understood that just fine, and from the start. Silas was a dilletante, Harald was the puppet master.

"Harald works directly with Moscow. I don't know with whom." His hands were shaking suddenly. "Telling you all this is going to get me killed."

I shook my head. "Gambling both with money and your integrity is going to get you killed. Telling me, might get you saved."

"Harald is protected. He does nothing himself. Nothing in writing. He conducts his business face-to-face," Maksim continued. "And if he wants something done that requires anything in writing, he gets Silas to do it."

"Like what?"

"Like signing documents that permit us to ignore SOX compliance in Estonia. Between Silas and Svend...and some other Copenhagen Bank lawyers, who keep changing, Harald keeps his hands clean." Maksim didn't like Harald, and

I didn't blame him, that man was definitely a puss boil on society.

"Who is the conduit to *The Ghost*?"

Maksim shook his head. "*The Ghost* is…fuck, there's only way to contract with him and that's face-to-face. He wants to know who you are and who you want killed. And then *The Ghost* decides if and how he'll do it."

"How does he get paid?"

"A Swiss bank account. There are many ways to hide money."

"Do you have proof of this?" I asked.

"Some. But like I said, Harald knows how to protect himself." Maksim sat down suddenly in an armchair. "I'm going to fucking die."

I felt for the man. But then I thought about Lucya Poletov who was convinced that Maksim had caused her husband's death. "Tell me about Nikita Poletov."

Maksim rubbed his face with his hands and looked at me. All his *chutzpah* was replaced by fear and a weary resignation.

"What's there to tell?"

"How did you set him up?"

He flashed me with a look of sheer pain. I ignored it. I was doing this for Lucya Poletov. I could give her this. A confession, so that Nikita's old man wouldn't feel the need to carry a gun at all times, scaring his family and himself.

"Nikita came to talk to me before he went to Copenhagen for a conference. He told me he knew what was going on with non-resident Estonian accounts, and he wanted it stopped. After that conversation, I called Harald Wiberg and told him. He told me to shut up and stay put, behave like nothing happened. A few days later…well, you know what happened."

Maksim stood up and went up to the window to look at the Copenhagen city lights.

"You believe Harald Wiberg was responsible for Nikita Poletov's murder?" My fingers were tingling with the desire to check my phone to make sure all this was being recorded. But I didn't want to spook Maksim.

"*I* was responsible. If I hadn't told Harald, Nikita would be alive. We'd have shut down the money laundering and—"

"You'd still be gambling, Maksim," I reminded him. "You'd still be up shit creek without a paddle, as you are now."

Maksim nodded and turned to face me. "What happens now?"

"Now, I call the cavalry and put you under protection."

"Right now?" Maksim asked.

"Yes," I said.

"No. I need to talk to my family and make sure they're safe, then I'll talk to the authorities. Until then, our conversation never happened."

"You know your life is in danger, right?" I was incredulous.

"The police come here, then everyone will know I'm talking. Not until my family is safe, Præst."

He was looking at me like *I* was supposed to keep his family safe. *How the fuck was I supposed to do that?*

"It may already be too late. What if someone saw us talking downstairs?"

"What if? You've been talking to everyone. Means nothing."

Well, that was a vote of confidence for my private investigator skills.

"You assure me my family is safe, and I will tell you anything you want, and I'll stand in court…or wherever you want," he vowed.

"Okay." I rose and donned my bag crossbody.

He came up to me. Looked me in the eye. "You'll make sure my family is safe."

"Yes."

Stop making promises, Præst, especially those you have no idea how to keep.

Chapter 50

Sunday Night, October 23, 2023

I met Johanne Juhl, per her instructions, at her apartment on Strandgade in Christianshavn, just a stone's throw away from the canals. I knew the Juhl's had a house in Klampenborg, but they kept an apartment in the city for convenience, especially when they were traveling.

The historic building had been completely renovated, and had large windows overlooking Wilders canal, with a bright kitchen-dining area where we sat at a counter. A *Morsø* wood-burning stove elegantly warmed the dining area, though not in the most environmentally friendly manner.

The living room was through the dining area and looked majestic, with gray painted walls, original abstract art, Dannebrog windows, and high wall panels.

"Elias is in Brussels," she informed me as she made me a cup of coffee in a De'Longhi machine. She was drinking a *very* nice Châteauneuf-du-Pape, which made me want to break my dry month.

The Clos du Caillou Chateauneuf-du-Pape Reserve Cuvee Unique 1998 was an outstanding bottle of wine, the kind you wanted someone else to buy for you because I rarely drank a two thousand kroner bottle of wine on a Sunday night.

"That's a good bottle of wine," I remarked.

"Would you like some?"

I shook my head.

"I had a friend over for dinner and we were having steak, so it seemed appropriate to open something nice from the cellar."

My cellar was a wine fridge in my kitchen that could hold about thirty bottles of wine, beyond that, my wine cellar was the wine store Kjær Sommerfeldt in Gammel Mønt.

Once I was settled with my coffee, and she with her perfect wine, she asked me how she could help me.

"Maksim Lõhmus is ready to come in and testify," I told her. "But he wants his family protected."

Johanne nodded. "What can he give testimony on?"

"Everything."

"Break it down for me."

And so, I did. It took a good two hours because she had many questions. I had to look up the transcribed audio recording, which I pretended were my notes. I would not share the recording with anyone until I had to.

I had had two cups of coffee, and the Clos du Caillou bottle was empty by the time we were done.

"Let me make some calls."

She went into what I thought was her office and closed the door behind her.

I had a sense of unease about leaving Maksim in his hotel room. I wished I could've brought him here with me. But he had been adamant about his family coming first, which I could understand. I knew Maksim had said no Danish police, but I trusted them, even if he didn't.

On impulse, I called Tommy.

"It's nearly fucking midnight. Who died?"

"I need a favor."

"Again?"

"I need you to send someone to keep an eye on a man in room 1912 at the Radisson Blu Scandinavia hotel."

There was a long moment of silence. "Who is staying there?"

"The head of Copenhagen Bank Estonia."

"And why does Maksin Lõhmus need protection?"

So much for being coy with Tommy, I thought ruefully.

"Just know his life is in danger. Don't ask me how I know, but I know. I'm right now...," I paused as I thought if I should tell him where I was, and then because I did trust Tommy, "at Johanne Juhl's apartment, and she's working the phone to make sure Maksim's family in Paris is protected. He won't come in until then."

"And you're worried someone might kill him in the meantime?"

"Yes."

"There's always drama with you." I could hear Tommy's exasperation. "How am I supposed to explain this? Eh? You know we can't just do things like send people around to protect people...." He trailed off.

"Tommy, I wouldn't ask if it wasn't—"

"Yeah, I know. I'll send someone," Tommy snapped, and hung up.

CHAPTER 51

Monday Morning, October 24, 2023

I KNEW AS SOON as my phone rang at five in the morning.

Afsana was dead to the world, fast asleep as I took the phone call and walked naked into my office.

"He killed himself," Tommy told me.

"No, he fucking didn't."

"There was a guy standing outside his room, Præst. And he was alive when I sent the man there. The hotel manager called the room and spoke to Maksim. But this morning...."

"How did they kill him?"

"He jumped out of the window, and there's absolutely no sign of anyone else helping him. I'm at the fucking scene, and I can assure you that he did himself."

"No." I was certain that the man I talked to wouldn't have killed himself. He was worried about his family. He'd make sure they were safe, and he would not die before he was certain they were taken care of.

"Come and have a look."

Tommy would never break protocol to ask me to a crime scene, but the fact he was, was evidence that Charlie had done an excellent job making Maksim's death look like suicide. But I had to see for myself, and so I took Tommy up on his offer.

I called Johanne Juhl and left her a voice message when she didn't pick up, telling her about Maksim and asking her to make sure his family was protected.

I then called Bør.

"Can you send someone to my place? Afsana is here and I have to go."

"You in trouble?"

"Maybe."

"Sophie?"

"I don't know."

"I'll send Small Bo. He knows you. He'll take care of your girl."

I changed quickly and sat on my bed next to Afsana. "*Skat*," I woke her up gently, and when she groggily opened her eyes, I smiled tightly.

"What's wrong?" Her eyes were wide open.

"I have to go," I whispered. "I want you to stay here. Small Bo is downstairs and—"

"What happened?" She sat up and cupped my cheek with her palm.

I felt a sense of desolation. I had gotten Afsana and Erik hurt, and now, Maksim was dead, probably because he talked to me. If I was a better detective and investigator, I'd have been able to protect these people.

"I'll tell you after I know more. You'll stay here?"

"Yes," she readily agreed, probably because she could see I was worried, and I was grateful that she didn't ask many questions.

I kissed her lightly.

"If I'm not back and you have to go to work, you go with Small Bo."

"Okay."

I kissed her again, and left.

I bicycled as quickly as I could to the Radisson Blu, and my lungs were burning by the time I got there. The police constable in the lobby directed me to the crime scene.

My heart broke slowly, pressured by guilt, as I walked around the building, going past the cops and hotel security.

I should've asked Tommy to insist the constable stay inside the room with Maksim. I should've insisted Maksim come with me to talk to Johanne.

They'd already put a tent over the body to prevent the elements from corrupting the evidence. I looked up at the building, determining the stories and the room that was Maksim's. The son of a bitch had pushed him out of the window.

They put crime scene tape around the area, but no one stopped me from going under it. Tommy was outside the tent, talking to the medical examiner. I walked up to him.

"Hey, Præst." Dr. Lise Pedersen, the ME, was friends with Tommy and his wife Nadia, and I had met her a few times socially.

I nodded. "I need to see him."

Lise looked at Tommy, who nodded.

"He talked to me, and then they killed him," I kept my voice low, but I felt like I was screaming to drown the clanging noise in my head.

"He jumped," Tommy tried to assure me.

Lise put her hand on my shoulder. "He left a note, Præst. Trust me—"

"I need to see him," I repeated adamantly.

"Fine." Tommy gestured toward the tent.

I hesitated for a moment as I extended my hand to lift the flap of the tent.

"You don't have to do this, Gabriel." When Tommy started using my first name, I knew it was serious.

"I don't have a choice."

"You always have a choice. You just choose the hard way, every fucking time," I heard him say as I went into the tent.

He fell headfirst, and the impact had cracked his skull open. Congealed blood surrounded his face like a halo. There was a contusion on the right side of his face, probably because of the way he landed. His left leg was twisted awkwardly beneath him. The bone at his elbow had shot through the flesh of his arm.

There was dried blood on his face, blood that had come out of his mouth. His skin was an ugly shade of blue and gray.

My knees wanted to give way, and I wanted to sink to the ground.

Maksim was a weak man who gambled, cheated, and was immensely corrupt. He was also a man who loved his family and wanted them safe. Flawed as he was, Maksim didn't deserve to die like this.

I grieved for a man I didn't know until I felt vomit rise up from my stomach. I went outside the tent, controlling myself so I didn't add body fluids to the mess inside. I took deep breaths to settle myself.

"Can I see his room?" I asked Tommy.

Tommy put a hand on my arm. "You're pale as a ghost, Præst. Go home—"

"I need to see his room and the fucking suicide note," I barked it out through a throat hoarse with unshed tears.

Tommy didn't argue and took my upstairs to room 1912.

"Forensics has not gone through the room. So, touch nothing," Tommy warned me at the door. "You have five minutes."

I nodded.

I walked in and saw the small empty liquor bottles next to the glass he'd been drinking from in front of me. His bed was not slept in. The window was open, pushed past the latch that should prevent it from opening fully. I looked at the window and noticed that some screws had been removed to make this happen. A Swiss knife lay on the coffee table that he'd used to climb up to the window.

It took me more than five minutes to look through the Maksim's room, but Tommy didn't object or even mention it.

"Suicide note?"

Tommy held up his phone to me. He had taken a photograph of the note.

"It's in Russian," I noted.

Tommy put his phone back in his coat pocket. "It's to his wife and children. He says he's sorry."

"He didn't kill himself." I was certain of it. "He wanted to protect his family and he wouldn't kill himself until he knew they were safe."

Tommy didn't entertain my suspicions. "Come on, let's go downstairs and you can tell me what's going on."

"Officially or unofficially?"

"You were the last man to talk to a high-profile suicide victim, Præst. This is fucking official," he told me.

We had the *official* conversation on the second floor in a meeting room the hotel had secured for this purpose.

Politikommissær Naja Andersen joined him. The police detective was a tall blonde woman, who had her hair up in a ponytail. She wore an elegant suit with sneakers, and a smile that probably drew men like bees to honey.

She shook hands with me, smiling widely. "I've heard so much about you," she beamed. "*Politiassistent* Freja Jakobsen is a friend."

I sat down, my faculties still not fully under control. Shock resonated through me, echoing like a loud clang in a silent room.

Tommy stood at the back of the meeting room, arms folded. His way of saying, this man is all yours *Politikommissær*.

"Why were you meeting Maksim Lõhmus?" she asked, her smile intact.

It was a nice tactic, I thought. It put people at ease.

"I was meeting with him to discuss a case."

"What case?"

"I've been hired to find out why Noor Mallik, an employee of Copenhagen Bank, died by suicide."

Naja made notes and, once in a while, nodded as if to herself. The dumb blonde tactic was a good one, too. Nico used it all the time when she interviewed people.

"Okay. *Wow*. And did you find out why she killed herself?"

I shook my head.

"I'm so sorry. It's always hard, isn't it with suicide? And here is Maksim Lõhmus killing himself. I can only imagine how upset you are. How did he seem when you talked to him?" She spoke earnestly, taking notes with meticulous care, as if dotting every *i* and crossing every *t*.

"Look, can you drop it?"

"Drop what?"

"The whole...," I shrugged. "I'm an ex-cop and a decent private detective, so I know every interrogation trick in the book. Here is what I will tell you about last night. I met with Maksim, he told me fuck all, and I left. Next thing, he killed himself."

To give her credit, she looked at me as if she were a wounded bird. "I can see you're upset. Even angry. I *absolutely* understand," she crooned.

I turned to look at Tommy, who was amused.

"Anything else?" I asked curtly. I was losing my patience, and anger surged through me. I needed to shut this down and now, before I did or said something I couldn't take back.

"Just a few more questions and you'll be on your way." She fluttered her fucking eyelashes at me.

I took my beanie off, because the meeting room was getting warm, and threw it on the meeting table. I then shrugged out of my leather jacket that I had put on in a hurry. I was wearing a pair of dark gray pants with sneakers and a T-shirt that I usually wore to paint my house in. It had stains on it.

"Fire away." I stood up and walked up to the coffee station. "Anyone want coffee?"

"I'll take one," Tommy said.

"Me too," Naja piped in.

I used the Nespresso machine to make three cups of coffee during which time no one spoke. I stood against the wall with my coffee and waited.

"What did you think Maksim Lõhmus could tell you?"

"You should talk to *Chefpolitiinspektør* Jorun Eskola at NSK."

She wrote that down, taking her time. "I certainly will."

"Does she ever break form?" I asked Tommy, incredulous that Naja Andersen continued to be cheerful and bubbly.

"Drives you up the wall, doesn't it?" Tommy said.

"Yeah."

"She's good."

I nodded in agreement. Naja smiled her thousand-watt smile. "After you spoke with Maksim, you called *Chefpolitiinspektør* Tommy Frisk. Why did you do that?"

I looked at Tommy and sighed. "Because I was worried that Maksim's life was in danger."

"Why?" Naja persisted.

I looked again at Tommy who stood stoic, unmoved.

"Because he was going to give evidence against Copenhagen Bank about money laundering in Estonia. I was worried someone might kill him. At no time was I worried that he'd kill himself. He was not suicidal," I emphasized.

"Oh, are you a psychologist?" Naja asked, and looked through her notes, as if searching for my credentials. "I see you have a Cand. Merc in Economics, not psychology."

"What else do you want to know?" I asked and looked at my watch like I was in a hurry, which I was. I needed to get away and get a fucking drink. *Fucking dry month!*

Naja craned her neck to look at my watch. "Rolex?"

"Omega."

"Very nice."

"Thank you."

I heard Tommy chuckle.

"And where did you go after you met with Maksim?"

"What was the time of death?" I asked and surprised her.

"We'll know once the ME—"

"What is Pedersen's preliminary conclusion?" I demanded.

"Between midnight and one," Tommy chimed in.

"And where were you between midnight and one?" Naja wanted to know.

I was *exhausted*, which was how Naja wanted me at, so I'd slip up and tell her more than I wanted. "As you know because I'm sure Tommy told you, I was having coffee with Executive Vice President of the European Commission Johanne Juhl."

"At midnight?"

"We're good friends."

"No, I meant, you were having coffee at midnight?" she mocked sweetly.

"It's my dry month, otherwise I'd have been drinking a very nice Clos du Caillou Chateauneuf-du-Pape Reserve Cuvee," I retorted.

"Why were you talking with her?"

"Like I said, we're friends."

"We will talk to her, Gabriel," Naja assured me.

"Knock yourself out. Are we done?" I put my empty coffee cup on the table. Put my jacket on, and my beanie. I picked up my messenger bag, and slung it across my chest.

"Yes. Thank you." Naja stood up and extended her hand to me.

I shook it.

"We'll reach out to you if we have further questions," she said politely.

I nodded at Tommy and walked out of the meeting room.

As I bicycled back home, Johanne called. "I heard about Lõhmus."

"They killed him, Johanne."

"It's not on you. His family is safe. I managed to get Europol to work with Paris Police Nationale," Johanne explained, and then, after a long pause, added, "I can't be officially involved."

"The police may come by; I told them we're friends."

She laughed. "Are we now?"

"Would you rather I told them the truth?"

"We *are* friends, Gabriel. Even if you don't like it. If you need anything else, let me know."

"Thanks."

I thought she'd hung up when she spoke. "You need to close this down."

"I know. I'm working on it."

Chapter 52

Monday Evening, October 24, 2023

He was at Hotel D'Angleterre.

Of all the names I'd looked through in all the lists, the one that I was convinced was Charlie was Krzysztof Komeda, who used to be a film music composer and jazz pianist, most known for writing the score for some of Roman Polanski's films, including the famous *Rosemary's Baby*. His album *Astigmatic*, which came out a few years before he died, is still considered one of the most important European jazz albums, as it changed the tone from American jazz to something entirely European.

I went to Kæmpe that evening after Afsana went to work with Small Bo. I hadn't worked out in the morning, thanks to rushing to the Marriott.

I used the treadmill when I got in, and then went to the boxing bag. By the time I finished sparring with Bør and had my ass handed to me in fifteen different ways, I was sweating and feeling every bone and muscle in my forty-one-year-old body.

As we sat on a bench in the locker by the boxing bag, drinking water, Bør, to my embarrassment, was barely winded and he'd been through the same workout as me.

"I'm going to meet him tonight," I told Bør.

"How?"

"I know where he is and I'm going to see him."

"And say what?" Bør asked.

"I'm going to play it straight."

"Can you?"

"Play it straight?"

"Yes," Bør muttered. "Because you're getting into one fucked up mess after another."

"I need to shut this down."

"Hopefully, you don't get shot this time."

"Hopefully," I agreed.

I told him my plan, and he grunted in disbelief when I was done. "You're just going to buy this asshole a drink at Marchal?"

"It's a nice restaurant and conveniently located in D'Angleterre."

Bør shook his head. "Fine. I'll be there."

"No. He knows you. Send someone else."

"No deal."

"Bør, you can't be there. You can't carry a weapon. You can't get caught. Malte will murder me." Bør's husband was an advertising executive, now, but in his time, he'd been a fighter and could beat the crap out of me, even though he was shorter and older than me.

"Malte would be here, if I'd let him," Bør said. "You know he loves you. I can't sit this one out. I won't. This is too dangerous."

"You stay in the bar. You don't carry a gun."

"Sure," Bør said. I knew he was lying. He knew I knew he was lying.

"Will you be carrying?" he asked.

"No." I wiped the sweat off my bald head with my towel, and rose. "What's the point? I can't win a gun fight with a man like him. I'm going to talk to him. I need him. He doesn't need me."

"He just wants to kill you."

"No. He wants to hurt me...or rather wants me to lay off this investigation. And now it's too late. The investigation has blown up. I need him to tell me what happened with Noor. That's all."

Bør groaned, "That's all? You want an assassin to tell you how he killed someone. Man, Præst. You're a piece of work."

"You take care of Sophie and Afsana. I'll take care of myself."

"I can take care of them *and* you." Bør squeezed my shoulder. "You do what you need to do. I got your back."

Chapter 53

Monday Evening, October 24, 2023

Despite what Bør thought, this would not be a dangerous situation. I knew in my gut that Charlie had had many opportunities to kill me and hadn't. I didn't know why. I didn't care why. All I wanted was to have a conversation with him.

At Hotel D'Angleterre, I asked the concierge, someone who I'd known for years, to hand deliver a note to the room of Krzysztof Komeda. The note was printed and simple. It listed the names of all his aliases that I knew of with an invitation to meet.

Charlie Turner, Zygmunt Karasinski, Henryk "Papa" Majewski, Tomasz Stanko, Adam Makowicz. Drinks at Marchal. Now.

I waited for three hours, as did Bør, neither of us drinking alcohol, and then gave up.

"Maybe it wasn't him," Bør suggested.

I shrugged disappointed. "I was so sure."

"You want me to get you home?"

I shook my head. "If he's following me...I want him to follow me. I need to...."

"Dude, this guy will kill you." And with that reassuring comment, we parted ways.

I felt a sense of dread fill me as I bicycled. I hadn't found *The Ghost*. I wouldn't be shutting this down. Eskola's investigation would take years. Nico's story would result in nothing more than Silas Haagen getting fired. Raisa Chaban wouldn't get her story for a long time. In the meantime, Harald Wiberg would get away, retire with millions of Danish kroner that he could luxuriously spend at a beach in the Cayman Islands.

It was ten at night when I got home. Afsana wouldn't be back until two in the morning, as was rote.

I threw my house and bicycle keys in a wooden basket I kept in the entrance, and was contemplating breaking my alcoholic fast. I was going to in a few days, anyway, how would a day or two, here or there, matter. And I'd smoke a fucking cigarette.

The kitchen light was on. I saw the opened bottle of wine first. "Oh, come on, that's a five thousand kroner bottle of wine I've been saving for an occasion," I muttered unhappily.

The bottle that *Charlie* had confiscated from my wine fridge and opened was a prized 2002 Lafite Rothschild, Pauillac.

Charlie who looked nothing like the men I had seen in New York, wore a pair of jeans and a black sweater. His hair was brown, stylishly fluffed up. His eyes were brown as well.

I couldn't place his age, face, or nationality, except that he was white. Or maybe Latin.

He stood at my kitchen counter, facing the living room. He raised his glass of wine.

"It's a beautiful bottle of wine." He spoke fluent Danish, like he was born and raised in Copenhagen. He'd spoken English with a Brooklyn accent when he was Charlie, and an Eastern European accent when he was Zygmunt Karasinski at the Met.

"Yes, I know."

"You don't have any music in your house, Gabriel."

When I looked at the small Bose speaker, he snorted.

"I'm in the process of replacing my record—"

"Ah, yes, the Molotov cocktail. You seem to know Polish jazz well."

"I like all blues and all jazz."

"Any Polish favorites?"

"Zygmunt Karasiński's *Jazz Jamboree '85 Vol. 2*."

He winced. "So, you knew at the Met."

"Yes," I said with more confidence than I'd had at the Met.

"I'm here. What can I do for you?"

"You can help me get Harald Wiberg."

He chuckled and sipped my good wine. "You sure you don't want to end your dry month, Gabriel?"

"I'm sure." Especially now when I have a professional fucking assassin in my house. I wouldn't touch alcohol with a gun to my head, *especially* with a gun to my head.

"Why should I help you?"

I ignored him, and continued, "And I want you to tell me what happened with Noor Mallik."

"Again, why should I?"

I smiled. "Because I found you."

He laughed this time. "I heard you have a dry sense of humor. I could kill you right here, right now, and finish this nice bottle of wine."

"It's too messy," I said with false bravado. "And then you'll have Tommy Frisk, Victor Silberg, Johanne Juhl, and half the fucking motorcycle gangs in Copenhagen on your ass."

"You think you're that important?"

"I know I am."

He poured himself some more wine. "This is not the best Lafite I've had, but it's in the top five."

"Your line of work pays well." I was wearing a suit, full uniform, so I took my jacket off and loosened my tie, and sat down on a barstool at the kitchen counter, facing him.

"This one is," he took a deep breath, "crushed berries, spices, and tobacco. Full-bodied, and the tannins are fucking velvet. You'd expect it to not have any fruit since it's twenty years old, but it does. This is what you'd call an elegant but wild bottle of wine."

Asshole!

"Are you going to help me?"

He shrugged. "What happens if I don't?"

"I found you once, I'll find you again. This time I'll find you with some people from the Danish and even the US government."

He nodded appreciatively. "I like a man with confidence. You got lucky once, Gabriel, you won't get lucky again."

He was right.

"How do you know I don't have someone waiting to arrest you right now?"

"Because that's not what you want," he said easily. "And arrest me for what? I've done nothing. I'm Krzysztof Komeda, a pharmaceutical investor traveling to Copenhagen for a seminar about affordable insulin. It's a polished identity."

"Then why the fuck are you here drinking my prized bottle of Lafite?"

"Professional courtesy."

"How far does this courtesy extend?"

He nodded. "This *is* a very nice bottle of wine."

"It's a fucking outstanding bottle of wine." I leaned over and picked up the cork to smell it, and sighed.

"I have a meeting with Harald Wiberg in two days."

"Okay."

"And I'll tell you where it is, and you can get your friends in Europol...I am assuming they're the ones who coordinated security for Maksim's family? Though they can stop doing that. I haven't been contracted to do them. And I don't like to harm families, which doesn't mean I won't." When I didn't respond, he nodded as if to himself. "In any case, you can ask Europol or PET or whomever else you're working with to join our meeting...ah...surreptitiously, of course."

"Won't you be incriminating yourself?"

He smiled. "And who am I, Gabriel?"

"Point taken." I looked longingly at the bottle of Lafite as he poured himself one more glass.

"Did you kill Noor?"

He shrugged. "I don't *actually* kill anyone, Gabriel. I am the gun, not the gunman. Harald Wiberg and Silas Haagen contracted me to kill her, *quietly*. And they wanted me to dissuade you from your investigation, *quietly*. They didn't want you to dead for the same reasons you mentioned I shouldn't kill you. But if you ended up in a hospital, that would not be too bad. While I was figuring out how to do that, the fuckers got impatient and hired someone else who botched it here in Copenhagen, and then botched it again in New York."

"And Maksim?"

"He was convinced to make the right choice to protect his family," he said with no emotion at all.

"And he believed you?"

"Yes. I always keep my word. His family is safe."

"How did he open the window?"

Charlie shrugged. "Maksim always carried a Swiss knife. A gift from his father. He even got it through airport security in his carryon...can you believe that?"

Since I knew much of airport security was theatre to make people feel safe rather than actually keep them safe, I believed it.

"And Noor?" I asked. I remembered her from her photos and felt a pang. She was so young. So beautiful and naïve. She had courage and integrity. She didn't deserve to die.

"She took too many pills, Gabriel," Charlie breathed. "Do you really need more detail?"

Did I need to know more? Maybe. But I wasn't sure what I'd do with that information. Telling Afsana and her family would only hurt them. The details didn't matter. She was gone because someone had wanted her dead.

"You didn't convince her?"

"She fell asleep. There was no…how do you say, violence, pressure, or manipulation of any kind."

"And the note she left?" I persisted.

He smiled then, and a shiver ran up my spine. This was not a good man. "I can't tell you all my trade secrets, now, can I? You can tell your girlfriend her cousin didn't suffer. She didn't even know it happened. I'm *that* good."

One thing was clear, he took pride in his work, as grotesque as his work was.

"And you can prove that Harald Wiberg and Silas Haagen hired you?"

"Yes. I'll make sure they confirm it during my meeting with them." I didn't have his confidence. I also was not an assassin.

"Okay."

"Let me understand this, you want to bring down Harald Wiberg and Silas Haagen, but you don't want *me* for Noor and justice?"

"Like you said, you are the gun. I want the guys who pulled the *actual* trigger."

He nodded and drank some more of my wine. "I give you the *trigger pullers* and I walk away. Is that a deal?"

He was probably going to walk away no matter what. "Yes."

"Okay, Gabriel, then we have a deal."

This seemed like a man who kept his word, which was incongruous for a man who was as morally flexible as Charlie had to be to do what he did.

"You're a pretty good musician," he surprised me by saying.

"You're mediocre."

"I know. I don't seem to have enough time to practice."

"So many people to kill," I mocked, "so little time."

"You and I have a lot in common, Gabriel." He waved a hand when I was about to protest. "Not our professions, but as people. You were raised by a loving mother and absent father. Your childhood was comfortable. Very blue collar, as was mine. You were a policeman. As was I. Though, I was also in the military and some other places. And you are a musician with a deep love for the art."

I wanted to stomp my feet and say I was nothing like this monstrous man, who probably would fit into a Beksiński painting. But I *knew* I was nothing like him, and what he thought didn't really matter to me, so I didn't protest. As Sartre said and I had learned early on, "*...it is senseless to* *complain since nothing foreign has decided what we feel, what we live, or what we are."*

As he finished *my* bottle of wine, he told me how and where he would meet Harald Wiberg and Silas Haagen.

"Why do you have to do this face to face? Isn't it safer virtually?" I asked.

"This is how I work. I need to have them tell me to my face what they want, so there is no confusion, no loss in translation. It's also for me to know who they are, and them to know who I am. This way no one fucks anyone over."

After he'd finished my one and only Lafite, he left.

He drank a whole bottle of wine in an hour and was not even slightly tipsy. I'd have been flat on the floor. You had to admire a man who could hold his liquor.

Chapter 54

Tuesday Morning, October 25, 2023

I came back from my run and workout at Kæmpe to find Valentin Jørgensen, Freja's on again-off again P.E.T. agent lover waiting outside my gate, leaning against an illegally parked BMW 5 Series that screamed asshole driver or unmarked police car. But Valentin had put who he was to rest as he wore a leather jacket that barely hid his weapon over a pair of jeans and police-issue boots.

Jorgen, my neighbor, was standing in front of his townhouse, smoking his pipe, and looking suspiciously at Valentin.

"*God morgen*," I said to both Jorgen and Valentin.

"You ready for the party this Saturday?" Jorgen asked as if it was code for, *do you need me to help with you with this asshole?*

"Yes, I am." How could I not be, with the street's WhatsApp group blowing up all the time.

Valentin waved at me and straightened as I opened the small gate to my postage stamp-sized lawn.

"You know him?" Jorgen asked.

"He's a friend," I replied noncommittally.

"The young woman, the one staying with you? Will she join the party? Is she Sophie's friend?"

Since I knew he'd seen me kiss Afsana before she got into a taxi to go to work, he knew she wasn't Sophie's friend. Another fucking comedian.

"No, she's leaving at the end of the week. You have a nice day, Jorgen," I cut him off, and opened the door for Valentin.

"Coffee?" I asked.

He nodded. I made him a cup and one for myself as well; and was almost going to open the back door to smoke a cigarette when I realized I had another four days to go before I could go back to my comforting rituals.

"Well?" I prompted. I'd expected someone from Europol once I'd let Johanne Juhl know I needed help in setting up an op to record the meeting Charlie was going to have with Harald Wiberg and Silas Haagen.

"Europol got in touch with us. We want a meeting with you, and I suggested I would pick you up since we know each other," he said flatly. I was standing where Charlie had stood the night before, and Valentin was sitting where I had at the kitchen counter.

"So, you're the point of contact for Europol?"

"For organized crime."

"This is organized crime?"

"Yeah, it is. We've had to loop in the *Prefekt* of Tallinn, since this is such a big fucking deal, and Maksim Lõhmus, an Estonian citizen, killed himself in Copenhagen." Valentin didn't show any emotion. He spoke flatly. I still couldn't reconcile this short, balding man with a slight potbelly, dating the tall, beautiful, and elegant Freja. Then again, people might wonder how a young and beautiful woman like Afsana had hooked up with an old, bald man like me.

"I need a shower." I picked up my phone to text Bør, asking him when Small Bo would come over to keep Afsana safe. "And I need to wait for a friend to get here before I can leave."

"Your girlfriend is here?"

I nodded and didn't bother to correct the girlfriend part. It seemed petty, especially since she was sleeping upstairs, naked, in my bed.

"How is she doing?"

"She's fine."

"Not upset about the attack."

"She seems to be fine with it." I paused thoughtfully. "I actually don't know if she's fine with it. She hasn't brought it up." *And I hadn't, either.* My therapist, Ilse, would say that was because I didn't want to deal with feeling guilty; of knowing that it was because of me she'd been hurt.

And my therapist would be right.

"Here is something I'm going to tell you off the record," Valentin said, stalling me from finding my bathroom. "They will want to know how you know about this meeting. They will want to know…hell, they know that you've had some contact with *The Ghost*. Now, Johanne Juhl is a politician, so she doesn't have to answer questions. She can just order people around. You are not, so you better have a good answer for how you've been in communication with *The Ghost* and not helped us catch him, and why he is feeding you information."

I nodded. "They think this might be a trap?"

"Don't you?"

I shook my head.

"You better have a good answer for why you're so confident, that this very fine assassin is not leading you and us to get killed."

"Thanks, Valentin. I'll give it considerable thought as I wash my hair," I told him, and took the stairs.

Chapter 55

Tuesday Afternoon, October 25, 2023

Felix Bergström, the Europol officer and apparent coordinator of the operation and merry band of the various agencies, was probably in his late twenties, early thirties. He wore tight black and green checkered suit pants, and a black T-shirt under, blasphemously, a black and green checked suit jacket. I believed that men who wore a suit jacket or blazer with a T-shirt were heathens. Wear it with a high neck pullover, a dress shirt…but a T-shirt that hadn't faced the dignity of an iron? It's like he just couldn't be bothered. What else didn't he bother with? *Sloppy, poorly dressed son of a bitch!*

It didn't help that he wore brown, pointed shoes with green socks, which I could see, because the suit pants were about an inch shorter than my sartorial sensibilities allowed, even if they were the right preferred length for current fashion standards. And if all that wasn't bad enough, he spoke Danish with a nasal-Swedish accent, so I could only understand about 70 percent of what he said.

I disliked him immediately.

We were in a conference room at the P.E.T. offices at Klausdalsbrovej in Søborg. This conference room had no windows, a slightly musty smell, a table that probably needed to be replaced since the start of the century, and six leather office chairs, two of which had duct tape over the leather seats to hold them in place.

"Let's get this started." I sat down on one of the chairs.

"*Politikommissær* Naja Andersen will join us," Felix said. "We should wait."

"Why is she joining us?" I asked.

Valentin was working on his laptop and didn't look up when he explained, "Because she has the Lõhmus case."

"I thought it was an open and shut case. He died by suicide," I scoffed.

"We have our suspicions that he may have had some help," Felix piped in, missing my sarcasm.

"Really?" I didn't bother to hide my disgust. "Can anyone elaborate why you think he may have had some help?"

Felix looked at Valentin who continued to work on his laptop. "It's an ongoing investigation. You're on a need-to-know basis, and you don't need to know."

I grinned and leaned back in my chair. "You have no reason but my suspicions. Damn, I didn't think she believed me."

"Who?" Felix looked confused.

"*Politikommissær* Naja Andersen." I was considerably cheered by that, and that feeling magnified when someone from the cafeteria brought in a big carafe of coffee, four plates, four forks, a very nice strawberry tart with a knife to cut it with, and a side of whipped cream.

"You guys have shittier conference rooms but better food than Polititorvet," I told Valentin after taking a bite of the tart. I hadn't eaten all day, so the sugar and caffeine were helping me sit upright.

Neither Valentin nor Felix had any dessert, sticking to coffee.

Naja Andersen arrived when I was on my second cup of coffee and slice of tart. Her cheeks were rosy, and she looked like the epitome of all things joyful. She wore a pair of skintight, black jeans, with military-style ankle boots, a high-neck pullover, and a very dashing gray blazer. Felix could learn something from her on how to dress casual and chic. Her blonde hair was tied in a ponytail as before, which accentuated her high cheek bones as they did her Georg Jensen daisy earrings. She wore a large watch that covered her right wrist, probably something she had inherited from her father or grandfather. It was ugly, not designer, so I deduced it must have sentimental value. On her left wrist she wore a Pandora bracelet laden with charms. She wore no makeup except for some mascara and lip gloss. She was the Danish girl next door.

"*Hejsa*. We meet again." It almost sounded like she was happy to see me. But then she said the same things in the same tone to Valentin and Felix and burst my bubble of feeling exclusive.

I poured her a cup of coffee that she took with milk and sugar. She also got a slice of tart.

Once we were all settled, she was the first to speak. "Isn't this *very* exciting?"

"How is this exciting?" I asked.

"Because we get to work with Europol and P.E.T., and catch the bad guys," she replied so sweetly that it gave me a toothache. Her baby blues sparkled.

Felix decided it was now time to show he was the guy with the biggest dick, so he stood up, and then, realizing that we were all sitting, relaxed awkwardly to slouch and lean against the table.

"Let me bring you all up to speed," he commanded. "Commissioner Juhl got in touch with us about Maksim Lõhmus. Our understanding is that he was going to give evidence against Copenhagen Bank—"

"*Whoa*," Valentin interrupted him. "Who the fuck told you that?"

"Yeah," Naja also wanted to know. "We didn't put that in any report. We're being *very* careful."

Felix looked uncomfortable. I leaned back and rocked myself on the chair, enjoying the show. Turf wars were nice to watch...from the sidelines.

"I was briefed that Maksim Lohmus had spoken to Gabriel, and had—"

"We're trying to keep Gabriel's name out of any official reports," Naja cut in. "It's for his and his family's safety. Do you know his girlfriend was attacked?"

Felix's Adam's apple bobbed as he looked nervously at me. I gave him my best, *My name is Paul, this is between y'all* look.

"Alright, what am I supposed to know?" Felix finally asked.

Naja smiled. Valentin's expression didn't change.

"Gabriel. Tell us what you know," she chirped.

"About what?"

"Don't get cute," Valentin warned.

I'd decided upon what I would tell them and what I wouldn't.

"I've been informed by a source who I'll not name," I raised my hand before anyone could protest, "for now. I can walk out of here if you want."

"Just try it, *pal*," Felix threatened, and then looked sheepish after both Naja and Valentin gave him a look of incredulity.

I grinned, feeling vindicated. "I was hired, as some of you know, to investigate Noor Mallik's suicide. My client wanted to know why she killed herself. She suspected Noor was being sexually harassed by Silas Haagen. Now, I did find out that Silas Haagen has been sexually harassing some women, but not Noor. But we'll leave that aside for now."

"Have you given that to anyone at crimes against persons?" Naja was furiously taking notes.

"Moving on," I got the conversation back on track mostly because I didn't want to tell them that Nico was working on the MeToo angle. "I spoke with Harald Wiberg and Silas

Haagen. Neither were pleased with my investigation. Soon thereafter, someone started following me. A car tried to run me over, destroyed my bicycle and my credibility with my insurance company. They didn't want to kill me, just send me to the ICU. Then, I found a phone at Noor's place that I used *another source,* who I will also not name, to look into it, because it was locked. I learned Noor was speaking with someone in the US weeks before she died."

I stopped to look at my audience for a moment, and then drank some coffee. I had their attention. *Gabriel Præst, private detective, hard at work.*

"I found out that Noor was a whistleblower. She had found evidence that Copenhagen Bank was using its Estonia branch to launder Russian money through bogus non-resident accounts. She suspected that nearly 200 billion euros were laundered, and the operation is ongoing. Evidence of this has been shared with *Chefpolitiinspektør* Jorun Eskola at NSK. Before he died, Maksim Lõhmus informed me that *The Ghost* conducts his business face to face. I have learned through yet *another* source—"

"Who I'm guessing won't be named?" Naja interrupted with a broad smile.

I grinned. "—that *The Ghost* will meet Harald Wiberg and Silas Haagen at Tivoli tomorrow."

Felix scrunched up his nose. "Tivoli?"

I wasn't surprised when Charlie told me about the location of the meeting. The world's second oldest amusement park, the Tivoli Gardens, which first opened in August 1843, offered a world of rides, restaurants and more, as well as several entrances and exits.

With nearly four and a half million visitors, almost the population of Denmark, the park would be just crowded enough to give our criminal collaborators anonymity, and sparse enough, because it was October, to give them the privacy they may need.

"It's an amusement park," Valentin said curtly.

"I know," Felix snapped. "It's a *huge* amusement park. How will we secure it?"

"Let's talk it through," Valentin replied.

They asked me a few more questions that I answered mostly truthfully and some I simply didn't respond to. After two hours of grilling, I was told my friendly interrogation had concluded.

"You're going to come right back here tomorrow morning and get briefed on the op. You're part of the op," Valentin reminded me.

I shifted uncomfortably. "I'm a civilian. I—"

"You're the only who has ever seen *The Ghost*."

I raised my eyebrows. "Valentin, I've never said I have seen—"

Valentin looked up at me then. "*Du bliver nød til at sluge en kamel denne gang*, Gabriel."

You're going to have to swallow a camel this time. In Danish, the idiom meant having to accept something that contradicts with your ideals and wishes. As much as I didn't want to talk about *The Ghost*, Valentin was right, I'd have to be there.

"I'll be here."

"Eleven, sharp." Valentin went back to his laptop.

Naja looked up from her notes then. "Just one more thing, Gabriel. I'm so sorry to bother you when you're helping us out so much."

Valentin was back to staring at his laptop, his fingers moving at great speed on the keys.

"Yes?" I asked patiently.

"Actually…I know you said you won't reveal your source on Maksim Lõhmus." She made a whole program of going through her papers.

Felix lost his patience. "We want to know who your source is."

Naja looked at him with narrowed eyes, her smile faltering for a good five seconds.

"I'm not talking about my sources." I put on my coat.

"Don't take that fucking tone with us, asshole," Felix thundered.

I didn't spare him a glance as I slung my Tumi messenger bag across my body. I'd hooked my bicycle on the back of Valentin's car, and I was keen on getting on the road.

Felix was about to speak again, when Naja raised her hand to silence him. "Felix…I don't know how to say this nicely so I'm just going to say it because I'm not in the mood anymore. Can you please shut up?"

Felix stared at her in disbelief.

Valentin didn't look up from his computer.

"You can talk to me like that," Felix roared. "I'm here with the P.E.T."

"Just listen to her, Felix," Valentin commented, his head down, his fingers on his keyboard.

I put on my Loro Piano, camel-colored shearling beanie, which was perfect for winter in Copenhagen, as it was water repellant, and smiled at Naja.

"It's going to rain, maybe even hail." Naja rose. "I can give you a ride."

"You have a bicycle rack?"

"Yes." Naja hurriedly started to pack up.

"Just a minute," Felix protested. "What's going on?"

Valentin, who was still plugging away on his laptop, doing God knows what, spoke softly, "The meeting has ended. We will meet again at 11 a.m. tomorrow morning to go through the op in detail."

"But what about *The Ghost*? Europol wants *The Ghost*," Felix blurted out, enraged.

Valentin looked up finally and stared down Felix. "If we do this right, we'll get Harald Wiberg and Silas Haagen for hiring a hitman to kill Noor Mallik and hurt our friend Gabriel here. And we'll get *The Ghost* for well...the good of all humanity."

Felix looked at me as if to ask if all this was true and if he had been at the same meeting as Valentin.

"Can we go?" I asked Naja, ignoring Felix. Any man who wore a t-shirt under his suit jacket was a moron, and he was just proof of that.

Chapter 56

Tuesday Evening, October 25, 2023

Naja drove a Police-issue Audi A5.

It was rush hour, so she avoided Helsingørmotorvejen and took Søborg Hovedgade all the way to the city. It was slow, but we kept moving and she kept her cheerful interrogation going.

By the time we were on Lyngbyvej, inching closer to Pastis where I'd asked to be dropped off, I finally had to ask. "Does it work?"

"What?"

"The dumb blonde thing?"

She grinned. "You can't even imagine how well."

"I can see that. I knew you were doing it and yet it worked on me," I confessed.

"I'm not trying to put one over on you. I just want to do my job and do it right. I know Freja *very* well and she'll vouch for me. And so will Valentin, even if he will eventually go back to his wife. The sorry son of a bitch."

"You think so?"

"I know so."

"Speaking of two people who are...well, nothing alike, I have to ask...."

"He must have mad skills in bed is my conclusion, because she's hot model material and he's a *total* nerd who hasn't met a treadmill he'd like to get on. And yet, they can't stay away from each other. And it's not *just* sex. It's," she shuddered, "a relationship."

Now, here was someone who got it. "Relationships are hard."

"Relationships are impossible," she exclaimed. "I don't do them. I hear you don't do them, either."

"I try not to," I said. "But once in a while...."

"You get tempted," she said understandingly.

"But then I come to my senses."

"Exactly, before there is serious damage," she finished.

We both stayed silent for a moment after that as we evaluated how fucked up we were to avoid relationships to prevent unknown future *damage*.

She parked illegally on Gothersgade and put a police sign on the windshield.

"May I buy you a drink?" she asked.

"It's my dry month," I told her.

She raised her eyebrows as if surprised. "And you don't cheat?"

"No."

"I like a man with will power," she remarked. "Then you can buy me a drink."

I liked her, so I agreed. We sat down at the bar at Pastis. I got tonic water, and she got a Kir Royale. Any other day, I would've gotten a champagne cocktail as well. They did it well at Pastis.

"What do you want to talk about?" I asked.

"How did he kill him?"

I wanted to pretend I didn't know the "he" or the "him," but it would be a waste of time, and besides, I found Naja Andersen *very* interesting. And she was nearer my age than Afsana.

"I thought you all believe he died by suicide," I mocked.

"That would be a bit too convenient, wouldn't it? He comes here and tells us that if his family is safe, he'll testify against the Copenhagen Bank gods…and *pist væk*, he's gone."

Not *just like that*, I thought, someone had interfered, someone had literally, if not physically, pushed him out of the window.

"Have you heard of the Sudden Russian Death Syndrome?"

Naja wrinkled her nose. "Maybe I read something. I have very little detail."

I'd read everything on the subject, wondering how many of these kills could be attributed to Charlie.

"The chairman of Lukoil, a company connected to Russian state-owned Gazprom, Ravil Maganova, died by falling out of a window at a hospital in Moscow. Another Lukoil executive, Alexander Subbotin, suffered from heart failure soon after. Leonic Shulman, the head of transportation for Lukoil, was found dead in his garage because of carbon monoxide poisoning. Alexander Tyulakov, an executive at Gazprom also went the carbon monoxide in the garage way. They both left suicide notes for their family," I shared.

Naja drank some of her champagne cocktail, and then looked at Oskar, the bartender. "Do you have anything to snack on?"

"He usually gets the olives and almonds," Oskar recommended.

"Let's do that, I'm starving," Naja lamented.

"And I'm paying for the snacks as well?"

Naja grinned. "If you insist."

I laughed softly. "I think Maksim was convinced to take the fatal leap to save his family."

"How? Someone talked to him over the phone. Face to face? How?" she pondered.

I shrugged. "I left there at ten in the night. I called Tommy around midnight...if only I had...."

The saddest words ever spoken were "if only I had."

"How do you think he did it?"

"I've no idea," I said, though I thought it was probably face-to-face, because I had gotten to know Charlie a little. He'd think that was bringing dignity to murder.

Oskar served our olives and almonds, and we both polished two olives off right away. We'd both missed lunch. In fact, I'd missed breakfast and lunch, and was surviving on two slices of strawberry tart.

"But how? He climbed up the side of the hotel? What?"

I shrugged. "He found a way to get into the room."

She nodded. "The Swiss knife? That's—"

"They knew he always carried one. His father gifted it to him," I told her.

Naja's eyes widened. "*He* knew a lot about Maksim."

"*He* does his homework."

"And now I'm going to ask you the really difficult question, Gabriel."

I looked at her, feeling weary, wishing that Afsana was home and not at work so I could spend some time with her and forget my day. I needed something good to happen today. Something to make me feel like there was hope.

"Did *you* talk to him face to face?" She picked up an almond and tossed it into her mouth, showing me that she had a pretty good aim.

I pulled out my phone, ignoring her question, and texted Afsana: *It's been a hell of a day. How can I spend this evening with you?*

"Gabriel?" Naja prodded.

I put my phone face down on the counter and shook my head. "No."

"You're lying." She sounded surprised.

"Okay," I said mildly.

"Why are you protecting him? He's an assassin. A *bad* guy."

Because he wasn't the enemy. Harald Wiberg and Silas Haagen were the enemy.

"I'm not protecting him. I don't have to. He can protect himself just fine."

My phone beeped, and I turned it to see a message from Afsana: *I can be home by ten and would love a bath in that sexy tub of yours.*

I grinned and replied: *I'll make sure it's ready for you.*

"Tomorrow, if you see him, will you help us catch him?" Naja demanded.

I looked up from my phone at Naja. "I don't have any more to say."

She drained her cocktail, and pushed her stool back. She stood up and held her hand out. I shook it.

"I look forward to working with you." Her smile was back on her face, genuine and beguiling.

"Me too." I smiled as well. I couldn't help myself.

Chapter 57

Wednesday Morning, October 26, 2023

I met Valentin by the lakes after my run. We walked up to Sortedam Dossering, and then crossed onto Tagensvej to get to Artisan Copenhagen. I got their classic pour-over coffee made with their dark roast. Valentin got a croissant and a latte. I was still feeling warm after the run, and Valentin was wrapped up in a coat, so we sat outside so that we wouldn't have to worry about eavesdroppers.

Valentin pulled out a pen and map of Tivoli from his coat, leaving croissant butter smudges on the paper. "There are only two entrances to Tivoli, the main one on Vesterbrogade, and the Central Station entrance on Bernstorffsgade."

"But many exits," I pointed at the several places where people could leave the park, albeit not re-enter.

"We'll have people at all the entrances and exits. However, we have other disadvantages. They're meeting at six in the evening, so it'll be dark, making it harder to keep an eye on them, even in brightly lit Tivoli," Valentin said seriously. "Harald Wiberg and Silas Haagen we can arrest anytime, but your *Ghost*, this will be our one and only chance. You understand?"

"Yes, I do." I bristled at Valentin referring to Charlie as my *Ghost*, yet I wasn't troubled by the idea of Charlie being caught. After all, he was a very bad man who'd done some very bad things. My skepticism about Valentin's success wasn't a reflection on his skills as an agent; he was undoubtedly competent. However, Charlie, a seasoned fugitive, had spent most of his life eluding police globally. His expertise in escape simply outweighed Valentin's in capture.

"We will need you to confirm his identity," Valentin warned me.

"I'll try my best," I said. "But you know he's going to be in disguise."

Valentin nodded. "We'll have plainclothes around the garden, and we will make sure to follow them. We have a long-range recorder in place so, once we know where they stop to talk, we can use the recorder. And we also recorders with all detectives to make sure we get their conversation."

I looked at the map as I drank coffee, now beginning to feel cold in my sweaty running clothes. "Silas Haagen and Harald Wiberg will probably come in through a restaurant."

Valentin nodded. "We will have people there as well."

"My guess is Nimb," I contended. "They'll meet there for a drink, and then pretend to go for a walk in Tivoli, meet *The Ghost*. After the meeting, they'll take any of the many exits to disappear into the streets."

Valentin watched me carefully and nodded. "Nimb?"

"Want to take a bet?"

He shook his head. "No, thanks. I'm getting divorced soon, I'm going to need my money."

I almost asked him if he was sure about the divorce but, even though I cared for Freja and she was my friend, there were boundaries, and this was none of my business.

Valentin walked me through the whole op twice.

"We have cameras all over the place. The control center will be at Balkonen, a Danish restaurant in the center of Tivoli. They're closed for remodeling; we'll have the place to ourselves."

"Questions?"

I shook my head.

"Great, I'll see you at eleven in Søborg."

"You felt you needed to give me extra coaching?"

Valentin smiled then, and I realized I didn't seem him smile often. "You're a civilian. It's my job to make sure you're prepared."

I grinned. "Well, as Thomas Edison said, *'good fortune often happens when opportunity meets with preparation.'*"

Chapter 58

Wednesday Evening, October 26, 2023

I watched P.E.T. agents and Danish police officers work in concert. This was Valentin's op from the P.E.T. side, and Naja was managing the Danish police end. Felix was there as well. I wasn't sure what he was doing.

We set up around one in the afternoon. I sat down with a copy of *Du côté de chez Swann*, Swann's Way, the first volume in Proust's novel in seven parts, *In Search of Lost Time*. I had purchased these volumes because Afsana had read them, and I had not.

We were spread across the restaurant. I sat at a table, trying to keep out of everyone's way.

Naja joined me, leaning against the table, my book was resting atop. "This is exhausting. We prepare and prepare and, even then, who knows what will happen."

I put the book aside. "If your enemy is secure at all points, be prepared for him. Attack him where he is unprepared, appear where you are not expected."

Who said that?"

"Sun Tzu in *The Art of War*."

"I have a quote for you. '*Nobody should pin their hopes on a miracle.*'"

"Who said that?" I asked.

"Vladimir Vladimirovich Putin."

"Well, we all need role models," I quipped.

Her earpiece crackled, and she rose. "Back to the grindstone, Præst."

"Better you than me." I went back to my book.

At five thirty, we observed Harald Wiberg and Silas Haagen being dropped off by a black Tesla Model S, captured on the CCTV footage along Bernstorffsgade. They were in a good mood as they walked into Nimb.

"You called it," Valentin said. "They're in Nimb," he spoke into his microphone, informing the rest of the team that the op was now on.

Naja watched the two entrances. "Where do you think *he'll* enter?"

"Doesn't matter." Charlie would not worry about being identified. "We won't see him. He'll be in disguise."

Each second ticked by extremely slowly in the command center. I felt the itch to go outside and breathe in some air.

"They're going through the back into Tivoli," Valentin said into his microphone. "I want eyes on these two."

We watched them in conversation, not a care in the world. They came down the stairs from Nimb, and went left toward the Ferris wheel and the Tivoli gift shop. They walked past the Tivoli Koncertsal, and went up to Ben & Jerry's ice cream.

"There," I whispered.

He wore a long coat, dress pants, and a bowler hat. I recognized the hat. I had one of those. Was it mine, I wondered. He had free rein in my house the evening he'd opened my bottle of Lafite. He could've easily taken my vintage Valentino bowler hat.

"Why can't we hear them?" Valentin yelled.

The audio video technician was playing with his computer. "I don't know. But we are getting static through the long-range recorder."

"Mikkel, get close to them. Order a fucking ice cream, now," Valentin growled.

"You didn't finish...crackle...crackle...he's still...crackle...causing problems," we heard Harald Wiberg say.

We couldn't hear what the man in the bowler hat said.

"Do we have photos of that man?" Naja called out into her microphone.

Someone else who was on a computer replied, "Yes, we do. I'm enhancing and I can then run through facial recognition."

We distinctly hear Silas Haagen speak. "We told you, you'd receive payment for Noor...crackle...only...crackle. Now, finish...crackle."

After that we couldn't even get much more because the three men began to walk. Charlie looked nothing like anyone I'd met before. This man looked Italian or Spanish. Definitely Latin. His hair was dark and long. His nose prominent.

His cheeks were nothing like the man who had drunk my Lafite.

"Is that him?" Valentin asked me.

"I don't know. It could be. It probably is but I can't recognize him, Valentin. He's in disguise. And he's good at it."

They were walking toward the lake, which meant they'd take the bridge across.

"They're going to go out H.C. Andersen's Boulevard," I cautioned.

"Yeah," Naja agreed, and gave orders, as did Valentin.

"Come on, come on. We can't have put all this money and resources into this and get fuck all," Valentin muttered.

We watched as they came by the Golden Tower ride. They shook hands and parted.

"Damn it," Naja cried out.

"Keep following that man in the bowler hat," Valentin cried out.

The said man went by the carousel as Harald Wiberg and Silas Haagen went back toward Nimb. And then, just as the carousel dipped and turned, the man with the bowler hat disappeared.

"Out, out, out, let's find this asshole." Valentin ran outside.

Naja and I followed him. We reached the carousel, Valentin was winded, Naja, who I realized probably ran daily as I did, was not.

"Where the fuck did he go?" Valentin looked around.

Not only on impulse, but also because I'd gotten to know Charlie, I went up to a nearby trashcan. On top lay the bowler hat. I picked it up.

"Fuck," Naja exclaimed. "Now, he could be anyone."

Yes, he was anyone, I thought.

I kept looking around as did Naja and Valentin, even though we knew it was a waste of time. This whole op had been a waste of time.

And then I saw him. He wore a black tracksuit. His hair was blond. But I knew it was him and he wanted me to know. He winked at me and then mimicked raising his hat.

I looked at the hat in my hand and grinned. Lodged in a hole in the front was a camera. I looked up again, he was gone.

"*Fuck*," Valentin screamed. Some children and parents glared at him, and someone asked him to calm the fuck down.

"We got nothing," Naja gritted her teeth. The smiles were gone.

They looked at me and saw my face wreathed in a large smile.

"What the fuck are you so happy about?" Valentin asked.

I pulled out the tiny camera recording device from the hat. "*The Ghost* left us a present." And as I peered inside the hat, I cursed, "Son of a bitch. This *is* my Valentino hat. He put a fucking hole in it."

Chapter 59

Thursday Night, October 27, 2023

I turned down Valentin's offer to be there when they arrested Harald Wiberg and Silas Haagen. But I gave a tip to Dag Sorgenfri Kjær, the journalist who'd helped me. I also introduced him to Kelsey Haines from *The Atlantic* so that they could work on this story from both sides of the ocean, Raisa's, and mine.

I called Raisa and told her everything that had happened. I gave her the recording I'd made of Maksim Lõhmus talking about Nikita Poletov's murder, and asked Raisa to share that information or whatever she wished with Lucya or whomever else she wanted.

"You're sure, you don't want a glass?" Afsana asked, holding up a bottle of Laurent-Perrier Cuvee Rose.

"Sure," I said.

Since Afsana had taken Thursday and Friday off, I'd gotten the keys to Clara and Eymen's Volvo and summerhouse in Kerteminde in Fynn. The house, which was mostly glass, was on the beach, with stunning views of *Storebælt*, the Great Belt strait.

I sat in the living room on a very comfortable mid-century Hans Wegner Papa Bear chair with my feet up on the ottoman, watching the waves crash gently onto the beach. Afsana slid onto my lap and put her arms around me.

"Thanks for bringing me here," she said, getting comfortable atop me.

I hugged her, nuzzling my chin against her. "Thanks for coming with me."

I was glad we were here. I needed to get away from Copenhagen and leave the case behind. It hadn't been easy to tell Afsana that Noor didn't kill herself, but very satisfying to add that there were two people going to prison for ordering her murder.

She'd told her family over a long phone call, and I was glad she'd be with them soon in London so they could heal together. She'd cried after the conversation, and the grief that had settled into gentle waves had once again become a raging storm.

She'd fallen asleep exhausted, which had given me the time to make the phone calls I needed to make, and check in with Tommy and Eskola as well. I called Flora and told her to expect a bill. She was grateful, she said, and that I'd absolutely earned my fee and then some. She was going to recommend me to all her HR friends!

Now, a glass of champagne, some caviar and blinis later, Afsana was in a better mood, as was I.

"Will you come see me in San Francisco?" She watched the beach as night claimed us.

"If I'm in San Francisco, I'll see you."

"Hmm...that's not what I said."

I hugged her tighter. "I know."

"Are you feeling bad at all that this is over?"

"Yes."

"Good."

We sat there for a long while, and then went to bed. The next day, the sun was shining, the sky was blue, and there was absolutely no wind. It was the perfect day to walk on the beach, which we did, and go to nearby restaurants, which we also did.

We didn't talk about her going away. We'd both accepted it, well, I had a long while ago, maybe even before it started, but she'd finally done the same. But accepting it didn't mean we didn't want to be together for just a little longer. That night, we drove back to Copenhagen and slept holding each other. One last night before she went her way, and I went mine.

Chapter 60

Saturday, October 29, 2023

Since we were going to have the block party that evening, Sophie canceled breakfast with me. But I knew she also did it because this was my last morning with Afsana.

I made French crepes, and served them with Nutella, as Afsana wanted and Sophie had always loved, along with fresh strawberries that I found at Irma at a ridiculous price, especially since they had been grown in a greenhouse and tasted more of water than strawberry.

"As you promised, this is exceptional," she said as we shared a carafe of coffee and ate our pancakes at the kitchen counter. "You know, you really need some music."

"I agree. I'm going to buy a Wrensilva as soon as I can afford it."

"What's that?"

"A turntable. I used to have a Victrola Jackson, but it got damaged."

"How?"

"I had some water damage last summer."

I helped her pack. She had a lot of stuff for two suitcases, one backpack, and a tote. When I was done packing, she was impressed. "How did you get it all in? Is that a skill you get as you get older?"

"Just like wine, everything gets better with age."

Afsana came to me and hugged me. "Well, you know that age makes the wine less fruity and more acidic."

"And smooths out the tannins and refines the flavors."

She looked up at me. "Will you take me to the airport?"

"Yes."

There was a loud knocking on the door. I went downstairs to find my neighbor Margrethe. "Remind Sophie—"

"Yes, she's bringing the potato salad," I interrupted her.

"We'll start setting up in the afternoon. You better get your ass over to help."

I looked upstairs, and then at Margrethe. "I can't. I have to drop a friend off at the airport."

Margrethe also looked up, and then nodded. "Is she going somewhere?"

"She's moving to the United States."

"Oh, like forever."

I nodded.

She patted my shoulder. "Well, we'll take care of you at the party."

We called for a taxi, catching it at the end of Øster Farimagsgade, since my street was closed off in preparation for the evening's festivities.

At the airport, we kept our goodbye short. I couldn't bear to see her cry, and truthfully, I felt a surge of tears myself, which threatened my sense of machismo. Brief as our time together was, it had been intense and filled with joy.

"Thank you for everything," she whispered when we hugged for the last time.

She waved as she went up the escalator to security. She was flying business, so check-in had taken all of five minutes, and her big suitcases were now all set to meet her in London.

As she got to the top of the escalator, she blew me a kiss. I raised my fedora, feeling a bout of sadness.

And watched as she disappeared through fast check-in.

I took the Metro back to Nørreport station, and then walked home, feeling blue.

Even before I reached Eckersbergsgade, I heard the sounds of the party. Beyoncé was telling the world she was comfortable in her skin and cozy with who she was.

The street glowed with a festive, Christmas-like illumination. Numerous tables were arranged, flanked by a mix of mismatched chairs and benches, with my picnic table at one end. Gas and electric heaters were strategically positioned for optimal warmth, complemented by two outdoor firepits that added to the cozy atmosphere for the revelers.

Sophie came up to me, holding a glass of wine, swaying to the music. "Welcome." She hugged me, and then pulled back. "You, okay?"

"Absolutely."

Jorgen waved to me. "Come here, Gabriel. And tell these bastards how I saved your life this summer."

I joined Jorgen on a bench, where he slid a can of Tuborg my way. As I popped it open, savoring the hiss of air and the aroma of fermented barley and hops, I took my first sip of alcohol in four weeks. Life was fucking good!

Jorgen was in the midst of fabricating a story about how he'd saved my life the one time I had gotten beaten up in front of my house.

Playing along, I embellished the story further, bolstering Jorgen's heroic image with a few more creative lies.

EPILOGUE

December, 2023

Nico and I celebrated the publication of the first exposé on the Copenhagen Bank scandal, featured in both The Atlantic and Politiken, with a byline shared by Raisa Chaban, Kelsey Haines, and Dag Sorgenfri Kjær.

This celebration came on the heels of Nico's earlier triumph, her inaugural #MeToo article, starting with Silas Haagen and Copenhagen Bank, with several follows in the pipeline.

Harald Wiberg and Silas Haagen were swiftly arrested for Noor's murder and their attempted hit on me, soon after Valentin, Naja, and their team reviewed and documented the incriminating recording made with my Valentino bowler cap. They now awaited trial in jail, with proceedings anticipated to commence in the spring.

Post-dinner, Nico and I strolled back to my place, basking in the twinkling charm of the Danish Christmas season, marking the first crisp day of Advent with a sense of accomplishment and anticipation.

"Are you traveling for Christmas?" I asked Nico, as she did that sometimes when her son was with his father.

"I have Sebastian this year, so we'll go to Loland to be with my parents. My sister and brother are also going to be there. How about you? Thinking of going to San Francisco?" she asked as we entered my street.

"I don't think so," I said.

Afsana and I had texted a few times, but it was mostly perfunctory and polite. If we had seen each other, maybe the chemistry would once again flare up, but already, the ardor had cooled as had the ache in my heart.

I heard the music as soon as I unlocked my door. I put my hand to stop Nico from going in. She looked puzzled. I knew what it was even before I walked into my living room. I recognized the music. It was Zygmunt Karasiński's *Jazz Jamboree '85 Vol. 2*.

Where my Victrola Jackson used to be stood a beautiful Wrensilva M1 turntable.

"Can I come in?" Nico called out.

I went back to where she waited, took her hand, guiding her inside.

Charlie was long gone.

We hung up our coats and made our way to the turntable, its sound quality surpassing that of my Victrola by a few light years.

"This is lovely," Nico exclaimed.

"It's a Wrensilva."

"I thought you were waiting to buy it."

"I was. This, I believe, is a present."

The light in the kitchen attracted my attention. On the counter stood one of the most beautiful sights in the world. A bottle of 1982 Chateau Lafite Rothschild, Pauillac.

Nico walked up to the counter and slid the wine away from the thick white note it stood on. I picked up the note.

It simply said: *Thanks for the Lafite. This one is better. But it needs to be drunk with music.*

He had signed it *Charlie*, the name we'd decided was his. I handed the note to Nico. She read through it and took a deep breath. "Wow."

"Yeah. This is a," I thought about it and did some calculations, "sixty thousand kroner bottle of wine."

Nico whistled. "You have *some* friends, Gabriel."

Friend? Mostly likely not.

"In his line of work, he can afford it," I remarked dryly.

"Well, what're you going to do?" Nico asked.

I walked around the counter and found my corkscrew.

"We're not drinking that tonight. It's for a *special* night," Nico protested.

I cut away the foil and screwed into the cork.

"Nico, *skat,* this is a special night, and I would drink this with no one but you. Now, why don't you increase the volume on the Wrensilva while I find us some Bordeaux glasses."

THE END

ABOUT THE AUTHOR

Amulya Malladi is the bestselling author of nine novels, including A DEATH IN DENMARK and THE COPENHAGEN AFFAIR. Her books have been translated into several languages, including Dutch, French, German, Japanese, Spanish, Danish, Romanian, Serbian, and Tamil. Currently living in California, she is a Danish citizen born and raised i
n India.

Website: www.AmulyaMalladi.com

Printed in Great Britain
by Amazon